ROYAL BLOOD

"No!" Rhys Michael cried weakly, instinctively trying to jerk away, even as Polidorus released the ligature that kept his blood from flowing. "Nooooo!" he groaned, as the hot blood began to stream around his arm and collect in a basin set beneath his elbow.

But a *Custodes* knight had one hand set firmly against his shoulder and the other on his upper arm. And Father Magan had that forearm in an unrelenting grip, to ensure that their unwilling patient did not twist against the padded wrist restraint that held the arm outstretched.

The horror and the helplessness of it all swept through Rhys Michael in less than a blink of an eye . . .

By Katherine Kurtz
Published by Ballantine Books:

THE LEGENDS OF CAMBER OF CULDI
CAMBER OF CULDI
SAINT CAMBER
CAMBER THE HERETIC

THE CHRONICLES OF THE DERYNI
DERYNI RISING
DERYNI CHECKMATE
HIGH DERYNI

THE HISTORIES OF KING KELSON
THE BISHOP'S HEIR
THE KING'S JUSTICE
THE QUEST FOR SAINT CAMBER

THE HEIRS OF SAINT CAMBER
THE HARROWING OF GWYNEDD
KING JAVAN'S YEAR
THE BASTARD PRINCE

THE DERYNI ARCHIVES
DERYNI MAGIC

LAMMAS NIGHT

THE BASTARD PRINCE

Volume III in *The Heirs of Saint Camber*

Katherine Kurtz

A Del Rey® Book

BALLANTINE BOOKS • NEW YORK

A Del Rey® Book.
Published by Ballantine Books

Copyright © 1994 by Katherine Kurtz
Map copyright © 1994 by Shelly Shapiro

All rights reserved under International and Pan-American Copyright Conventions. Published in the United States by Ballantine Books, a division of Random House, Inc., New York, and simultaneously in Canada by Random House of Canada Limited, Toronto.

Library of Congress Catalog Card Number: 93-47131

ISBN 0-345-39177-2

Manufactured in the United States of America

First Hardcover Edition: June 1994
First Mass Market Edition: August 1995

10 9 8 7 6 5 4 3 2 1

For
my very dear friend,
DENIS O'CONOR DON,
Prince of Connacht.
If Ireland were still a monarchy,
he would be High King.

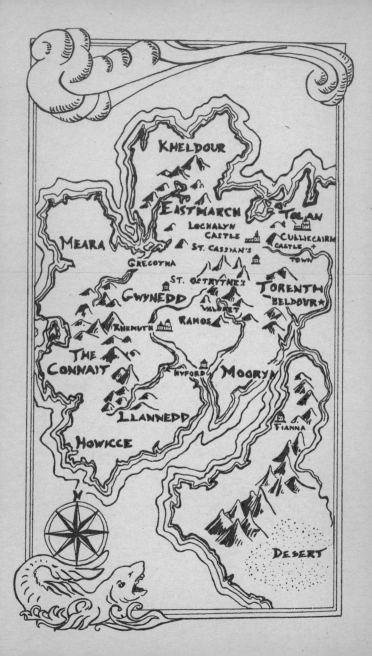

Contents

PROLOGUE

He hath put forth his hands against such as be at
peace with him; he hath broken his covenant.
—Psalms 55:20

The nagging drizzle of the night before had yielded to clearing
skies at dawn, but a persistent overcast remained even at noon-
time on this chill day in early June of the Year of Our Lord
928, now seventh in the reign of Rhys Michael Alister
Haldane, King of Gwynedd. Climbing to the castle's highest
rooftop walk, two women had braved a cutting wind to seek
out a sheltered angle between cap-house and rampart wall, a
natural sun trap that was warm enough to shrug off fur-lined
cloaks and begin to thaw chilled bones while they resumed
their watch of the day before.

It was a better place than most to await the return of their
men, now several days overdue. To the south they could see
for miles across the vast plain of Iomaire—and a lesser distance eastward, to where the mists of the Rhelljan foothills obscured the approach to the vital Coldoire Pass. It was toward
this pass that their men had ridden, more than a week ago, and
it was toward Coldoire that the elder of the pair now turned
her gaze yet again, shading her dark eyes against the glare of
sunlight on persisting tatters of fog.

She had kept this kind of vigil all too many times before.
Sudrey of Eastmarch had been chatelaine of this castle for
fully twenty years. She was hardly more than a child herself
when she first came to Lochalyn as a bride and, within the
year, bore the daughter who would become the taller, redheaded young woman fretting at her side. Apart from the death

1

of a beloved brother, a decade ago, the intervening years had been mostly kind, though she and Hrorik had never been blessed with any more children. Stacia was their only child and sole heir, herself now a mother, suckling an infant son but hours old when his father and grandfather had spurred urgently toward the Coldoire Pass to investigate reports of Torenthi troop incursions.

"D'ye think it's only yesterday's storm that's delayed them?" Stacia suddenly blurted, startling one of the wolf-hounds basking at her feet as she rose to peer out over the rampart again, clasping her son closer. "Dear God, what if sommat's happened to Corban? They should hae been back days ago. Oh, sommat's happened—I know it has!"

"Hush, child. We don't *know* anything yet."

But as Sudrey of Eastmarch gazed out at the Coldoire mists, her lips compressing in a tight, expectant line, she very much feared that she did know more than she cared to admit. Not of Stacia's beloved Corban, but of her own dear Hrorik.

The dread confirmation would come soon; she could feel it. She carried but little of the blood of the magical race that once had ruled this land, and she had denied what she had for more than half her life, but it was enough to give her sudden, blinding flashes of unsought knowledge when she least expected or wanted it. Nor had she ever received but rudimentary training in the use of the powers that might have been hers to command, for she and her brother had been orphaned young and brought up by their uncle, a Deryni lordling whose abuse of *his* power and privilege eventually had led his tenants to turn on him and kill him.

That had been just on the eve of the overthrow of King Imre of Festil and the Haldane Restoration. After that had come the turmoil and wars that left her and her brother hostages of Hrorik's father, the fierce but kindhearted Duke Sighere of Claibourne, for she and Kennet were both of them distant kin to the royal House of Torenth. In those days, she had deemed it the better part of prudence to pretend that she had no powers at all; and after a time, she had almost forgotten that she ever did. She had never expected to fall in love with one of her jailer's sons . . .

Her wistful recollections had distracted her from her watch across the castle ramparts, so that it was Stacia who first saw the riders, first only a handful and then dozens of them, picking their way slowly and painfully along the muddy, winding track that led down from the mist of the Rhelljans to approach the castle gates.

"They're comin'!" Stacia breathed, pressing hard against the rampart edge as she squinted against the glare. "Look ye, there's Da's banner!"

Sudrey's breath caught in her throat as she, too, began to make out the battle standard borne by one of the lead riders—a silver saltire and two golden suns against an azure field.

"Mother—I dinnae see Corban's banner," Stacia cried. "Mother, where is't? Corban—"

She was turning to careen down the turnpike stair before Sudrey could stop her, moaning and clutching her son fearfully to her shoulder, the wolfhounds lumbering after. Behind her, Sudrey cast her own anxious gaze over the approaching riders again, now seeing what her daughter had failed to notice: the dark, irregular shape bound across the saddle of one of the horses nearer the banner, wrapped round in a greeny tweed cloak that she herself had mended before her husband rode out, what seemed like an eternity ago.

Later, she would not remember her own numbed descent of the narrow, winding stair; only that, all at once, she was down in the castle yard with men and horses churning all around her, the din and the stench of blood and death almost beyond imagining. Across the yard, her son-in-law all but tumbled from his spent mount to stagger toward her, one bandaged and blood-stained arm braced around the shoulders of his weeping but relieved young wife.

He was grimy and exhausted, young Corban, his helmet gone, his sweat-matted black hair mostly pulled free of its border clout, his leather brigandine showing the signs of heavy battle survived. As he reached Sudrey, he collapsed to armored knees at her feet, his broad, leather-clad shoulders heaving with a dry sob as he crushed her to him with his free hand, burying his bearded face against her skirts.

"Forgive me, I couldnae save him!" he gasped. "They've ta'en Culliecairn—God knows why! We lost dozens, an' most of those returnin' carry wounds. They lured us wi' a flag o' truce, then o'erran us. We must get word tae Sighere an' Graham an' beg reinforcements—an' from the king!"

"Is it invasion?" Sudrey heard herself calmly asking.

"I cannae say." Corban raised his head and drew back a little, dark eyes as bleak and empty as her heart. "They wore the livery o' Prince Miklos of Torenth. It *could* be one prong of an all-out invasion. We must see if Sighere's outposts hae seen activity in the Arranal region or along the coast."

Her mind flicked back at once to a private meeting several months before at Lochalyn: herself, Hrorik, and the strikingly handsome Prince Miklos—who was technically a distant cousin—and another, slightly younger man, as dark as Miklos was fair, then presumed merely to be the prince's aide. Hrorik had reluctantly encouraged the meeting, not out of any love for Torenth but in hopes of putting to rest nearly seven years' worth of letters sent periodically from the Court at Beldour, the Torenthi capital, badgering his wife about her hostage status.

She had answered *that* question quite firmly: that she was no longer hostage or Torenthi, but gave her loyalty to her husband's liege lord in Rhemuth. The Torenthi prince had been quietly furious. Hence, this present conflict probably was not really about border disputes; it was Miklos' response to her refusal to espouse the cause of his companion, finally revealed as Prince Marek of Festil, Pretender to the Crown of Gwynedd. And now Sudrey's refusal had cost her her beloved Hrorik and the lives of many other loyal Eastmarch men.

"I do not think there will be activity farther north," she whispered, raising her gaze above Corban's head to where Eastmarch squires and men-at-arms were loosing the lashings that held a sad, tweed-wrapped shape across the saddle of a spent bay mare. "This is not the true invasion—though eventually, that will come. Hrorik and I had feared that such might happen, but not so soon. Prince Miklos tried to win me to his cause some months ago, appealing to my Torenthi blood. I refused, and this is the result. It has to do with the Festillic Pretender."

"A feint, then, for testin' the waters?" Corban asked, leaning heavily on Stacia to get to his feet.

"Aye—and perhaps a deliberate provocation, to lure the young king out of Rhemuth. They will know, or at least suspect, that he is not a free agent. I pray that, in meeting this new threat, he is also able to come into his own."

"God grant it!" Corban said fervently. "But meanwhile, I must see that Eastmarch doesnae become the Pretender's own." He bent to press his lips to his son's forehead, then thrust his bewildered wife from him as he called to several of the Eastmarch captains.

"Attend me, men of Eastmarch. We must ride for Marley, to seek Sighere's aid. Elgin, I need those fresh horses *now*. Nicholas, have ye seen to those provisions? Murray, I give ye command o' the garrison here at Lochalyn. I'm takin' half a dozen men, in addition to Elgin. Will that leave ye enou' tae hold the castle?"

Stacia looked thunderstruck, though Sudrey knew that Corban was only doing what he must, under the circumstances. He was a good commander, the son she had never borne. Behind him, some of the fittest-looking men were already mounting up again, others shouting answers to his questions.

"But, ye cannae just leave!" Stacia wailed. "What about my da? What about our bairn? What about *me*?"

"*Mo rùn*, my heart, your da is dead. I share yer grief, but I cannae change fate." He turned aside to nod gruff thanks as a man brought up a fresh horse, setting foot to stirrup and springing up into the saddle. The animal was fractious, and nearly unseated him as another man offered him the flapping Eastmarch banner.

"But—that's my father's banner!" Stacia gasped, clutching her son closer and barely avoiding the horse's hooves as her husband fought his mount and deftly footed the banner's staff at his stirrup.

"Stacia, my daurlin', have ye no been listenin'?" Corban said. "This is *your* banner, now that yer father is dead. 'Tis you who are Countess of Eastmarch. An' that makes me *Earl* of Eastmarch, so 'tis also *my* banner. An' one day, if we all live through this, it will be *his* banner." He jerked his bearded chin toward their now squalling son, then cast a beseeching look at his wife's mother.

"My lady, I beg ye to make her understand. I cannae delay more. See to the wounded. Bury Hrorik. Hold this castle, howe'er best ye can. I'll bring ye help as soon as I may. Murray's sendin' messengers on to Rhemuth to inform the king. God keep ye."

He was spurring back out the castle gates at the head of his tiny escort before either woman could gainsay him, the bright blue and gold and silver of the Eastmarch banner fluttering boldly above his head. Watching him go, Sudrey of Eastmarch, née of Rhorau, found herself already shifting into that calm, passionless efficiency that must be her bulwark for the next little while, setting aside the grief that would render her useless if she let it take over.

"Jervis, please start bringing the wounded into the great hall," she said to her household steward, turning her back on the men now carrying the long, tweed-wrapped bundle toward the castle's chapel. "That will serve the best as infirmary, until we can get everyone taken care of. Have the kitchen start boiling water and tell the women to gather bandages. And summon Father Collumcille and Father Derfel and that midwife from down in the village. She may be some help. And Murray—"

"Aye, my lady?"

"Did my husband's battle surgeon come back from Culliecairn?"

"He did, my lady." Murray was instructing the two messengers about to leave for Rhemuth, and looked like he, too, could use the surgeon's services—or at least a woman's hands—to clean and bind his wounds. "He's already working on some men o'er in the stable entrance."

"Well, have him move everything and everybody into the great hall as soon as he can. I want some order to this."

"Right away, my lady."

As she turned to deal with her daughter, she saw that Stacia, too, had rallied to necessity and training and was tearfully entrusting her baby to Murray's eldest daughter, with instructions to take the bairn upstairs to her bower and stay out of the way.

"I have to be strong now, for my da," Stacia told her mother tremulously, lifting her chin and wiping away her tears on the edge of a sleeve. "He raised me tae be his heir. He'd be shamed if he thought I couldnae take care o' his men—of *my* men."

In the din of milling horses and clanking armor and shouting and moaning men, the two made a tiny island of calm as, arms around one another's waists, they began to head purposefully toward the great hall. Behind them, the messengers chosen to carry word to Rhemuth swung up on fresh mounts and galloped out the castle gates.

CHAPTER ONE

Therefore pride compasseth them about as a chain;
violence covereth them as a garment.
—Psalms 73:6

The Eastmarch messengers exhausted a succession of mounts in the days that followed, galloping into Gwynedd's capital less than a week after the taking of Culliecairn. Almost incoherent with exhaustion, the pair made their initial report to a hastily gathered handful of Gwynedd's royal ministers, then were whisked away for further interrogation in private by Lord Albertus, the Earl Marshal, and certain members of his staff. The king was told of their news, but was not invited to join the impromptu meeting now in progress in Gwynedd's council chamber.

"Aside from the military implications, this is going to raise certain practical complications," Rhun of Sheele said, sour and suspicious as he sat back in his chair. "For one thing, the king is going to want to go."

Lord Tammaron Fitz-Arthur nodded patiently. As Chancellor of Gwynedd, it was his duty to preside over meetings of the king's council when the king was not present—and in fact, he presided even when the king *was* present—but formalities hardly seemed necessary with only four of them seated around the long table.

"Of course he'll want to go," Tammaron said. "It's only natural that he should wish to do so—and were the decision up to him, there would be no question. There's a risk involved, of course. Not only might he be killed, but he might be tempted to assert his independence. However, I believe that both pos-

7

sibilities pale beside the very real prospect that this is the challenge we've been hoping to postpone."

At Tammaron's right, quietly imposing in his robes of episcopal purple, Archbishop Hubert MacInnis nodded his agreement, one pudgy hand caressing the jeweled cross on his ample breast. Those who did not know him well saw what he wanted them to see: an affable if oversized cherub, ostensibly godly and devout, rosy face framed by fine blond hair cut short and tonsured in the clerical manner, tiny rosebud lips pursed in a languid pout.

But the apparent innocence of the wide blue eyes was deceptive, and the cunning mind behind them had contrived the death of more than one person who stood in his way. In the last decade, the Primate of All Gwynedd had become the single most powerful man in the kingdom.

"This is damnably inconvenient, if it *is* the challenge," Hubert muttered sullenly. "*Damn*, why couldn't they have waited even another year? A second son would make all the difference."

"You're assuming that the queen carries another son and not a daughter," said the archbishop's elder brother, Lord Manfred MacInnis, seated across from Hubert. He was a beefy, red-faced man in his mid-fifties, muscled where Hubert was merely fat, his sunburned hands scarred and callused from years of wielding a sword. "I wouldn't worry so much about potential heirs as I would about the man who wears the crown right now. If this *is* the challenge we've been dreading, 'tis we and the present king who will have to meet it. And if he can't do that, not even another prince will be enough to ensure the continuance of the Haldane line in power—and us as the power behind the throne."

It was no more than a simple statement of fact. The men seated around the table, the core of the Royal Council of Gwynedd, had been virtual rulers of Gwynedd for six years now, since plotting the slaying of the sixteen-year-old King Javan Haldane in an "ambush" far to the north—blamed on Deryni dissidents—and simultaneously masterminding the coup that put his brother, Rhys Michael, on Gwynedd's throne, though king only in name.

The cost had come high, for the hollow crown this youngest Haldane prince had never sought. Not alone had he lost a beloved brother and king, but the shock of the sudden and brutal slayings surrounding the coup at Rhemuth had caused his young wife to miscarry of their first child—a supreme irony, for eventual control of an underage Haldane heir had been a large part of the ultimate purpose behind the coup.

The new king had not truly comprehended the scope of his captors' ambitions in the beginning. It was horror enough that *he* must fall under their control. Drugged nearly to senselessness during the coup itself, he had been kept drug-blurred for some months thereafter, all through the public spectacle of his brother's burial and then the sham of his own coronation.

Only when he had been safely crowned did they make their intentions clear—and underlined their demands with threats of the most abhorrent nature concerning the fate of his queen if he did not comply. He had been spared to be a puppet king and to breed Haldane princes who, in due course, would fall totally under the sway of the great lords—and under the sway of regents, if their father made himself sufficiently troublesome that he must be eliminated before a tame heir came of age.

Fortunately for all concerned, especially the king, the prospect of another regicide became less and less likely as the first few months passed. Though dispirited at first, the new king gradually seemed to become reconciled to the inevitability of his situation, allowing himself to be shaped as the docile and biddable figurehead they required.

Compliance slowly bought small indulgences. Once the king ceased to be argumentative or to display stubborn flashes of independent thinking, permission was granted for him to attend routine meetings of the council. A satisfactory history of behavior at council meetings earned him the privilege of presiding over formal courts, though always closely attended and working from a carefully rehearsed script. Very occasionally, the queen and later their young son were allowed to appear at his side on state occasions. After the first year or so, when it appeared that he had accepted the restrictions placed upon him and decided to make the most of royal privilege, they had even allowed him to resume his training in arms, against just such a threat as now seemed to be materializing. The queen's new pregnancy seemed to confirm Rhys Michael's capitulation, though there were some seated around this table who still had reservations.

"Let's get down to specifics," Tammaron said. "This hardly comes as any great surprise, after all. We've been aware of increased Torenthi troop movements up along the Eastmarch border since last fall."

Several of the others nodded their agreement, and Rhun muttered something about having warned them long before that.

"It's just the sort of beginning we might have expected," Tammaron went on. "A test incursion into—"

The door to the council chamber slammed back without preamble to admit Paulin of Ramos, black-clad and predatory-looking as he stalked into the room. The mere presence of the Vicar-General of the *Ordo Custodum Fidei* produced no dismay, for he was as heavily involved in intrigue as the rest of them, and one of the architects of their rise to power, but he had been expected to remain with his brother Albertus, questioning the messengers.

"A Torenthi herald has just arrived under a flag of truce," Paulin announced, flouncing angrily into his usual place to Hubert's right. "The man demands an immediate audience of the king and declines to reveal his business except in the king's presence."

"Do you think he comes from King Arion?" Manfred asked.

"No, I do not. I thought so at first, but the Torenthi arms on his tabard are differenced. The black hart is gorged of a coronet. That's Arion's brother."

"Miklos!" Rhun muttered.

"And the Eastmarch messengers claim that Miklos was behind the taking of Culliecairn," Tammaron said, enlightenment dawning on the angular face.

"Precisely," Paulin agreed. "I'd say that the timely arrival of Miklos' herald tends to confirm their story. The question now becomes, is Miklos acting alone, or for King Arion, or for Marek of Festil, as he has in the past?"

Uneasiness murmured around the table at that, for the prospect of an eventual Festillic bid to take back the throne of Gwynedd had loomed with increasing probability since 904, when Cinhil Haldane, the present king's father, had ended a Festillic Interregnum of more than eighty years by ousting and killing the unmarried King Imre. There it might have ended, except that Imre's sister, the Princess Ariella, had been carrying his child when she fled. Later legalists had tried to claim that the royal pregnancy derived from a dalliance with one of her brother's courtiers, by then conveniently dead, for mere illegitimacy was not necessarily a bar to inheritance in Torenth, but everyone knew that Imre was the father.

The child born of this incestuous union the following year

had been christened Mark Imre of Festil, though he now went
by Marek, the Torenthi form of his name, and was accorded
the title of prince among his Torenthi kinsmen. The House
of Festil was descended from a cadet branch of the Torenthi
royal line—Deryni, all—and Torenth had provided troops for
Ariella's unsuccessful attempt to take back the throne lost by
her brother. Following her death in that endeavor, her son and
heir had been brought up among the Deryni princes of Torenth,
biding his time until conditions were right to make his own try
for his parents' throne. Prince Marek now was twenty-three, a
year older than his Haldane rival in Rhemuth, recently married
to a sister of the King of Torenth and lately the father of a son
by her.

"I would think it very likely that Marek is, indeed, behind
this," Tammaron said thoughtfully. "Having said that, however,
I am not altogether certain we can assume that this is a serious
bid to take back the crown. Marek is yet unblooded. He has an
heir, but just the one; and many's the infant that dies young."

"Yet Culliecairn *has* been taken," Manfred pointed out.

"Yes, but I suspect Miklos has done it on Marek's behalf,"
Tammaron countered. "And I seriously doubt that King Arion
supports it. *He* certainly doesn't want a war with us right now,
because he hasn't got adult heirs yet either.

"No, I would guess this to be a drawing action, almost a
field exercise, to see what we'll do. Marek hasn't the support
to make a full-scale invasion and won't until his heir is of age.
I think he wants to flex his muscles and size up his enemy—
and perhaps test to see whether it's true, that the King of
Gwynedd is not his own man."

"Which means," Hubert said, "that the king must be seen to
be his own man, and a competent one, by riding with an expeditionary force to free Culliecairn. I'll grant that there is
some small risk, if he should take it in his head to actually try
to lead," he added, at the looks of objection forming on several
faces. "On the other hand, he knows full well that if he should
meet his death in such a campaign—*for whatever reason*—
young Owain would become the next king, with the certainty
of an actual and open regency until the boy reaches his majority."

"I can't say I'd mind a ten-year regency," Manfred said,
grinning as he leaned back in his chair.

"No, but the queen would," Tammaron said. "And she'd sit

on the regency council by right. Would her brother sit as well, Hubert? He's the boy's uncle; it's customary."

"The king, ah, has been persuaded *not* to name his brother-in-law to the regency council," Hubert said, pretending to study a well-manicured thumbnail. "Something about concern for the young man's health, I believe—the strain of the office, and so forth."

"And it won't be a strain to keep him on at court?" Rhun said archly. "If I'd had my way, he would have been killed six years ago."

Hubert favored the younger man with a droll smile. "Fortunately for him, dear Rhun, you were away supervising another killing at the time. But rest assured that Sir Cathan understands the precarious nature of his position and will do nothing to jeopardize his access to his sister. Nor will she do anything that might endanger his life—or even worse, from her perspective, force us to forbid her access to her son. So long as both of them maintain the utmost discretion and circumspection, I am content that Cathan Drummond should remain in the royal household, if only for the sake of appearances. Besides that, his presence reassures the queen, who will bear stronger princes if her mind is at ease. 'Tis a small enough inconvenience, I think—and one that is open to immediate reassessment, if either of them should abuse the privilege."

Rhun snorted and shook his head. "I'd still rather he were dead."

"That's as may be, but at very least, nothing must happen to him during the queen's pregnancy. Do I make myself quite clear?"

"You do."

"Good. Because whatever else happens, she carries the second Haldane heir, our backup for Prince Owain. Worry about that, if you insist upon worrying about something. Whether or not the king survives this current crisis, Michaela could die in childbed—or worse, the child might die. And if the king should die, whether on a campaign into Eastmarch or as a result of his own folly, the shock could cause her to miscarry again; it happened before."

"Aye," Tammaron breathed. "So all Haldane hopes ultimately hang on one small four-year-old."

"Precisely. For that reason, and to prevent the boy being brought untimely to the crown, I rather think that the king, his lady wife, and her brother will continue to do whatever we require of them."

Hubert's words brought nods of agreement. That the king was a devoted father was hardly any secret, but of the five men seated around the council table, the archbishop perhaps knew the king best of any of them. Though Tammaron and Rhun had been among the original regents appointed to rule Gwynedd during the minority of King Alroy, Rhys Michael's sickly eldest brother, it was Hubert who, because of his office, had been in a unique position both to interact with the three Haldane princes himself and to require detailed reporting from the priests who were the princes' teachers and confessors.

Nor had his influence ended with the end of the regency. For it was also Hubert who, with Paulin of Ramos, had been responsible for the plot that eventually put Rhys Michael on the throne. Accordingly, Hubert's opinion held weight in proportion to his physical size, among these men who shared with him the governing of Gwynedd.

"Well, then," Manfred said, "I suppose we'd better let the king receive Prince Miklos' herald."

"Indeed, yes," Hubert replied. "I'd already informed him of the news from Eastmarch. Before court is convened, I shall be certain that he understands both the political and personal implications of any independent action he might contemplate and that he knows precisely what is expected of him."

CHAPTER TWO

Be not deceived: evil communications corrupt good
manners.

—I Corinthians 15:34

Following Hubert's second briefing, the king could harbour no
illusions regarding what was expected of him. As he dressed
for Court, however, he reflected that he probably understood
the implications of the coming audience far better than any of
his great lords supposed.

Still a little stunned, nonetheless, he considered his situation
as he crossed the fronts of a clean white shirt his body squire
had just put on him, stuffing the tails into the waist of close-
fitting black breeches and then holding out his arms for the
sleeves to be fastened at the wrists.

At least the afternoon was mild, not at all like that other
June, when his brother Alroy lay dying and his brother Javan
had come back to Court, forever changing the destiny of the
fourteen-year-old Prince Rhys Michael Alister Haldane. Seven
years had passed since then, and Rhys Michael had been king
for six of them—king in name, at least.

For now he knew, though he had not wanted to believe it at
the time, that Javan's own great lords had conspired to be rid
of him, the king they could not control, and to set Rhys Michael in his place. It had cost the youngest of the Haldane
princes his innocence and the lives of his brother and the child
who would have been his own firstborn son. It had also cost
him his freedom for the future and sentenced whatever further
progeny he might engender to a life dictated by the great lords.
As King Rhys, he now came and went at their behest, all but

worn down by the intervening years of subjugation, both physical and mental, with even the thought of further resistance almost battered into resignation and acceptance of what they required, if he wished to survive.

This latest development might not set too well with their long-range plans, though. Already, a faint pang of hope had flared in his breast, where he had thought all chance of deliverance nearly stifled.

He had a fair idea what the waiting Torenthi herald would say, based on Hubert's briefing and the news brought earlier by the Eastmarch messengers. The seizure of Culliecairn, with its castle and garrison and town, could not be tolerated. Culliecairn guarded the Torenth-side entrance to the Coldoire Pass, the most direct route through the northern Rhelljan Mountains between Eastmarch and the Torenthi Duchy of Tolan. Hubert had already mentioned the likelihood of an immediate campaign to free Culliecairn, even conceding that it probably would be necessary for Rhys Michael to go along. The king had been forbidden to make any official commitment without first clearing it with his advisors—which rankled, as such constraints always did; but the developing scenario also reminded Rhys Michael most pointedly that he was still an anointed king.

At least they had never forbidden him to *look* like a king. Indeed, they demanded it, whenever they trotted him out for some state occasion that required his official presence. The great lords approved of keeping up appearances. The body squire kneeling at his feet had given his boots a final buff with a soft cloth and now was buckling golden spurs to his heels.

"Beg pardon, Sire," his senior aide murmured, easing past the squire with a plain white belt in his hands.

Faintly bemused, the king lifted both arms away from his sides to allow it. Dark-haired and dark-eyed, Sir Fulk Fitz-Arthur was several years his junior, obliging and loyal enough in most things, but loyal first to his father, Lord Tammaron, if pushed to a choice. Rhys Michael tried to avoid forcing that choice whenever possible, for he honestly liked Fulk and sensed that the liking was mutual; but not for an instant did he believe that mere fondness might make Fulk overlook forbidden deviations from what the great lords permitted.

Far more certain was the loyalty of his other aide, who was shaking out a scarlet over-robe over in the better light of an open window. A year younger than Fulk, and brother to Rhys

Michael's beloved Michaela, Sir Cathan Drummond had been a towheaded squire of twelve on that awful day of the coup, witness to much of the slaughter, nearly a victim himself, and as helpless as Rhys Michael to prevent any of it.

Fortunately, the great lords had stopped short of killing the queen's brother the way they had so many others of those loyal to the Haldanes. After several months' confinement following the coup, upon giving his solemn oath never to speak of what he had witnessed that day, Cathan had been permitted to return to the royal household, the token member actually to be chosen by the new king and queen and the only person, other than themselves, on whom they could always and utterly rely.

It had not taken Cathan long to discover what he must do in order to stay alive, even if he *was* the queen's brother. Grudgingly permitted to resume his training in arms, as well as the gentler accomplishments expected of noble young men headed toward knighthood, he had quickly learned not to do *too* well at anything that might suggest a threat to those who were the true masters at Rhemuth Castle. His eventual knighting, the previous Twelfth Night, had been one of the few acts as king that Rhys Michael had performed gladly, of his own volition. Permission to appoint Cathan as a second aide had been an unexpected dividend of the evening, though the king suspected expediency rather than charity to have been Hubert's motive. Now a belted knight as well as brother to the queen, Cathan was least apt to cause trouble if he continued directly in the royal household, where he could be watched. It kept Cathan himself under scrutiny, but at least it allowed Rhys Michael an adult confidant and ally besides his wife.

As if sensing the king's fond gaze upon him, Cathan came smiling now to lay the scarlet over-robe around his sovereign's shoulders. The fronts were stiff with gold embroidery, as were the wide cuffs of the sleeves, and the broad clasp Cathan snapped closed across the chest resembled the morse of a bishop's cope. He had pinned to the robe's left shoulder a large, fist-sized brooch with the golden lion of Gwynedd embossed upon it, the background inlaid in crimson enamel—Michaela's gift to the king on the birth of little Prince Owain. For the three of them, it had come to symbolize their hopes of a House of Haldane no longer fettered by the great lords.

Blessing Cathan for having thought of it, especially today, Rhys Michael let his fingertips brush the brooch in passing as he adjusted the hang of a flowing sleeve, knowing

Cathan would catch the significance. Fulk had turned away briefly to fetch a burnished metal mirror, so missed the gesture entirely.

"A good choice, Sire," Fulk declared, as he angled the mirror to reflect the royal image.

"Yes, I thought so."

Critically the king studied the overall effect, nervously ruffling one hand through the short-cropped black cap of his hair as he turned to view himself from several angles. He would have preferred to wear his hair longer, perhaps pulled back in a queue or braid, but for some reason the great lords insisted that he keep it short—almost clerical in its severity, though without the shaved tonsure. He had often wondered why— further assertion of their control over every aspect of his life, he suspected. But it sometimes had occurred to him to wonder whether they thought that, as with Samson, they could keep him from gaining strength by cutting his hair.

At least the stark barbering let the Eye of Rom be seen. The great ruby glowering in his right earlobe had belonged to his father and both his brothers before him and was regarded as part of the official regalia of Gwynedd. King Cinhil had been the first Haldane to wear the stone, but the men who eventually became the great lords of Gwynedd remained unaware that it had been given to Cinhil by the Deryni mage later to be known as Saint Camber. Ancient tradition, likewise unknown to the great lords, identified the stone as one of the gifts of the Magi to the Christ Child, later sold to finance the flight to Egypt. Whether or not that was true, Rhys Michael regarded it as one of his few true links with the kingship he feared he might never wield in fact.

"This will do nicely," he said, turning back to Cathan. "Let's have the crown, then."

From a handsome wooden casket studded with brass nail heads, Cathan carefully lifted out the gold and silver State Crown of Gwynedd, with its leaves and crosses intertwined. Cabochon rubies the size of a man's thumbnail had been added to the crown since the coronation six years before, with lesser gems also gleaming among the crown's interstices. Against the sable Haldane hair, as Rhys Michael ducked his head to receive it, the effect was truly majestic.

"Yes, indeed," Fulk murmured approvingly, as he surveyed the king over the top of the mirror, and Cathan also grinned his agreement. "That should make the Torenthi herald sit up and take notice."

"Let's see, shall we?" the king replied, smiling.

Before that question could be answered, though, he must first submit to a final briefing, back in the little withdrawing room behind the dais of the great hall. Afterward, he was told to delay his entrance while the great lords took their own places and the hall had a chance to settle—which also gave him opportunity to survey his audience before he went out. He reviewed his instructions and prayed for courage as he cautiously twitched aside a fold of the heavy velvet that curtained the opening through the screens to the dais beyond.

The high-beamed hall was not as crowded as it might have been—which was just as well, since he expected this would be a rather less congenial court than most, based on the news from Eastmarch and that assumed to be borne by the Torenthi herald. Accordingly, he was a little surprised to see a fair number of ladies present—mostly the wives and daughters of the great lords or ladies from the queen's household, twittering anxiously among themselves as they settled on benches in the window embrasures that overlooked the castle gardens. A few were even carrying baskets of embroidery.

He supposed this did concern them, if Gwynedd went to war. Michaela had wanted to attend, but Hubert had forbidden it. He and Paulin were standing along the right side of the dais, Paulin apparently briefing the seated Archbishop Oriss, who had been specially summoned from his sickbed for the occasion and who looked as if he might not make it through the court. Behind them, Tammaron was instructing a captain of archers, surreptitiously indicating the long gallery that overlooked the right side of the hall. Farther to the left, just off the dais, Rhun and Manfred appeared to be lecturing an angry-looking Lord Richard Murdoch. Albertus was not in evidence. Out in the hall itself, scores of knights and lesser courtiers were also drifting toward the dais where the king shortly would emerge.

And far at the back of the hall, carefully watched by guards in Haldane livery, the legation from Torenth was waiting: half a dozen men-at-arms in eastern-style armor, cloaked in the tawny orange of the Torenthi House of Furstan. One of them bore a flagstaff trailing a banner of white silk. Beneath that banner stood a short, dark man who must be the Torenthi herald. As expected, his tabard bore the springing black hart of Furstan on a silver roundel, differenced of a golden coronet around its proud neck.

"I think they're about ready for us, Sire," Fulk murmured close by his right ear.

With a grunt for answer, Rhys Michael let fall the curtain and held out his hand to Cathan for the sheathed Haldane sword, laying it in the cradle of his left arm with the hilt like a cross at his elbow. At his nod, Fulk grasped an edge of the heavy curtain and drew it aside, following when the king and then Cathan had gone through.

Those first to notice his entrance stirred and then grew silent as he crossed the dais, turning to follow his progress and bowing when he passed, but not giving his arrival the formality of a state entry, lest too much ceremony acknowledge the importance of the men waiting. Rhys Michael acknowledged their bows with an air of preoccupation, settling stiffly into the throne-chair set under the Haldane canopy, and then handing off the Haldane sword to Cathan again. Not for the first time, he found himself wishing it were Javan still alive to sit here in his place, but he made himself dismiss the thought as futile. Javan was dead, and he was alive; and if he hoped to stay alive, he must be very, very careful how he handled this.

And as Constable Udaut came forward to inquire about the visitors seeking audience at the back of the hall, another reason for caution suddenly became clear. Lord Albertus was entering through the screen entrance at the other side of the dais, accompanied by the two haggard-looking Eastmarch messengers and a handful of his staff, mostly black-robed *Custodes* knights. Among the latter, similarly garbed in black, was a small, dark man known only as Dimitri, said to be Deryni, though few at court were aware of that. Though ostensibly employed by Paulin and the *Custodes Fidei*, his exact allegiance was unknown, the last time Rhys Michael heard—and it had been Javan who had told him that, in one of their last conversations before Javan rode off to what was to be his death. In the back of his mind, Rhys Michael had always wondered whether the mysterious Dimitri was at least partially responsible for the treachery.

It was certain that Javan's Deryni allies had not counted Dimitri an ally; and whether he was working *only* for Paulin and his *Custodes* remained an unanswered question. Not for the first time, Rhys Michael lamented the fact that not one of

Javan's Deryni allies had managed to make contact with him since Javan's death, though reason reminded him of their small numbers even then; and the few that he knew of personally had died by the same treachery that took Javan.

The one ray of hope that made him keep believing that there had ever been Deryni backing for the House of Haldane was the fact that, as Javan had predicted, Rhys Michael gradually had learned to discern whether a man was telling the truth. This usually was a Deryni talent, he knew, and ordinary humans could not detect or prevent its use against them—a decided advantage in his present circumstances, except that even if Dimitri had not been present, the Torenthi herald and at least some of his escort undoubtedly were Deryni.

This rather canceled out any advantage his meager talent might have given him; for Deryni, though they could not prevent being Truth-Read, sometimes could detect it. It would not do for the Torenthi herald to know what Rhys Michael could do, even if he could keep it from Dimitri.

He dared not Truth-Read during court today, then—and he must guard his own words, for both the herald and Dimitri undoubtedly would seek to Truth-Read *him*. As Albertus and his party came to stand just behind Rhun and Manfred and Richard, the king shifted his attention back to Udaut, who had started purposefully toward the back of the hall.

Udaut did not announce the visitors waiting there; merely gave them leave with a gesture to approach, turning then to proceed back up the hall in the assumption that they would follow. They did, but the men-at-arms made their own statement of their presence, drawing to attention with much stamping and clashing of arms in martial drill, then pacing behind Udaut with heavy tread, the banner bearer and a bemused herald following almost indolently behind.

When the six guardsmen reached the dais before the throne, they came to a halt with another stamping of steel-shod feet and clashing of mailed fists on ornate breastplates, then parted to make an aisle through which their leader might proceed. The man with the banner footed his staff with a clash of metal against the wooden floor, dipping the white silk in salute as the herald gave a restrained, formal bow.

"Rhys Haldane of Gwynedd," the herald said, the clear voice lightly accented as he drew himself erect from his bow. The man's dark hair was cut short around his long face, the severity emphasizing high cheekbones and slightly canted dark eyes above a thin moustache and a small, close-clipped beard. "Hear the words of my master, the Prince Miklos of Torenth, who acts in behalf of his kinsman, the royal Marek of Festil, rightful king of this realm."

"Sir, you stand before the rightful king of this realm!" Richard Murdoch said, hotheaded and belligerent as he took a step forward, one gloved hand wrapped taut over the pommel of his sword. "You will observe appropriate courtesy."

The herald inclined his head indulgently toward the younger man. "My master has not sent me to debate titles, my lord. His message is for the Haldane."

"Then, speak," Rhys Michael said, before Richard could reply. "The Haldane is listening."

"My lord." The herald inclined his head again. "My gracious prince bids me instruct this court on the antiquity of the noble House of Festil, which sprang from the royal line of Torenth and ruled in Gwynedd for nearly a century. Prince Marek of Festil is the current representer of that noble house. Through his marriage last year to the Princess Charis, Duchess of Tolan and sister to my lord Prince Miklos and King Arion of Torenth, Prince Marek has confirmed, ratified, and strengthened his royal heritage. Already, the royal and ducal line is renewed and secured in the person of his firstborn son, the future Duke of Tolan, who also will rule one day in Gwynedd as King Imre the Second."

A low mutter escaped Rhun's lips, but Hubert slightly raised a pudgy hand in forbearance. Rhys Michael felt a cold chill of dread churning in his gut, spiced by anger, but the herald was not yet finished.

"To that end," the man went on, "and in celebration of the birth of the young prince, my lord Prince Miklos would invite the Haldane court to attend his nephew's christening at Culliecairn, which castle and town my lord Miklos means to present to the royal child as a christening gift."

A murmur of outrage began to ruffle through the hall, but the herald's voice rose above it as he continued.

"If the Haldane would dispute the giving of Culliecairn to this heir of Prince Marek, let him present himself before the city gates within ten days, no later than Saint John's Eve, prepared to show legal proofs why Culliecairn should not become the birthright of Prince Imre of Festil."

"By God, he goes too far!" Manfred muttered dangerously.

"He has some cheek!" Tammaron declared.

"This is an outrage not to be borne!" Rhun roared.

Though in total agreement for once, Rhys Michael kept his anger in check, staying further uproar of his great lords with an upraised hand which, somewhat to his surprise, was heeded.

"Peace, gentlemen. We must not confuse the messenger with the message. What is your name, sir herald?"

"Eugen von Roslov, my lord," the man replied, with a curt inclination of his head.

"Eugen von Roslov." Rhys Michael repeated the name, giving its pronunciation the same accent as its owner did. "Pray, forgive me if I appear to have missed something, but is it Prince Miklos or Prince Marek who affronts my sovereignty by laying claim to my property?"

Smiling faintly, the herald favored Rhys Michael with a graceful inclination of his dark head. "Why, 'tis not intended to affront Gwynedd's sovereignty, my lord, but to ameliorate a slight, no doubt unintentional, incurred when Gwynedd neglected to invite a representative of Torenth to your Highness' coronation. No doubt the precipitous timing of that event contributed to the oversight, following hardly a year after your predecessor's coronation. Nonetheless, my lord's advisors felt certain that your Highness would wish to make amends by attending a similarly auspicious royal event in Torenth."

"The christening of my rival's heir in Culliecairn, sir herald?" Rhys Michael replied. "Surely you jest. Not only that, your geography is faulty. Culliecairn is in Gwynedd."

The herald spread his hands in a dismissive gesture. "No longer, my lord. Furthermore, its giving to my Lord Marek's heir satisfies the social obligation of presenting suitable gifts at the christening of a royal heir. Having designated the castle and town of Culliecairn as a sufficiently princely endowment for his royal nephew, my lord Prince Miklos took possession last week, thus sparing you the effort of bringing a gift along."

"I prefer to make my own decisions regarding the giving of gifts," Rhys Michael said quietly, "and while I understand a father's pride in the birth of a son, you will excuse me, I hope, if I do not share your enthusiasm regarding a further pretender to my throne.

"Furthermore"—he gestured toward the messengers—"I am informed by these good gentlemen that your master's seizure of my property has cost the lives of many good men, including my loyal Earl of Eastmarch, to whom Culliecairn's security had been entrusted."

"No loss of life was intended," the herald said smoothly, "but alas, some men did die."

"Indeed, the death of the Earl of Eastmarch is the only thing that would have permitted your master's entry into Culliecairn," Rhys Michael retorted. He drew a deep breath before going on.

"I therefore must regard the action of your master as an act of unwarranted hostility on the part of a foreign prince. If Miklos does this as a private individual, then I shall appeal to his brother the King of Torenth, who is his overlord, for King Arion surely will not wish his vassal to threaten the borders of a neighbor with whom Arion himself is at peace. If it is done as a prince of Torenth, with King Arion's knowledge, then Miklos risks war between our two kingdoms. And if he does it in behalf of Marek of Festil, then he supports a rebellious and illegitimate claimant against my throne—which, again, could be construed as a formal declaration of hostilities between our two kingdoms. Pray, what is his intention, sir herald?"

The herald inclined his head. "My master has not confided his deeper motivations regarding such matters, my lord. I am instructed merely to convey his intentions regarding Culliecairn."

So saying, he reached casually to the small of his back, up under his tabard, and slowly withdrew a brown leather gauntlet, which he tossed almost offhandedly on the carpet at Rhys Michael's feet.

"If you wish a more formal declaration," the herald went on, "there is a gage in token of my master's claim. You may take it up or not, as pleases you, but to take back Culliecairn, you will have to discuss the terms with my master."

The gage lay a handspan from Rhys Michael's left boot. The challenge was not unexpected, and he had in mind what he must say, once he picked it up, but he knew he must confirm the terms with the great lords before he acted. He must also make himself calm down.

"Let my ministers attend me," he said, getting smoothly to his feet and glancing at Hubert, who nodded minutely. "The Lord Constable will see to our guests while we confer. Let refreshment be brought if they desire it. My lords, attend."

Within minutes, he was facing the agitated handful of them in the little withdrawing room behind the dais, one forefinger punching the air for emphasis as he argued his point.

"This news changes the entire focus of what was told me before court," he was saying. "It's a direct challenge to the sovereignty of this kingdom. You must let me answer it. If I don't, I lose all credibility; *Gwynedd* loses all credibility."

"Sire, we aren't prepared to go to war with Torenth," Tammaron began.

"That's fine, since this isn't about a war with Torenth. Arion isn't behind this. It's Miklos, on behalf of Marek of Festil, and it isn't even a war with Marek. Do you really think *he'd* make a true bid to take back the throne? Not now. Not with only one infant son between him and the obliteration of his house."

"Has it occurred to you," Paulin said, "that this could be a ruse to lure *you* from safety? You aren't that much more secure than Marek, with only one heir living and hope of another. The man is Deryni, Sire. So is Miklos. So is Arion. What if they mean to use their accursed magic against you?"

Rhys Michael turned away with a faintly sick feeling in the pit of his stomach, for he had no answer for that argument.

"I can't worry about that just now," he said softly. "As an anointed king, I believe and hope that divine grace will be granted me to withstand even their magic. It may also be that, against an army, magic is not so effective as it is against an individual man. 'Tis said that an arrow or a sword can be faster and more deadly than a spell—I don't know.

"But this I do know: If you allow any foreign prince to take and keep Culliecairn, which belongs to Gwynedd, then the very sovereignty of the Crown of Gwynedd is a sham, never mind the man who wears that crown. I've learned to accept my own impotence as a man, but I beg you not to further hollow away the crown you hope someday to put upon my son's head. What kind of a kingdom would you leave to *your* sons?"

The question took Richard sufficiently off guard to silence him. Rhun and Tammaron were also at a loss for words, for all three had sons who stood to inherit the power wielded by their fathers. Manfred exchanged a glance with Hubert, for his sons, too—Hubert's nephews—had also benefited from the power wielded by their kin at court. Even Albertus became more subdued, for in order to become Grand Master of the *Custodes* knights, he had resigned his title early to a son already at court—Bonner Sinclair, the young Earl of Tarleton, who was also nephew to Paulin.

Of all the men in that room, only Robert Oriss had attained his position of influence without the connivance of the former regents and had been uninvolved in the coup. Unlike Hubert, Rhemuth's archbishop had no relatives who stood to benefit from his high office; but seeing the royal house purified of its Deryni taints was an aspiration all of them shared.

"No one wishes to impugn the sovereignty of the crown, Sire," the old archbishop said slowly. "But perhaps Culliecairn does not represent an erosion of royal authority so much as an erosion of royal loyalties—in this case, loyalties *to* the Crown. What of the Earl of Eastmarch, who should have protected and held Culliecairn for you? He has a Torenthi wife. It is even said she comes of Deryni stock. Who is to say that it was not Eastmarch's connivance that helped betray Culliecairn to its captors?"

"If so, he has already paid with his life," Rhys Michael said quietly. "But Hrorik would never betray me. I trust my northern vassals, and especially the Earl of Eastmarch and his kin. However, I betray *him*, if I do not ride to the aid of his widow."

"Perhaps we ought to send a viceroy," Manfred said, clearly with himself in mind for such an appointment. "I like not the thought of putting your Highness at risk."

"If it were Culdi taken," the king replied, "and a taunting challenge came, would *you* send a mere deputy? No, you would go. And this is the theft of a fortress at the northern gateway to my kingdom, to be handed over to the heir of my arch-rival, a man who would seize my throne. I will abide by your guidance, gentlemen, as needs I must, but surely you see why I must go."

They disputed the prospect for several minutes more, Tammaron and then Hubert sketching out the details of what he might say in his reply. Before they went back in, he slid the Haldane sword into its holders on his belt, setting his hand on its pommel as he returned through the curtained doorway that Fulk and Cathan parted for him. Up in the gallery, the watching archers lowered their bows and stepped back from sight, though their arrows remained nocked.

"I trust you will pardon the brief interruption," Rhys Michael said mildly, remaining standing as he faced the Torenthi herald once more. "I further note that the gage of your master's challenge yet lies before my throne. I find his belligerence most distressing, for I have never wished him ill, but I am prepared to respond in the way that I must, if he persists in this folly. Is he determined to press this futile attempt to give my castle of Culliecairn to the pretender's heir?"

"Not futile, my lord, since he does possess it," the herald replied. "What answer shall I give him?"

"Why, that I refute his claim and have taken up his gage," Rhys Michael said quietly, "for it is certain that neither your master, the Festillic Pretender, nor any other person outside Gwynedd shall keep Culliecairn." He bent and scooped up the gauntlet almost before anyone could react, hefting it briefly in one hand before tossing it deftly back to the herald, who caught it against his chest.

"Tell your master that I shall meet him at Culliecairn no later than the Eve of Saint John, at which time he shall render up my property," Rhys Michael said. "Tell him that I regret he has forced us to meet under arms, for I remember him kindly from my brother's coronation and would rather have counted him as a friend."

"When friendship would diminish a king's crown, he needs must discount it, my lord," the herald replied.

"Aye, that is true. I cannot count as friends those who befriend my enemies. If your royal master would assist the Festillic Pretender, who seeks to wrest back the crown my father restored after seventy years of usurpation, then he declares himself my enemy as well. Tell him what I have said and warn Marek of Festil that I shall ask and give no quarter where he and his are concerned. You may go in safety."

Without further comment, he turned on his heel and strode from the dais to disappear through the curtained doorway in the screen behind. Cathan and Fulk followed, nearly colliding with the king, who had stopped just inside to draw a deep breath, shivering in after-reaction.

"Well said, Sire!" Fulk whispered fiercely, as Cathan urged the king farther from the screen so other of the great lords could come through. Glancing back a little dazedly, Rhys Michael saw the Torenthi contingent making an uncertain withdrawal, for their audience had suddenly evaporated.

"You handled that very well, your Highness," Hubert said, suddenly beside him, his touch bringing back the king's focus in a flash. "Why don't you rest for half an hour or so? Be assured that Lord Albertus will see our visitors safely out of Rhemuth. Meanwhile, I'll have Lord Tammaron convene the council. You'll be called when we're ready for you again. Having made our decision, I would hope that the royal party could leave first thing in the morning. You'd best advise the queen. Fulk, Cathan, would you please accompany his Royal Highness back to his quarters?"

If the king objected to this cavalier treatment, he gave no outward sign of it, merely drawing deep breath and setting his hand resolutely on the hilt of the Haldane sword before mounting the turnpike stair that led back to the royal apartments. Hubert watched him go, joined a moment later by his brother, who also had been watching the exchange.

"He did that far better than I expected," Manfred said.

"Aye, there's a great deal to be said for Haldane blood," Hubert replied, "even when it's been suppressed. Imagine what the sons will be like, who will never have been exposed to corruption from outside."

Manfred nodded thoughtfully. "It's just possible that we may have gotten to him in time. I wouldn't have predicted it, after our rocky beginning." He snorted, with an ironic little smile. "Not that he has any choice but to follow our guidance, does he? Still, it's for his own good."

"And ours," Hubert reminded him.

"And ours, granted," Manfred agreed. "But it's for the good of Gwynedd, too, if we're to keep the Deryni taint out of Court. And isn't that what keeping the Festils at bay is all about?—besides preserving the Haldane line, of course."

Hubert nodded grimly. "Never the Festils again, no matter *what* else we have to do to ensure it," he said emphatically. "But, go ahead and help Tammaron begin summoning the council. Take Archbishop Oriss with you. I want to have a word with Paulin. I'll join you directly."

Paulin was waiting for him in the little withdrawing room behind the dais screen, with several of his *Custodes* brethren and the wiry little man known to them as Dimitri. The latter was cloaked and cowled in black, so that he looked almost like one of them, but he was not—not of their Order, not strictly of their faith, and not even fully human, by their reckoning, for he was Deryni.

Especially for this last reason, Paulin's *Custodes* companions were giving him wide berth, bunched a little uneasily to one side of the fireplace while Dimitri stood before it, hands folded in the sleeves of his robe, gazing into the flames. He glanced around slowly, almost as if awakened from a sleep, as Paulin pulled two chairs closer for himself and Hubert and they sat.

"Tell us about the herald and his party," Paulin said without preamble. "All Deryni?"

"Aye, my lord, but very well behaved." Dimitri made them a profound bow, then folded to his knees before them to sink back on his heels, hands resting on his thighs. "It was almost as if they—sensed another Deryni presence in the hall besides themselves. Not I, my lord," he added, before Paulin could ask. "I kept my shields damped; they cannot have known. This meant that I dared not essay beyond the simplest Truth-Reading—but nor did they. That is what I meant by 'well behaved.' In fact, none but the herald even sought to Truth-Read. I would have expected more—some attempt to Read beyond the mere words of the king's responses, to catch any hint of bravado or bluff."

"Is it possible *he* was bluffing?" one of the black-clad monks asked. "The herald, I mean."

Dimitri slowly shook his head. "I think not," he said thoughtfully. "The herald at least *believes* that Prince Miklos holds Culliecairn for the Pretender's son and that the challenge has only to do with the future ownership of the castle."

"Then, could this be an excuse to draw our strength up to Coldoire while Torenthi forces make more serious encroachments elsewhere?" The speaker was a dark-haired *Custodes* knight called Cloyce, who was one of Albertus' aides.

Dimitri inclined his head.

"I cannot rule out such motivations, my lord, based on what I perceived," he allowed. "You must rely upon more conventional information to confirm or deny such possibilities. All I can say for certain is that the herald spoke no direct lie in what he told the king—and that, beyond confirming that the king also did not lie, he did not press whatever advantage his blood might have given him, by attempting to probe beyond simple truth."

Hubert grimaced. "What about the king, then? Is it possible," he asked slowly, "that something in the king himself deterred closer scrutiny? You did mention another possibly Deryni presence in the hall. We've always believed Rhys Michael was untainted in that regard, but Javan or someone close to him was skilled enough to manipulate me briefly, all those years ago."

Looking almost perplexed, Dimitri shook his head. "Why do you persist in this questioning, my lord? You have never permitted me to examine his Highness—and I accept that it is because you fear I might somehow seize control and then manipulate him for my own ends, whatever you can think those might be, after so many years of loyal service—but some ability to shield is not that uncommon in humans, especially if the subject has been exposed to Deryni. Since all three Haldane brothers were in the care of Deryni tutors and Healers in their early childhood, it may be that the king retained some residual benefit from that time."

"I would hardly call it a benefit," Paulin muttered.

Dimitri shrugged. "If the herald was deterred from employing advantages he *might* have utilized, then I should count it as a benefit, my lord," he replied. "But be advised that such shielding ability as is sometimes encountered in humans usually yields readily to physical contact. Had the herald had occasion to touch the king, the outcome might have been quite different—though, of course, any serious encroachment would take time, especially if one wished one's efforts to go undetected."

The Deryni agent's attempt to defuse any threat that might be perceived from himself did little to reassure most of the men listening, though Hubert, at least, did not seem alarmed.

"The king knows better than to let a Deryni touch him," the archbishop said flatly. "He fears those of Torenth far more than he fears us."

"So long as he fears us both," Paulin murmured, casting Hubert a sour look. "Shall we adjourn to the council chamber? They'll be mostly gathered by now, and we should agree on a plan of action before we summon the king to join us."

"Quite true," Hubert agreed, lumbering to his feet with difficulty. "Dimitri, you will hold yourself in readiness for the afternoon, but for now, you may go."

As he and Paulin headed out of the room, the two *Custodes* men falling in behind them, Dimitri bowed low to touch his forehead to the floor, remaining thus until they had gone.

CHAPTER THREE

And if it be meet that I go also, they shall go with
me.

—I Corinthians 16:4

In the royal apartments, meanwhile, the king was stealing a
few minutes with his wife before duty called him back to the
great lords' business. When he came striding into the solar that
linked their respective sections of the royal apartments, he
found her sitting in a pool of sunshine near the window while
the youngest and prettiest of her maids combed out her freshly
washed hair.

"My lord!" she cried, her face alight with the joy of him as
she sprang to her feet. The royal blue of her overgown was a
shade darker than her eyes, and the damp mane of her hair fell
like a wheaten curtain nearly to her hips, shifting heavily as
she handed off a towel to the maid.

Beyond her in the wide bay of the window, interrupted in
their needlework and gossip, three of her ladies-in-waiting also
rose—all of them chosen by the great lords, wives and daughters mostly, and also their agents and spies, not really friends.
They fell silent and dipped in formal curtsies as he entered,
civil enough after six years, and the little maid also bowed and
backed away from the queen, her comb clutched to her breast
and eyes downcast.

"Ladies," the king murmured.

He allowed himself a slight smile, but he ventured no further comment as he crossed the room and led Michaela into
the privacy of their bedchamber. He had left the State Crown

with Cathan when he came through his own quarters, but he still wore the crimson over-robe with the Haldane brooch.

"I'm to go," he said, the words falling with the threat of unknown peril as he drew her to sit beside him on the edge of the great state bed.

Like all the Court, she had known of the Eastmarch messengers who arrived earlier that morning, and her troubled gaze never left his face as he related the gist of what had just transpired in the great hall and the room beyond. She said nothing as he spoke, but he could sense her growing fear.

"So that's as much as I know, for now," he concluded, when he had outlined his intentions. "I don't *think* this is the full-blown challenge we've been fearing—Marek of Festil wouldn't chance it, with only the one heir—but on the faint chance that it is, it's essential that I go in person. Not even the great lords could disagree. Shall you be very brave while I'm gone? If—anything should happen, you must be a strong regent for Owain and—"

His voice broke off as his gaze and one suddenly trembling hand dropped to caress the gently rounded curve of her abdomen. Shuddering, she stifled a sob and drew him to her, pulling him down on the bed atop her, seeking reassurance in his embrace. The faint perfume of her damp hair invited him to bury his face and hands in it, to drown his own apprehensions in loving her, but the knowledge that a summons from the great lords was imminent made him push such temptations to the back of his mind and draw apart a little. Raising up on his elbows, he took one pale hand to press a tender kiss to its palm.

"God, how I adore you, Mika," he whispered, searching her blue eyes. "I can hardly breathe for wanting you, but Cathan or Fulk will be knocking on the door any second. It's what I've been longing for—a council meeting where they may actually credit what I have to say—but it also means parting from you. Maybe forever, when I go tomorrow."

She summoned a brave smile and brushed trembling fingertips along the line of his jaw, letting them linger then on the Haldane brooch pinned to his shoulder.

"Have we not prayed for this day to come, my lord?" she whispered. "Not the parting, but the chance to assert your kingship. 'Tis so sudden, though—but a night away. Must you really leave so soon?"

He closed his eyes briefly, desperate fear churning at his gut, then sighed and sat up, turning slightly from her gaze.

"If I let them delay, they may find some new reason not to let me go," he said bleakly. "Besides that, if Culliecairn really is taken, as seems certain, then best to resolve the situation before Torenthi forces get too strongly entrenched there."

"I know you must go," she whispered, brushing her hand down his arm. "I would ride with you if I could. You know I would."

"Aye, my love, and I would take you with me," he replied. He dropped his gaze briefly, then held her close again.

"Oh, God, Mika, what if I don't come back?" he whispered. "What will become of you? What will become of our sons?"

"I will—try to be strong for them and for you," she said softly, tears welling in her eyes. "I will give my life, if need be, to see that they survive—and that they do not forget their Haldane legacy. The crown *will* be free again, someday, my love—I swear it!"

"Ah, my fierce, proud queen," he murmured. "Now I *really* don't want to go. And I especially don't want to go tomorrow, even though I've lived for this day for six long years now—the chance to actually be a king. I wish you could have seen me at court, Mika."

"I wish I could have been there," she countered softly. "Would that I could be at your side now—and tomorrow. We must—make tonight suffice for all our tomorrows."

She would have said more, but an enormous yawn caught her by surprise. After indulging it, she stretched and drew him to her for a quick, hard kiss, then flashed him a sheepish and apologetic smile.

"I must be certain to have a nap this afternoon," she said. " 'Tis no reflection on the company, I assure you, but growing this baby seems to take such a great deal more energy than Owain—"

A knock at the door made them both freeze, and Rhys Michael reluctantly turned his gaze in that direction, though he kept his arms around her.

"Come."

Cathan poked his head into the doorway, tentative and immediately apologetic as he saw them. One of his hands clutched the sheathed Haldane sword, the other a thin gold circlet chased with Celtic interlace.

"Sorry, Mika," he said, glancing at his sister. "Rhysem, they're ready for us."

Closing his eyes briefly, the king heaved a heavy sigh and got to his feet, drawing Michaela with him.

"I don't want to go," he whispered.

"You must, my love," she replied, lifting her face to his. "Go with my love and my prayers."

With only her brother as witness, Rhys Michael felt no need to forgo a proper kiss of leave-taking. Pressing his lips to hers, he let himself drown for a few seconds in the bliss of their joining, more than usually aware that any parting might be their last, if that proved most expedient for the men who held their fate. When, at length, he finally raised his head from hers, his body ached from wanting her. He held her close a moment more, feeling her heart pounding beneath his, then resolutely kissed first the tip of her nose, then her forehead.

"Right, then. I'm off." His voice was a little hoarse. "We'll dine privately, I think. Cathan can join us for supper, because I know you'll want to say good-bye, but he goes to bed early." He grinned. "Make sure you get that nap. I should be back in a few hours."

Bravely blinking back her tears, Michaela followed him into the solar and watched him continue on into his own apartments with Cathan, ruffling one hand through his hair with a familiar gesture that made her throat constrict with the loving of him. She caught a sob as she turned away from the closing door, determined not to let her ladies see her distress.

Over in the window bay, her ladies had risen as the king passed through the room, but they settled back to their needlework at a gesture from the queen. As one of them held a hank of silk to the light, drawing out another long strand, the queen's young maid emerged from among them. After casting a questioning look at her mistress, she picked up an ivory-backed brush and came back to the sunlit stool where the queen had been sitting, testing a damp strand of hair as the queen sat down again.

"It's very nearly dry, my lady," she said. "Shall I brush it a little?"

"Yes, thank you, Liesel," the queen replied. And as the girl began to brush, her mistress closed her eyes and gave a contented sigh.

"That feels wonderful," she murmured after a few seconds,

eyes still closed. "I could sit here and let you do that all afternoon."

A faint smile tugged at the rosy lips of the girl addressed as Liesel. Pert and pretty, she was a little younger than the queen and shorter by a head, with hair a slightly paler shade of gold braided and pinned close under the white kerchief that bound it. The pale oatmeal color of her close-sleeved gown was not flattering to most women—which was precisely the intention of the great lords, in choosing it for the castle's female servants—but Liesel's high color made it a perfect foil for beauty yet to ripen fully. Her eyes went golden in the sunlight, lit against the pale raiment—eyes that shone with genuine affection for the woman whose hair she continued to brush.

"My lady has beautiful hair," she said quietly. "Caring for it gives me pleasure as well."

"Does it?" Michaela smiled dreamily but did not open her eyes. "Aye, it must be something like stroking a cat. It pleasures the cat, but the stroking is also pleasing to the one who does it."

" 'Tis like heavy silk that catches the shimmer of the sunlight, my lady," Liesel replied. "Small wonder that the king prefers it unbound."

"Aye, he does."

Michaela's smile evaporated as she opened her eyes to glance sidelong at her maid, a haunted look flashing briefly in her gaze.

"Liesel, you must help me do something special with it tonight," she murmured. "The king dines with me, and tomorrow he rides for Eastmarch. God alone knows if I shall see him again in this life."

Liesel had stopped brushing and stared at her mistress with pity in her golden eyes.

"Oh, my lady," she breathed.

Reaching back to pat the girl's hand, Michaela conjured up a brave smile, suddenly very weary.

"Now, don't *you* get weepy, or you'll make me cry as well," she whispered. "He must not know how much I fear for him." She looked about to say more, but then she sighed heavily and felt at her hair again. "I think I'm dry enough now. I really do need a nap."

"Yes, my lady," Liesel murmured, eyes downcast.

Covering a yawn with one graceful hand, Michaela bestirred

herself to glance over at the women in the window bay as she rose.

"Dear Lady Estellan, why don't you and Lirin and Adelicia enjoy the gardens for an hour or two? I'm going to have a nap, so I shan't need you for a while. Liesel will help me undress."

She did not linger to see that they went. She did not much care for them anyway, but she had to maintain a facade of geniality. As she made her way back into the bedchamber and watched Liesel turn back the coverlet on the high, canopied bed, with its hangings of crimson damask and gold-shot yellow silk, another heavy yawn claimed her.

"I don't know why I get so sleepy carrying this baby," she murmured, as the maid helped her shed the blue over-robe. "Owain didn't make me this tired."

"Perhaps this time my lady is more preoccupied," the maid replied, as her mistress climbed up onto the bed. "But lay you down and rest awhile, your Grace. Sleep is a remedy for many ills."

Yawning again, Michaela did as she was bade, her eyes closing even as she lay down in her undergown. A deep sigh soon told of her shift into sleep, and the maid, after laying the blue over-robe across the back of a chair, came treading softly back to the bed to lean close to her sleeping mistress.

"Sleep deeper now," she whispered, as she laid one hand lightly across the royal forehead.

Her own eyes closed briefly, and after a moment a faint gasp escaped her lips. She was shaking her head as she gazed at her mistress once more, concern in her golden gaze.

"God give you gentle rest now, sweet queen," she whispered, as she withdrew her hand. "Sleep well and wake refreshed. You gave me leave to go and fetch a book of poetry from the library. If you should wake before I return, you also bade me fetch fresh flowers for your hair tonight."

The ladies in the solar had gone when Liesel came quietly out of the royal bedchamber, though another maid called Elspeth lay napping in the sunshine of the deserted bay, not stirring as Liesel passed through. The usual guards were at their posts in the corridor outside.

"Merry greetings, Mistress Liesel," their captain said, sauntering over to smile down at her.

She had to tip her head back to look up at him, for she came only to his shoulder, but she had the measure of the man and knew this one could be manipulated.

"God give you grace, Captain," she said boldly. "My lady is sleeping. Pray you, see she is not disturbed."

He stepped aside with a courteous salute and let her pass without a word. He had been one of the more brutish of the regular guards when first she came to royal service a few months earlier, but now he was as tame as a fireside tabby in the presence of this bold-eyed slip of a girl.

For the name of the queen's favorite maid was not Liesel at all, nor was she only a maid. Just now, this golden-eyed daughter of the Healer Rhys Thuryn and Evaine MacRorie was also the sole interface between the royal couple and certain Deryni working behind the scenes to extricate them from their indenture to the lords of state.

Not that either Rhys Michael or his queen were yet aware of "Liesel"'s true identity or her mission—though she knew, as she headed briskly down the corridor toward a turnpike stair, that this would have to change, and soon.

The eventual plan had been to gain access to the king and awaken his Haldane powers—a task for which Rhysel Thuryn was one of the pivotal players—then stage a sudden coup such as put the king's father on the throne nearly a quarter century before, spearheaded by Deryni-backed pro-Haldane forces who even now were beginning to gather in remote parts of Gwynedd. The target date had been some five or six months hence, when the queen's new pregnancy would have progressed to the point that safe delivery of a second heir was likely—as was the increased danger that the king would be eliminated by his captors, once his dynastic duty had been done. That danger was dire enough to hazard making their move despite its attendant perils—for the king could perish in any attempted coup—but his impending departure for Eastmarch on the morrow suddenly placed him in far more immediate danger, if he must face Torenthi magic without a way to counter it.

Fighting down a wave of sick fear, Rhysel gained the welcome dimness of the turnpike stair and started down, left hand trailing along the newel post for balance. Not for the first time, she found herself regretting the circumstances that had kept her mentors from moving in the king's behalf long ago.

But it simply had not been possible to establish contact with the new king during those precarious days and months immediately following the death of King Javan. Not only was Rhys Michael closely guarded, but no one was sure what reception a Deryni contact might receive, for no one knew how much Javan had confided to his brother before riding out on his final journey north.

Furthermore, the reshuffling of power that had put Rhys Michael on his brother's throne had also cost his would-be supporters dearly. Though several well-placed Deryni had established a precarious foothold in Javan's court, keeping their true identities secret and slowly beginning to erode the great lords' influence, Javan's fall had brought their deaths as well. It was believed that the great lords had not suspected the Deryni presence; and, indeed, they must never learn of it, else Rhys Michael himself must fall under closer scrutiny—if that were possible.

It also had become clear, once those critical first months were past, that the new king probably was relatively safe where he was, for the time being—at least until he produced an heir or two, and so long as he did not take too long about it. Even the great lords did not desire the extinction of the Haldane line. They wanted another long regency, heralding a succession of grateful and biddable monarchs who would support the dispersal of royal power among the great lords who had engineered their very existence.

But here, theory and expediency might well diverge. Preserving the legitimate succession was most desirable; but if Rhys Michael had declined to cooperate, the great lords had decided very early that it was sufficient for their purposes merely to keep the king alive until some willing surrogate ensured that the queen did, indeed, bear offspring that would be taken for Haldane. What the great lords most desired was a puppet Haldane king; but a puppet bastard carrying the Haldane name would suit them well enough, if it came to that.

Rhysel guessed that the king would have come to understand this all too well, as the months spun on into years. From clandestine probes of Queen Michaela, she knew that the royal couple had delayed conceiving an heir as long as they dared, but the birth of a son in the second year of the king's reign had made Rhys Michael's continued survival that much more precarious. He now was no longer the only Haldane. The birth of a second heir, especially another prince, might well push the great lords to a second regicide, once they were certain the second child thrived; for a regency for a four-year-old heir, with a spare in the royal nursery, would require far less effort than maintaining the illusion that a grown king actually ruled his kingdom. Whenever it suited the great lords, whether sparked by actual transgression or mere pique, Rhysel had no doubt that the king would meet a convenient "accident," as many had done before him.

Thus had it become urgent that the king be brought to his full Haldane powers before the birth of his next child—and now it became essential that he be awakened before he left for Eastmarch, lest he perish at the hands of a Deryni enemy before he had a chance to clean his own house. The prospect would have been daunting enough with time for preparation, months from now, as they had planned. But if they were even to try, on such short notice, the king must be willing to cooperate without reservation, to give himself totally into the guidance of his Deryni allies with little time for wariness or explanations, for there *was* no time except for trust and the doing of what must be done.

From what Rhysel had learned of the king by her own meager observations, securing that trust would be no easy thing. He had little reason to trust anyone besides his wife and her brother, and certainly not the Deryni who seemed to have abandoned him these past years. What Rhysel thought might swing the balance was a factor she did not believe even her mentors had considered. Both Queen Michaela and her brother possessed Deryni blood of their own; it was diluted and had been rendered impotent in early childhood, but what potential they once had possessed could be restored—*if* the blocking process could be reversed.

So far as Rhysel knew, only one person now alive could do that—her own brother Tieg, not yet fourteen. She did not want to think about the danger of bringing him here to Rhemuth— for Michaela and Cathan certainly could not go to him—but she and Tieg had already discussed the possibility. She found herself wondering whether Tieg's unique powers could also catalyze a Haldane's powers. She knew from reading Michaela that the king had shields and perhaps could Truth-Read— which had kept Rhysel herself from probing more directly— but he would need far greater skills than those to keep him safe from a trained Festillic adversary.

Pale skirts gathered close about her ankles, Rhysel glanced left and right as she emerged from the spiral stair that led down to the library floor. The corridor was deserted, as she had hoped it would be at this time of day, and her slippered feet made no sound as she moved quickly along the expanse of diagonally set black and white tiles. Her true destination was a disused chamber just beyond the library, but to be seen entering it might arouse unwelcome curiosity. So she would go into the library first, fulfilling the errand she had set herself from the queen and also disarming whatever potential betrayal might be lurking there.

The precaution proved to be well taken, for she sensed a presence in the room even before her hand touched the door latch. Forewarned, she opened it boldly and entered. Over at the far left end of the room, glaringly lit by a wash of sunlight from one of the bay windows, a black-clad back was hunched anonymously over one of the writing desks, intent on his scribing. He glanced back over his shoulder as he heard the door, then scrambled awkwardly to his feet, the sunlight casting rusty highlights on a familiar black scholar's robe, worn and much-patched.

Thank God. She had been expecting one of the sour *Custodes* scribes. She could deal with this young man.

"Why, Master Donal. God give you grace," she said lightly, as she closed the library door behind her. "Hard at work, I see."

He bobbed his head and blushed to the roots of his short-cropped dark hair. The gangly lay scholar adored her and usually became tongue-tied in her presence—a reaction that Rhysel did not try too hard to discourage, since a smitten suitor was far more malleable than a rejected one. Simple courtesy cost nothing, and she did not *dis*like Donal, for all that he seemed to work willingly for those who were her enemies.

"M-mistress Liesel," Donal stammered. "Your unexpected p-presence fulfills the promised fairness of a glorious day."

She favored him with an inclination of her head and an appreciative smile that made him blush even more, then turned her attention to a casual inspection of the room, her gaze brushing lovingly over the manuscripts and bound volumes scattered across another library table. There were more stored in the ceiling-high range of shelves and pigeonholes that occupied the right-hand wall of the room, and the familiar scent of leather and ink was like a heady perfume.

Masking her pleasure, she moved a little closer to the table stacked with books and ran a finger along a spine stamped with gold. Donal knew she could read and write, but he had no notion that her passion for learning probably surpassed his own—one of the many legacies of her beloved parents. That she had put it aside in a greater cause, he probably would never know. All her recent years had been spent trying to absorb the practical knowledge and training to enable her to function as she did now.

"Pretty words, Master Donal," she said softly, a smile still playing at her lips as she glanced up at him. "But if you think to deter me from my errand with compliments, I must warn you that I will not be swayed. I come at the queen's behest. My lady bids me bring her the book of Lady Kyla's poetry, whose binding was to be repaired. Is it ready?"

Ducking his head in happy affirmation, Donal scurried over to the wide library table and sorted quickly through several stacks, finally selecting a vermilion-bound volume from among the rich jewel-tones of leather bindings.

"Aye, here it is." He burnished the book's spine against a sleeve, then held it out for her inspection as she came nearer. "Brother Lorenzo brought it back only yesterday."

As she took the book from him, it was no difficult thing to brush his hand with hers. The instant of contact reinstated controls used several times before, sufficient to forestall any possible interference.

"Thank you, Donal," she whispered. "The queen will be pleased. Now go back to work and have a lovely dream." She briefly closed her hand around his slack one, still poised from having given over the book. "Remember only that I came to fetch this. Go now."

He turned without a word and went back to his desk, settling on his stool to gaze dreamily out the window, his chin propped on one hand, a grey-mottled quill slack in his other. As she opened the library door to slip back out, he was already sinking into the pleasant memory of an old daydream—a gentle fantasy just wishful enough to ensure that the fastidious Donal would never dream of mentioning it to anyone, even a prying *Custodes* confessor. Pleasant enough for Donal, harmless enough for both of them, and far less intrusive than other measures she might have employed to divert his notice of whatever he might hear from the room next door.

The corridor outside was still deserted as she closed the door quietly behind her. She cast with her powers in both directions, but no one was about. Hugging close the volume of poetry that was her ostensible reason for being in this part of the castle at all, she moved silently to the next door to the left. She already knew the room beyond was unoccupied, but as she gently turned the latch and slipped inside, she wondered what she would do if someone were assigned permanent quarters here. The location would be ideal for some avid scholar.

As she always did, she breathed a faint sigh when she had eased the door closed behind her, her visual inspection confirming that the small, lime-washed chamber remained disused. A sheen of dust blurred the surfaces of the table and chairs set before the cold hearth in one corner, and the mattress on the simple bed remained folded up against the head, hard against the wall to the right of the door. Despite the austerity of the room thus stripped, she could almost imagine the man who briefly had occupied this room and guarded what it contained, even though she had never met him.

His name had been Etienne de Courcy, and only a handful of men and women knew, or would ever know, how he had aided the Haldane cause. Because he had been loyal to King Javan, the great lords had executed him following the coup that put Rhys Michael on the throne, but they had never guessed that he was Deryni; never guessed that it was he who had spirited away the Deryni wife and daughter of a slain Healer during those first hours of confusion.

And though he might have stayed with them in safety, it had been Etienne's own choice to return, his powers and memories blocked, to let himself be captured, tortured, and eventually killed rather than risk that the great lords might discover how Deryni had been inserted into the midst of Javan's court. For that, and to keep this avenue open, Etienne de Courcy had given his life. Guiscard, his elder son, had also died in the Haldane cause, fighting at the side of King Javan.

Breathing a silent prayer of thanksgiving for the lives of both de Courcys, two more martyrs for the survival of her race, Rhysel moved quietly into the center of the room, trying to disturb the dust as little as possible. Stepping onto the only square flagstone for a full arm's length all around, she braced her feet and bowed her head over the book clasped against her breast. As she let fall her shields, she felt the powerful tingle of a Transfer Portal under her feet, and she drew on the Portal's power as she warped the energies.

CHAPTER FOUR

Miss not the discourse of the elders: for they also
learned of their fathers, and of them thou shalt learn
understanding, and to give answer as need requireth.
—Ecclesiasticus 8:9

Many miles north and east, a fair-haired youth assigned to
keep watch beside another Portal leaned back in his chair and
chewed thoughtfully at the feathered end of his quill. As he
glanced casually in the direction of the Portal, briefly probing,
the hazel eyes went a little unfocused. Though baptized Camber Allin MacLean, he had been known as Camlin since childhood, to distinguish him from the illustrious and now sainted
MacRorie kinsman in whose honor he had been named. At
twenty-two, exactly the age of the king, he somewhat resembled Camber's son Joram, in whose exile household he now
resided—except for the tough white scars scribing both wrists,
front and back.

He could remember a time before the scars, half a lifetime
ago. Memory of the scarring itself was mercifully blurred,
though he knew, from later conversations with those who
found him, that he had been nailed to the timber portcullis of
his father's burning castle. Within the range of atrocities committed that day at Trurill, crucifixion had been one of the
milder examples; at least Camlin had survived.

Most at Trurill had not, including his father. Appallingly tortured and maimed by his captors, the dying Lord Adrian
MacLean had even been compelled to watch while they im-
paled the boy they had mistaken for his son and heir—young
Aidan Thuryn, cousin and fosterling of his house, beloved el-

der brother of the same Rhysel whose arrival was expected later today.

Dazed with shock and disbelief, the eleven-year-old Camlin had been witness to all of it, shivering with terror in a pitifully inadequate hiding place beneath the kitchen stairs. The raiders, when they finally found him, had assumed him to be a mere squire, and had settled for stripping and scourging him before dragging him out to the castle gate to crucify him, just before they set fire to the castle and rode away. A snowstorm had saved him from the fire; and the slain Aidan's mother and younger brother had arrived in time to save Camlin his life and at least the limited use of his hands.

He grimaced as he laid down his pen and massaged gently at the knotted scars on his right wrist, gazing unseeing at the empty Portal square as he fondly remembered "Aunt" Evaine and little Tieg. He still wondered how they had done it, for a Healer's gifts normally did not begin to manifest until age ten or so. Tieg had been only three at the time and totally untrained; and his mother, though a powerful Deryni, had been no Healer at all. How had *she* managed to harness and channel her young son's healing potential and effect even a clumsy healing of injuries that should have left Camlin crippled, if he survived them at all?

Of course, she had been Saint Camber's daughter. And perhaps her years of working with her Healer husband, the unsurpassed Rhys Thuryn, had given her some special insight; though so far as Camlin knew, no other Deryni had ever duplicated her feat—or Tieg's.

He couldn't even bring himself to resent that the result had not been perfect; it should not have been possible at all. Because of the scarring, he would never again possess sufficient wrist strength to wield the sword that should have been his birthright; but since his father's murderers believed him dead as well, and one of the great lords now possessed the lands that should have passed to Camlin, that question was moot at best.

What he *could* still wield with fair panache was a pen—so long as he did not wax too wordy. Even here, in the underground sameness of the sanctuary, changes of weather outside made his wrists ache, and writing for too long almost always had its price. Some days, even the effort of lifting a cup to his lips produced such excruciating pain that he must seek a Healer's easing.

Such physical limitations encouraged an economy of words

that, of necessity, must cut to the heart of any question. His growing proficiency in this regard had impressed even the most demanding of his very exacting teachers here in the haven. In a rare flash of old rivalries among the Deryni religious orders, the Gabrilite-trained Dom Rickart and Dom Queron avowed that Camlin was acquiring an almost Michaeline militancy in his sharpness of reasoning; Joram and Bishop Niallan, who had been Michaelines, professed that this was no bad thing. Whatever the middle ground might be, Camlin was building a useful niche for himself, here in the close-knit environment of the sanctuary, at last able to begin giving back something to those who had given him so much.

Smiling wistfully, he picked up his pen again and returned to his work. For something to do while he took his turn at monitoring the Portal, he had been annotating Bishop Niallan's history of the Haldanes since the Restoration, begun shortly after the death of King Alroy.

The piece in progress dated from just after King Javan's death—Tieg Thuryn's transcription of the eyewitness memories he had read from Etienne de Courcy before blurring other memories and blocking Etienne's powers. It was one of the few inside accounts they had of the events surrounding the great lords' seizure of power and the person of the then-Prince Rhys Michael Haldane, and it still chilled Camlin to read it: the cold-blooded treason, masterminded by trusted ministers and so-called men of God, that had seen the prince's aide brutally murdered before his eyes, another loyal lord slain while trying to escape, and a third so gravely wounded that he later would die of his wounds, though it took him several pain-racked months.

Etienne himself would never know that, of course. Not for the first time, Camlin found himself wondering what kind of loyalty would make a man like Etienne choose to go back to certain capture, probable torture, and almost inevitable death. Camlin was sworn to the Haldane cause, and to a prince he had never met, but he doubted he would have had the courage to do what Etienne had done . . .

Shaking his head, Camlin made a note to inquire further on a reference to a particular *Custodes* knight, then skipped over Etienne's rationale for returning. An indecipherable word jumped out at him, and he bent closer to puzzle it out. Tieg's handwriting was clear enough, but his spelling sometimes bordered on the whimsical. Camlin put it down to laziness; Tieg maintained that a Healer had better things to do with his time than worry about exact spellings, so long as his meaning was clear. Camlin countered that proper spelling helped convey proper meaning, and so the debate continued. It was an ongoing but good-natured dispute that had occupied the pair of them increasingly as Tieg grew into young manhood. Camlin had just set his pen to another correction when the door to the outer corridor eased open.

" 'Lo, Camlin," came a low-voiced greeting, as Tieg himself slipped inside. "Uncle Joram said I should relieve you, if you're ready for a break."

Camlin smiled and laid his pen aside as he turned around. Tieg's voice had broken only a few months ago, and though the change had not been unexpected, Camlin still found himself listening for a familiar boyish treble, not this deep-voiced young man.

Tieg seemed to grow visibly from week to week. Yet a few months short of his fourteenth birthday, he already stood half a head taller than Camlin, who was not short, and his hands looked to belong to a far larger individual. A spattering of freckles across his nose still reinforced a first impression of boyish innocence, but the hazel eyes were wise far beyond his years.

His attire likewise proclaimed his emerging adult standing. Though Healers usually did not qualify until about the age of eighteen, Tieg had already earned the right to wear full Healer's green—at least here in sanctuary. Recently, in imitation of Dom Queron and Dom Rickart, he had also begun pulling back his wavy reddish hair in a four-stranded Gabrilite braid—a capital offense outside these walls, if the wearer was Deryni, and even humans sporting such a braid risked having their heads shaved. The law also allowed for human transgressors to be flogged to unconsciousness, if circumstances suggested that the offense had been meant to show support for Deryni. Fortunately Tieg rarely ventured outside the sanctuary, and never in green or wearing a braid.

"Well, you're looking very official today," Camlin said, restraining a grin. "Did Joram really send you, or did you just get bored?"

Tieg chuckled and shook his head, looking down sheepishly. "He didn't exactly *send* me—but I guess I did get bored. They're busy talking about levies and supply lines and the strategic weaknesses of Rhemuth Castle. I don't mind relieving you, though."

"Well, it's very kind of you to offer, but I think I'd just as soon stay a while longer and finish what I'm doing. I'm not that tired."

"No, but your hands are," Tieg replied. Looking faintly smug, he came over to catch up Camlin's two wrists in his big Healer's hands. "When are you going to stop trying to mask your pain, when you know I can do something about it?"

Camlin caught his breath as Tieg probed gently at the scarring on one of his wrists, then exhaled softly and closed his eyes, almost going boneless as blessed healing poured into swollen tissues and dissolved away his discomfort. He had never felt a Healer's touch like Tieg's, and he wondered whether it had anything to do with his blocking talent.

"I don't think so," Tieg said aloud, answering the unasked question. "Dom Rickart told me one time that, back when he first started his training, one of the oldest brothers at Saint Neot's had something of the same feel, but Dom Queron says he detects a little of my father's flavor."

He shrugged as he shifted his attention to the other wrist. "I haven't had contact with that many other Healers, so I really couldn't say. And unfortunately, I'm afraid I don't remember very much about my father."

Only half listening, Camlin let the bliss of Tieg's healing wash all around him as the second wrist was eased. He wondered how Tieg did it. He could only compare it to the feeling he sometimes got when meditating, when he thought he had made a better than usual connection with the rhythm of the Spheres. Bishop Niallan had suggested that perhaps Camlin was tapping into the energies that sometimes called one to a life of contemplation and prayer. Camlin was not certain he had such a calling, but many aspects of such a life were definitely appealing—and suited to his physical limitations.

"I remember your father fairly well," he said, reluctantly dragging his focus back to the here and now. "Of course, I was only eleven when he died." He sat back in his chair and let his healed hands rest easily in his lap. "I really liked Lord Rhys; everyone did. I wish I'd had the chance to know him as a man."

"So do I," Tieg said softly.

The very tone of his words conveyed several shades of meaning, but before their conversation could digress into useless conjecture on what might have been, a faintly discordant surge in the local energies rippled at the edges of consciousness.

"Rhysel's coming," Tieg said, instantly refocused as he turned away to move closer to the Portal.

Catching a little of Tieg's sudden tension, Camlin also got to his feet. The permanent Wards built into the sanctuary Portal were supposed to prevent unauthorized access, but solo Portal duty always put him a little on edge, on the chance that magical protections must be augmented with physical force. It was not likely—the Portal's defenses probably would hold against any psychic trickery most intruders might try, at least until help could be summoned—but Camlin's Deryni abilities were not particularly strong, never mind that his hands would be all but useless in any physical altercation. Still, that first instant of temporary disorientation upon arrival would render any newcomer vulnerable as well.

She was there even as he thought it, not looking vulnerable at all, the sheer psychic impact of her sudden presence making Camlin recoil a step even as he drew a startled breath. For all that both he and Tieg towered over her, she was cool and self-possessed, golden eyes scanning and assessing over the book she clasped to her breast. Even in the drab, colorless gown worn by the queen's maids, with her spun-gold hair mostly covered by a white kerchief, Camlin thought her quite one of the loveliest creatures he had ever seen—though here, in the cloistered seclusion of the sanctuary, he had to admit that his experience was somewhat limited.

"What's happened?" Tieg demanded, as her look of concentration shifted to a worried smile. "You weren't expected for hours. Does this mean there's news?"

Sighing, she stepped from the Portal niche to deposit her book on the table where Camlin had been working.

"More like intimations of disaster, I'm afraid. Hello, Camlin. I don't know whether we can move fast enough or not. Messengers from Eastmarch arrived at Court this morning with news that Torenthi forces have taken Culliecairn, up by the Eastmarch-Tolan border. Then a Torenthi herald arrived. It seems that Miklos of Torenth intends Culliecairn as a christening present for Marek of Festil's new son. The king leaves for Eastmarch in the morning. This could be Marek's bid for the throne."

Camlin could only stare at her, openmouthed. Tieg had gone

a little pale beneath his freckles, obviously fathoming far better than his elder cousin what the news meant in more immediate terms.

"It's too soon," Tieg muttered. "Dear God, we'd better tell Uncle Joram. He's with Ansel and Jesse. They've only just begun compiling troop commitments for six months from now."

"Well, I think it's going to take more than that and far sooner than six months from now," Rhysel replied. "Are they in the staff room? I need to get back as soon as possible, but if we're to salvage anything from this, we'll need to move quickly."

"I'll take you," Tieg agreed. "Camlin, I'll have to back out on that offer to relieve you."

Rhysel gave her brother the gist of her plan en route, in quick rapport that spared nothing of the dangers inherent in what she proposed. She and Tieg had always been close, and they had discussed a similar scenario before, unbeknownst to their elders.

A few minutes later, she had conveyed just her news to her uncle and the other four men gathered with him around a table strewn with maps and papers. She had not expected Niallan and Queron, but she knew them all very well, and the arguments they were likely to raise—and that any argument could come to only one conclusion, once she told them what she proposed. But she still had to convince them.

Her Uncle Joram would have the final say, of course, even though Bishop Niallan was his senior in years and ecclesiastical rank. Joram was the only one of them to have been there from the beginning, back when his father, the sainted Camber, had orchestrated the Haldane Restoration. Only Joram had firsthand knowledge of how it had been done, and only Joram could shoulder that ultimate responsibility for deciding what must follow.

He had paid a price for the weight of such authority. The silver-gilt hair grew a little more tarnished with each passing year, even receding a little at the temples of late, cool silver now against the plain black cassock that was his usual working attire instead of the Michaeline blue he once had worn. The planes of the handsome face, once merely lean, had been honed to something more akin to ascetic.

But the Michaeline knight remained. Though the distinctive blue cassock of his former order had been abandoned some years ago, save for ceremonial occasions, he had taken to

wearing the white sash of his knighthood at all times, in un-
spoken declaration of his self-assumed role as inheritor of the
trust his order had borne before their suppression. Had the Order still existed in Gwynedd, he might have been their vicar-
general by now. At forty-three, though no longer battle-fit
because of the forced exile of the last decade, he was only now
approaching his intellectual prime.

Nor were his companions any less formidable. Close by Joram's right hand sat Niallan Trey, the exiled former Bishop of
Dhassa. Before his elevation to the episcopate, Niallan had
been a Michaeline like Joram. Even now, though in his early
sixties, something of the former warrior remained in the way
he carried himself, in the cant of the proud grey head, in the
military precision of the close-clipped grey beard. He, too,
wore the white sash of Michaeline knighthood.

Dom Queron was one of their two resident Healers besides
Tieg, steel-slender and intense, his wiry hair gone nearly white
and once again grown long enough to display the four-stranded
braid of his original religious order, though he had been a Servant of Saint Camber and a disciple of the preacher Revan
since. A priest and Healer he remained, and always at heart a
Gabrilite, though he wore the grey robe of the Camberians
under a green Healer's mantle rather than the white of the
Gabrilites; either would have meant his death outside these
walls.

Then there were Ansel and Jesse, only in their mid-twenties,
Ansel looking much as his famous uncle must have looked at
that age, light-eyed like Joram, but fairer than Joram had ever
been. He wore his hair close-cropped to make it less memorable, for the sun had bleached it almost to white. His riding
leathers were well cut, but plain and patched in several places,
molded to his lean frame by years of wear in all kinds of
weather. His homespun shirt could have done with a wash.

Jesse, shorter and stockier than Ansel, was dressed much the
same, with brassy highlights streaking the brown hair queued
back with a rawhide thong. Both men had unbuckled their
swords and laid them across one end of the trestle table—
serviceable-enough weapons by mere appearance, unremark-
able by their mountings and well-worn scabbards, but bladed
with the finest R'Kassan steel. The pair had spent most of the
last six years looking like what they were not, ferreting out the
information and contacts that would eventually enable them to
assist a Haldane coup in Rhemuth.

When Rhysel had finished her initial report, Ansel scowled and moved around to the far end of the table to consult one of the lists he had brought to Joram, glancing at his uncle in speculation. Jesse was silently turning a map marker in suntanned, callused fingers, emotion stirring golden flecks in the depths of his brown eyes.

"I wonder why they're letting the king go to Eastmarch," Jesse said quietly. "They've never even let him go on a progress before, much less a military campaign. It's too dangerous—aside from the question of his physical safety. What if he tried to take the bit in his teeth and break free, in front of witnesses?"

"Maybe they don't mean for him to come back," Ansel retorted. "With another heir in the offing, maybe they'd just as soon he died in glorious combat with the enemy, the way his brother did. They might even find a way to blame it on us again."

"It doesn't matter *why* they're letting him go, don't you see?" Rhysel said, leaning both hands on the table in front of where she stood. "The point is, he's going—and he's going to be in grave danger. Now, what are we going to do about it?"

"A bit more warning would have been useful," Niallan said quietly, bestirring himself to turn one of the maps for a better look at the area of Eastmarch. "But whatever the great lords' long-term plans may be, we'd better have a presence there secretly, at least. If we're lucky, maybe we can help counter dirty tricks, if Marek decides to try any arcane unpleasantness."

Ansel swept aside a stack of papers and flounced into his chair. "A lot of good that's going to do," he muttered. "Uncle Joram, are you going to say something?"

Sighing, Joram tossed aside the remains of the quill pen he had been shredding while the others argued, avoiding Queron's gaze.

"Our original scenario is impossible," he said. "It would mean moving our timetable forward a full six months. It can't be done."

"Not all of it—no," Rhysel said.

To the man, other than Tieg, those present turned to stare at her aghast.

"I hope you aren't suggesting what I think you're suggesting," Queron murmured.

Rhysel pursed her lips, bracing for their objections. "There's only one option open to us, if we hope to have a king six months from now," she said quietly. "We must try to bring the king's powers through. Tonight."

Joram closed his eyes, drawing a slow, deep breath. Queron was shaking his head. Ansel and Jesse glanced at one another uneasily. Tieg sat forward eagerly in his chair on Joram's other side. Niallan watched and said nothing, only his nervous turning of his bishop's ring betraying his tension.

"It's out of the question," Joram finally said, not looking at her.

"No, that *is* the question. Hear me out. We know that he can Truth-Read; we also know he has shields. That's as much as Javan had, when you brought him to power. He's got to have access to his powers before he heads off for a war in which his enemy might use magic against him. Whether it's Marek himself or only Miklos he has to face, neither of them will stop at anything to kill him, if they get the chance. Aside from the fact that we don't want it known that he has Deryni backing, he may need more protection than Ansel and Jesse are able to provide."

"The need is not at issue!" Joram replied. "The means is another matter entirely. Just whom did you have in mind to accomplish what you're asking?"

"You. Me. Tieg. Michaela."

"Michaela?" Joram said.

"What *about* Michaela?" Ansel asked, almost simultaneously.

"Oh, Ansel, she's your half sister; you needn't sound so shocked," Rhysel replied. "We've all tended to forget, because she's been blocked, but she *is* Deryni. Not a very powerful one, even if she weren't blocked, and without any training— but that could be remedied."

"By Tieg," Ansel said disbelievingly. "You'd have him unblock her, and she's suddenly the equivalent of a fully trained, experienced Deryni."

"Of course not. But the king trusts her more than any other living person. She might be able to help us catalyze him."

"I can't even consider such a notion," Joram said, not looking at Tieg, whose expression had a hopeful look. "We daren't risk Tieg on something so uncertain."

"You'll need a Healer," Rhysel countered.

"Queron. Rickart," Joram replied.

"But they can't unblock Michaela."

"But they *are* trained Deryni and experienced ritualists," Joram pointed out. "Besides, what makes you think Michaela could be useful, if she did have her powers?"

"I know that she'd do anything to help her husband," Rhysel said simply. "Incidentally, she's carrying another boy; Tieg showed me what to look for, and I finally was able to read it."

Queron groaned, and Joram merely shook his head.

"That gives the great lords their 'heir and a spare,' " Ansel murmured, looking stricken.

"True enough," Jesse agreed, "but they don't know that yet—and won't, until the child is born. A lot could happen between now and then."

Niallan turned him a droll look. "I don't think we can count on another miscarriage to save us this time, Jesse."

"It won't matter much anyway, if Marek launches magic at the king and he has no protection," Ansel said.

"Which is why he must have power," Rhysel replied. "Surely you see that. Joram, I haven't got time to argue with you. We've got to try. It's his only hope."

Joram only closed his eyes for a long moment, turning his head aside to bury his face in one pale hand briefly.

"I confess to being very nearly daunted," he said quietly, as he raised his head and forced himself to draw a deep breath. "All our planning has been geared to a schedule six months away—first an attempt to bring the king's power through, and then the follow-up with loyal troops shifted into the castle by Portal, the way we did for Cinhil. There's no way we can move our men that fast, even if the first could be done. I'd be throwing away lives for nothing."

"Then, we won't worry about that part until *after* Eastmarch is resolved," Rhysel replied. "I agree that there's no way we can move the full operation forward so quickly. But meanwhile, we do what we can to bring the king's power through *tonight*. If it isn't tonight, it may not happen at all. And if it doesn't, and Marek of Festil brings magic to the meeting in Eastmarch, we may lose another Haldane. I thought that's what all our sacrifices have been for—to keep the rightful Haldane kings on the throne of Gwynedd and give them every possible chance to reign independent of great lords or regents. If Rhys Michael is killed, it's *ten years* before his son is of age."

"I *have* dealt with a regency before, you know!" Joram snapped. "I do have some idea what would be involved."

"Then give the king the best possible chance to survive this," she replied. "We can't let him ride off to Eastmarch without at least *trying* to bring through his powers. We've discussed the theory often enough, and you've personally helped bring other Haldane kings to power."

"With *preparation*," Joram agreed. "With an experienced team who knew precisely what they were doing. And it didn't work for Alroy."

"Only because you never got a chance to finish what Cinhil started," Rhysel retorted. "It worked for Cinhil, and it worked for Javan. As for an experienced team—well, none of you were experienced when Cinhil came to power. You learned as you went along. This time, at least *you* have experience."

Joram sighed heavily and looked away from her, shaking his head, clearly preparing another objection, but she set a hand on his wrist and drew his gaze back.

"Joram, we can't hope to succeed without you," she said. "Tieg and I are as ready as we *can* be, under the circumstances, but we need you to direct us. And Michaela can be drafted to help, once Tieg reinstates her powers—and Cathan, too."

Ansel snorted, a short bark of mirthless laughter. "Rhysel, they were only children when they lost what scant powers they had; it was I who had it done, to protect them. And before that, they'd had no training. My dear mother forbade it."

"I know that," Rhysel replied. "But I've taken the liberty of laying some groundwork, at least with the queen. I've blocked all memory of what I've done, but she has the full background of what she is and was, and what she must let be done to help her husband survive. I can release that in an instant. Cathan is less certain, because I haven't had opportunity to probe him or work with him, but I know that he's utterly devoted to his sister and the king. There's absolutely no question of that. I'm sure he'd cooperate as best he's able."

"And what about the king?" Joram asked.

Rhysel glanced down at her hands, surprised to find them nervously pleating a section of her skirt.

"I haven't dared to try touching him yet, for obvious reasons. The shields are going to be his biggest obstacle—and ours. He'll be suspicious, as well he should be. That's why I think that Michaela will be the key to gaining his cooperation, especially with so little time to prepare and explain. I know there are excruciating risks, just to confront him with the possibility, but it can work, Joram. It *has* to work."

"And if it doesn't?" he asked.

She drew a deep, fortifying breath and met his gaze unflinchingly.

"If it doesn't work," she said softly, "you and I and whoever else is involved probably will not survive to worry. We've waited for my generation to be ready for this day; perhaps it will be for the next generation to try again."

"If we do it right," Tieg said, speaking for the first time, "it won't be necessary for the next generation to try again. I know we can do it, Uncle Joram."

"Ah, the optimism of youth," Joram murmured. He closed his eyes briefly, then nodded.

"Very well. We're left with no choice. Queron, the rest of you, am I going to have your full support in this? We'll have a lot to do in the next few hours."

The two younger men nodded, wide-eyed, and Niallan sighed and whispered, "Aye," as Queron lifted a hand in reluctant agreement.

"All right, then. Rhysel, go back to the queen and make the basic preparations you outlined. You daren't tarry here any longer, or you'll be missed. I'll work out a format with Tieg and Queron in the meantime. Be alert for a contact late in the evening. And be very, very careful."

CHAPTER FIVE

There is no fear in love; but perfect love casteth out fear.

—I John 4:18

Rhysel returned to the royal apartments to find the queen in the solar, reading to young Prince Owain, while the boy's nurse visited with some of the queen's ladies in the window bay. Mother and son were cozily ensconced in a large wooden chair well cushioned by embroidered pillows, and both looked up as Rhysel came in. Grey-eyed Owain was the image of his Haldane father, with a shining cap of jet-black hair cut close around his face.

"Ah, there you are, Liesel," the queen said, closing her book. "What have you brought?"

The sweet fragrance of the garden accompanied Rhysel as she came to let the queen see into the flat basket over her arm.

"Fresh-cut blossoms to grace the Queen's Grace," Rhysel said, smiling, as she held a golden jonquil close to the queen's wheaten hair. "Your Highness asked if I could do something special with your hair for tonight. I thought I might pull the sides back into a loose braid down the back and weave in a cascade of flowers."

"Hmmm, the king would like that, I think," Michaela replied, selecting a pale yellow rose and inhaling deeply of its perfume. "Owain, do you think your papa would like some of these braided into Mummy's hair?"

The four-year-old sniffed critically at the bloom, then shook his head and pushed it away.

"Papa likes red ones best," he declared, reaching for a

smaller, more delicate tea rose of vibrant crimson. "Put red ones in Mummy's hair, Liesel." He gave it an appreciative sniff and smiled wide. "Mmmm, smells nice."

Both Michaela and Rhysel grinned at that, and the queen gave an accommodating shrug as she took the flower from her son.

"Well, that would appear to settle the question," she said. "Apparently the men in my life prefer red roses to any other color. Perhaps it comes of being Haldanes." She allowed herself a resigned sigh. "Ah, well. I prefer pastels, but have Agatha choose something suitable to go with *red* roses, would you? Come back when Owain's had his supper and gone to bed."

Later, while Rhysel dressed the queen's hair, she had ample time to set her instructions in place for later in the evening. It would hardly be the leisurely and romantic leave-taking that Michaela was anticipating, but Rhysel saw no remedy for that—not if they continued to hold any hope that the king might be brought to full access of his Haldane powers on such short notice. She wished there had been opportunity to prepare Cathan as well, but he and Fulk had been closeted with the king all afternoon, down in the council chamber. At least Fulk was dining with his parents this evening, since he, too, would be riding out with the king on the morrow.

She made a last adjustment to the queen's coiffure, teasing loose two wispy tendrils at the temples, then laid aside her comb and picked up a mirror to hold for Michaela's inspection. The queen had dressed with care, in a loose-fitting night shift of ivory silk with a rose damask over-robe. She had clasped it at the throat with the Haldane brooch, borrowed back from Rhys Michael when he returned from his meetings to bathe and change. The color complemented the claret-colored roses twined in her hair and gave her a rosy glow of her own.

"It's perfect," she said softly, smiling as she glanced at Rhysel above the mirror. "Thank you, Liesel. Now hand me those pearl drops for my ears, and I'll be ready."

A little later, having overseen arrangements for dining in the solar, Michaela welcomed husband and brother to the rare experience of a truly private meal. Ample candlelight made of their table an island of cozy reassurance, set apart from the uncertainties of the morrow. During a simple and leisurely meal that Cathan both served and shared, the three of them were able to discuss the day's implications with far more candor than was usually possible, none of them yet aware of the measures set in motion by the queen's maid.

"Oh, my dearest darlings, this is almost like being a real family," Michaela said softly, setting one hand on her husband's hand and the other on her brother's. "Do you know how I treasure nights like this? I can hardly remember the last time when just the three of us were able to sit down to a meal together, without Fulk or somebody else lurking about, hanging on our every word."

Cathan snorted softly, permitting himself a wan smile. "Fulk isn't *that* bad. We could do far worse."

Sighing, Michaela squeezed his hand and managed a brave smile. "Aye, we could—and have done, in the past, haven't we? I wish him well on the campaign. The potential replacements are all far worse."

"Well, I'm still glad he had somewhere else to go tonight," Rhys Michael replied, idly picking up a wine bottle and rejecting it when he saw that it was empty. "He would have wanted to serve table, if he'd been here."

Rolling his eyes heavenward, Cathan leaned back in his chair and indulged in a heavy sigh, briefly affecting the jaded court drawl becoming common among his peers.

"The man can be *so* tiresome. But it's mainly his father's fault, of course. You'd think the council would have given up by now. We're not about to discuss plans for an insurrection when Fulk is around, even if there were any hope of *staging* an insurrection."

"And we're not about to plot an insurrection tonight, in any case," Rhys Michael agreed, turning his gaze on Michaela and quirking a wicked smile at her. "Actually, my dear, my intentions for this evening were of a more—personal nature."

As he lifted her hand to nibble on her fingertips, Michaela broke into delighted giggles of mock scandal.

"What, with my brother present, sir?"

"Well, you *did* say it was a family evening," Cathan retorted, grinning roguishly as he brought her other hand to his lips.

Where this might have led, Michaela was never to know, for any further development was curtailed by a knock at the door. As she burst into giggles anew, Rhys Michael rolled his eyes and glanced toward the door.

"Please go away," he called.

"Sire, 'tis Liesel," a low female voice came. "Her Grace did bid me bring her a book of poetry. Shall I simply leave it?"

Smothering a laugh, Michaela pulled her hands away and shook her head, getting to her feet.

"You two are incorrigible!" she whispered sotto voce as she headed for the door. "I *did* want to show you this book, though. The binding is a work of art. Don't worry, though. I'll send her away."

She smoothed her skirts in an automatic gesture as she made her way across the room, glancing back at her husband and brother to blow them a kiss just before she set her hand on the latch. Liesel was waiting a little anxiously outside the door, arms clasped around a large leather-bound volume.

"Pardon the intrusion, my lady," the girl murmured, eyes averted as she dipped in a nervous curtsey.

"Nonsense. I asked you to come."

Neither Cathan nor the king could see how the girl brushed her mistress' hand as she straightened from her curtsey, but the touch seemed to freeze Michaela's thoughts in her head.

You cannot resist me, but you have nothing to fear, came a voice in her mind, though Liesel's lips did not move.

Michaela blinked, a part of her aware that this was familiar, that Liesel was a friend, an even more deeply buried part of her remembering what was about to be set in motion.

"I've been waiting a long time for this," she whispered, closing her eyes briefly. "But, come in and show the king and my brother. Cathan, I want you to see how beautifully Brother Lorenzo replaced this binding."

Cathan looked at her a little oddly, but Liesel was already heading across the room to show off the book, diverting the men's attention from the fact that Michaela locked the door before following. The queen reached her chair between husband and brother just as Liesel proffered the book for Cathan's inspection—and took control of him as her hand touched his.

"Rhysem, Liesel is a friend," Michaela found herself whispering urgently, as Cathan breathed out with a faint sigh and his eyelids fluttered closed. "She's come to help us. Please don't raise an alarm until you've heard what she has to say."

"Hear me, Sire," Rhysel joined in urgently, not breaking gaze with the king, keeping one hand on Cathan's wrist as she set her book aside. "Read the truth of what I say. I promise you that I am not an enemy. What I am, I think you know."

The stunned Rhys Michael had half risen from his chair, instantly on guard, but at Michaela's nod of reassurance, sitting calmly in her chair between them, he partially subsided. Still watching him, Rhysel came around to stand between Cathan and Michaela, relaxing their controls. Cathan blinked, then turned to look up at her in awe. Michaela swallowed nervously, but could not seem to summon up any fear.

"I apologize to all of you," Rhysel said softly. "It isn't usually done, to take control of friends without their permission. But I had to be certain you wouldn't raise an alarm before you realized I wasn't a threat. And I am *not* a threat—not to the three of you, at any rate. The great lords are another matter, entirely."

"You're Deryni," Rhys Michael breathed, wide-eyed. "Someone's come at last. Javan promised me you would, but it's been so long—"

Rhysel let herself relax just a little, briefly turning away to pull a stool closer.

"They hurt us badly when they killed your brother, Sire," she said quietly, sinking down on the stool. "Those few Deryni who had successfully infiltrated the Court were killed—though at least no one ever knew for certain what they were. After that—well, we have never been very many, Sire, who could work at the levels necessary to do you any serious good— which is partially why we had to wait for my generation to grow up a bit. My mother was Evaine MacRorie, and my father was the Healer Rhys Thuryn, for whom you are partially named."

"Rhys and Evaine's daughter," Rhys Michael murmured, taking it all in. "I remember both of them. That makes you— some kind of a distant cousin to Mika and Cathan." He looked at her uncertainly. "Are you a—a Healer, then?"

Rhysel smiled and shook her head. "Alas, no, though my brother and sister both have that gift."

"And what gift do *you* have, Mistress Liesel?" Michaela found herself asking, not by compulsion this time, but out of genuine curiosity.

Their fair captor smiled. "Actually, my name is Rhysel— though I've made, ah, certain 'adjustments' to ensure that you and your brother won't slip and call me that. That's part of my gift." She shifted her gaze back to the king. "I must ask that you guard your own tongue in that regard, Sire."

"Then, you—haven't tried to influence me," Rhys Michael whispered.

She shook her head. "Almost certainly, you would have felt my touch. But if you hope to survive what may wait for you in Eastmarch, you must allow my touch tonight. Do you know of the power that your brother bore?"

"What good did it do *him*?" the king replied, looking down at his clasped hands. "The great lords still killed him, in the end."

"King Javan had some appalling luck and made some unfortunate decisions that had nothing to do with whether or not he had that power," Rhysel retorted. "But if you aren't prepared to meet Prince Miklos or Marek of Festil on their own terms, it's quite possible that your son will never even get to be a puppet king!"

Rhys Michael looked up sharply at that, and Michaela gasped and set a hand of entreaty on Rhysel's forearm.

"Can you really help us?"

"I can try." Rhysel turned her golden gaze directly on the king's. "But everything hinges on your willingness not to resist what is asked of you tonight, Sire—and even that may not be sufficient."

Rhys Michael breathed out a heavy sigh.

"If you're asking me to open my mind to you, I don't think I can," he whispered. "I have shields. Javan tried to get past them, but he couldn't."

"Because you were trying to prevent it," Rhysel breathed. "But you *can* learn to lower them. We'll show you how."

"*We!*"

Rhysel nodded. "Joram and my brother Tieg. There's a way to smuggle them into the castle in disguise. If they should be caught and found out, it's death for both of them—and probably death for the rest of us as well, if anyone draws the correct conclusions—but we're willing to take the risk, if you agree to do your part."

"And what—what would I have to do?" Rhys Michael whispered.

"Whatever they ask you to do—*whatever* they ask, no matter how strange it may sound or how much it might frighten you. That goes for all three of you," she added, including Michaela and Cathan in her glance.

Michaela swallowed, not taking her eyes from Rhysel's. "I'll do it," she whispered. "You have my word."

"And mine," Cathan agreed.

"And what about you, Sire?" Rhysel murmured.

Hardly even breathing for a few seconds, Rhys Michael stared at her searchingly—he had been Truth-Reading her for some time—then turned his gaze neutrally to his wife.

"Mika, give me the Haldane brooch, please," he said.

As she slowly unclasped the brooch with trembling hands, the king got to his feet, the grey Haldane gaze meeting Rhysel's unflinchingly.

"You shall have my word as well," he said, as Michaela handed him the brooch. "But for a pledge as important as this, I wish to make it on something more important than even a holy relic." He cupped his two hands around it and held it slightly toward Rhysel, who also stood.

"My lady, are you aware what this means to us?" he asked softly.

Rhysel nodded. "Your aspirations for a Haldane throne that's free."

"Then, believe me when I say to you that this is my most sacred oath," the king said, shifting his right hand to cup over the top of it. "By the life of my son who is and the child who shall be"—his glance darted briefly to Michaela—"I pledge you my word as an anointed king that I shall do everything in my power to assist you and those who shall come."

"I swear it also," Michaela whispered, laying her hand atop his.

Cathan also had risen as he saw what his brother-in-law intended, and as the brooch was extended to him in turn, he kissed the fingertips of his right hand, then laid them over the brooch now cupped again in the king's hands.

"My faith as well," he said, glancing aside at Rhysel. "There is no holier oath I can swear to my liege and king."

Tears were glittering in Rhysel's eyes as Cathan's hand fell away, and she nodded tentatively toward the brooch.

"May I, Sire?" she whispered.

Nodding, he held it out to her, still cupped in the hollow of his hands, locking his gaze with hers as she laid both her hands lightly atop it, one overlapping the other.

"I pledge you my word that I am your true servant, Sire," she said, "and that I and mine shall never play you false. What we shall do, we shall do only for good and for the good of this kingdom. So help me God." She swallowed at his nod and withdrew her hands.

"I'll go now, to bring the others. Cathan, if Fulk should return before I do, be certain to leave the door ajar to warn me."

"That I will, my lady," Cathan murmured. "But, is there anything else we should do while you're gone? Any preparations we should make?"

She quirked him a wry smile and picked up her book. "Your prayers would not be amiss."

The bored guards outside the royal apartments did not question her departure and would not cause problems when she returned. Soon, a torch in one hand and book hugged close in the other, she was cautiously exiting the turnpike stair on the library floor—sent by the queen to exchange the book for another, should anyone inquire.

The Haldane man-at-arms and gangly squire waiting in the room adjacent to the library wore the faces of Joram and Tieg, though no one in the castle was likely to recognize either. Joram had never spent much time at Court, and he had covered his distinctive silver-gilt hair with a quilted arming cap and mail coif. In addition, the Haldane crimson of the surcoat over his leather jazerant was very different from the Michaeline blue that had always been associated with him.

As for Tieg, he had been a child of two or three on his last visit to the castle, a far cry from this lean, long-limbed youngster kitted out in the livery of a Haldane squire. Since midafternoon, someone had barbered his reddish hair in the stark pudding-bowl style expected of young gentlemen in squire's training, reinforcing a disguise that would enable him to move about the castle almost invisibly. As a final touch, Tieg was cradling two dusty, grey-glazed bottles of wine, ostensibly brought up from the royal cellars, and the thoroughly bored-looking Joram raised a laconic eyebrow as he held up a third.

It was a scenario not likely to be questioned, for one of the illusions that Rhys Michael had taken pains to maintain during the years of his incarceration was that of a prodigious capacity for alcohol. In fact, far more wine had gone down the royal garderobes than had passed the royal lips, but he had quickly learned that when the great lords thought him less than sober, they sometimes tended to talk more freely in front of him. Sending down to the royal cellars on the eve of separation from his wife and son was not at all out of character.

Nodding silent approval, Rhysel sent both of them a quick assessment of her progress with her royal charges. Then, after scanning the corridor outside, she scurried back the way she had come, so that she might arrive back at the royal apartments before them. The guards took only bored note of her return, and a brief word with each ensured that the two men soon to arrive would not be challenged. She left her torch in a wall cresset before going inside.

She found the door ajar between the outer anteroom and the solar, as she had feared—though at least that meant that Fulk had returned now instead of later, to interrupt important work. As she slipped into the solar and saw Fulk sitting with Cathan at the table, Fulk in the chair the king had occupied, she reflected that she had been looking forward to what she was about to do for nearly as long as she had been resident at the castle.

"Oh, good evening, Sir Fulk. The queen bade me fetch her a book."

Fulk came to his feet and bowed, casual and smiling, and Cathan glanced around with a silly grin. The table had been mostly cleared in her absence, but a silver goblet stood before Fulk, and another was in Cathan's hand. The latter had his feet propped up on the near arm of the queen's empty chair.

"Too late," Cathan said cheerily, raising his cup in salute. "The King's Grace has already changed his plans for the evening. I don't suppose you'd care to change yours as well?"

Rhysel smiled and arched an eyebrow as she came closer, a little surprised—and flattered—at his choice of a ruse, but playing along. Despite his slightly slurred speech, Cathan was not drunk.

"Indeed," she replied, "the thought *is* tempting—and 'tis a passing fine book of love poetry that's set to go to waste. But with *two* handsome gentlemen to choose from—"

Chuckling good-naturedly, Fulk came over to pluck the book from her hands.

"Here, now. Let's see what—"

One of her hands closed over one of his, and she had him. As his eyes fluttered closed, and he started to sway, she steadied him and glanced at Cathan, indicating the outer door with her chin. At the same time she tightened her controls and guided the oblivious Fulk to a seat back at the table—but *not* the king's chair.

In a matter of seconds, while Cathan went into the outer chamber to await the others' arrival, she had made the necessary adjustments to ensure that Fulk Fitz-Arthur henceforth would be the king's man first, and not his father's. Other than that, he was no worse than most young men of his class, and far better than most. And now that he would be unable to remember or tell of anything unusual that he might see or hear . . .

She got him back on his feet just as the connecting door from the outer chamber gently opened, and Cathan glanced in, standing aside then to admit Joram and Tieg. Rhysel shot them a relieved smile as she ushered Fulk past them, and Cathan came in and closed the door behind them.

"Come and sit down, Cathan," Joram said quietly, sweeping off his mail coif and arming cap and tossing them onto the table.

Cathan looked around at the sound of his name, his breath catching in his throat as Joram's grey eyes caught and held his.

"Sit, please," Joram repeated.

A little stiffly, Cathan came to sit in the chair that Joram pulled out from the table. Behind him, the door to the royal bedchamber slowly opened to reveal the king and queen. Rhys Michael had changed from his more relaxed attire of supper and now wore a scarlet Haldane tunic, secured at the throat with the Haldane brooch. And of course he wore the Eye of Rom.

"Come in, please," Joram said softly. "I hope you won't mind if we don't stand on ceremony, but we have a great deal of work to do in a very short time, if we're to minimize the danger of interruption. Cathan, Michaela, I don't know whether you remember that you were born Deryni."

Cathan could react but little, still caught in Joram's control, but Michaela paled and gave a faint gasp.

"I see that Tavis was very efficient," Joram said, flicking a glance at her, then back to Cathan as he sat easily on the edge of the table. "It's going to be a bit tricky putting *back* the memories that were taken away, so we'll do Cathan first, since there's less to do; he was younger when it happened. The two of you may come closer and watch, if you wish. I'll try to explain as I go, so it won't seem so frightening. Cathan, look at me, please. There's nothing to fear."

Cathan obeyed without hesitation.

"Now. We haven't the time to go into great detail, but believe me when I tell you that both you and your sister used to have some Deryni powers, or at least the potential to be developed. To protect you both, when you were still very young, it became necessary to block those powers and to bury the memory that you ever had them. I apologize for that, because it cut you off from your heritage, but it also made you immune to the Deryni-specific effects of *merasha*, which probably saved your lives. We would have restored you sooner, but not just anyone can do it. Tavis had the ability, and another man you never knew, but they're both dead. Tieg is the only one left that we know of.

"He's going to unblock those powers now. You needn't be anxious. I think you'll have shields and a bit more, but Tieg is going to turn control over to me after he's put things back. Then I'll come in with a deep briefing to catch you up on what you need to know now, as an adult."

As he glanced at Tieg and gave a slight nod, the young Healer moved into place behind Cathan's chair, big Healer's hands cupping gently atop Cathan's sandy head. Cathan's eyes closed of their own weight, and Tieg's went dreamy and unfocused.

"Good natural shields," Tieg said softly, after a moment, "a bit more that can be developed, though not instantly. No training at all, though. Over to you, Uncle Joram."

As he lifted his hands, flexing his fingers several times, Joram bestirred himself from his perch on the table edge and moved in. Cathan had not moved under Tieg's touch, but the closed eyelids flickered as Joram set his hands to the younger man's head. After a moment, as Joram drew back, Cathan gave a long sigh and opened his eyes.

"C-Cathan?" Michaela asked, flinching as he raised his eyes to hers.

"I'm all right," he said softly, searching first her face and then Rhys Michael's with his blue gaze. "It's as if—as if someone has lit a lamp inside my mind."

He got to his feet as, with a sob, she came to him, burying her face against his chest while he made awkward little stroking motions on her hair, dislodging several of the roses. Apart, Rhys Michael watched helplessly, not daring to move closer or to say a word as Joram came to take her from her brother. She looked up at the Deryni as he put his hands on her shoulders to draw her away, not taking her eyes from his as he urged her to sit where Cathan had sat.

"I promise, there's nothing to fear," he whispered. "Your husband will need your help. Just close your eyes now, and relax."

Her eyes seemed to close of their own accord. She felt Joram's hands fall away, and then the hands she knew must be the boy's were resting gently on her head, the fingertips pressing lightly against her temples. She could feel all resistance draining out of her, and then a deep, throbbing silence punctuated by a single, crystalline resonance and the flare of warmth and light behind her eyelids.

"Good shields here, too," she heard the boy's voice say, as if through layers of cotton wool, as his hands lifted and others took their place. "See what you can do."

The next thing she knew, she simply *knew* a great deal about them and what they planned. As she opened her eyes, she found herself already considering how best to help Rhysem. Her first thought was to reach out her hand to him, smiling as she bade him come to her. There were tears in the grey Haldane eyes as he knelt at her side, taking her hand to cradle it to his lips.

"Mika?" he managed to murmur.

"I'm fine," she whispered, fighting back her own tears. "Rhysem, what do you see, when you look at me now?"

"I see—a sort of brightness. It's shields, isn't it?" His face fell. "But, if *I* can see them, what about other Deryni? What if Dimitri sees them?"

Smiling, she damped the shields, watching the look of awe come over his face.

"I know how to do that much, at least," she said. "I'm not sure what else, but—I'll figure that out some other time. Maybe while you're gone. As for Dimitri, I suspect he'll be going along with you, so we'd better see about getting *you* some protection. Father Joram?"

Joram had drawn Cathan with him to the door to confer with Rhysel as the royal couple spoke, and now he motioned them toward the royal bedchamber.

"We'll move in there now, where there's a better chance of privacy," he said. "I've pared the formalities to the bone, but the rest of our work will require a bit more intensity. An interruption could be literally fatal. Cathan will keep Fulk occupied and make certain no one else gets past them."

As Cathan passed on into the anteroom, Tieg was already moving into the bedchamber, taking something out of the small pouch at his belt. Rhysel fetched a ball of white wool from one of the sewing baskets in the solar window and followed as Rhys Michael got up from his knees and helped his wife to her feet. Joram briefly withdrew to confirm that Cathan knew his part. When he shortly joined the four of them, Rhysel was unwinding the ball of white wool, laying it down to mark out the circumference of a large circle centered on the Kheldish carpet at the foot of the royal bed.

"Sire, could you come over here, please?" Tieg called softly, from where he was pouring water into a cup on the little table beside the bed.

Though the king complied, he cast a wary glance at the small blue glass vial in one of Tieg's hands. It seemed almost to glow in the light of the single candle lit there.

"What's that?"

"Just something to relax you a little, to take the edge off your nervousness. It's perfectly harmless. You aren't going to lose consciousness or anything like that."

Rhys Michael swallowed with an audible gulp, looking at Joram in appeal as the older man came to join them.

"Joram, I don't think I can do this," he whispered, watching as Tieg unstoppered the little blue vial and began counting drops into the cup.

"I don't think you can *not* do it," Joram said quietly. "You've got very rigid shields and very little control, and we haven't a great deal of time to take things gently. This should make our work a lot easier—and yours."

Rhys Michael had gone a little pale as Joram spoke, and he glanced with growing horror at the cup Tieg now extended.

"Joram, I can't," he whispered. "You don't understand. You don't know what it's been like. They kept me drugged for months after Javan was killed."

"This won't be like that," Joram replied, taking the cup from Tieg and holding it out to the king. "We want to enhance your perceptions, not dull them. This is similar to what was given to you and your brothers the night your father died. I assure you, there's nothing to fear."

As the king turned away, trembling, Michaela came to him, gently laying a hand on one taut shoulder.

"Rhysem, you must trust them," she said softly. "Joram is right; we haven't a great deal of time. If he says this will help, we have to believe him. Drink it, my love. Do it for me, for Owain—"

He closed his eyes, shaking his head. "Please, don't ask this of me. I can do it without."

"I *am* asking, Rhysem," she went on. "I'm asking the same way *you* asked, many years ago, when Cathan and I had to do something similar. Do you remember?"

He opened his eyes and looked at her in question.

"I know *I'd* forgotten, until Joram gave me back my memories," she went on. "I was ten. It was the morning after Cousin Giesele died in her sleep, and the regents wanted to find out if Cathan and I knew anything. We didn't, of course. But then Archbishop Hubert said we couldn't see our parents until after we'd drunk a sleeping potion. We didn't want to; we were afraid. But then you came over and took the cups from Hubert, and you said, 'Mika, don't be silly. It's for your own good. It will only make you sleep for a while.' "

She could see by his expression that he remembered, and she quietly took the cup from Joram, to hold near her husband's hand.

"I have to say the same sort of thing to you now, Rhysem," she whispered. "Don't be silly. It's for your own good. And it won't even make you sleep; it will only help you relax a little. Isn't that right, Tieg?"

As the young Healer nodded, Rhys Michael glanced at him, at the cup, then back at Michaela. He said nothing as he took the cup from her, and his hand was trembling, but he drained it in one long draught, wiping his mouth with the back of a hand before setting the cup back on the little table.

"Good man," Joram murmured, as Tieg grinned and touched the king's hand in thanks and reassurance, then moved past him to join Rhysel in the circle. "Now, try to relax for a few minutes, until we're ready for you. Try gazing into the candle flame—or lie down, if you wish."

As Joram likewise led Michaela to join Tieg and Rhysel in the circle, Rhys Michael drew a deep, shuddering breath and did his best to follow Joram's instructions. He knew he had made a fuss over something that should have been very minor, but he could not summon up any guilt about it. Even though he believed he trusted these Deryni who had risked so much to come to him, the incident had smacked far too much of the sort of treatment he had had at the hands of the great lords in those early days, and the threat of more such treatment if he ever crossed them.

He sat himself down on the edge of the great bed and made himself draw another deep breath, gazing into the candle flame. He thought he could begin to feel Tieg's drug working in him, but he wasn't sure. He did seem to feel a bit less anxious now, and he found his heart rate had slowed when he pressed his fingers to the pulse in his neck.

He closed his eyes, letting the slow, steady pulse beat take him deeper, trying to put his fear aside, and gradually became aware that the edge of his hand was touching the Haldane brooch at his throat. Covering it with his hand, he bowed his head and dared to breathe a prayer that what they were planning would work.

After a while, the prayer drifted into stillness, and remaining upright seemed to require too much effort. It was pleasant and floaty behind his closed eyelids, so he drew another deep breath and let himself lie back on the bed, legs still dangling off the edge. As he outflung his arms to either side to stretch, a more fearful and cynical part of him marked the symbolism as acknowledgment that he, like his brothers, was very likely to become another sacrifice for the great lords' ambitions, just as the Christ had stretched out His arms upon the Cross; but a sterner part of him rejected such defeatist notions and brought his hand back to the brooch, like a talisman against the great lords' power over him—the Haldane lion, bold and fierce and proud. He could feel the cool of the metal and enamel under his hand as he made his resolve, and he hardly even flinched when someone lightly touched his other wrist.

"Sire, we're ready for you," Joram said quietly.

CHAPTER SIX

Then a spirit passed before my face; the hair of my
flesh stood up: It stood still, but I could not discern
the form thereof: an image was before mine eyes,
there was silence, and I heard a voice.

—Job 4:15–16

Rhys Michael felt a momentary rush of light-headedness as he
sat up a bit too quickly, and he gratefully accepted Joram's
steadying hand as he stood down beside the bed. It took a few
seconds for his vision to settle. He was not exactly dizzy, but
he surmised that Tieg's drug probably was responsible for the
faint distancing he seemed to be experiencing as he glanced
around the room.

The very silence was imbued with a clarity, a sense of expectation, that he had never experienced before. Beyond the
foot of the bed, he could just make out the others gathered in
the circle marked out by Rhysel's wool—Rhysel closest, Mika
to her right, between him and the door, and Tieg opposite
Rhysel, with his back to the curtained window bay. The arrangement seemed to strike a familiar chord in Rhys Michael's
memory, but he could not quite remember why. It occurred to
him that the window faced east, and that this was significant.

The light seemed odd, too, not so much bright as—different.
Only two other candles were burning in the room besides the
one on the bedside table: one by the door and one on the floor
in the center of the circle, next to what looked like a small
glazed cup. The latter was hard to make out, as were the occupants, but if Rhys Michael squinted his eyes just so, he
thought he seemed to detect a faint silvery sheen wrapping itself over and around the circle, like a huge, almost invisible
bowl upturned over it. The hazy glow obscured his vision al-

most like looking through a fine veil, cobweb-fragile, and he shook his head slightly to try to clear it as Joram led him forward, heading them between the circle and the foot of the bed.

Instinct warned him not to try to touch it. Even passing close to it, he felt his skin seem to crawl. Just past the bed, he noted that the circle was incomplete. The two ends of white wool that should have closed it had been folded back to either side to leave a gap wide enough for a person to pass. The Haldane sword lay on the floor just outside, with its point just touching the more easterly side of the gap and angled to suggest an open door. Peering more closely at the opening, Rhys Michael thought the air seemed slightly clearer there, as if there really was a door through something just beyond his ability to see.

"Go into the circle and wait in the center, Sire," Joram said quietly, as he indicated the opening. "I'll join you when I've let Cathan know we're starting."

Rhys Michael could feel the hackles rising at the back of his neck as he passed uneasily into the circle. Mika came to him as he entered, gathering him to the center in a silent embrace that needed no words. He kissed her gently, and as they drew apart, she kissed her fingertips and pressed them lightly to the Haldane brooch at his throat, tears in her eyes. Smiling, he did the same, the wonder of her loyalty and love lending him courage and determination as Joram returned, passing again between the circle and the foot of the bed. As Joram bent to pick up the Haldane sword, Rhys Michael noticed a small silver cross now hanging outside his crimson surcoat, a tangible reminder of the Deryni's priestly calling.

Somehow reassured by that, the king let his wife withdraw to her former place and turned back to the opening. As soon as Joram had entered, Tieg crouched down briefly to bring the ends of white wool together and loosely knot them, symbolically completing the circle.

But it was Joram's action that actually completed it, Rhys Michael knew. Setting the point of the sword to the floor at the left side of where the doorway had been, Joram drew the blade smartly across the former threshold three times. Each stroke seemed to make the fog intensify in the opening, so that when he finished, bending briefly to lay the sword just along that part of the circle's arc, only the weapon's position remained to indicate where the opening had been.

"You stand now in a warded circle, Sire," Joram said softly, coming to turn him toward Tieg now, but well back from the candle. "I believe you sensed something of its power when you passed through its gate, which now is closed. The circle is guarded by the holy archangels, upon whom we shall call again shortly. A few small preparations are required first, however. Give me your right thumb, please."

Heartbeat quickening despite his determination not to be afraid, Rhys Michael gave Joram his right hand. As he did so, young Tieg produced a small piece of parchment from his belt pouch and, surprisingly, the Haldane Ring of Fire. Joram, meanwhile, had drawn a small silver dagger from a sheath at his belt. Somehow, Rhys Michael had the feeling he had seen it before, but he could not quite remember where.

"You've gone through part of this before," Joram said, compressing Rhys Michael's thumb beside the dagger's blade. "The sacrifice of blood and at least a token test of courage have been elements of all the empowering rituals in which I've assisted. The form we have used has differed, according to the circumstances, but the blood baptism of the Ring of Fire seems to be a constant, as is the formal naming of the king. The words you are about to hear were chosen by your father. Tieg?"

With a casual gesture of one Healer's hand, Tieg conjured a fist-sized sphere of greenish handfire and set it hanging in the air slightly above their heads. The suddenness of it startled Rhys Michael, especially so close, but he knew what it was; he had seen Javan conjure handfire once. But even had he wished it, he could not have pulled back, for Joram's hand held him fast, his thumb imprisoned close by the shining blade. He forced himself to lower his eyes from the handfire as Tieg tilted the square of parchment toward its light and read.

"I will declare the decree. The Lord hath said unto me, Thou art my Son: This day have I begotten thee. Ask of me, and I shall give thee the heathen for thine inheritance, and the uttermost parts of the earth for thy possession."

Rhys Michael blinked at the words. He had heard them before, he was sure, at a time just beyond the range of recall. He was still trying to remember where, when Joram drew his captive thumb sharply across the dagger's razor edge, to the accompaniment of other words that struck a chord somewhere deep inside him.

"Rhys Michael Alister Haldane, King of Gwynedd, be thou consecrated to the service of thy people."

He could not move. He seemed frozen in this instant of time. Into the thrumming silence that followed came the faintly rasping sound of Joram twice drawing the flat of the blade across the thigh of his breeches to clean it, then the cool, metallic snick of it being sheathed. The blade had been sharp enough to cause no immediate pain or much bleeding, but Rhys Michael's jaws clenched as Joram compressed the cut from the ends and it gaped open, welling with blood in which Tieg carefully rolled the dark red stones of the Ring of Fire. The touch of the stones against raw flesh made the king bite back a gasp of real pain, all his body tensing, but then the wounded thumb was being pressed to the parchment Tieg handed to the elder Deryni, mere pressure that allowed the cut to close.

The action gave the young Healer brief respite to pull a bit of clean linen from his pouch and wipe the thumb clean, then clasp it in one hand for a few blurred seconds. The pain ceased; and when Tieg opened his hand a moment later, releasing the king's thumb, the wound was completely healed.

Joram, meanwhile, had bent briefly to retrieve the cup at their feet. Rhys Michael guessed that the liquid half filling it was water, but by the greenish light of the handfire above, he could not be sure. Joram looked very focused as he slightly lifted the cup between them in his left hand, the parchment held over it on his open right palm. He did not even blink as the parchment burst into flames and, within a few heartbeats, was reduced to a mere snippet of ash. This he tipped into the cup, watching the ash disintegrate as he spoke again.

"Give the king Thy judgments, O God, and Thy righteousness unto the king's son."

Rhys Michael breathed a fervent "Amen," and let the words sink into his soul as Joram held the cup closer to Tieg. The Healer carefully slipped the bloodstained Ring of Fire into the cup, then summoned the handfire down beside the cup while Joram gently swirled the ring around the bottom to stir the contents. When it was done to both their satisfaction, Tieg drew the handfire back into his hand and quenched it, leaving the circle lit only by the candle near their feet and the two elsewhere in the room.

"You drank of a similar cup once before, Sire," Joram said quietly. "As we proceed, I expect you'll begin to remember. We shall now reiterate the blessings that made it potent by more than blood, calling upon our archangelic guardians to witness our intent. Stand where you are and attend. It's customary to turn as we invoke the various Quarters, beginning in the East."

So saying, he passed the cup to Tieg, then stepped back to the edge of the circle closest to the foot of the bed as Tieg likewise retreated to the easternmost limit of the circle. Clasping the cup between his Healer's hands, Tieg briefly bowed his head over it, then lifted his face heavenward, eyes closed. His deep voice was low and musical, almost singing words Rhys Michael had heard before—he could almost remember when.

"O Lord, Thou art holy indeed: the fountain of all holiness. In trembling and humility we come before Thee with our supplications, asking Thy blessing and protection on what we must do this night."

Slightly elevating the cup, he shifted his right hand to extend the palm flat above it, lifting his eyes to a Presence that only he seemed able to see.

"Send now Thy holy Archangel Raphael, O Lord, to breathe upon this water and make it holy, that he who shall drink it may justly command the element of Air. Amen."

Shifting the summoning hand to support the foot of the cup, he raised it just above eye level and threw back his head, eyes closing as a faint breeze stirred his reddish hair, swirling once around the circle's confines and then subsiding. Rhys Michael, standing at the circle's center, felt the ghost-breath of the stirring as a crawling of the fine hairs on his forearms and a chill along his spine. As Tieg lowered the cup, the king found himself joining his hands in an attitude of prayer, fingers pressed to his lips, only now beginning to realize the magnitude of what they Called.

The young Healer smiled faintly, bowing slightly to the king before moving slightly to his left to hand the cup to Michaela. Rhys Michael turned to face her, but she did not seem really to see him, so intent was she upon young Tieg. She received the cup as if it bore the Blessed Sacrament, reverently bowing her head over it before lifting it as he had, with palm extended flat above it, drawing upon the knowledge they had given her of her heritage.

"O Lord, Thou art holy indeed: the fountain of all holiness. We pray Thee now to send Thy holy Archangel of Fire, the Blessed Michael, to instill this water with the fire of Thy love and make it holy. So may he who drinks of it justly command the element of Fire. Amen."

Rhys Michael fancied he could see blue flames flickering above the rim as she lifted it in further offering, though he could not imagine that she had the power to craft such fire herself. Whatever its source, her face seemed aglow as she carefully passed the cup to Rhysel. Only reluctantly did he take his eyes from her as she backed into her place and the younger woman bowed briefly over the cup, then lifted it in supplication.

"O Lord, Thou art holy indeed: the fountain of all holiness. Let now Thine Archangel Gabriel, who rules the stormy waters, instill this cup with the rain of Thy wisdom, that he who shall drink hereof may justly command the element of Water. Amen."

Rhys Michael flinched as thunder seemed to rumble softly all around him, glancing instinctively at the door beyond Michaela, for surely they must be able to hear it in the next room. A glittering mist seemed to gather above the cup as Rhysel spread her hand higher above the cup, almost-lightnings crackling and spitting from hand to contents.

A whiff of the sharp, clean scent of summer thundershowers prickled briefly at his nostrils, and when she lowered the cup, beads of moisture were streaming down the outside, dripping on the carpet as she took it to Joram. The priest appeared nonplussed, as did Rhysel, only wiping his right hand against the tail of his surcoat before extending it over the cup he raised. Despite their apparent nonchalance, the king felt a shudder of fear tighten along his spine, and he had to clasp his hands tightly together to stop their trembling as Joram spoke.

"O Lord, Thou art holy indeed: the fountain of all holiness. Let Uriel, Thy messenger of darkness and of death, instill this cup with all the strength and secrets of the earth, that he who shall drink hereof may justly command the element of Earth. Amen."

Very suddenly, in an instant of unexpected vertigo, Rhys Michael seemed to feel the floor lurch under his feet. Though it ended almost as soon as begun, he had to scramble to regain his balance, arms briefly outflung in mindless dismay until the room stabilized. He could hear the hollow, tinkling sound of the Ring of Fire rattling against the inside of the cup as Joram lowered it, and his heart was still pounding as the Deryni bade him turn to face Tieg again.

The young Healer had come forward to take up the candle, remaining deeper in the circle as Joram moved in beside him with the cup, and Rhys Michael found himself sinking to his knees before them. The candlelight lit their faces eerily from below, also lighting the cup with merciless clarity, and he knew he was trembling again.

"I can't tell you exactly what to expect next," Joram said quietly, studying the taut, upturned face of the young man kneeling before him. "I think you realize that this cup is now potent with far more than water and Haldane blood. Drinking it should be sufficient to take you past whatever has prevented your assumption of your father's power—but if it isn't, I'll step in. Possibly Tieg, as well. Try not to resist whatever happens. You probably *can*, if you're determined not to let anything past your shields, but it won't be in your best interests."

Rhys Michael nodded dimly. He was very much aware of the power in the cup Joram now held out to him, a power whose promise he knew he had tasted before, at his father's hands. But as his own hands clasped around it and brought it to his heart, a flash of the futility of it all nearly made him drop it.

"Rhys Michael Alister Haldane, you are the true King of Gwynedd, God's anointed," he heard Joram saying softly, as if through a fog. "Drink. By this mystery shall you come to the power that is your Divine Right, as king of this realm; and even so shall you instruct your own sons, in due time."

Rhys Michael raised the cup in shaking hands and drank it to the dregs, wanting it to be true, praying that it *was* true. The draught was bitter with ash and despair, flat with the faint salt-taste of his blood and his mortality. All too briefly, he thought he sensed *something* vaguely stirring deep within him, the ghost flickers of unfamiliar images teasing behind his closed eyelids, but he could not seem to bring it to focus.

Choking back a sob of frustration, frantic to catch and hold the Sight, he sank back on his hunkers and blindly scrabbled the Ring of Fire out of the bottom of the empty cup, shoving the ash-smeared band of it hard onto his left hand. The momentary discomfort as it grazed across his knuckles flared as a fleeting glimpse of psychic clarity that made him gasp, came and was gone almost before it could register.

No! Come back! a forlorn part of him pleaded, sightless eyes straining at the darkness.

Hands huddled to his breast half in prayer, he found himself rubbing at the knuckle he had scraped in donning the ring. In that instant he became acutely aware of another presence in the circle, both familiar and strange—not Joram or Tieg or either of the women—One who had the power to give him his Sight, if only he could focus, could bring the vision through. But how?

"Please, help me," he whispered, slowly collapsing over his clasped hands. "Help me, whoever you are. Help me to See, for the sake of my Crown and my kingdom!"

As he huddled there in a miserable ball of hopelessness, shaking his head in denial at his seeming impotence, he felt the cool sleekness of the Haldane brooch hard at his throat. Suddenly something Joram had said earlier came clear as crystal in his mind: *The sacrifice of blood ... the test of courage ...*

In that instant he knew what he must do. Reason shrank from the performing of it, but his fingers were already fumbling at the clasp of the brooch, easing the sleek length of shining metal pin from the throat of his tunic, testing the sharpness of it against a questing thumb.

"Sire?" came Joram's tentative query from somewhere far away.

He shook his head emphatically, shrinking away from the other's touch, opening the clasp wide so he could get a firm grip around the brooch itself as he poised the point of the sharp metal pin against the palm of his left hand.

"Don't touch me!" he whispered. *"I have to do this!"*

He felt the pulse pounding in his ears and the surge of hopefulness welling up within him. Merely mortal flesh shrank from the certainty of the pain to come, but he offered up his fear in a heartfelt entreaty to Those who watched, of whose presence he had no doubt; to that Other who he prayed would be his salvation; and to Him in Whose service he had been anointed as king. Unlike his father or his brother Javan, he had never considered himself particularly religious, but he sensed the fitness of some formal seal on what he now did.

"In the name of the Father, and of the Son, and of the Holy Spirit," he whispered, pouring all his will and longing into the invocation. "Not my will but Thine be—*done!*"

He jammed the clasp home on the final word, a part of him detached and almost surprised at how hard it was to force such a slender sliver of metal between bones and sinews.

And the pain of it—a blinding, burning agony centered in his palm but racing up his arm to lance into his brain in an explosion of white-hot light. The mass of the brooch itself was like molten metal in his hand, but far worse was the raging inferno that kindled in his head.

The fire illuminated old, long-buried memories—standing fearlessly before his father and draining another cup, his father's hands laid upon his head as power came surging through in a fountaining of light and heat, stirring the power and setting its access in place, then reimposing Blindness, setting constraints that should have loosed six years ago and more, when Javan died . . .

But besides his father's hands in memory, other hands suddenly were on his head here and now, and they were not Joram's hands, or Tieg's. He could feel the presence behind the hands pushing, probing, insisting, entreating, but his own defenses surged up in rebellion. He sensed the benign intent of that Other and knew he must not resist, but he could not seem to summon up the will to yield. In desperation, he jammed the brooch harder against his palm and gave a twist, shifting the impaling shaft of gold between the bones of his hand.

The new pain brought his intention abruptly and sharply to a focus, blossoming out like a flower of light, pushing back his shields, baring his soul to that Other who waited. As he felt the weight of ghost-hands upon his head, light exploded behind his eyelids with a white-hot brilliance, and his brief awareness of illumination faded smoothly into oblivion.

CHAPTER SEVEN

Thanks be to God for His unspeakable gift.
—II Corinthians 9:15

Joram briefly had glimpsed that other presence in their circle and knew that Tieg had seen it, too, by the startled look on his face. But as the king gave a little moan and collapsed onto his side, twitching alarmingly, Joram relegated any personal dismay to that deeply guarded inner place reserved for things he did not understand or entirely approve of. He doubted whether Tieg had recognized the figure as his Grandfather Camber, Joram's father, but the boy would surely ask about it later. Much to Joram's dismay, "Saint" Camber had acquired a disconcerting tendency to make unexpected appearances during magical workings, at least for Haldanes. Whether this betokened merely an ongoing interest in that royal House's well-being or was sign of more far-reaching intent, Joram had no idea; but with the king's life hanging in the balance, this was not the time or place to debate the issue, even with himself.

"Don't touch him!" he ordered, as Tieg started to go to the stricken king. "Let it run its course!"

Tieg drew back, though obedience clearly was at odds with the Healer's instincts urging him forward. Rhysel had gone to the queen as Rhys Michael collapsed, preventing her intervention, and glanced at her uncle in query as the king's movement ceased and Joram finally dropped to his knees beside him.

"All right, it's done," he murmured, darting a glance of summons at Tieg as he rolled the king onto his back. "I think he'll be all right. This follows the same pattern as other

Haldane empowerings. Rhysel, please close down the circle while we see how he is. Your Highness, you'll help most if you don't interfere."

White-faced, Michaela nodded and sank to her knees where she stood, freeing Rhysel to take up the sword and set about closing the circle. Tieg had already come to crouch at the king's head, setting his candle aside to lay both hands across the pale forehead.

After a moment, he turned his attention to Rhys Michael's left hand, grimacing as the length of gold protruding from its back briefly snagged against a fold of scarlet tunic. Turning the hand palm-up, he gently unbent the fingers still clasped around the heavy enameled brooch, then carefully drew it free. Two small, almost bloodless puncture wounds remained, in the palm and on the back of the hand.

"That can't have been easy, on several counts," Tieg said as he handed off the brooch to Joram. "Hands are tough, and very sensitive to pain. At least what he did seems to have accomplished what was necessary. Were you expecting this?"

Joram shook his head. "Not this, precisely," he said, "but it was clear very quickly that something more was going to be necessary to focus him. He obviously figured out what it was."

Shaking his head, Tieg clasped the wounded hand in one of his own, fingers covering the two small punctures. When he released it, after a few seconds of concentration, both wounds had disappeared.

"How long will he be unconscious?" Joram asked, as the young Healer shifted his attention back to the king's head.

"Hard to tell. And when he does come around, all he's going to want to do is sleep. We'd better get him into bed. I do want to see him stirring before we leave, though."

"But he does have full powers?" Joram asked, as Tieg slid an arm under the royal shoulders to lift him to a sitting position.

"Well, I don't know how full is full, in the case of a Haldane, but there's certainly a lot more there than there was before."

"And could you block it, if you had to?" Joram persisted.

Tieg shot him an incredulous look. "If you're asking whether he feels like one of us, the answer is yes. And I can sense the triggerpoint. You don't really want me to touch it, though, do you?"

"Good God, no. I'm just trying to figure out how this all works. Let me give you a hand with him."

Together they pulled the unconscious king to his feet, an anxious Michaela also rising, though she did not try to interfere. Behind them, Rhysel had closed the circle and was briskly winding up the length of white wool that had delineated its boundaries. Rhys Michael began to revive as they manhandled him toward the bed, legs moving jerkily at first, then starting to support a little of his weight as he tried to lift his head and look around.

"You're going to be fine, Sire," Tieg reassured him. "Don't try to exert yourself. We're going to put you to bed now."

They braced him against the edge of the bed so they could begin undressing him, letting Michaela help. He was an almost dead-weight at first, but he seemed to be aware of his surroundings by the time they drew the sleeping furs up around his chest. Michaela had crawled up onto the other side of the bed and was sitting cross-legged beside him, watching fearfully as her husband's eyes scanned around him and gradually began to register reason.

"I know you must be very tired, Sire," Joram said, as the king's bleary gaze met his. "That's completely to be expected. The best thing you can do now is sleep. There will be a lot of demands on you tomorrow and in the days to come, and you'll want to tread slowly and cautiously as you explore the limits of your power."

Rhys Michael managed a weak nod and reached out to take Michaela's hand. She was smiling and crying, both at the same time.

"Mika, it worked," he whispered.

"Yes, my darling."

"Why did I fight this? How could anyone *not* want it?"

"What you do *not* want," Joram said grimly, "is any extra scrutiny. Unfortunately, I can't stay around to help you ease into wisdom on how to use your powers. I can only beg you to go slowly and be very, very careful, until you can find ways to shift the balance safely. The great lords did not achieve their positions of influence overnight, and you aren't going to get rid of them instantly, either. If all of them were to disappear right now, you wouldn't have the experienced support you'll need to reign effectively—especially if Eastmarch should turn into a full-blown war, God forbid. That support can be gathered, but not all at once.

"For now, your primary concern is to meet the challenge of Miklos of Torenth and stay alive. Remember that you're still mortal. Magic you may have, but swords and arrows, poison—they can all still kill you, if you aren't careful."

"I'll remember," Rhys Michael murmured, earnest resolution in his eyes. "Thank you, Father Joram—and Tieg. And please—thank that other man who was in the circle with us, there at the end. I'm not sure I could have done it, if it hadn't been for him."

Joram closed his eyes briefly, knowing he had not heard the last of this, then nodded. "We'd better go," he murmured, glancing at Tieg. "We don't want to press our luck—or yours. I wish there were time to establish a contact link for future communication, but you're in no condition right now. Later, perhaps, after you've returned. Meanwhile, Rhysel will continue to be your go-between. God keep you, Sire—and your Highness. You'd both best sleep now."

As he and Tieg slipped out of the room, Rhysel following, Michaela snuggled down to lay her head against her husband's shoulder. He smiled as he let his arm encircle her, reaching out drowsily with a tendril of thought to gently brush her mind. To his pleased surprise, he felt the feather-brush of her response in kind, fragile but exquisite. It was thus that he allowed himself to drift into sleep, enwrapped in her love and secure in the expectation that, at last, he had a weapon to use against his enemies.

One of those enemies even then was prowling the darkness not far away, bound on an errand for other masters besides those to whom he answered in the castle. Unseen, the Deryni Dimitri made his way along a dim-lit range of vaulted cellars, silent as a wisp of fog. Torches burned here and there along the stone-flagged corridor, but the pools of light they cast were far apart, leaving wide areas of darkness between.

The alcove Dimitri sought was well screened by one of these patches of darkness, and here he hid himself to wait. Very shortly his intended victim came sauntering along the corridor as expected—a bored and gullible young guard named Iosif, who had served Dimitri's purposes before.

He was bigger than Dimitri, and much younger, full-featured and powerfully built, with a mop of curly black hair above the scarlet surcoat that covered body armor of boiled leather. He was armed with short sword and dagger. One big hand bore a torch aloft, and the other swung a large ring of keys. Though his mere size would have made him a formidable opponent, Dimitri had no intention of ever letting their relationship become adversarial on any level.

Poised to make his move, he waited until the young man had come just abreast of the alcove, then reached out one hand to seize the man's nearer wrist, at once securing control and drawing him into the alcove, his free hand catching up the ring of keys before they could fall. His victim's eyes had closed at Dimitri's touch, and he offered no resistance as his torch hand slowly sank.

"Good evening, Iosif," Dimitri whispered, smiling slightly as he rescued the torch and snuffed it against the wall. "You do not remember me, but I promise you shall remember your reward, if you survive this night's work. Sit and be at ease now. I must reach very far tonight."

Oblivious to his mortal danger, the younger man sank at once to a sitting position against the wall, booted legs splayed wide to brace himself, head lolling against the rough stone at his back, big hands lying open and motionless beside his leather-clad thighs. His captor bent to set keys and torch within easy reach to either side, then folded to sit cross-legged between the younger man's knees. Drawing a deep breath then, Dimitri leaned slightly forward and reached up to lay hands on either side of the curly head, fingers slipping through the thick hair and thumbs coming to rest on the temples.

"You cannot resist me," he whispered, dark gaze fixing on the blur of his victim's closed eyes. "I regret that it may be necessary to hurt you, but I shall try to be brief. Look at me, Iosif. Open your eyes . . . and now open your soul . . ."

The young man's breath caught in a little gasp, but he obeyed. The Deryni's thumbs tightened. Ignoring the brief flash of dread in his subject's eyes, Dimitri at once breached the puny human defenses, quelling the stifled moan that passed the other's lips as he forced the pathways open wide and pushed deep into the other's mind, to the very core of lifeforce. He could taste the pain he caused as he began to pull the power to drive his intent, but he balanced his speed to a level that was safe enough, if less than comfortable. If he had to draw too deeply or for too long, true damage would be done, but that was a calculated part of the risk—Iosif's risk.

Steely-willed, Dimitri drove his call outward then, tight-focused toward the mind that should be waiting for his contact.

Finding the connection he sought took longer than he would have liked—Iosif was tiring quickly—but once the link was secured, the communication itself was quick and smooth, briefly giddying as the other probed deep and then withdrew enough to pass on further instructions before dismantling the contact.

In the space of a heartbeat, Dimitri was alone in his subject's mind once again, blinking dazedly back to normal awareness. The pounding of his own heart indicated that the operation just completed had taken far more out of him than it usually did, so he drew a long, slow breath and pulled a bit more energy from Iosif to stabilize himself, breathing out then with a relieved sigh. The young guard looked pasty-faced and almost feverish as Dimitri assessed the cost, and the pulse in the side of Iosif's neck fluttered weak and thready under his captor's fingers.

"A near-run thing, eh, my hapless young friend?" Dimitri whispered, shifting a little energy back to better balance the younger man. "Now you shall have what you desire, but consider carefully what dream you shall wish for in the future. Succubi are passing fickle, and sometimes cruel. Pleasure they may give, but not always do they reckon well a mortal mount's endurance."

A sly smile curved at his lips as he set the old scenario in motion, for well he knew what men like Iosif desired, in the loneliness of the long night watch. The erotic fantasy starting to stir at the edges of the younger man's awareness was tailored to fuel the most profound of carnal longings.

The dream would be brief but vivid, after which a shaken and exhausted Iosif would be off on his rounds again. If he did not actually ascribe his condition to a literal visitation by the delectable succubus of nocturnal memory, he certainly would be convinced that his exhaustion came of an exquisitely satisfying dream—clandestine bliss stolen while he sought a catnap in one of the several hiding places he had discovered were safe from his sergeant's prying. And it was something he would never report to his superiors or even a confessor.

So Iosif would keep his secret—and Dimitri's—and the odd partnership would continue as long as Dimitri had need of him—or until the night came, as it could at any time, when Dimitri must drain his subject past recovery. A less skilled mage might simply have killed his subjects after each night's work—supplying such an illusion as Dimitri's required extra effort and a bit of imagination—but Dimitri was savvy enough to realize that a series of mysterious deaths would have aroused suspicion.

No, far better to use the same subject again and again, and give the workman generous compensation for his labors. As Dimitri got to his feet, the younger man already was beginning to breathe more heavily, face flushing with anticipated ecstasy.

Smiling slightly as he shook his head, Dimitri put the man from his mind and glanced out into the main corridor, scanning left and right. He had his orders; time enough to begin implementing them tomorrow, as opportunities presented themselves. Several ideas had occurred to him already . . .

His master, meanwhile, had also paid a price for the night's work. Far away, in the cool darkness of a sparsely furnished tower room of a castle called Culliecairn, Prince Miklos of Torenth lay still as death and set himself the welcome discipline of running slowly through a spell to banish fatigue. These far contacts necessary to maintain input from his agent in Rhemuth always left him drained, even when he augmented his energies, and it was hard on the subjects from whom he borrowed those energies. The sturdy captain sprawled unconscious in the chair beside the camp bed was accustomed to serving his prince in this wise, but even with a Healer's ministrations, he was apt to require a day abed to fully recover. But the extra power had to come from somewhere, and a subordinate could spare it far more easily than Miklos.

Stirring a little stiffly, the prince opened his eyes and carefully stretched each long limb before sitting up with a sigh. Long blond hair tumbled loose around his shoulders as he bent his head to press the heels of both hands hard against his forehead. At this sign of life, a shorter, darker young man of a similar age came over to pour wine into a pair of silver goblets, handing one to the man just awakened before flouncing down in another chair beside the narrow camp bed.

"Well?"

"It proceeds according to plan," the fairer man replied, lifting his cup in salute and then drinking it down. "The Haldane has taken the bait and will be here within a fortnight."

The younger man laughed aloud and lifted his own cup in answer. "Well done, Dimitri! I really didn't think they'd let him come out. I thought they'd simply send an army."

"They are sending that, too," Miklos said mildly. "And it remains to be seen whether he can be lured into a confrontation of the sort you seek, once he arrives."

Marek of Festil snorted and set his cup beside his chair.

"I don't see why not. If he thinks he can get Culliecairn back by negotiation, why should he wish to risk men's lives in battle?"

"True enough. However, he seems rightly to have deduced that we have not my brother's support in this venture, and that you are as yet in no position to make him a serious military challenge. These insights show a far keener understanding of political realities than we had been led to expect. We may have been mistaken in assuming that he is controlled by his great lords."

"Dimitri swears that he is," Marek said.

"I prefer to judge that for myself, I think. We can afford to go slowly."

"Miklos, I've been going slowly for twenty-three years," Marek said, exasperation in his voice. "I'm the same age my father was when the Haldane's father killed him. It's time I found out whether the Haldane magic that killed my father passed to his son. I don't think it did, or he would have used it by now to free himself from his great lords."

"I am inclined to agree; and if you are correct, I shall kill him for you."

"I can kill him myself."

"You probably could. However, if we both are wrong, and the Haldane magic is his, it is best that I be the one to find this out. The House of Festil can ill afford the loss of its head at this time. Your heir is less than a year old, Marek."

"And you *have* no heir," Marek pointed out.

Miklos shrugged and smiled. "The gamble of a younger son, cousin. I have yet to establish *my* dynasty, but if it's to be done, better on the basis of lands won than lands merely given, however generous one's benefactor."

"When I am king," Marek murmured, reaching across to clasp his cousin's arm, "when we have won back my lands, I shall make you Duke of Mooryn, holding all of southern Gwynedd. And it will be because you have won it, not because anyone deigned to give it."

"Which is precisely why I am willing to be a little reckless in your cause," Miklos replied with a sly smile. "Now, here is what I have asked Dimitri to do."

* * *

At that moment, what Dimitri had been asked to do was of far less concern to him than making his way back to the privacy of his own quarters for some much-needed sleep. Soul-weary from his work of the past hour, and grown at once arrogant and complacent through several years' supposition that he was the only Deryni at large in Rhemuth Castle, he hardly noticed or cared that his shields were sloppy as he began to climb a turnpike stair leading upward. What mere human would notice his vulnerability, should he chance to meet anyone?

But others noticed. Nor were they merely human. En route back to the Portal room beside the library, just emerging from the turnpike stair that had led them down from the level of the royal apartments, Joram and Tieg paused to glance quickly along the corridor and then back down the stairwell as they sensed the flare of undisciplined shields somewhere nearby. Simultaneously came the faint, padding whisper of soft-shod footsteps ascending the turnpike stair from farther below, confirming the source of the flare. But there should be no other Deryni here!

Hardly breathing, Joram set a hand on Tieg's forearm, tight-shuttered communication passing between them. By keeping their own shields locked down, they should be able to avoid betraying their identity as Deryni; but they stood little chance of going unnoticed, for Tieg carried a torch. Nor dared they risk being seen entering the little room beside the library.

But their mere appearance should arouse no suspicion, dressed as man-at-arms and squire. As such, they had every right to be about the castle at this hour. Could the intruder say as much? Who was he?

The only way to find out was to brazen it out. Shields pulled close, they turned back onto the landing to await whoever was coming, Tieg holding his torch aloft in simple courtesy. The footsteps continued up the stairwell, torchlight now breaking around the newel post, preceding the one who bore it.

Against the glare of the other man's torch, Joram could make out but little of his features, but his raiment was black and monkish. Joram felt the other's flare of interest as he became aware of them, but no suspicion. And before simple interest could shift to suspicion, Tieg boldly reached out to grasp the hand holding the torch, at the same time plunging deep for the triggerpoint, stripping the other's powers bare and plummeting him into oblivion.

The man had no time to cry out, even in his mind. Consciousness simply ceased. He went rigid rather than buckling at the knees, for Tieg's controls held him immobile. After a taut instant to confirm his work, the young Healer handed off first one torch and then the other to Joram, shifting his hands then to either side of the man's head to Read him. Within seconds he glanced back at Joram in consternation.

"Good God, Joram, this is Dimitri!"

Joram moved in beside him immediately, glancing around surreptitiously as he stubbed out one torch against the wall and then conducted his own quick probe of their captive's mind. The breadth and depth of Dimitri's ongoing deception was so vast as to be almost unbelievable, except that Joram had seen the results all too clearly. That the Deryni double agent was no longer capable of any deception or subterfuge hardly mattered, for his work for the great lords had cost the lives of scores of innocent men and women, over the years. His work for Prince Miklos of Torenth and the Festillic Pretender, Prince Marek, bespoke even more convoluted plots and betrayals.

We'll take him back to the haven, Joram said in Tieg's mind. *I plan to strip him dry before I kill him.*

That's risky, Tieg returned. *If he just disappears, awkward questions are likely to be asked, maybe even of the king.*

If no body is ever found, his disappearance will remain a mystery, Joram replied. *They have no other Deryni to investigate it, and Fulk will verify that Dimitri never came near the royal apartments and the king never left them—which is all quite true. Help me get him up.*

CHAPTER EIGHT

Who causeth the righteous to go astray in an evil
way, he shall fall himself into his own pit.
—Proverbs 28:10

With but a few hours remaining before dawn, Joram finally decided *not* to kill Dimitri.

"The temptation is almost irresistible," he said to his closest
advisors. "God knows he deserves to die. But considering what
we've learned, I think he can serve our purposes far better if
we return him precisely where Paulin and Hubert think he
ought to be—with his orders suitably redirected, of course."

Bishop Niallan sat back wearily in his chair, absently rubbing one hand over his short-clipped grey beard.

"I just don't know, Joram. Granted, he'd be in a position to
do us several very large favors, but this does complicate an already precarious situation."

The subject of their discussion still lay where he had been
deposited some hours before, oblivious even to their presence,
stretched out motionless on the long table previously taken up
by maps and strategy papers. Still stripped of his powers and,
therefore, quite humanly vulnerable, Dimitri had been sub-
jected to the most thorough and rigorous examination of which
the very proficient Deryni ranged around this table were capable. The full extent of his service to the great lords now was
known, as well as the superior allegiance he owed to Miklos
of Torenth—and had owed, from long before he allowed himself to be recruited by Paulin of Ramos.

"Well, it was an incredible double deception," Dom Rickart
said, glancing toward the head of the table, where Jesse

MacGregor was still immersed in trance, fine-tuning Dimitri's new orders while Queron and Tieg observed. "And what incredible luck, that he should just walk into your hands like that."

"What incredible luck, that one of *our* people hasn't just walked into *his* hands, over the last few years," Joram countered. "And if he'd ever gotten his hands on the king, it would have been the end of him. We've all seen what suspicions he already had."

"Which is all the more reason to simply kill him and be done with it," Ansel said. "The very thought of letting him go back alive, even controlled—"

"Ansel, the idea doesn't exactly thrill me either," Joram said sharply. He was still wearing his Haldane harness and looked taut and irritated. "I'm quite aware of the risks. But his disappearance just now, on the eve of departure for a major military expedition, would raise far too many questions—as would his death by 'natural causes.'"

"Didn't we eliminate some *Custodes* priest just before Javan's coronation and make it look like natural causes?" Dom Rickart said thoughtfully.

"Yes, and Paulin was suspicious at the time, even though he was never able to put a finger on anything," Joram replied. "I don't think we dare use that ruse again, at least not in this instance. A convenient and fatal 'accident' would be useful, but that's far more difficult to arrange so that it's convincing, especially on short notice. And needless to say, we daren't even consider any form of killing that would be recognizable as murder."

Niallan gave a resigned sigh and bowed his head on one hand, rubbing at his eyes.

"So, if we do send him back controlled, how effective do you think he'll be?"

"Not very, and not for long, but he might have time and opportunity to eliminate at least a few of the opposition," Joram said. "Miklos will be the biggest limiting factor in that regard. The nature of the contact link he's forged with Dimitri ensures that he'll spot our tampering, if Dimitri makes the expected contact. So we can't allow that. And if Dimitri *doesn't* make the contact, Miklos eventually will become suspicious and try to force it—which he's quite capable of doing. Either way, Dimitri's a dead man."

"What if the great lords get suspicious first?" Ansel asked.

Joram shrugged. "A lot depends on the circumstances, but the end result is pretty much the same. Since they know what he is, they're sure to dose him with *merasha* before the questioning goes very far. Given the zeal of *Custodes* inquisitors, they'll probably employ torture if he doesn't break fairly quickly—which he won't. His final defense is set beyond a very high pain threshold. I don't much care whether he tells about working for Torenth, so long as he dies before revealing that he's also become a triple agent."

"I gather he has a death-trigger set," Dom Rickart said.

Joram nodded. "Quite a powerful one. It's a mark of his devotion to Miklos that he willingly allowed it to be set, so there could be no possibility of him betraying Miklos under pressure. Fortunately, with his powers temporarily suspended, it's possible for Jesse to—adjust it."

"Just like that?" Ansel said indignantly. "A nice, clean death-trigger? You mean that after all the deaths he's caused, he just gets to suicide out?"

"He'll still be dead," Dom Rickart pointed out, faintly disapproving. "And suicide is hardly a clean way out, if you accept the teachings of the Church on taking one's own life."

Bishop Niallan waggled a hand in a yes-and-no gesture. "Actually, we may be saving him from that, Rickart. It can be argued that since he didn't agree to the changed terms we're imposing, his death won't technically be suicide anymore. Call it an indirect execution, if you prefer. Personally, I would as soon send his unrepentant soul straight to hell, but my office as a priest forbids indulgence in vengeance. I salve my conscience with the knowledge that at least he's going to have a chance to make some restitution before he dies—even if he's forced to do it."

A little taken aback at the vehemence of Niallan's response, Ansel sat back in his chair as Rickart raised an eyebrow and asked Joram, "How long are we talking about, then? How long do you think he'll have?"

Joram folded his arms across his chest with weary resignation.

"He's to contact Miklos again when the Haldane levies are about two days' ride out of Culliecairn—say, in about a week. That's assuming, of course, that Miklos doesn't decide he needs to initiate a contact sooner, for some reason. Keep in mind, though, that it takes a great deal more energy if the contact isn't expected and assisted, especially across such a distance. Naturally, such a contact becomes increasingly feasible, the closer together they get."

"Having said that," Queron interjected, speaking up for the first time, "the chances are that Miklos *won't* attempt a contact for the first four or five days. With the kind of power outlay that's required, why bother, when the royal forces can't have done anything to threaten Miklos anyway? And if Dimitri tries to carry out his orders from Miklos and fails, what could Miklos do about it? Meanwhile, Dimitri can do a lot for *us*."

Niallan nodded reluctantly. "I agree with your logic. You may well be right. But I'm still not happy about turning him loose totally without supervision and without the king knowing. So much could go wrong."

"Nothing can be done about the lack of supervision, if we're going to try this," Joram said, "but we'll see what we can do about alerting the king. It will have to be through Rhysel, and she may not have an opportunity to pass on the information, but it's worth a try."

"I'll see to it," Tieg said, rising.

Joram nodded. "Be as quick as you can, then. The longer we keep Dimitri here, the greater the danger that he'll have been missed."

The dawning light that morning was fitful, for rain had moved in over Rhemuth during the night. The steady drumming of it against the leaded window glass woke Rhys Michael just as Cathan was pushing back the heavy curtains covering the window bay, but the absence of proper daylight made him burrow back under the sleeping furs for a few seconds, seeking warmth nearer Michaela, before he remembered what had happened the night before.

He sat up with a start, causing Cathan to turn to him in question and Michaela to sigh sleepily in protest. Instinctively he reached out a tendril of thought to brush her mind, though he kept his shields close. Her startled query shifted almost immediately to a tender feather-brush of response that felt almost like butterflies in his mind, so intimate as to be almost physical, echoed by her hands as she snuggled closer under the sleeping furs. Glancing back at Cathan, Rhys Michael could only manage a sheepish grin.

"Oh, it's you," he murmured, affecting nonchalance as he partially reclined back onto the pillows. "Aren't you a bit early?"

"The rain makes it darker than it should be," Cathan said cheerily, coming closer to lay a robe across the foot of the royal bed. "Your squires are drawing a bath in your dressing room—and I'll remind you that you aren't likely to get another while we're on the march—but I think I can stall them for a little while, if you—ah—aren't quite ready to get up yet. I should point out, however, that you're both expected at Mass in about an hour, and Archbishop Hubert will be very cross if you're late."

He grinned as he handed over a cup of morning ale, deliberately touching his hand to the king's, and the brief contact enabled Rhys Michael to confirm from Cathan that, indeed, he had not dreamed the night before.

Laughing delightedly, Rhys Michael waved Cathan out of the room with a shooing motion and set the ale aside, then turned to take Michaela in his arms, soon losing himself in the sweet bliss of their joining. Almost from the beginning, there had been an urgency to their lovemaking that went beyond the mere physical, knowing that each time might be the last.

Now that urgency was heightened by the knowledge that he soon would be riding into a much more tangible and immediate danger than had been their constant companion for the last six years. Though they pleasured one another gently this morning, lest her pregnancy be endangered, their passion carried a new poignancy that left Michaela softly weeping in his arms when they were spent. Only a determination not to let him leave with this impression enabled her to summon up a tremulous smile as he drew apart from her at last, in response to Fulk's knock at the door, to shrug into the robe Cathan had left him and pad off to his bath.

Somehow, Michaela managed to keep further tears at bay as she set about her own ablutions and allowed her ladies to help her dress. She found their fussing and endless chatter even more irritating than usual, although Lirin, the youngest of them, was also a trifle subdued this morning, perhaps because her Richard also was set to ride out with the king. Lady Estellan's husband was going, too, but they had been married for more than thirty years and had not shared a bed for decades.

"Your Highness, you're very pale this morning," Estellan said, holding first one gown, then another near her face, though trying to judge color by the grey morning light and candles was difficult. "I thought you were through with the morning sickness."

"I'm fine, Estellan. Just a little tired."

"And missing the king already, I'll warrant. Well, you just concentrate on bringing that bairn to term. The king will do what he must, and God willing, they'll all come home safe."

To counter the grey of the morning and offset her pallor, Estellan brought her a loose-fitting gown of deep rose silk, with a wide border of interlaced golden lions chasing one another around the hem and trailing sleeves. It pleased Michaela well enough as she pulled it on over her shift—the gown was one of her favorites, and Rhysem's—but not until Rhysel came to do her hair could she begin to feel the grey lethargy lift from her mood.

"Oh, *there* you are," Estellan said, as Rhysel approached with her basket of combs and brushes and pins and bobbed a quick curtsey. "She's looking a little peaked this morning, but the hair must be formal. The right veil will give her some color, I think. She's to wear her State Crown."

"Yes, my lady."

Making a deeper reverence to the queen, Rhysel set her basket on the dressing table and began brushing the tangles from the long, wheaten hair. After seeing Joram and Tieg safely on their way the night before, she had come back to Michaela to check on the king. Dead asleep, the newly empowered Rhys Michael had not stirred, but Michaela had greeted her like a sister, clinging to her for a long moment while she simply shook in after-reaction.

After, Rhysel had helped the queen ready for bed, then soothed her into dreamless sleep before returning to the sparse garret chamber she shared with another maid. She, too, had slept for a while after that—until Tieg's message roused her out of sleep and left her staring at the ceiling for what remained of the night.

"Pretend to be preoccupied while I braid up your hair," Rhysel whispered, as she divided off three thick sections with an ivory comb. "Whatever you do, don't react."

The officious Lady Estellan had disappeared momentarily, presumably to fetch the crown and a suitable veil, and Lirin and Lady Nieve were out of earshot, brushing up a drab-colored cloak by the wan light of day, over in the window bay, but Rhysel still shifted to mind-speech.

There's been a new development—potentially, a very good one. You must pass this on to the king, if you possibly can.

As her nimble fingers quickly plaited a thick braid to pin at the back of the queen's head, she silently imparted what portion of the news Tieg had instructed her to pass on. Rhysel had the whole of it, but too many details could only alarm Michaela and make her role that much more difficult to play, at least until she settled into her newly regained powers, such as they were. Michaela received the news of Dimitri's capture with amazement and a growing flare of hope, a little of it lending a new light to her eyes, though no sign of it showed in her expression.

Now make some critical comment about the way I've done your hair, Rhysel sent silently, as Estellan returned with the crown and a rosy handful of gossamer veil. *We don't want the dragon lady wondering why you suddenly look much perkier than when I first came in.*

Michaela sighed and picked up a hand mirror to inspect Rhysel's work.

"I wish we could leave at least part of it down," she said, smoothing a side strand for Rhysel to pin. "The king likes to see it loose."

"Queens do *not* wear their hair loose in public," Estellan said, handing Rhysel the veil with a sniff of disapproval. "Here, cover her Grace's hair with this before we put on the crown. It will give her some decent color."

"Yes, my lady," Rhysel murmured dutifully. The veil was a rose silk shot with gold, and actually did suit Michaela's coloring very well, but as Estellan momentarily turned her back to check on progress in the window bay, the queen stuck out her tongue, in a rare show of pent-up exasperation.

The old cow! came her spirited expletive, fortunately only caught by Rhysel.

Biting back a smile, Rhysel arranged the veil close around Michaela's face, with part of it cascading back from the crown of her head, then set the crown in place—leaves and crosses intertwined and set with rubies like the king's. As Rhysel held up the mirror so the queen could get a better view, Estellan returned with Lady Nieve, bearing a grey wool cloak lined and hooded with grey rabbit.

"I'm afraid it's still raining, your Highness," Nieve said, as the queen rose and let herself be helped on with the cloak. "A pity to cover that lovely gown, but on a day like this—Never mind, though. You look beautiful. We'd best go now. Mustn't keep the archbishop waiting."

"Thank you, Liesel," Michaela murmured, as she turned to go, knowing Rhysel would understand that her thanks were not only for the service just performed with the royal tresses. She wished she could send her thanks directly into Rhysel's mind, but she seemed to require physical contact for that. Perhaps, in time, she would learn how to extend her strength.

But meanwhile, what she *could* do had enabled Rhysel to pass on the news about Dimitri in safety, and she knew that she could pass it on to Rhysem in the same way, without anyone else being aware. That knowledge gave her hope that her husband's plight might not be nearly as desperate as they both had feared, for Dimitri's intended presence on the expedition to Eastmarch had been a source of some anxiety the previous afternoon. She hoped he would be greatly relieved to learn that Dimitri had been neutralized.

The bells were ringing for Terce as she went into the solar, where Rhys Michael also had just emerged. He was accoutred for his journey, in supple scarlet riding leathers under a tough, metal-studded scarlet jazerant, with scarlet gauntlets stuck into his white belt and the Haldane sword hanging at his side. The State Crown was on his head, and golden spurs were on his heels. He had left the Ring of Fire in Michaela's keeping earlier, for it was state regalia not suitable for the field, but the Eye of Rom was in his ear and his Haldane signet on his hand. He came to kiss her when she came out, then led her from the solar preceded by Cathan and Fulk, both clad in grey but armored much the same as he, with the badge of his service bold on their sleeves.

A squire bore a torch before them as they carefully descended the dim newel stair, and Michaela's ladies followed with another torch. The sounds of voices drifted up on the damp air to meet them as they approached the screens passage, whence they would enter the dais end of the great hall. Just as they reached the landing, little Owain broke away from an indulgent nurse and came running to join them, crimson-clad and joyous, miniature Haldane lions emblazoned bold across breast and back, though differenced by a label of the eldest son. He shrieked with delight as his father scooped him up to ride on his shoulders.

Thus did King Rhys Michael Alister Haldane make his way through the great hall and on to the Chapel Royal, with his queen on one arm and his laughing young son overseeing all from his superior height. Those gathered in the hall gave them reverence as they passed—courtiers and officers and a few of their ladies, some of the latter sniffing back tears to see the young prince thus. Those set to accompany the king on his expedition fell in behind, to join him for the Mass of Dedication that would send them blessed on their way.

Not until Mass was well in progress did Michaela find the opportunity to pass on Rhysel's news. Owain had gotten fidgety very quickly, once the Mass began, so Lirin had taken him out to be handed back to his nurse. Hubert was intoning a seemingly endless Gospel.

". . . The harvest truly is great, but the labourers are few; pray ye therefore the Lord of the harvest, that he would send forth labourers into his harvest. Go your ways: behold, I send you forth as lambs among wolves . . ."

Close your eyes and don't react to this, Michaela sent to Rhysem, as they stood with hands clasped between them in the folds of her cloak, and Hubert's voice droned on and on. She wanted to bow her head, to retreat further into the hood of her cloak, but one could not incline one's head too far forward while wearing a crown.

Rhysel had more news this morning, she went on, hoping her concentration would be taken for attention to the reading. *Joram and Tieg ran into Dimitri after they left us last night. They took him prisoner and—did things to him. It wasn't only the great lords he was working for—but he serves our purposes now. Rhysel says he won't be useful for very long—his conflicting loyalties are going to catch up with him, probably before you reach Eastmarch—but meanwhile, don't be surprised if things happen.*

He had managed not to react as she passed the message, but he did dare a glance at her before averting his eyes again and pretending to be caught up in the service.

What do you mean, if things happen?

She squeezed his hand more tightly and swallowed.

He was supposed to kill people. He still will. Except that Joram has changed some of the targets.

Who chose the original targets? Rhys Michael demanded.

Miklos of Torenth, acting for Marek. That's all I know.

He withdrew from her then. He still kept hold of her hand, but she sensed he had retreated to some intensely private place deep inside his mind where, at least for now, she was not welcome. He remained tightly shuttered until, at the offertory, he squeezed her hand, with a whisper bade her stay in her place, and went forward to remove his crown and lay it on the altar before the startled Archbishop Hubert.

"Your Grace, as I prepare to embark upon this journey, I offer up this endeavor to the greater glory of God and for the continued freedom of this kingdom from those who would usurp her sovereignty," he said quietly, hoping Hubert would not guess the double meaning in his words. "May Culliecairn be freed, and may God give us victory."

With that he retreated to the lowest altar step and knelt there for the remainder of the Mass, head humbly bowed over clasped hands. Later, he could not have said he exactly spent the time in prayer, but he certainly found much food for contemplation in the news Michaela had brought him. To his surprise, when the time came for Communion, Hubert gave him the Cup as well as the Host.

It was meant as an honor and sign of approval from Hubert, he knew, but for some reason he found it profoundly disturbing. It had nothing to do with religion. Drinking of the Sacred Blood brought more personal images of blood flashing through his mind—his own blood of the night before, shed by Joram and then by his own hand; the blood of friends slain on the day of the coup, six years before; Javan's bloodless body when they had brought it home, *his* royal blood soaking a field Rhys Michael had never seen, by a river ford north of Valoret, where his slayers had cut him down untimely; and more blood on Rhys Michael's hands—a great deal of it—whether his own or that of others, he could not tell. At one point, the sensation of wetness was so intense that he even wiped his palms surreptitiously on his thighs. Then he had to clasp his hands again to keep from shaking.

Hubert must have taken his trembling for fervor, for after the Mass was concluded, with Michaela called to kneel beside him, he blessed Rhys Michael with a special benediction and put the crown back on his head, leaving them then for a final moment alone before they must make a public parting. Speaking briefly with Paulin afterward, while they waited for the king and queen to appear on the great hall steps, Hubert remarked that he thought it boded well for the expedition that the king voluntarily should offer up his crown upon the altar of God.

"It bespeaks a dedication I had not expected," Hubert said.

"I am also forced to wonder whether receiving the Cup sparked some sort of religious conversion. Hitherto, I would have described the king's attitude toward religion as indifferent. Oh, he goes through the motions readily enough—but you know what I mean."

Paulin was noncommittal, but assured Hubert of his ongoing concern for the king's spiritual welfare—so long as that did not compromise the great lords' intentions for Gwynedd.

"A tame king is an altogether useful thing," Paulin said, "but this particular one occasionally shows disturbing flashes of independence. I begin to think that he may well become expendable, once the new heir is born."

"Has something happened to make you more wary?" Hubert asked.

Paulin shook his head. "Nothing specific that I can point out to you. But guard the young prince well, Hubert, and pray that his mother is granted safe delivery of another healthy son. I do not trust his father. I shall have Dimitri keep a close watch on him."

Chapter Nine

Rejoice not against me, O mine enemy: when I fall,
I shall arise; when I sit in darkness, the Lord shall be
a light unto me.

—Micah 7:8

Rhys Michael had not expected even the ragged cheer that
went up as he and Michaela came out onto the great hall steps.
The castle yard was packed with rows of bright-clad men on
horses, from heavy cavalry and lancers to mounted archers and
scouts—but no infantry, for the great lords had decided that
men on foot would slow the army's pace too much. For like
reason, only a modest baggage train waited outside the open
gates to accompany the campaign; provisioning and additional
men would come from the estates through which they passed
en route north.

The cheer receded into the general din as king and queen
slowly descended the steps. Cathan was waiting to lay a thick
woolen cloak around the king's shoulders—Haldane crimson,
with the Haldane brooch to clasp it at the throat. Rhys Michael
drew it gratefully around him, for a fine mist still hung on the
air and a pewter-colored sky promised more rain to come. As
Michaela fastened the clasp, Rhys Michael cast his gaze over
the waiting men, trying to read their mood.

His commanders were waiting for him at the foot of the
steps, mounted and ready. He had chosen none of them.
Albertus, the earl marshal, had several of his *Custodes* officers
around him, and Rhun sat his horse beside Fulk Fitz-Arthur,
who had the Haldane battle standard footed in his stirrup.
Fulk's younger brother Quiric held the reins of the reliable
grey destrier Rhys Michael was to ride, and other squires

tended Cathan's bay and an ill-tempered roan that belonged to Earl Udaut, the castle's constable, who was consulting with Earl Tammaron off to one side.

Others of the great lords who would be going along were also gathered in the yard behind Albertus and Rhun: Hubert's brother Manfred, instructing the captain of a smart-looking contingent of lancers in Culdi livery; Richard Murdoch, husband to Michaela's Lady Lirin, with a company of archers in the colors of Carthane, perhaps a score of them.

Farther back, Paulin had joined a handful of black-clad men whose red-and-gold cinctures marked them as *Custodes Fidei*. Rhys Michael recognized a few of the faces, but he did not spot Dimitri—though he had no time to really look for him. Behind Paulin were ranged at least thirty black-clad *Custodes* knights in their red-fringed white sashes. Other lesser lords also sat beneath their banners at the head of more modest contingents—Lord Ainslie, Richard's brother Cashel, and others Rhys Michael did not recognize. He guessed their total number at about a hundred, not counting servants and support personnel—not many, to defy a Torenthi prince and a bastard pretender. But several hundred more would join them as they passed close to Valoret and Caerrorie and Sheele, in addition to whatever men were already massing from Eastmarch and points north.

Quiet began settling on the company as old Archbishop Oriss tottered out onto the great hall steps in cope and mitre, supported by Hubert and leaning on his crozier, for as Archbishop of Rhemuth, it was he who had the honor of blessing the troops. Tammaron approached Rhys Michael, ready to summon him before Oriss, but the king was already removing his crown, giving it into Michaela's keeping. Owain's nurse had brought the boy back to rejoin his parents, bundled in a miniature scarlet cloak against the damp, and Rhys Michael bent to pick up the boy and kiss him.

He turned to face the archbishops then, kneeling with the boy in his arms. A hush fell over the assembled men as they realized he intended so to receive Oriss' benediction.

Into the settling silence came the rustle of pennoned lances being lowered in salute, the mounted archers saluting with their unstrung bows, cased in oilskin to keep away the damp. Helmeted heads bowed as Oriss lifted a palsied right hand, and the Haldane standard dipped.

"Benedicat vos omnipotens Deus: Pater, et Filius, et Spiritus Sanctus."

"Amen," Rhys Michael responded, with a hundred other voices, as he crossed himself in blessing, repeating the sign over his young son, then got slowly to his feet. Out of the silence behind him arose a cheer from a hundred throats, as lances again were lifted and bows were brandished. After kissing his son on both cheeks, Rhys Michael gave the boy back into his mother's care, then chastely took her hand and kissed it, meeting her eyes only briefly in final, wordless farewell.

Then he was turning to descend the steps, pulling on his gauntlets, and mounting up on the big grey stallion that Cathan now held for him. He dared not look back at the pair standing on the steps. Quiric handed up the open-faced helm circled by its coronet of gold, and as Rhys Michael settled it on his head, he became suddenly aware of the Haldane standard close by in Fulk's hand—and that only once before had he ridden under that banner in his own right, as king, on that murky and best-forgotten day of his coronation, with his brain dulled by the great lords' drugs and his heart still aching for his slain brother, who should have been king instead of him.

The old grief caught at his throat, and he longed to take the standard in his own hand, the way he often had seen Javan do, but he knew such an act of independence would only earn him a sharp dressing-down when they camped for the night—if Albertus could restrain himself from making a public reprimand for that long. Still, the banner that symbolized Gwynedd's sovereignty now was his to guard and defend, and now, at last, perhaps Rhys Michael would have a chance to assert the freedom for which Javan had died.

Not immediately, of course; but soon. At least in the field, a king might win by valor what caution and timidity had not been able to secure under the close confinement he had endured these six years. There was much to lose, not least of which was the grey-cloaked woman clutching the hand of a very small boy cloaked in crimson, the pair of them watching him from the great hall steps—but there was also much to win, including their freedom as well as his own.

Behind him, Cathan and Udaut were both mounting up, Udaut fighting his mount for a moment before he could force it ahead to join the eight castle guards detailed to escort the royal party as far as the city gates. Balanced between excitement and melancholy, Rhys Michael lifted a gauntleted hand in farewell to those waiting on the great hall steps, imprinting his final glimpse of them in memory, then turned his steed's head toward the castle gate to follow Albertus and Rhun, not looking back.

The cavalcade moved out at a smart pace, for the mist had turned to drizzle, and the horses were eager to be off. Several ranks ahead of him, Udaut's roan was still being fractious, even crow-hopping a few times until Udaut slugged it hard in the neck and forced its obedience. Fulk commented airily that had the animal been his, he would have put the horse down long ago, or at least turned him out to stud. Cathan avowed that this would only perpetuate a bad bloodline.

Leaving the two to debate the issue, Rhys Michael gigged his own mount a few paces ahead of them, then settled in half a length before, happily putting Udaut and his misbegotten horse out of mind. Despite the desperate prospects he might face in the days to come, he already felt freer. He had ridden regularly for years, to keep fit, but not in all that time had he been allowed more than a few leagues from the city. Despite the rain, cheering crowds lined the streets, cheering for *him*, the way they had done in the old days even before Javan, when Alroy had been king.

He was rejoicing in his growing freedom as they approached the city gates, beginning to relax a little, refusing to think too much about what might lie ahead in Eastmarch—for that was nearly a week away. He had even begun tentatively casting about with his powers to start getting a feel for what he might perceive with them, somehow knowing that the crowd was large enough to hide him, if some other Deryni chanced to catch a psychic glimpse of a probe.

Afterward, he realized that the odd shimmer around Udaut's stallion should have warned him; he had thought it a fluke of errant sunbeam on raindrops at the time. But when it first began, he doubted anyone had considered the animal's behavior that surprising. The big roan had an evil reputation and had been acting up from the moment its groom led it into the yard.

Now, spooking at God knew what, the animal suddenly exploded in a screaming, spine-wrenching series of bucks that hurled the startled Udaut over its shoulder to slam into one of the gate pylons with bone-breaking force. Apparently not satisfied with merely ridding itself of its rider, the squealing beast then proceeded to trample the unfortunate Udaut and several screaming bystanders who could not retreat fast enough, biting and kicking in a killing frenzy, until a crusty guardsman with more courage than good sense managed to force his own mount close enough to fling himself across, wrench the stallion's head around by an ear, and cut its throat.

The animal screamed once more and collapsed. Blood sprayed wide in its death-throes, spattering onlookers and running red on the rain-slick cobblestones, and the guard sustained a bone-bruising kick before the thrashing subsided. The sharp smell of the blood sent several more horses into momentary fits of nervous jigging and snorting until their riders could regain control; but by the time anyone could get near the now motionless Udaut, nothing could be done.

Rhun and Cathan were the first to reach the constable's side besides the now limping guardsman, but Cathan's grim glance back told of the futility of it, even as Rhys Michael calmed his own wild-eyed steed. Around Udaut, his men were moving the crowd back with practiced ease, making room for Albertus to dismount and run to Udaut's side as Paulin and a grey-haired battle surgeon called Stevanus began pushing their way forward from behind the king.

"Let the surgeon through!" Paulin ordered, as Stevanus elbowed his way past several more riders and dashed ahead to crouch beside the victim.

But Stevanus' brisk examination could only confirm that death had been a mercy for Rhemuth's hapless constable, for Udaut's back was broken, one arm was mangled almost beyond recognition, and one leg lay twisted under him at a sickening angle. The head was mostly unmarked, other than for a small trickle of blood that ran from the gaping mouth. The staring eyes looked almost more surprised than pained. Paulin caught up with his surgeon as Stevanus was closing the dead man's eyes and crossed himself with every evidence of genuine sorrow as the battle surgeon gently straightened out the twisted leg, then moved on to see to the injured spectators.

"I've never seen a horse go berserk like that," Paulin muttered, almost a little awed.

"I have," Albertus said, going back to prod the stallion's steaming carcass with a booted toe. "Never quite like this, though."

As he bent down to begin uncinching the animal's saddle, motioning one of the guardsmen to help him, Paulin remembered himself and crouched down beside the dead man's head to trace the sign of the Cross on his forehead. Cathan had come back to stand beside Rhys Michael's grey, catching hold of the reins and stroking the animal's neck to gentle it, and though they pretended attention to Paulin's prayers, both watched surreptitiously as Albertus pulled the saddle free.

"In nomine Patris, et Filii, et Spiritus Sancti," Paulin murmured. *"Requiem aeternam dona ei, Domine, et lux perpetua luceat ei."*

"Offerentes eam in conspectu Altissimi," came scattered responses from around him, though most everyone else within sight was watching Albertus curiously. The earl marshal was running his hands along the sheepskin lining of the saddle, sniffing at his fingers, his assistant removing the stallion's bridle to inspect the bit, shaking his head, mystified.

"Kyrie, eleison," Paulin intoned.

"Kyrie, eleison. Christe, eleison," the response came.

As Albertus finally ran his hands across the sweat-matted hide on the stallion's back, tight-lipped as he, too, shook his head, Paulin again signed Udaut's forehead with the sign of the Cross.

"Tibi, Domine, commendamus animam famuli tuae, Udauti, ut defunctus saeculo tibi vivat." To Thee, Lord, we commend the soul of this Thy servant, Udaut, that when he departs from this world he may live with Thee. By the grace of Thy merciful love, wash away the sins that in human frailty he has committed in the conduct of his life. *". . . Per Christum, Dominum nostrum."*

"Amen," came the murmured reply.

Paulin sighed then, and gestured for one of the guardsmen to cover the body with his cloak as he and the others got to their feet. As the man obeyed, a slight commotion from farther back in the now stalled cavalcade heralded the agitated approach of Richard Murdoch, who was married to Udaut's daughter. Recognizing the big roan sprawled with legs akimbo at Albertus' feet, and not immediately seeing Udaut, Richard hastily dismounted and started forward, concern writ large on his handsome face. Albertus now was inspecting the roan's bloodied hooves, using one of the quillons of his dagger to pick out the mud from around each vulnerable frog.

"It's too late, Richard," Rhun said, catching him by the shoulders to stay him. "His horse threw him and then he was trampled. He's there." He indicated the cloak-shrouded form with his chin. "There's nothing you can do."

Richard sagged against Rhun's hand for just an instant,

catching up a moan, then pulled away, shaking his head slowly as he came to lift an edge of the cloak. Stevanus had seen him approaching and came to crouch beside him.

"I'm sorry, my lord," Stevanus said quietly. "I—believe he felt very little after the first impact. And had he survived, any one of his injuries would have left him a hopeless cripple."

Richard swallowed and let fall the edge of the cloak, then glanced back dully at Albertus, who was wiping his hands on the corner of his cloak.

"Do you know what caused it?" he said. "What were you looking for?"

Albertus shook his head and shrugged. "A burr, some trace of an irritant—I don't know. But there's nothing. It just—happened."

He came to stand awkwardly beside the younger man as another guardsman joined the first and, together, they wrapped the cloak more closely around the body and picked it up. One of the *Custodes* clerics had brought up another horse, and the two laid the cloak-wrapped body across its saddle and began tying it in place.

"This, ah, does leave us with an awkward logistic problem," Albertus said to Paulin in a low voice, almost as if he hated even to mention it. "Rhemuth now has no constable."

"Well, we can't delay our departure, and we can't leave Rhemuth undefended," Rhun said.

His gaze flicked appraisingly to the still dazed-looking Richard, then back at Albertus and Paulin, both of whom gave slight nods of assent. With a sick feeling in the pit of his stomach, Rhys Michael realized what they were about to do.

"So I suppose it's fitting that we appoint a new constable and get on with things," Rhun went on quietly, setting a hand on Richard's forearm, which made the younger man look up with a start. "Do you think you're ready for this, Richard? It isn't a hasty offer. We've been watching you for some time—since your own father's death, in fact. We need someone loyal and reliable to hold Rhemuth in our absence and to guard the safety of the queen and the king's heir. Also," he added, in a milder tone, "your wife will need you to help bury her father. We could hardly ask you to come with us as planned, under the circumstances. If you wish, I'll take personal command of your archers."

Richard swallowed, then nodded tentatively. "Yes, I—thank

you. You do me great honor. I shall try to prove worthy of your trust. But—dear God, what am I going to say to Lirin?"

Gravely Paulin came to lay a sympathetic arm around Richard's shoulders. "I am so sorry, Richard. If it will give your dear wife comfort, remind her that her father will have gone straight to Heaven. He came from Holy Communion not an hour ago."

As Richard gave a choked nod, turning to take the reins of his horse and remount, Rhys Michael thought the remark might have been one of the more hypocritical ones he had ever heard. Nor had he even been consulted about Udaut's replacement—not that they had ever consulted him before.

Cathan must have sensed his resentment, or at least shared it, for he cast the king a wry glance before catching up his bay and remounting. Watching him, Rhys Michael paid scant attention to the mounted *Custodes* man who was leading up Paulin's mount and the dun gelding that Master Stevanus rode. But as the two came back to claim their steeds, Rhys Michael could not miss recognizing the man. Dressed like Stevanus in the red and black tunic of a battle surgeon, the dark, slightly built man with downcast eyes looked like any of a number of others riding among the *Custodes Fidei*, but the king had no doubt that it was Dimitri. He had not expected that the Deryni would be riding so close.

The little man apparently sensed the royal scrutiny, for when he had handed over his charges, he turned slightly in the saddle, made what might have been a slight bow in the king's direction, then turned deliberately to go back to his place.

In that instant, Rhys Michael knew that the first "thing" had happened through Dimitri's instigation. It had looked entirely like an accident, and he could not regret the death of Udaut, who had turned on him so traitorously the day of the coup. But to replace Udaut with Richard Murdoch, whose betrayal had been at least as treacherous—

Then he saw the logic of the move, which surely had been orchestrated by Joram. If anything, Richard was an even less acceptable constable than Udaut, but appointing him to that post just now would keep him from accompanying the army to Eastmarch. And that meant one less powerful enemy for Rhys Michael to worry about in his immediate vicinity.

"My condolences to your lady," the king murmured, as a tight-jawed Richard took his leave of Albertus and Rhun and passed nearby, starting to lead the squires back toward the castle with their grim burden.

As the cavalcade began to move out again, Rhys Michael reflected that this was likely to prove an even more interesting journey than he had anticipated.

CHAPTER TEN

Look to yourselves, that we lose not those things which we have wrought, but that we receive a full reward.

—II John 1:8

In the days immediately following the king's departure for Eastmarch, Joram and his colleagues in sanctuary began setting in place such measures as might give their fledgling Haldane additional support when he reached his destination. From Joram's own agents in Torenth and the Forcinn came repeated opinions that Marek himself was not capable of a serious incursion into Gwynedd this season and that Miklos had fewer than three hundred men backing him. If the taking of Culliecairn was but a feint to draw the king out of Rhemuth, as it appeared to be, it was not to test his military strength.

Logic and the agents' past reliability suggested that their assessments were correct. Though a full-scale armed encounter seemed increasingly unlikely, when viewed in light of the reports, it was Bishop Niallan who pointed out that Miklos could have offered few greater provocations than to have the Festillic Pretender's heir christened on Gwynedd soil. That he had informed Gwynedd's king of his intentions in advance only served to reinforce suspicions that the true object of the exercise was to lure the king onto ground of Miklos' choosing where, presumably, he would have no protection from more subtle testing that Deryni might employ against an enemy.

Against that possibility, as well as to augment the physical force available to the king when he confronted the intruders, Ansel and Jesse quickly gathered a troop of nearly forty former Michaelines and other loyal men, some of them Deryni.

Though none dared flaunt that lineage these days, many of the men had built themselves admirable reputations in the last decade for helping keep the peace in the borders and were somewhat known in Eastmarch as men to be trusted. With these men in the forefront, and Ansel and Jesse disguised among them—and Tieg riding as squire, for they must have a Healer among them—the troop set out for Lochalyn to offer their services to Sudrey of Eastmarch, who was herself of Deryni lineage.

Not that shared blood was any guarantee of a warm reception. Though Sudrey might have been born Deryni, distant kin both to Miklos and Marek, she had never been known to evidence the slightest hint of possessing any powers—whether because they were minuscule or because she simply declined to use them, out of respect for the human sensibilities of her husband and his people, no one knew. But the killing of her husband by forces under a prince of her own Deryni kindred could have done nothing to revive her Torenthi connections in any positive way. It was hoped she would turn a blind eye to the fact that some of the benefactors come to help avenge her husband's death might be Deryni like herself.

In fact, the composition of Ansel's band never became an issue, for he and Jesse were able to present themselves and their men to one of Sudrey's captains, who was happy to accept the offer of an extra forty mounted men with no questions asked. Casual inquiry around the camp that night disclosed that with the slain Earl Hrorik now in his grave, the Lady Sudrey had called her husband's captains to her and personally taken their vows of allegiance, never mind that Corban, her daughter's husband, now was technically Earl of Eastmarch.

Nor was she solely dependent upon the men remaining from her husband's disastrous foray up to Culliecairn, where Miklos' forces showed no signs of withdrawing. Hrorik's nephew, the twenty-year-old Duke Graham of Claibourne, had rushed to her assistance as soon as he heard the news, with two hundred men now encamped round about Castle Lochalyn. Sighere, Hrorik's brother, had brought another hundred from Marley to add to the scores who were continuing to pour in from the farther reaches of Eastmarch itself. Rumor had it that the king was bringing another two to three hundred and would arrive within a few days—news brought by fast messengers from along the line of the king's march, not by magic.

In Rhemuth, meanwhile, Queen Michaela could gain little

news of what went on beyond the walls of the royal apartments. The sparse reports she had from Rhysel from time to time assured her of Joram's ongoing efforts to place agents among the forces massing in Eastmarch; but as she had no real knowledge of military thinking and what was appropriate preparation for war, such reports meant little. She received the odd, brief letter from the king as he made his way north and east by stages, but she knew the letters were read before they left his encampments, and again before being placed in her hands. Accordingly, the letters spoke only of missing her and Owain and concerns for her health and that of the child she carried.

Nor did her domestic situation alter much, other than to accommodate the brief upheaval of Court routine caused by Udaut's death. Because it was expected, she made herself put on mourning and attend Udaut's semi-state funeral in Saint Hilary's Basilica, at the foot of the castle, but she hardened her heart to the prayers offered for the dead man's repose. Let God forgive the man who had been part of the conspiracy that murdered King Javan and put her husband on the throne; she would not. Kindness toward the grieving Lirin came more easily, for she well remembered grieving her own father, and she readily granted Udaut's only daughter leave from royal service to mourn.

Other than this brief deviation from normal court routine, the days that followed passed with little variation, each one much like the one before. Especially with the king absent, Michaela chafed increasingly under the emptiness of the life imposed on a captive queen. Only at day's end did joy touch her heart, when a bathed and fed but inevitably sleepy little Prince Owain was brought by his nurse for an all too brief visit.

But never in private. The nurse had orders to remain always in attendance, and usually at least a few of her ladies-in-waiting also remained. Nor were visits to the nursery permitted, being thought disruptive to the young prince's routine. Even discussion of her unhappiness with the situation could result in the loss of any visiting privileges at all.

Thus denied even the pretense of mothering her child, Michaela was expected to join her ladies in "suitable" pastimes during the remainder of the daylight hours—listening to one or another of them read or sing, plying her hand at needlework, which she was growing to detest, and pretending to find diversion in the idle gossip that passed for intellectual stimulation in this stifling environment. Occasionally, when the weather was fine, she was allowed to escape to the gardens for an hour's stroll, for walking was deemed beneficial for an expectant mother, but usually the incessant chatter followed her even there.

At least one of her ladies must accompany her to Mass, as well—though at least they must keep silent during the service. With concentration, Michaela could use the murmur of the Latin to foster an illusion of silence, provided she put from mind that most of the celebrants were priests of the detested *Custodes Fidei*—and if not a *Custodes* man, Hubert himself was apt to be presiding. Michaela had no idea whether she derived any spiritual benefit from so shifting the focus of the Mass, using the silence to dream dire fates for her oppressors, but at least it offered respite from mindless chatter; and in that semi-privacy, when she did turn her thoughts to prayers for Rhysem's safety and deliverance, she sometimes thought she caught a glimmer of what might have driven Javan to seek out refuge in the monastery, when it was he who was plotting how to free Gwynedd's crown.

Rhysel was able to provide more active encouragement in this regard. Though her place as maid within the royal household did not permit her unlimited access to the queen, at least it was regular, morning and night. The queen's increasing propensity for afternoon naps gave added excuse for Rhysel to be much about the royal apartments, there to take down the queen's hair and brush it after lunch, in preparation for the royal nap, and then to arrange it again for the evening, especially if the queen was expected to preside at table in the great hall.

Michaela came to treasure the time when Rhysel was working on her hair, for the physical contact permitted the two of them to hold silent converse under the very noses of Estellan and the others who vied for the honor of serving in the queen's entourage. In more private moments, when Rhysel helped the queen retire for her naps, occasional instruction could be imparted in further refinement of such powers as she had.

"We must be very, very careful in this," Rhysel whispered, one afternoon when the other ladies all happened to be out of the room momentarily. "I know this is heady business, but just remember that if we're ever discovered, it can mean both our deaths."

Michaela tossed her tawny mane. "Do you think I haven't

been living with that threat for the last six years?" she said. "Not yours, of course, but Rhysem and I have always been that close to the edge."

As she indicated a hair's breadth between thumb and forefinger, Rhysel nodded.

"I know that, and you're both incredibly brave. Just remember that even Deryni are vulnerable. You can't help anyone if you're dead."

Lady Estellan returned at that with a cup of cool wine, ending their verbal exchange, but the stark truth of Rhysel's warning tempered Michaela's enthusiasm thereafter, though at least this turn of events had given her a new glimmering of hope.

En route to Eastmarch, meanwhile, Rhys Michael was concerned with his own stark truths. Udaut's death had left a breath of uneasy speculation within the royal entourage that never really died down. Though not even Albertus could point to foul play, some whispered that such a freakish accident was a portent of ill luck to come. Cathan noted that the chaplains seemed to be doing a brisk business in confessions and the blessing of arms and steeds and holy medals, and at least for the first few days, Fulk reported that the men talked of little else around the campfires at night.

Rhys Michael's own observations tended to confirm the sense of ill ease. In the sparse leisure time that remained to the great lords between the end of each day's march and finally seeking out their beds—the ongoing chores of regular inspection of the men and dealing with the dispatches that caught up with them daily, both from behind and ahead of march—the king knew that Rhun and Manfred, at least, continued to expend a fair amount of time and energy rehashing the circumstances of Udaut's death. Dimitri seemed somewhat more in evidence than usual, but he never approached the king; fortunately for him, it did not seem to have occurred to his masters that he could have had any part in the death. Rhys Michael continued warily to test his powers as they rode along, but nothing occurred to necessitate even thinking about action that might uncloak his newfound abilities prematurely.

Thus did the first few days pass uneventfully, as the expedition sped north and eastward, skirting the southerly bank of the Eirian, overnighting under the stars or sometimes at establishments of the *Custodes Fidei*, where the king and at least his great lords found proper lodging and the troops encamped in the fields round about. They made good time, and only one other incident marred their progress, again having to do with horses. What made it stand out particularly in Rhys Michael's mind was that it involved another of the great lords.

It had happened three days out, while they were riding along an embankment that skirted the Eirian. Albertus had been riding at the front with some of his *Custodes* knights when a swarm of bees suddenly attacked the lead riders, stinging men and beasts and scattering that end of the march. Though both Albertus and his mount avoided being stung, one of his companion's efforts to escape sent him careening into Albertus' mount, and both animals went sliding and scrambling down the embankment and into fairly deep water.

Albertus managed to keep his seat, sputtering and swearing as he swam his horse toward shallower water, but his companion was not so fortunate. Still swatting at bees, the man flailed for balance but lost it as his horse scrambled for footing, dragged under by his armor and sinking from sight even as Albertus turned to try to aid him. By the time Albertus and others could find him and drag him out, he could not be revived.

This second freak accident of the campaign put a further damper on spirits as the column re-formed and continued on, the body of the dead *Custodes* man tied across his horse's saddle for delivery to his brethren at the next *Custodes* House they passed. Quickly supplied with a dry cloak by one of his squires, Albertus seemed shaken but none the worse for wear as he gigged his horse with his spurs and headed farther back along the line of march to bully stragglers, keeping a wary eye out for further swarms of bees, but the oddness of the incident was sufficient to make the king wonder whether Dimitri had attempted to strike again and gotten the wrong man. The accident was totally unlike the one that had claimed Udaut and would have been entirely plausible, had it been Albertus who drowned, but who could say? He certainly was not going to seek out Dimitri to ask.

They passed near Valoret later that day, pausing only long enough to dispatch two men to Ramos with the body of the drowned man and to pick up the troops promised by Hubert from the *Custodes Fidei* garrison there: eighty *Custodes* knights and men-at-arms under Lord Joshua Delacroix, Hubert's commander-general. They camped under the stars that night, but very near Rhun's seat at Sheele. When Rhun's levy of twenty knights joined them that evening, they were accompanied by his castellan, Sir Drogo de Palance, who brought several wagonloads of roasted meats, cheeses, fresh bread, and wine for the enjoyment of his lord, the king, and their staff.

A festive mood prevailed in the camp that night, at least among the officers, who were invited to dine in Rhun's command tent, but Rhys Michael was sober as he retired to write his daily letter to Michaela. He dared not voice his suspicions regarding Albertus' mishap, just as he had not dared to commit his suspicions about Udaut's death to writing, but he did relate the incident in as straightforward a manner as he could manage, in a tone that almost applauded the earl marshal's unfortunate luck—a reaction that would arouse no suspicion at all from those who read his correspondence before he sent it or Michaela received it. Perhaps Rhysel would be able to read between the lines and draw more discerning conclusions.

The growing royal cavalcade headed slightly easterly with the dawn, picking up Manfred's levy of fifty lancers at a rendezvous point near Ebor and passing well onto the plain of Iomaire, where they camped under the stars once again. Commanding Manfred's levies was his son Iver, the Earl of Kierney, who had gained his title by marrying well. Now in his thirties, Iver MacInnis had become his father's hand in the north, dividing his time between his wife's estates in Kierney and his father's lands in Culdi, for Iver would own both, once his father died. His addition to the growing royal party only underlined Rhys Michael's despair that he would never break free.

The last day but one saw them pressing north and east at speed across the vast heartland of Iomaire. They were more than two hundred strong by the time they encamped that evening in the fields around Saint Cassian's Abbey, another *Custodes* House. As was customary, the king and his great lords and officers were given accommodations in the abbey guesthouse. Messengers were awaiting the king's arrival with new maps and dispatches from Lady Sudrey, who promised a full four hundred men when the royal forces joined them on the plain before the Coldoire Pass.

Following a quick perusal of the messages waiting, clerks were set to work drafting responses, and shortly the king and his officers went in to a frugal supper in the abbey refectory, hosted by the abbot and his obedientiaries. Attendance at Compline followed, obligatory in return for the hospitality shown, and thereafter, Rhys Michael retired to the single room assigned him and his aides at one end of the guesthouse.

The accommodations were as sparse as the meal. Two pallets had been added to the usual stark configuration of one narrow bed and a functional washstand with earthen pitcher, wooden bowl, and rough grey towels. Out of deference to the special needs a king might have for dealing with dispatches and the like, a round table and three mismatched chairs had been provided nearer the room's single high window, feebly lit by rushlights in a standing rack beside it. More general illumination came from several iron lanterns hung from metal hooks set into two of the walls. The place smelled faintly of sweet herbs and the new straw that had been strewn on the flagstoned floor.

"We've slept in far worse," Fulk said good-naturedly, as he slung his saddlebags onto one of the pallets.

"Aye, and eaten far better," Cathan replied. "I can't say I envy the abbot his cook."

"Well, it was better than camp fare," Rhys Michael said.

It was early yet for sleeping, so the king sent Cathan for a bottle of wine while he and Fulk spread out the maps he had brought from their pre-supper briefing, intending to review the terrain of the Coldoire Pass and the fortress of Culliecairn, perched on its rocky crag. A knock at the door summoned Fulk to answer it, expecting Cathan, and he fell back in some dismay as Albertus swept into the room, followed by a second man bearing a torch to light their way.

"Sire, it's Lord Albertus," Fulk announced, though a pinched tone in his voice made Rhys Michael look around and then get slowly to his feet.

"My Lord Marshal," he murmured, his blood running cold, for Albertus' torch-bearer was none other than Dimitri.

Albertus made him a curt bow, hands clasped behind his back, hidden in his scarlet-faced black mantle.

"Your Highness. I wished to inquire whether you had any questions regarding the maps you took away with you. From some of your comments at supper, I was not altogether certain you approved of our plans."

The statement was a blatant lie. Rhys Michael knew it at once, without any benefit of Truth-Reading—which he dared not employ in Dimitri's presence, even though he knew the Deryni supposedly was neutralized. Affecting an expression of wide-eyed mystification, he gestured to one of the other chairs as he took his own seat.

"I can't imagine why you would think that," he said easily. "But please, be seated. Perhaps you would care to go over the plans again and question me on my understanding. I am the first to admit that my knowledge of strategy, alas, is totally theoretical. Pray, be seated, my lord."

"I prefer to stand, thank you," Albertus said coolly. "And do not presume to patronize me. Don't think I am not aware how you mouth the platitudes you know are expected of you, while secretly you plot to overturn the established order. Did you have anything to do with Udaut's death?"

The sudden question stunned him. Carefully setting both hands on the arms of his chair, Rhys Michael sat back and slowly shook his head. He was too new to his powers to know whether Dimitri was Truth-Reading him, but there could be no other reason for the Deryni agent's presence. This question he could answer without danger of being caught in a lie, but what about the next, and the next? Dimitri supposedly had been "neutralized," but what did that really mean? How far could he actually be trusted?

"Of course I had nothing to do with Udaut's death. Why would you even ask such a question?"

"Perhaps because there has always been rumor about the Haldanes," Albertus murmured. "Your father was friendly with Deryni and was said to have borrowed their magic from time to time, in the early days of his reign. Your brother Alroy was free of the taint, but Javan—well, we were never able to prove anything, but I have always had my suspicions. I would like to believe that we intervened in time to spare you such contamination, but recent events make me wonder."

"What recent events?" Rhys Michael said boldly. "Udaut's accident? Your own? I assure you, I had nothing to do with either. How could I? Ask *him*, if you don't believe *me*."

He gestured toward the impassive Dimitri, taking a big risk if Dimitri had *not* been neutralized. The Deryni's dark eyes caught the light of the torch in his hand and almost seemed to glow. Rhys Michael all but held his breath as Albertus glanced at Dimitri, who shrugged and shook his head—but whether from knowledge confirmed by Truth-Reading or a shift in his loyalties, Rhys Michael could not tell.

"He speaks the truth, my lord," Dimitri said quietly.

Albertus stared at him for a long moment, considering,

glanced at the king, then took the torch from Dimitri's hand and turned partway toward the door, where Fulk was waiting nervously.

"Fulk, bar the door and then come and assist Master Dimitri. I should have had this done long ago."

"Sir Cathan will be returning any moment, my lord," Fulk said in a low voice, not moving. "If you intend what I think, and you wish to keep this private, you'd best wait until he's come back, or an alarm will be raised."

Fulk's logic was inescapable and wholly in keeping with his original obligation of loyalty to the great lords, but it was also a welcome delaying tactic. Quite clearly, Albertus had not sought permission of his fellows to do what he obviously intended, which was to have Dimitri probe him at last; but just as clearly, Rhys Michael himself could not raise the alarm, protesting *too* much that he did not want to be probed, lest the ensuing commotion convince the other great lords that perhaps the king had good reasons of his own to avoid Dimitri's touch.

"Go and find Sir Cathan and bring him back here," Albertus said, jamming his torch into an empty wall cresset. "And say nothing of this to anyone."

Fulk gave a nod and turned to go, but before he could even get out the door, Cathan returned on his own, a dusty wine bottle tucked in the crook of one arm and several wooden cups balanced atop it. His cheery whistling ceased abruptly as Fulk drew him inside and he saw the king's visitors.

"Sir Cathan, you will remain there by the door and see that we are not interrupted," Albertus said, as Fulk relieved Cathan of his bottle and cups and set them on the floor. "Bar the door. Fulk, come and be ready to assist Master Dimitri."

"I won't be held!" Rhys Michael blurted, half coming to his feet as Fulk headed toward him.

Albertus whirled and stabbed a forefinger at the king. "Sit down!" Rhys Michael sat. "You will do what you are told. Whether or not you are physically restrained depends entirely upon your cooperation."

Rhys Michael swallowed and made himself take a deep breath, trying not to shake. He had almost let pride and blind panic stampede him into open defiance of Albertus, which would never be tolerated. Cathan was standing taut and anxious by the door, poised to move on command, but Rhys Michael shot him a restraining glance. He was going to have to allow Dimitri's touch. Whether that would prove his betrayal remained to be seen. He could only pray that the information he had received about the Deryni was correct.

"I didn't say I wouldn't cooperate," he murmured. He kept his eyes downcast as he clasped his hands in his lap, aware of Fulk moving in to stand behind his chair. "It wasn't my intention to defy you."

"I am very glad to hear that," Albertus said, raising a dark eyebrow. "May I take it, then, that you do not object to letting Master Dimitri resolve the question of your innocence, once and for all?"

"My objections obviously have no bearing," Rhys Michael said quietly. "I think that what you're proposing is extremely ill-advised, but I'll do what's required of me, as I've always done. I know my place, and I know my vulnerability. I don't have to *like* some of the things I'm obliged to do, but that doesn't mean I'm ready to throw everything away in a childish show of pique."

A smile quirked at a corner of the earl marshal's long, cruel mouth, and he signaled Fulk back from the king's chair with a negligent wave.

"Gracefully spoken—Sire," he said, though disdain tinged the honorific title. "Sir Fulk, I doubt your services will be required. Master Dimitri, I would know whether our brash young king bears any traces of the kind of power you wield. You know the rumors concerning the Haldanes. I would have them confirmed or denied."

Rhys Michael drew a deep breath, briefly closing his eyes.

"Albertus, I beg you not to do this," he whispered, averting his gaze from the compulsion of Dimitri's dark eyes as the Deryni started to move toward him. "You know why he hasn't been permitted to touch me in all these years. What if he works his own mischief? Does Rhun know what you're doing?"

"That is not your concern," Albertus said, and gestured with a curt nod for Dimitri to proceed.

With a slight bow, Dimitri came to perch casually on the right-hand arm of Rhys Michael's chair, flexing his fingers once as he lifted them toward the king's head.

"It will be easier for both of us if you do not resist this, Sire," Dimitri murmured, as he laid his hands across Rhys Michael's eyes.

CHAPTER ELEVEN

Keep thee far from the man who hath power to kill
... lest he take away thy life presently.
—Ecclesiasticus 9:13

"It will be easier for both of us if you do not resist this, Sire," Dimitri murmured.

At the same instant that his hands covered his subject's eyes, curving around the temples, more specific instruction came slamming against the edges of Rhys Michael's rigid shields.

Give a human reaction, or I cannot help you, Haldane! Appear to lose consciousness. Read the truth of what I tell you. I am ordered to protect you, regardless of the cost to myself.

Knowing it to be so, Rhys Michael did his best to convey the desired impression, eyes closing and taut limbs twitching as he made them relax, even allowing himself to slump forward so that the top of his head rested against Dimitri's chest—for it also shielded any telltale expressions from Albertus' view. He could feel the Deryni's hands slipping around to cradle the back of his head and the sly insinuation of the other's thoughts settling into a more stable link, and he focused his intent on a reply.

How can you help me?

That remains to be seen. Albertus has been gathering his suspicions for some time, but something has persuaded him to demand this confrontation just now. I shall know what it was before he leaves this room. We have not time for extensive alterations to his memories, but if his suspicions hang upon only a few points, I may be able to make adjustments that will spare

*his life for now. I am ordered to kill him, but his death must
not be traceable to you.*

So saying, Dimitri pushed Rhys Michael back into an upright position, though he kept a hand set on one shoulder so
that his fingers remained curled around the back of the king's
neck.

Slowly begin to show signs of regaining consciousness, he
sent. *Pretend still to be lightly controlled.*

"Well?" Albertus demanded, moving closer as the king
stirred and softly moaned, and Dimitri turned his head to
glance at the earl marshal.

"I do not know what you expected me to find, my lord, but
he is simply—a Haldane. He does not wear the yoke of his
submission lightly, but surely you did not expect that he
would."

"I know all that," Albertus muttered. "What about Udaut?"

"He was as surprised and mystified as you, my lord."

"Well, what about the bees?"

"Do you truly think he can command bees?"

"But the Haldanes *do* have—can he Truth-Read?"

"Can a *human* Truth-Read, my lord?" Dimitri asked, scorn
touching his tone of voice.

"Don't provoke me, Deryni!" Albertus snapped. "His father
knew how to do it, and so did Javan. Now, *there* was a *human*
for you! Jesus Christ, *you* were the one to confirm that someone had managed to tamper with Hubert's memory, and that
Javan prob—"

Without warning, Dimitri seized Albertus' wrist and jerked
him off balance, surging into the other's mind even as he released Rhys Michael, rising to guide the earl marshal's collapse as his knees buckled. Fulk had started forward in alarm,
not certain what was happening, but Cathan was already hurtling across the room to wrestle him away from the king, taking him into control as Rhys Michael scrambled from his chair.

Meanwhile, Albertus swayed on his knees and then toppled
onto his side, while Dimitri still maintained dogged contact. As
the king crouched down beside the kneeling Dimitri, the
Deryni was already forcing his mind deep into that of the unconscious Albertus, less and less mindful whether he ripped it
as he searched out what he must know.

"It is as I feared," the Deryni murmured, as he withdrew
enough to speak, the black eyes almost glowing as he glanced
at Rhys Michael. "He suspects too much, and the threads run

too deep. His life was already forfeit, but I had hoped for better cover for the deed. Still, *you* will not be suspect."

"Wait!" Rhys Michael whispered. "What are you going to do?"

"Merely stop his heart. It will be an easier death than he gave most of his victims. Easier than your brother's death."

Chilled, Rhys Michael grabbed Dimitri's sleeve.

"Did *he* kill my brother?"

"His was the direct order that permitted it. He watched him die. See for yourself, if you wish, but be brief."

Rhys Michael could not turn away from that invitation. Trembling, he laid his hand on the earl marshal's forehead and let Dimitri guide him to the specific memory that lay bare beneath their scrutiny. With a tiny mental wrench, he was *in* Albertus' memory, reliving those final moments of treacherous battle lust on a killing field beside a river ford, when a king had fallen to well-planned treason by his own lords of state.

From Albertus' vantage point astride a great black brute of a battle charger, he saw a hail of arrows rain down on the red-clad figure farther across the field. Beyond the king, the Haldane standard faltered as the valiant Guiscard de Courcy went down at last. Though Javan himself appeared to escape unscathed, his horse went down with half a dozen wounds, bright blood blossoming against the animal's creamy coat.

Somehow the king managed to throw himself clear, landing on his feet. Bareheaded, he laid about him with the Haldane sword like a man possessed, but not so nimble afoot as he had been mounted. Sir Charlan, the king's favorite aide, tried to ride alongside and pull the king into the saddle behind him, but more of Albertus' *Custodes* knights cut down that horse as well. King and aide fought together as a team then, and with Charlan now guarding the king's back and Javan himself maintaining a deadly net of steel before him, no one seemed able to breach their defenses—until more arrows began to find their marks.

"Take him!" Albertus screamed, thrusting his bloody sword toward the distant figure and trying to fight closer.

Another flight of arrows whispered off in the king's direction, and this time the king fell. The arrow he took in the chest probably was fatal, even if lesser wounds had not already delivered enough *merasha* to kill him within minutes. Sir Charlan caught him as he fell, himself now wounded, and Albertus spurred his horse toward the spot where he had seen them go down, several of his *Custodes* knights clearing a path.

It was all but accomplished. His sword running with the blood of good Haldane men, Albertus dismounted and strode exultantly through the carnage of dead and dying men. The wounded Charlan was cradling the dying king against his chest and weeping. In that sudden stillness amid the continuing battle around them, Albertus was not even certain they were aware of his presence.

Prolonging the moment served no purpose. As Albertus gazed down at them pitilessly, one of his men moved in behind Charlan with sword poised to finish the young knight. At Albertus' nod, the sword plunged downward to pierce Charlan through the lungs. Blood gushed from his mouth as he collapsed across the king with a mortal gasp, still trying to protect his prince, even in death. But Javan, too, was dead by the time they could shift Charlan's body aside . . .

If you desire his life for this, take it, Dimitri's thought came. *You are his king. He killed your brother. You have the right.*

Show me how!

I will do it, then. There is no time. Learn by observing, even—so.

Before Rhys Michael could object, the spell was welling up in Dimitri's mind, spilling over into Rhys Michael's consciousness but forbidding interference. He flinched from the power now uncoiling from reserves deep inside Dimitri, surging down a muscled arm as Dimitri lifted a cupped right hand above Albertus' chest. He could sense the energy filling Dimitri's palm, spreading out to his fingertips; and as that puissant hand turned toward Albertus, he could almost see a ghost-hand of fire plunge downward from the physical one to penetrate the earl marshal's chest, fiery fingers curving around the pulsing heart and squeezing.

Though unconscious, Albertus fought it. Pain contorted the angular face, and his body arched against it, one booted foot agitating the straw as his limbs went into spasms. He seemed to take a long time to die, though when Rhys Michael blinked himself back to normal consciousness, now shaking in after-reaction, he realized that the entire thing, both the killing and the Reading before it, had taken less than a minute.

"I will deal with this now," Dimitri said, glancing up at Cathan, who immediately brought Fulk closer. He reached up and touched Fulk's hand, closing his eyes briefly, then returned his attention to the still form before him.

"Sir Fulk, you had best summon another surgeon," he said quietly, beginning to loosen the neck of Albertus' garments and perform the other tasks one would expect of a physician. "He has suffered a seizure of some kind. I think it was his heart."

As Fulk raced off to obey, Cathan following as far as the doorway, Rhys Michael glanced at the Deryni.

"I know you had no choice in what you did, but I want to thank you," he said in a low voice.

Dimitri shrugged. "I have worked in the cause of my prince; you are struggling to retain your Haldane crown. I cannot resent you for that, and I hope you do not begrudge me my loyalty to *my* prince. I thought I knew the risks I ran. I still do not comprehend how I was taken, or how I am compelled now to serve your interests above my own. But rest assured that I will not betray you, for I cannot. I will die before I allow you to come to harm."

The pounding of footsteps in the corridor outside forestalled any further discussion, and he set a hand urgently on Rhys Michael's sleeve.

Stand up. You should not be seen kneeling here beside him or me. Remember that you are meant to fear Deryni. When you are questioned, keep your answers vague but tell as much of the truth as possible—that Albertus brought me here to Truth-Read you regarding Udaut's death; that he bade me probe you as well, which you protested. You remember nothing of that experience, save that only a short time elapsed. Of Albertus' death, you know only that he appeared to suffer a seizure, and I tried to aid him. If pressed, wonder whether I might have had a hand in his death. Go now!

The instructions were conveyed in the blink of an eye. The approaching footsteps still had not yet reached the door as Rhys Michael lurched to his feet and staggered far enough away to flatten himself against a wall, trying to make himself as inconspicuous as possible. He had to keep reminding himself that Dimitri was an enemy, only doing what he did because he had no choice. That did not alter the fact that the Deryni was about to sacrifice himself to divert suspicion from Rhys Michael.

Rhun was the first to arrive, closely followed by Paulin and Master Stevanus, but the second battle surgeon could do no more than Dimitri apparently had been able to do. Manfred brought the abbey's infirmarian as well, but by then the room was getting far too crowded. Paulin confessed himself too shaken to give his brother the Last Rites and had to summon another of his *Custodes* priests to come and administer that Sacrament.

"How can this have happened?" Paulin murmured, trembling as Rhun drew him into the corridor, where the king and his aides had withdrawn with Manfred. "What was he even doing here, Sire?"

Affecting to be dazed and a little confused himself, Rhys Michael gestured vaguely toward the maps still spread on the table, aware that every word he uttered was likely to make Dimitri's death more certain.

"He—said something about wanting to make sure I understood the strategy planned for Culliecairn," he said. "I suppose he noticed that I brought the maps with me after supper."

"And then he just—collapsed?" Paulin asked, disbelief still mixed with shock.

Rhys Michael let his gaze go a little unfocused, hoping his questioners would read the reaction as uncertainty, something not quite right.

"I—can't quite remember clearly," he murmured. "We'd been talking, and suddenly he—was on the floor, going into convulsions of some kind. He clutched at his chest and—started gasping for breath. Dimitri tried to help him, but—"

"Why was Dimitri here?" Rhun demanded, picking up on the cue.

Rhys Michael swallowed audibly, all too aware how very vulnerable he was. "He—Lord Albertus wanted him to T-Truth-Read me."

"What about?"

"Udaut's death."

Manfred snorted and glanced back into the room, where a priest called Ascelin was bent over Albertus' body, signing the forehead with holy oil.

"He wouldn't let it go," he muttered. "He just didn't want to accept that Udaut's death was an accident."

"So, he had Dimitri Truth-Read you," Paulin said.

Rhys Michael nodded.

"And what else did he have Dimitri do?" Paulin suddenly looked at Rhys Michael in more avid speculation. "Dear God, he's been wanting to have Dimitri probe you for some time. Did he?"

Swallowing, Rhys Michael looked away, knowing that the truth—the only answer that would turn suspicion from himself—would probably seal Dimitri's fate.

"I—think so," he whispered.

"What do you mean, you *think* so?" Rhun demanded. "Did he touch you?"

"I—don't—I can't—"

"He did, my lord," Fulk offered. "Only for a few seconds, but he definitely touched him."

Rhys Michael closed his eyes briefly and swayed a little on his feet. He had hoped to avoid so direct an accusation, but Fulk had taken the decision out of his hands—perhaps on Dimitri's own orders, he suddenly realized. The Deryni had controlled Fulk briefly before sending him for help and must have set the instructions he knew were needed to carry out his own priority—that of protecting the king at whatever cost.

"Sweet *Jesu*, Albertus, how could you be so *stupid*?" Paulin murmured, his gaze shifting disbelievingly to the still form of his brother. "On the eve of a confrontation with Torenth, you allow—nay, you *invite*—a Torenthi Deryni to probe the king, with no way for us to check and see what he's done *besides* probe—"

"What are you saying?" Rhys Michael whispered. "He can't have done more than that. It was only a few seconds, I'm sure. Wouldn't I know?"

"You weren't even sure he touched you," Rhun said coldly, keeping his voice very low. "We'll hope no serious harm was done in so short a time, but I suggest we try to find out before he realizes we're suspicious. It's even possible he had a hand in Albertus' death. Paulin, have a word with Master Stevanus, would you?"

His subtle gesture with the first two fingers of his right hand sent a chill up Rhys Michael's spine, for he knew Rhun was referring to a Deryni pricker, which would administer a debilitating dose of *merasha*. Though it was intended for Dimitri, not himself, the thought of helping deliver any Deryni to the great lords' ministrations made him almost physically ill.

Back in the deathroom, Dimitri was quietly conversing with Stevanus and the abbey's infirmarian, away from where Father Ascelin was reciting prayers over Albertus' body. As Paulin briefly diverted to kneel with the priest and join in a prayer for his brother, Rhun stepped into the doorway and raised a beckoning hand in Dimitri's direction.

"Master Dimitri, would you come over here, please?"

With a nod to Stevanus, Dimitri came to join Rhun and Manfred and the king, making them a deferential bow. "My lords, Sire."

"Tell me, Master Dimitri, why did Lord Albertus ask you to accompany him tonight?" Rhun asked.

Dimitri's glance flicked to Manfred, then to Rhys Michael, carefully neutral, but the brief thought that brushed the king's mind confirmed that Dimitri was prepared to play out what now appeared to be inevitable.

"Am I to speak freely before Lord Manfred, my lord?" Dimitri asked in a low voice.

"I would not have asked you in front of him if I did not expect you to speak in front of him," Rhun said sharply. "Why did Lord Albertus bring you here?"

"He wished me to be present while he questioned the king concerning Lord Udaut's death."

"To Truth-Read his answers?" Rhun asked.

"Yes, my lord."

"Why should that be necessary?" Manfred interjected. "Did Lord Albertus have any reason to suppose that the king knew something about Udaut's death?"

"Not to my knowledge, my lord."

"Very well," Rhun said. "And did you Truth-Read the king?"

"I did."

"With what result?"

"Why, the king was telling the truth, of course. How could it be otherwise? Lord Udaut's death was an accident."

"Was it?" Rhun asked.

Dimitri did not even blink. "I have said that the king had nothing to do with it, my lord. Why do you question me this way? Have I not served you faithfully these many years and never given you cause to doubt my word?"

"Perhaps we were led to overlook such cause," Paulin said, slipping back into the conversation beside the Deryni. "What else did you do to the king besides Truth-Read him, Dimitri? Did you perhaps probe him, as you've been wanting to do for some time? And what did you do to my brother?"

Dimitri had led the questioning in this direction. It was the only possible scenario that would satisfy the great lords' questioning and totally divert suspicion from the king, and Rhys Michael knew it—and knew that Dimitri knew it.

"To your *brother*?" Dimitri asked, scorn in his tone. "Surely your grief has made you mad."

"Dear God, did you kill him?" Paulin whispered, now convinced that he had stumbled onto the truth. "Brother Serafin died of 'heart failure' a few days before Javan's coronation, and we always wondered about that. You weren't around then, but there were other Deryni who were capable. That's one of the more insidious Deryni spells, isn't it? You can kill a man without even touching him. We'll never know if Udaut actually died of 'heart failure,' but you could have reached out with your mind and done that—and also made his horse go mad and trample him, to cover your tracks. Did you summon up that swarm of bees, too? Was it my brother who was meant to drown?"

Dimitri shook his head disdainfully, turning to Rhun in appeal. "My lord, I am given far more credit than I deserve. If such conjectures seem plausible to you, small wonder that your people fear mine. Regardless of what answers I may give you, I am damned merely for being what I am. For what good it will do, I remind you that my kind have limitations, just as all men do. Physical contact is almost always required. We—"

In that instant, at a nod from Paulin, Master Stevanus made physical contact with Dimitri via a Deryni pricker, jamming its double needles into the taut muscles at the base of the Deryni's neck. Dimitri gasped and clapped a hand to the pain, dislodging the device as he whirled in dismay to throw off the hands already trying to restrain him, but his eyes told Rhys Michael that the Deryni was well aware of his plight.

In the seconds remaining before the *merasha* rendered him powerless, Dimitri might carry out one more order besides the very last—and over *that* one, he had no control, for it must wait until the very end. Before the drug could begin to diffuse his powers, even as Rhun and Manfred were grabbing at his arms to take him prisoner, he turned the full strength of his magic on Paulin, twining his hands in a death-grip in the neck of the prelate's black robes to pull him closer and will invisible hands of fire to clutch not at Paulin's heart but at his mind.

Paulin screamed and kept on screaming, a bloodcurdling wail of mortal agony that rose on a higher and ever higher pitch, until Rhys Michael thought that vocal cords of mere human flesh could not sustain such a sound. Yet even that was but a poor reflection of the true anguish of a mind being ripped. Surely Cathan must have felt some of the spillover, but he and Fulk boldly dragged Rhys Michael back from the physical struggle to shield him with their bodies, lest Dimitri attempt some attack on the king.

And all the while, unaware of the true magnitude of Dimitri's attack, the others were wrenching at his arms and shouting conflicting orders, Manfred bellowing for them to kill him, Rhun screaming that, no, they must take him alive. Cringing behind Cathan and Fulk, helpless to prevent any of what was unfolding so rapidly, Rhys Michael sensed a faltering in the energies and guessed that the *merasha* must be starting to erode Dimitri's control. Just then, Rhun managed to place a precise blow behind Dimitri's left ear with the pommel of his dagger.

CHAPTER TWELVE

Whereas thy servant worketh truly, entreat him not
evil, nor the hireling that bestoweth himself wholly
for thee.

—Ecclesiasticus 7:20

The flow of power ceased utterly as Dimitri crumpled like an
ox felled with a poleax, arms trailing limply down Paulin's
chest as he sagged to his knees and was dragged apart by
ready hands.

But merely subduing Dimitri did not end Paulin's agony.
Though his shrieking choked off in midscream, his body
arched in a strangled convulsion, still flailing as it pitched to
the floor.

"Stevanus, see to him!" Rhun shouted, as he and Manfred
stripped the belt from Dimitri's own waist and began to lash
his wrists together.

Stevanus was already scrambling to Paulin's side. The convulsions were weakening, but Paulin's eyes were vacant and
staring. His rigid chest kept heaving with the effort to draw
breath, but clearly no air was reaching his lungs.

"He's dying! He can't breathe!" Stevanus gasped, rolling
Paulin onto his side and prying the rigid jaws apart.

In the corridor, Rhys Michael clung to the door frame and
craned his neck to see what was happening. Blood gushed
from Paulin's mouth as Stevanus thrust his fingers inside, apparently probing for whatever was obstructing the airway.

"Jesus, he's swallowed his tongue!" the king heard him
gasp.

As Stevanus forced his fingers deeper to dislodge the ob-
struction, the abbey's infirmarian came creeping timidly from

under the table where he had taken refuge. Together, the two of them quickly managed to get Paulin breathing again, albeit shallowly, but Paulin had bitten his tongue nearly through as he convulsed. The bloody lump of it lay in the blood-soaked straw beside his head as Stevanus cast his knife aside and shakily shifted a gory hand to the pulse point in his patient's neck. The infirmarian was pressing a wadded edge of his scapular to the stump of Paulin's tongue to staunch the bleeding, keeping the head turned so he would not choke on his own blood.

"Dear God," Rhys Michael murmured, slumping weakly against the door frame. He had not expected anything of this magnitude.

Meanwhile, Paulin's spine-chilling screams had brought men running from either end of the corridor, wide-eyed monks and soldiers with swords in their hands. Crowding anxiously around the doorway, trying to peer in, most hardly noticed how they jostled the shaken king and his aides, pressing them back into the room. The priest Ascelin was cowering in shock beside the body of Albertus, farther toward the shuttered window, and both Stevanus and his erstwhile assistant looked white-faced and shaken.

"Is he still alive?" Rhun demanded, glancing around from the still unconscious Dimitri as Manfred tightened a belt around their captive's ankles.

"Yes." Stevanus grimaced as Paulin's pulse fluttered beneath his bloody fingers.

"Jesus, where did all the blood come from?" Rhun said, rising to come closer.

"His tongue." Stevanus gestured toward the bit of bloody flesh in the straw. "Even if he survives whatever else Dimitri did to him, he'll never speak again."

"God in heaven," Rhun murmured. "Then, he may still die?"

"I don't know. Since I have no idea what the Deryni did to him, I can't even tell you which to hope for."

"Damn the Deryni and their powers!" Rhun said, uneasily glancing back at Dimitri. "I *told* Paulin something like this would happen one of these days, if he insisted on continuing to use Deryni."

Brother Polidorus, the infirmarian, glanced toward Dimitri and fought down a shudder.

" 'Tis black magic," he muttered. "Woe be unto all of us, if the Deryni has summoned evil spirits under this roof."

Rhun rolled his eyes heavenward, though he, too, darted another nervous glance back at Dimitri. Manfred had shifted nearer the Deryni's head, his dagger pressed to the upturned throat. He flinched at the monk's words and blanched even paler, his free hand fumbling at the open neck of his tunic until it could close around a substantial gold crucifix.

"Good God, you don't really think—"

"I think," Rhun said, "that Brother Polidorus ought to see about getting Father Paulin to the infirmary. Stevanus, I need you here with me. Let the priests deal with Paulin and make sure *he* can't do anything when he comes around." As he prodded Dimitri's bound form roughly with a booted toe, he finally noticed the men crowded into the doorway behind the king and stabbed a forefinger at the soldiers in the front.

"You, you, and the two of you, come and help get Father Paulin to the infirmary. What are the rest of you gawking at? Go back to your quarters, all of you. Everything is under control."

As the four selected edged warily into the room, giving distance to the dark-clad form Manfred guarded, the others reluctantly began to disperse. Directed by Brother Polidorus, the four briskly lifted the unconscious Paulin onto their shoulders and carried him out. Stevanus was bending over Dimitri.

"Now, Fulk," Rhun went on, spotting Fulk beside the king and beckoning him nearer. "Inform the abbot what's happened, then fetch me Father Lior, Father Magan—and Gallard de Breffni. Tell Gallard to bring his tools. Go!"

As Fulk threw a salute and ducked out the door, Rhun turned next to Cathan.

"You, help Father Ascelin see about taking Lord Albertus' body to wherever the mortuary chapel is, then find Lord Joshua Delacroix and tell him what's happened. Tell him he's acting Grand Master of the *Custodes* knights until the Order can make an official appointment of Albertus' replacement—or is there someone more senior, Stevanus?"

"No, he's suitable," the battle surgeon said. He had come away from Dimitri momentarily to wash the gore from his hands, over at the washstand beside the single bed.

"Right, then. Delacroix is acting Grand Master. Acting vicar-general, too, for that matter, unless it has to be a priest. You *Custodes* will have to sort that out. Go, Cathan. Meanwhile, as Albertus' designated second-in-command, I take the office of earl marshal to myself and hereby assume command of this campaign—unless you want it back, Manfred. You were earl marshal before Albertus."

"And I resigned," Manfred said. "But I'll serve under you as vice-marshal, if you wish."

"Thank you. I'll welcome your experience. Now, let's get this Deryni secured before he regains consciousness. We've got a long night ahead of us, but I intend to break him before dawn."

Neither Rhun nor Manfred seemed to have any particular instructions for Rhys Michael, as they now proceeded to turn the room into an impromptu interrogation chamber. The king had no desire to stay and watch what was going to happen, but since they had commandeered his room, he really had nowhere else to go. Nor did he think he ought to go very far, at least until one of his aides returned. And the question remained of whether Dimitri would reveal anything that might endanger Rhys Michael, even though the Deryni had *claimed* that he was ordered to protect him.

Apparently all but forgotten by the two, as men came and went to do Rhun's bidding, the king soon found himself eddied into a dim corner of the room where the torchlight did not really reach—which at least was a vantage point from which he might watch and not himself be noticed. Now, if he could just avoid doing anything that might shift attention back onto himself . . .

After a few minutes, *Custodes* monks came to carry Albertus' body away. Soon after they had departed, Fulk returned with Father Lior, the *Custodes* inquisitor-general, who was accompanied by a younger man in priest's garb and a greying, blondish man wearing the black jazerant and red-fringed white sash of a *Custodes* knight.

As Fulk came over to join him, Rhys Michael found himself staring at the knight, squinting against the dimness and trying to recall where he had seen the man before. The context had not been good; he was sure of that. Not that he held any *Custodes* knight in high regard.

"What's happened?" Lior demanded, as his companions came in and set down leather satchels on the table, the knight clearing the maps from it with a sweep of his arm.

At Rhun's direction, Manfred had stripped the bedclothes and thin mattress off the narrow bed and dragged it out from the wall. As he turned it upside down, Rhun said, "It appears the good Dimitri has turned on his masters. Or perhaps he's been serving different masters all along. He killed Albertus, and he's half killed Paulin. I want him broken. I want to know what he did to the king, and I want to know who he's been working for."

Lior was already crouching beside Dimitri, peering under an eyelid, then feeling at the pulse in the captive's neck. Kneeling on Dimitri's other side, Stevanus had a Deryni pricker in his hands again, nervously twisting the cap as he awaited further instructions.

"How much has he already had?" Lior asked.

"Just a single dose, Father. Rhun managed to tap him behind the ear before it could take effect, but I think he's going to need more when he comes around."

"Which is going to be soon," Lior said, wiping his hands on his thighs and glancing around behind him. "Gallard, let's get another of these beds in here. One is too narrow to be effective. Sir Fulk?" He summoned the aide with a beckoning gesture. "Come and help the surgeon strip him."

With Lior standing back to supervise, the men went about their preparations with an efficiency that spoke of ready acquaintance with what the inquisitor-general intended. Very shortly the abbot showed up with one of his subpriors and a *Custodes* captain-general and briefly drew Rhun aside for an update on the situation. Watching from his shadowed corner, Rhys Michael tried not to think about the tortures they were preparing, glad he could not get a clear look at the instruments and vials the younger priest was taking from one of the leather satchels, laying them out in neat rows on the table.

Fulk and Stevanus had Dimitri stripped by the time the knight named Gallard dragged another wooden bedstead into the room, Manfred helping him upturn it beside the first and lash the inside legs together. Though Dimitri had served an enemy prince, Rhys Michael felt the gorge rise in his throat as he watched them shift the helpless Deryni onto this improvised bed of torture and begin tying him spread-eagled to the bedposts, stretching the flaccid limbs taut.

In that instant, as he watched the knight named Gallard securing one of the bonds, he suddenly remembered where he had seen the man before. He had never learned the man's name, and he had never again seen the man at Court in the six years since, but certain it was that Gallard de Breffni had been the cold-eyed *Custodes* knight at Hubert's side when the great lords turned on him in council and seized control of the castle, the same day that others of their number had treacherously slain an anointed king. It was Gallard who had murdered the loyal Sir Tomais d'Edergoll before his very eyes, Gallard who had dared to lay traitorous hands on Rhys Michael's own person when they marched him up to see Sir Sorle and the Healer Oriel slain, and to take Michaela into custody.

And that had been but an extension of earlier treason, for the man whose name he only tonight had learned also had been his principal keeper while, months before those other murders, he lay abducted by the great lords' agents. They had been *Custodes*, all of them, though Rhys Michael had been induced to think them Ansel's men at the time—that it was Deryni who had turned against him and the great lords who had rescued him. And all the while, the great lords had been working toward that moment when Javan must be slain and Rhys Michael set in his place, but as a puppet king; and in his youthful arrogance and blindness, Rhys Michael had never even suspected until it was much, much too late.

Long-banked anger smouldered into flame. In this one man was embodied much of the treachery and betrayal of a lifetime, finally given name and form. Gallard de Breffni's life was forfeit in that instant, just as Albertus' had been. Rhys Michael Haldane was an anointed king, entitled to dispense justice. He had the right and the means to take de Breffni's life. Dimitri had shown him how. He could feel his newfound power starting to stir within him, tendrils of energy uncoiling down his arms as his hands clenched into fists and the spell began to take shape. Even from here, all he had to do was reach out and—

"Sit down and have a front-row seat, Sire," Rhun said in a low voice, suddenly beside Rhys Michael.

Taken totally by surprise, Rhys Michael started back violently and went into a crouch, one hand going instinctively to the dagger at his belt, even as he recognized Rhun's voice. He frantically pushed the power back down. In the concentration of his anger, he had not even noticed Rhun's approach.

Weak-kneed with relief, he made himself stay his hand and straighten up, trembling in after-reaction as he cast a shaken glance at Rhun. What had he been thinking? Tempting though it might be to slay de Breffni, to slay Rhun—to slay everyone in this room, for that matter—he knew he dared not.

Not with *merasha* in so many hands. Not on the eve of a confrontation with a Deryni pretender. Not without a man to call his own, save Cathan, who was not even here.

"Good reflexes," Rhun commented, totally unaware how close he had come to death. "He must have given you a good scare. Here." He pulled the nearest chair closer and shoved it against the wall. "You're entitled. I suppose you're as anxious as we are, to find out whether he got into your mind. But don't worry; we'll break him. His days of playing both sides have just come to an end."

He did not wait to see whether the king sat, for Dimitri was starting to come around. A moan escaped the Deryni's lips as Manfred tightened down one of the wrist restraints, trailing off as the dark eyes opened and the bleary gaze slowly found focus. Pain was in that gaze, but also resignation. As Stevanus moved the standing rack of rushlights nearer his head, their sickly glow gave Dimitri's dark visage an oddly jaundiced pallor. The torchlight from the walls cast a paler, flickering light over his naked form and on the faces of the hard-eyed men looking down at him. The abbot, a round little man with beady eyes and not a hair on his head, crossed himself and drew back into the corridor with his two attendants.

"Dear, *dear* Dimitri," Lior said softly. Flanked by the younger priest and Gallard de Breffni, he shook his head and made a soft *tsk*ing sound with his tongue as he folded his arms across his chest. "I had so hoped never to meet you this way."

Just visible in one of his hands was the cap end of a Deryni pricker—an unusual one, cased in ebony and inlaid with mother-of-pearl. His knuckles showed white upon it as he gazed down at his captive, betraying his tension. Though sick anticipation churned in Rhys Michael's gut, he could not but watch. Every muscle taut, he made himself ease down on the edge of his chair as Fulk came to stand beside him.

"You have broken faith, Dimitri," Lior said more coldly. "In times past, you have *seemed* to serve, but now I worry that deception drove you from the start. In asking myself what seeds of treachery you might have sown in *my* mind, I have asked Father Magan to assist me tonight." He fingered the Deryni pricker as he glanced at the younger priest beside him. "You have never met him, so you cannot have tainted him with your foul magic. But rest assured that he knows how to deal with your kind."

Dimitri flicked a glance of utter disdain at both men, then turned his face away, his wrists testing at his bonds.

"No good, Deryni," Lior said sharply. "You have killed one of your masters and probably a second. Before you are paid in kind, as you surely knew must be your fate, we require information regarding your *other* masters." He smiled without a trace of mirth. "Naturally, you will not wish to give us this information. Just as naturally, we must insist."

Dimitri closed his eyes briefly, a faint grimace twitching at the sensuous mouth as he swallowed with difficulty. Though he still seemed determined to put up a defiant front, Rhys Michael guessed that it was becoming more and more difficult, with the *merasha* in his blood. Sweat sheened on the lean torso, and muscles corded in his outstretched arms and legs flexed as he continued to test at his bonds.

"A ridiculous game, isn't it?" Lior said. "You are required by your masters to resist unto death, and I am required by mine to press you as hard as I can, your mind addled by my drugs and your body pushed by most exquisite pain to the very brink of death, but not beyond—until you have told me what I want to know."

His expression hardened as his words seemed to have no effect on his prisoner.

"Very well. I know that we are not nearly to that point just yet. While Master Stevanus' sting denied you access to your powers, you still have most of your faculties of reason and the will to resist. Regrettably, Lord Rhun's method of rendering you senseless spared you from what I understand is a unique sensation, as the drug disrupted your control and stripped away access to your powers. Rest assured that such respite will not be granted again. I intend that you should experience the further erosion of your senses to the fullest."

So saying, Lior handed the Deryni pricker to Father Magan, who unscrewed the cap and carefully withdrew the twin needles embedded in its underside. A tawny drop of liquid quivered in the torchlight, suspended between the needles, as Magan raised an eyebrow and calmly bent closer to their captive's lean torso.

Expecting the usual quick jab of the needles, Rhys Michael stifled a gasp and nearly came to his feet as Magan instead touched the needles lightly to the shadowed hollow of Dimitri's navel. In the same instant, as the act registered, Dimitri groaned and threw himself against his bonds in a frenzy, trying to roll away, rocking the wooden bedsteads to which he was bound and nearly breaking free.

"Hold him!" Lior ordered, even as Manfred and Gallard were throwing their weight across the ends to keep him fast, and Rhun was pinning his shoulders back against the wooden slats.

Rhys Michael forced himself to sink back into his chair, though his own heart must be pounding nearly as wildly as Dimitri's was. He could see the hard muscles of the Deryni's belly rippling in spasm as he made another halfhearted attempt to twist free, but clearly the drug so oddly administered was having its effect. He was panting as he ceased struggling, his body now running with sweat, and his eyes were glazing, the pupils wide and dilated as Rhun roughly turned the face toward the rushlights.

"Is that a new way of administering *merasha*, Lior?" he asked, as he released the captive's head and stepped back, looking at the inquisitor-general.

"Absorption of the drug through the skin is slower but steady," Lior said, drawing a deep breath and exhaling. "The umbilicus provides a handy receptacle, and the skin lining it is very thin. A somewhat limited method of delivery, but it has its uses. Father Magan discovered it. Obviously, it had not occurred to Dimitri." He glanced at the faintly twitching captive, whose eyes had closed.

"I know you're still conscious, Deryni," Lior said, in a slightly louder voice. "Nor need you bother to hope that your ordeal will be cut short by a miscalculation of the drug's dose. We know precisely how much *merasha* a Deryni can tolerate before the dose becomes lethal, or even before sleep gives temporary respite.

"But before that comes the pain. Just as Father Magan is conversant with the drugs we can use to help break you, so Sir Gallard is well versed in the various methods of causing pain. Do not look for your other masters to save you from either."

Dimitri's other masters even then were debating the numerous possible reasons why their agent had not yet made contact. In the tower chamber at Culliecairn, Prince Miklos of Torenth was sitting on the edge of a narrow camp bed with his head in his hands. In a chair opposite sat Marek of Festil, wide-eyed and impatient-looking.

"But we know they're close," Marek said. "We've had conventional dispatches since they left Rhemuth. Besides the death of Udaut, there's been no hint that anything odd has happened—certainly nothing to indicate that Dimitri's been found out. Believe me, if a Deryni spy had been discovered in the bosom of the *Custodes Fidei*, we would have heard."

"We *should* have heard from *him*," Miklos said, raising his head. "I like it not. In more than six years of service, he has never been more than a few hours off, if a contact was prearranged. Given the uncertainties attendant upon forced march, I could understand a delay of a day or two. Privacy could be hard to come by. But the scouts predict arrival at Lochalyn tomorrow. That means they shall be *here* the day after. And we have not the foggiest notion where we stand, what other key men he has been able to eliminate or subvert, what he has found out about the Haldane—"

"Then, let's go ahead and force the contact," Marek said. "If he's that close, it won't take that much more energy to initiate the contact, instead of just standing by to receive. It's late enough now that he's probably asleep. We'll go in tandem, with a human backup. If everything's all right, we can find out what we need to know. If he's captured, or he's turned, we can kill him. And of course, if he's dead, we'll know that, too."

Miklos, Prince of Torenth, rubbed his hands over his face, then nodded with a heavy sigh.

"Very well." He stood. "I shall go and fetch someone for backup. I don't wish to use one of my regular sources; this may kill whomever we use, if the power drain is too heavy."

With that he went out of the room, closing the door softly behind him. Marek rose and paced the length of the room a few times, then went to the window and looked out over the valley below the castle.

Beyond the valley lay the Coldoire Pass; and between the pass and the castle, the watchfires of Miklos' Torenthi levies sparkled in the cool night air like jewels flung across a bolt of velvet. It was the gateway to Marek's kingdom, stolen from his parents by the father of the king riding to meet him out there in two days' time. It was close enough that he could almost smell it.

He turned as the door opened behind him and Miklos returned, now accompanied by a short, stocky guard wearing Miklos' livery.

"Sit there," Miklos said, pointing to the floor beside the narrow camp bed. "Lean your back against the bed."

The man obeyed the odd command without hesitation, obviously already controlled. Wearily Miklos went around to the other side of the bed and sat down, drawing a deep breath, then totally emptying his lungs before reclining and swinging his booted legs up onto the thin mattress.

As he briefly laid an arm over his eyes, Marek came to join him, sitting in a chair on the opposite side of the bed from the guard and performing the same deep-breathing exercise that Miklos had done. After a moment Miklos raised his arm to tip the guard's curly head back against the bed, his hand briefly cupping over the eyes. Then he shifted it down to let his wrist lie against the man's shoulder, the V of his thumb and fingers lightly clasped around the man's throat.

"All right, he's ready," Miklos murmured, upturning his other arm along his side. "Whenever you are."

Marek had been disciplining his own trance already and linked in easily with the Torenthi prince, as he clasped his hand around the other's wrist. Marek was powerful and very well trained, perhaps the match of his older cousin, but this was Miklos' working, so he let himself take a subordinate role as Miklos wove the spell. In the background, he could feel the vibrant life-force of the guard pulsing in synch with the power Miklos was coiling to unleash, not even accessible to its owner but now set in potential and ready to be drawn upon.

Powerful and focused, their call went forth, fine-focused only to the mind of the agent they sought, sweeping a far smaller area and lesser distance than Dimitri had spanned, a week before, when last he communicated. It took some time to locate him, because his trace, when they finally picked it up, was odd.

Merasha! came Miklos' stark pronouncement. *Someone has found him out!*

Bracing himself for even the secondhand taste of *merasha* disruption, Miklos thrust the contact home, seeking no permission and needing none, for Dimitri's shields were in tatters, no impediment at all. Stark on the very surface of his mind lay drug-addled snatches of the event that had precipitated his undoing: Lord Albertus killed, as ordered, but under circumstances that inadvertently had betrayed Dimitri as well . . . and the despicable Paulin mind-ripped even as Dimitri succumbed to his captors' power.

Dimitri was not unconscious; indeed, he was in a great deal

of pain. But not yet near the breaking point; not yet near the trigger Miklos had set against just such a contingency.

Yet something was wrong here—something about the trigger. To Miklos' consternation, other minds had been deep in Dimitri's. Alien traces showed like faintly wrong-colored threads against the subtle, complex pattern Miklos had laid down. He could not quite make out their source, but he could see glimpses of the work—and where at least a few of the threads seemed to lead.

Trigger alterations, Miklos noted. *Let us see if we can discover who has done this. Could it possibly have been the Haldane . . . ?*

He drove his probe closer toward the source of the alteration, himself causing pain; drawing heavily on his backup now, ignoring *his* pain, starting to catch a glimpse, a glimmering—

In that instant, more powerful and more recent compulsions slammed into force, tripping the death-trigger that Miklos himself had set. Though aware what it would cost to delay the effect, Miklos locked Marek into the link and drove all their considerable power and all the last reserves of their backup into one final, desperate attempt to force the trigger back and keep the channel open just a little longer, relentlessly seeking explanation, *willing* the linked mind to yield its information.

Who? Tell me who!

CHAPTER THIRTEEN

Rejoice not over thy greatest enemy being dead, but
remember that we die all.

—Ecclesiasticus 8:7

Dimitri had yielded nothing to his interrogators, despite a diverse range of tortures applied to shrinking flesh over the
space of several hours. Efficient and apparently unaffected by
the pain he caused, the inventive Gallard de Breffni had presented him with varied inducements calculated to push him to
the very brink of what he thought he could bear and then
beyond—though never to the point that he might escape into
unconsciousness. Diverse stimulants kept him alert, periodically reviving sensations pushed to overload and countering the
sedative effect of the *merasha*, but these did nothing to ease
the disruption of his mind and powers.

Nor could Dimitri choose either to surrender the information
they demanded or to end his agony, for he had given that
choice into another's hands when first he offered himself as
Miklos' agent. Though the decision of when to activate a
death-trigger usually was reserved to the subject, the protection
of extremely sensitive information sometimes required that absolute levels be set, over which the subject no longer retained
control. With Dimitri's own concurrence, Miklos had set the
triggerpoint against an almost unimaginably high pain threshold; for the longer Dimitri could keep from breaking, against
the worse coercion, the greater the chance his interrogators
would doubt their findings, even if bits of the truth should
manage to slip through.

But now new pain probed into the very depths of Dimitri's

awareness, totally apart from what Gallard de Breffni was doing to his body. Vaguely he recognized the touch; weakly he strained to reach toward it—or at least toward the triggerpoint, to give him blessed release. As the probe drove ever deeper, either the pain or his yearning finally tripped the long-sought trigger. An instant of relief immediately gave way to a rainbow brightness erupting in his mind, obliterating all else, hurtling him toward oblivion at last.

Dimitri's bloodied torso suddenly arched in spasm, his breath catching in his throat and his whole body going rigid.

"What's happening?" Rhun demanded, as Stevanus laid an ear against the bloody, straining chest and Magan tried to get a look at the prisoner's pupils. The others were throwing themselves across arms and legs to restrain the convulsion. Rhys Michael had retreated as far as the corridor some time before, unable to bear the Deryni's screams and the stench of blood and urine and burnt flesh, but now he anxiously pressed back into the doorway with Cathan and Fulk. The abbot and his two attendants were watching with undisguised horror.

"We may have hit a death-trigger," Magan murmured, hunting in vain for a carotid pulse. "They can make themselves die, you know."

"Give him more *merasha*!" Lior ordered, fumbling to open his Deryni pricker. "If he's doing this himself, it may break his concentration."

"I don't want him killed yet!" Rhun barked.

"It won't kill him. He hasn't had that much. We're nowhere near a lethal dose."

"We're going to lose him if we don't do *something*," Magan said, snatching the Deryni pricker from Lior's hands and plunging it into Dimitri's neck.

Whether or not this new outrage was the cause, the fragile balance shifted enough in that instant to let Dimitri's death-trigger snap closed at last. His back arched once more, then relaxed utterly, his limbs going limp as the dark eyes rolled upward until all but the whites disappeared. The final breath sighed gently from between slack lips.

"He's dead," Stevanus whispered, hollow-eyed and grey as he lifted bloody hands from Dimitri's chest to stare at them in the torchlight.

Another was passing into death in a darkened tower room in Culliecairn. In the same instant that the death-trigger released

Dimitri, Marek tumbled out of the disintegrating link with a gasp, hands clapped to his temples, and Miklos of Torenth lost the pulse in the throat of the man under his hand.

Unperturbed, Miklos shifted a portion of his focus to deal with the suddenly dwindling flow of backup energy, the while riding out the psychic backlash generated by Dimitri's death-trigger. That the backup was dying was regrettable but not un-expected, for no human could have survived the drain Miklos demanded, once he had determined to seek out the source of the alien threads. While a part of him sealed off the last of the aborted connection, Miklos relentlessly stripped out the final increments of energy the dying man could give, using it like oil to still the last reverberations of psychic storm. He only wished the effort had borne better fruit. Sending men to their deaths was a part of command, but he disliked sacrificing them for so little return.

Meanwhile, the infusion of energy was having the desired effect. With heart rate already slowing to more normal levels, Miklos laid an arm across his eyes and made himself run through the usual set of checklists employed by Deryni after an arduous working. Remaining in another's mind at the time a death-trigger tripped was never pleasant and often profoundly unsettling—far different from easing a soul's passing when death came more gently.

He felt groggy and a little light-headed as he opened his eyes, but at least he knew that a few hours' sleep would finish restoring him. Drawing a deep breath, he shifted his arm to glance aside at where Marek sat, head bowed in his hands and breathing a little shakily.

"Are you all right?"

Marek raised his head and took a deep breath before he turned his face to Miklos.

"I will be. What the devil did they do to Dimitri?"

"Physically? The sorts of things one might expect. He knew the risks."

"That isn't what I meant."

"I know. And I have no answer for you."

Sitting up, Miklos swung his feet to the floor next to Marek, pausing with hands set to the edges of the bed on either side before he pushed himself to his feet and staggered to the table and two chairs set under the window. Wood screeched against stone as he pulled out one of the chairs, and he had to catch his balance against its back before passing a hand over a rack of candles to produce light.

He sat down heavily, pulling a tray nearer to pour himself a cup of wine. He managed not to spill any, but he had to use both hands to lift the cup and drain it. While he drank, Marek came to join him, pouring a cup for himself, then refilling the other's.

"Who do *you* think got to him?" Marek asked. "Was it the Haldane?"

Miklos shook his head, then took another quaff of his wine. "I cannot say. He should not be capable of such a thing, but if not he, then who? Camber's kin again? Dimitri had seen no evidence of Deryni infiltration at the Court in recent years, but remember that he has never been allowed direct contact with the Haldane himself."

"Who else might have done it, then?" Marek asked.

Shrugging, Miklos set his cup aside. "We know that some of those Deryni who had aided King Cinhil were still in evidence when Javan came to the throne, even though they dared not show their faces in Rhemuth. Paulin and Albertus even had their suspicions about Javan." He raised an eyebrow and shook his head almost regretfully. "I shall almost miss them, I think. They have done us many favors, over the years—they and their *Custodes Fidei*."

Marek suppressed a shiver, then took a deep draught of his wine. "I mistrust religious fanatics, no matter what the religion. I'm just as glad they're gone."

Miklos' pale gaze flicked away momentarily, even as memory shied from the echo of Paulin's anguish he had read from Dimitri. Paulin, at least, was *not* gone; indeed, he might linger in a living death for many days or weeks or even months. He would know nothing more of pain, but that was small recompense for the unspeakable agony of having his mind ripped while still conscious. After such an experience, what mortal flesh could possibly ever register mere pain again?

"You don't look particularly pleased," Marek noted, breaking in on Miklos' distraction. "They stood in our way."

"So they did," Miklos said, recovering himself. "Still, they have served our purposes, though they knew it not. Not only did they rid us of Javan Haldane, who would have made you a formidable adversary, but now I begin to wonder about his replacement. Perhaps they did us no favor at all."

"What are you saying?"

"Only that we should not underestimate this son of Haldane," Miklos said quietly. "We have believed him to be a puppet in the hands of his great lords, these six years. We have assumed that he is not the man his brother Javan was shaping to be—or his father was."

"You think he has the Haldane power?"

Miklos shrugged. "I know not. But *someone* exposed Dimitri. *Someone* guessed his dual loyalties. You saw the traces of their work. I find it a curious coincidence that Dimitri should be unmasked on the very eve of this Haldane's first public venture in nearly six years."

When Marek did not speak, Miklos went on more tentatively.

"Perhaps we should consider whether this may not be a timely warning, a sign that we should draw back somewhat from our original plan and rethink our strategy until we have learned more of this Haldane. It is just possible that he may have come into the same powers his father wielded. If so, and if he reveals them, his own great lords may kill him—nay, *will* kill him, if he has not supporters to protect him."

"That may take time."

"True enough. But time we have. What we do not have—what *you* do not have—is a sufficiently secure succession, if we were to take him on now, and you should fall. This is further reason for waiting, for biding our time."

"I'm tired of waiting! We can take him now; I know we can."

"Perhaps. But perhaps not. Consider the risks. My sister Charis has given you a son and heir in whom the blood of Festil is rejoined to Torenth—a magnificent birthright!—but the child is yet young."

"He is strong!" Marek blurted. "He will make a noble king one day."

"He is an infant," Miklos said calmly. "Infants sometimes sicken and die, for no apparent reason. Do you truly wish to risk all just now, with but one puny princeling to carry on the line of Festil, if you should fall?"

Anger flared in Marek's dark eyes as he turned to look at his elder cousin, but then, after a taut pause, he shook his head.

"I thought not," Miklos said. "Nor do I."

"What is it you propose?" Marek asked, after another silence.

"Simply this," Miklos said. "We tread softly. Let us see how

this Haldane is minded to respond to our challenge, besides bestirring himself to come to us. We must lure him to a face-to-
face meeting. Perhaps the Lady Sudrey may be useful in this
matter. I am stricken with remorse over the accidental killing
of her husband and desire to make amends. I might even be induced to withdraw from Culliecairn without further loss of life,
as a sign of my contrition."

"Pull out of Culliecairn?" Marek began indignantly.

"We shall *talk* about pulling out of Culliecairn," Miklos
amended. "If opportunity presents, and he does not display the
defenses we fear, we can still try for the kill, but I think it best
we devise several contingency plans. Perhaps the young prince
your son has taken cold, and the christening must be post-
poned. That justification will speak to the Haldane, since he,
too, is father of a young son. If he can be induced to bring
Sudrey to the meeting, additional possibilities become feasible.
That situation has been maturing quite long enough."

Marek nodded, beginning to become caught up in his cousin's reasoning.

"But our ultimate aim must be to assess the Haldane's
strength," Miklos went on. "Hence, we must be prepared to
negotiate, to back down with at least some grace. Culliecairn
was a convenient ruse to get the Haldane to show his face, but
I think it is not worth the cost of a kingdom. There will be
other days, other battles. If expediency requires, we have lost
nothing by giving it back."

"I suppose not," Marek said sullenly. "I want him, though,
Miklos. I want him dead. I want my father's throne back."

Miklos grinned and shook his blond head, looking suddenly
years younger.

"And you shall have it, cousin—all of it, I promise you—
but all in good time. For now, let us merely expect to lay more
groundwork—and be ready, if fate should offer some unantici-
pated opportunity."

Elsewhere, other Deryni were reacting to the implications of
Dimitri's passing. Assigned to monitor the death-trigger they
had altered, Dom Queron Kinevan stirred groggily from trance
and ran through a brief spell to settle his nerves, then turned
his gaze to the crystal sphere suspended above the table in the
Camberian Council chamber, using it as a focus to amplify his
Call to Joram.

There could be no mistaking what he had picked up. They

had kept no actual link established with Dimitri since returning him to Rhemuth with his new compulsions, but a constant watch had been set to scan for any major working he might attempt. Niallan had caught the ripples from Udaut's "accident," and Joram himself had intercepted the lesser ripples that should have resulted in Albertus' death. Thereafter, Dimitri apparently had been lying low—until a few hours ago.

Alerted by the deviant burst of energy that had killed Albertus and then the second that had ripped Paulin's mind, Queron had dipped briefly into Dimitri's *merasha* disruption and then pulled back to a more bearable level to observe, well aware what the final outcome must be, with Dimitri having provoked sufficient mistrust to warrant dosing him with *merasha*.

Only after several hours of physical torture did Dimitri finally escape, released by the death-trigger that Miklos had set and Jesse had adjusted. The reverberations of Dimitri's suffering had been bad enough, especially for a Healer of Queron's sensitivity; but worse by far had been the intimation, shortly before Dimitri died, that Miklos himself somehow had forced a link while the torture was underway, his alarmed query adding to Dimitri's agony—until the death-trigger snapped shut. Queron's one consolation, aside from knowing that Dimitri now was beyond pain, was that he did not think Miklos had been able to identify the traces left behind, to know who had tampered with Dimitri since Miklos had set his initial imperatives.

"What's happened?" Joram's voice asked.

Bestirring himself, Queron turned around in his chair to glance back at the great, ceiling-high bronze doors that Joram was closing. By the light of the single candle burning in the center of the table, Joram looked almost spectral. Obviously rousted from sleep, he had paused only to draw on a mantle over his white nightshirt. His feet were bare; the silver-gilt hair was tousled, sticking up in back where he had slept on it oddly, and the eyes were darkly hollowed.

"You got here quickly," Queron observed.

"You did indicate that it was urgent."

Queron nodded. "Dimitri's dead. So is Albertus, and Paulin's mind-ripped. And Miklos forced a link through, just at the end. That's probably what snapped the death-trigger."

"Is the king safe?"

"He was when the link was severed. Dimitri did everything he could to protect him."

"You'd better give me all the details you have," Joram said, pulling one of the heavy chairs closer to Queron's and sitting.

Not waiting for further invitation, the Healer reached out to lay his hand on the one upturned on Joram's nearer chair arm, closing his eyes then and slipping into rapport with the ease of long practice. The requested information was conveyed within seconds, in a powerful and steady flow of psychic impression. As Queron dismantled the contact, Joram sighed and leaned back in his chair.

"I never thought I'd say this, but I find myself feeling sorry for Paulin," he said.

Queron turned his face toward the hanging crystal. "It isn't one of the more pleasant ways to go," he agreed.

"I suppose that's what's bothering me," Joram replied. "He *isn't* really gone."

"Isn't he?" Queron said. "When a mind has been ripped the way Paulin's was, what's left? The body could keep on going for quite a while—but is the soul still there?"

"Are you equating soul with mind?" Joram said with a faint smile.

Queron shrugged, returning the smile. "It's a question I've long considered—and never answered." He sighed. "I wonder why Dimitri did it."

"What, attack Paulin? Paulin was on his hit list, just like Albertus."

"Yes, but why rip his mind? He could have stopped his heart, the way he did with Albertus. Mind-ripping is hardly subtle. He must have realized that such an act would only reinforce anti-Deryni feeling—regardless of who ends up on the throne."

Joram raised an eyebrow. "I doubt that ever crossed his mind. When every other power has been taken away from you, or is about to be, I suppose it makes a kind of sense to lash out with as much destruction as you can."

"Then, why just Paulin? Why not Rhun and Manfred, Stevanus? Why not the whole roomful?"

"The king, for one thing," Joram replied. "He was forbidden to harm Rhys Michael or Cathan. The more practical reason probably is that he couldn't be sure of having enough power long enough to wreak destruction on a larger scale. Better to accomplish one definite kill than to attempt several and accomplish none of them."

"I suppose you're right." Queron sighed and rubbed wearily at his eyes. "So, shall I contact Ansel and let him know what's happened, or do you want to do it?"

"I'll do it," Joram replied. "You've been through enough tonight. Send Rickart to relieve me, and then go to bed."

Even an hour later, the king had not yet been given leave to seek out his bed. As soon as Dimitri's body had been taken away, all the principals had been obliged to adjourn to the abbot's lodgings, there to endure the inevitable debriefing that the abbot required. Fortunately, any ambiguity in Rhys Michael's statements before the attack on Paulin seemed to have been lost in the drama of the attack itself, so no question of the king's willing involvement ever arose.

"I've never heard anyone scream like that," Stevanus murmured, still badly shaken as they huddled around the abbot's table and a servant poured wine.

Manfred shuddered, his hand again closing around the crucifix at his throat. "You would have thought demons were rending his soul," he whispered. "God help him."

The comment elicited a flurry of self-conscious signs of the Cross and an order for more light. As servants brought candles for the table and set several torches in wall cressets, Rhun steered the discussion in less hysterical directions.

"I think it's fair to conclude that Dimitri probably has been working for Miklos all along," he said, after he had given the abbot a more objective account of the attack on Paulin. "I can't tell you what made Paulin recruit him. Personally, I've never been comfortable with the idea of using Deryni, even when we had them bound by hostages, and I misliked this arrangement from the first time I heard about it. By then, it was too late. You *Custodes* were convinced that Dimitri was reliable, and you'd come to depend on him."

"Father Paulin assured us—" Lior began.

"Yes, I know. So did Albertus." Rhun sighed and rubbed both hands across his face, then set both elbows on the table.

"All right, forget about what Dimitri may have done in the past," he said. "Let's consider what he's probably done recently and how that may affect us. Aside from any subtle influence he may have had on those with whom he had direct contact over the years, he'll have been reporting regularly to

Miklos, almost certainly by means of a magical link of some kind. That means that Miklos knew precisely what had been said at Court when his herald came, long before the herald could return."

Gallard de Breffni pushed his cup away, a scowl creasing his blond brows. "Conventional spies could have done the same, sending messages by relays. Even so, it doesn't give Miklos any particular edge, just to know that we're on our way."

"Perhaps not. But what new orders did Dimitri receive, once he'd reported?"

"To begin killing off key figures in Gwynedd?" the abbot guessed. "You all seem fairly certain that this Udaut was not the victim of an accident."

"But, why would Miklos of Torenth want Udaut dead?" Stevanus asked. "It isn't as if Udaut was a brilliant commander whose loss would cripple our military strength. He wasn't even coming along on this venture."

"No, but I replaced him with Richard Murdoch," Rhun said, "so we lost *his* services on this campaign. And now I feel certain that Albertus was meant to drown at that ford."

"Dimitri still got him," Manfred pointed out. "It just took a few more days. He got Paulin, too. I wouldn't necessarily regard those as crippling losses for the campaign—losing *you* and Albertus would have been far worse—but the *Custodes* have been badly damaged."

Abbot Kimball nodded dismally. "Father Paulin was our founder and a man of great faith. Replacing him will not be easy."

Thereafter, the discussion digressed to concerns mainly of interest to the *Custodes*, though the hint of hysteria kept intruding. The king's part in all of it became less and less an issue, and he gradually concluded that he probably had gotten through the incident relatively unscathed. As Lior and Magan launched into a brief but heated philosophical debate on the relative wickedness of merely being Deryni, Rhys Michael found himself starting to drift off and even yawn. The abbot eventually noticed and spoke up as soon as a lull in the conversation allowed.

"I think we might allow the king to retire now," he said, himself covering a yawn. "Our remaining business mainly concerns the Order. Sir Gallard, perhaps you would be so good as to show his Highness and his aides to the guest chamber here in my lodgings. Sire, I doubted you would wish to return to the scene of tonight's—ah—unfortunate occurrence, so I took the liberty of having your things brought up."

Indeed, Rhys Michael had never intended to return to the room where two men had died and a third should have done, and was able to offer the abbot gracious thanks for the courtesy. The choice of escorts was unfortunate, but he firmly squelched his distaste and allowed Sir Gallard de Breffni to escort him and his aides out of the abbot's parlour and down a short corridor to a well-appointed chamber half again the size of the one they had vacated.

"They could have given us this room at the start," Fulk said, when the door had closed behind the retreating Gallard. "That other wasn't proper accommodation for a king."

"Just lead me to the nearest bed," Rhys Michael murmured. "As long as we aren't sleeping in a torture chamber, I don't really much care."

He let Cathan pull his boots and managed to stay on his feet long enough to get out of his riding leathers, but he was asleep almost as soon as his head hit the pillows.

Except that he dreamed, fitful and restless, for all that was left of the night. Vivid images of Dimitri's tortured body intermingled with others older but no less potent: Gallard de Breffni coldly running his sword into the gut of the astonished Sir Tomais, that day of the coup . . . and Sir Sorle and Master Oriel, cut down by arrows a while later . . .

And more arrows slamming into his brother's body . . . and Javan sinking back into the arms of the loyal Sir Charlan, who died at Albertus' order, as one of his *Custodes* knights stabbed him in the back, and blood gushed from his mouth . . .

And blood pouring from Paulin's mouth as Stevanus probed deep with his fingers and pulled loose the tongue, bitten almost through . . . Stevanus' knife flashing as he finished the job, lest Paulin choke . . . and Paulin screaming, shrieking mindlessly, as Dimitri ripped his mind, and ripped . . .

CHAPTER FOURTEEN

I have seen the foolish taking root.

—Job 5:3

The dawn tolling of a single, deep-throated bell finally intruded enough to drag Rhys Michael from restless sleep. The cheerless cadence would have rendered further sleep impossible, even if memory of the previous night had not come tumbling back into consciousness.

He sat up with a start. At the foot of the bed, Cathan was laying out a clean tunic for him to put on before donning riding leathers and armor, himself already armed and dressed for departure.

"Lord Mánfred has been asking for you," Cathan said, as Fulk brought in hot water and a basin and towels. "They're burying Albertus here, this morning, before we leave. Mass will be as soon as they can get everyone organized."

Groaning, Rhys Michael fell back on his pillows and rubbed at his eyes, then blearily rolled over and staggered to his feet, well aware that it was useless to hope for any reprieve.

"What's the word on Paulin?" he asked, as he padded over to the garderobe. "Did he make it through the night?"

"Well, he's still alive," Fulk's terse reply came. "Whether that's a blessing remains to be seen. We'll have to leave him here with the brothers, of course. He hasn't stirred, hasn't regained consciousness. Father Lior says it's by no means certain that he ever will."

Emerging from the garderobe, Rhys Michael stripped off his stale tunic of the day before and tossed it to Cathan on his way to the basin and pitcher. From what had spilled over during Dimitri's attack on Paulin, he suspected that, if anything, Lior was being overly optimistic. His newly acquired Haldane wisdom suggested that those few who survived mind-ripping on the scale he had witnessed the night before sometimes lingered for weeks or even months, but usually as little more than vegetables. He was not certain even Paulin deserved that—though after what had been done to Dimitri, he could not imagine that the scales were much out of balance. Death would be a mercy for Paulin, as it had been for the Deryni.

The funeral bell continued to toll as Rhys Michael quickly washed and dressed and his aides packed up the few personal items that had emerged from saddlebags for morning use. He questioned whether it was necessary to don armor until after they had heard Mass, but Fulk informed him that the new earl marshal wanted to be ready to ride out as soon as they had buried Albertus.

"They *are* going to let us eat before we go, I hope," Rhys Michael said, letting them help him buckle on the red brigandine over his riding leathers.

"Only travel fare, in the saddle," Cathan replied. "We're already going to be several hours later riding out than was planned."

The king finished arming in silence, belting on the Haldane sword while Cathan knelt to adjust one of his spurs. He pulled on his cloak before following Cathan down the stairs and into the abbot's yard. Fulk brought up the rear, with the saddlebags slung over one shoulder. Waiting in the yard were Lord Joshua Delacroix and six *Custodes* knights. The new acting Master of the *Custodes* looked underslept and a trifle uneasy, which probably described the condition of just about everyone at Saint Cassian's this morning. Rhys Michael was certainly on edge.

"Be pleased to come with me, Sire," Lord Joshua said, snapping to brisk attention. "I have orders to escort the three of you to Lord Rhun."

Something in the tone made Rhys Michael wonder briefly whether some new suspicion had surfaced in Rhun's mind after they parted the night before—but then, courtly courtesies had never been a particular attribute of either the *Custodes* or Rhun. That Cathan and Fulk were included in the bidding suggested that this probably was just a guard of honor to convey them to the abbey church, Rhun flexing his muscles as earl

marshal. Still, Rhys Michael set his hand on the hilt of his
sword as he gave Joshua a sparse nod of assent and fell in with
him and his men, Cathan and Fulk flanking him a half a pace
behind.

Passing through a narrow slype passageway, they emerged
into bright sunshine and the not unexpected bustle of men and
horses beginning to assemble in the open yard before the abbey church, which loomed grey and squat on their left. The
tolling of the bell was louder here and damped the usual banter
that would have accompanied mere preparations to be off.
Alerted to the king's presence by his crimson brigandine amid
all the black of his *Custodes* escort, men gave way with grave
deference, a pinch-faced squire coming immediately to relieve
Fulk of the saddlebags. Many of them were heading up the
steps and into the church, mostly *Custodes* knights, but to the
king's surprise, Lord Joshua continued to lead them straight
across the yard.

"I thought we were going to Mass," Rhys Michael said,
holding back a little. "Isn't that the church?"

"It is, Sire, but Lord Rhun desires you to join him in the infirmary first."

"To see Father Paulin?"

"So I would assume, sir."

Rhys Michael let himself relax just a little. Joshua Delacroix
was a man of maddeningly few words, but it made sense that
the king should be brought to pay a courtesy call on Paulin's
sickroom, since the expedition would be riding out directly after Mass. Seeing the stricken vicar-general was not a duty
Rhys Michael particularly relished, but he supposed it was the
least he could do. Paulin was not likely to give him trouble
ever again.

They crossed the remainder of the abbey yard without further exchange, accompanied only by the solemn tolling of the
bell and the quiet milling of the gathering *Custodes* men.
Above the arched entrance gate to the cellarer's yard, which
would admit them through the stores range to the inner cloister, he could see the dense black smoke of something burning
in the yard beyond. They had come back this way the night before, from the refectory, and Rhys Michael assumed that the
infirmary must lie somewhere beyond. Because of the tolling
of the bell, he could not hear the crackle of the flames as they
passed under the arched gateway, but he caught a whiff of the
smoke just as they emerged into the sunlight again.

He stopped dead, left hand clenching tightly around the pommel of the Haldane sword, abruptly thankful he had not yet broken his fast. Over near the yard's outer wall, the source of the greasy black smoke now became all too obvious. The sight sickened him, never mind that Dimitri would have been dead for hours by the time they chained him to the stake and lit the pyre. Kindling and bundles of fagots were mounded waist-high all around, well ablaze, and the body itself was engulfed in flames.

The *Custodes* were responsible for this, without doubt, exacting the last measure of petty vengeance on an enemy now beyond their reach. Several were standing close by, prodding at the pyre with long poles to encourage the flames. Forcing down the gorge rising in his throat, for he knew this fate also was meted out to living men, Rhys Michael crossed himself and averted his eyes.

"They didn't have to do this," he muttered, well under his breath.

Ahead of him, Lord Joshua suddenly had realized that he no longer had an entourage and turned to glance back at the king. Seeing the king's expression, he returned immediately, hand set on the hilt of his sword.

"Please come along, Sire. They're waiting for you."

"Why are they doing this?" Rhys Michael demanded. As he gestured toward the pyre, Lord Joshua moved a little closer, reluctant to meet the royal gaze.

"Sire, they say he loosed black magic in the abbey last night," he murmured, keeping his voice low so that only Rhys Michael could hear. "The abbot feared contamination, if the body was not burned."

"That's superstitious nonsense," the king retorted. "The man was dead."

"Fortunate for him, Sire. If he'd survived his interrogation, he would have been burned alive."

"I thought spies were hanged, drawn, and quartered."

"Aye, sir, but burning is the penalty for sacrilege. The Deryni killed a professed Christian knight with magic and also used it to attack a mitred abbot. That gives the Order precedence in dealing with the crime."

It was useless to argue with the single-minded Joshua, who was only a tool. Biting back a number of highly satisfying retorts, none of which would endear him to his *Custodes* keepers, the king glanced reluctantly at the fire again. Though the face was no longer recognizable, for which Rhys Michael was thankful, the limbs were starting to contract in the heat, moving eerily. With a shudder, he turned his back on the blaze.

"We were on our way to see Father Paulin, I believe," he said quietly.

With a smart salute, Lord Joshua turned to lead the way, taking them through the cellarer's stores and on into the cloister garth, along the south range, past kitchens and refectory and thence through another arcaded passage that led to the very steps of the infirmary hall. Still a little numbed by the scene in the cellarer's yard, the king paid no special note to the chanting he could hear as he entered and followed Lord Joshua down a long central corridor.

To his consternation, the scene in Paulin's sickroom was perhaps even more grotesque than what they had just witnessed. They had shed their escort knights at the door, but Cathan and Fulk were at his heels and nearly ran him down when, just at the open doorway, he stopped dead.

Because so many men were crowded inside, the room seemed far smaller than it actually was. Two beds occupied the center of the chamber, on the nearer of which lay the still, deathly pale form of Paulin. To the king's astonishment, Albertus' body lay on the other, decked out in the full ceremonial robes of his former office. Two monks with thuribles were censing the beds from either side, and six more were ranged along the side toward Albertus, chanting the responses to an antiphon being sung by the abbot. Aspergillum in hand, the abbot was punctuating his verses with sprinkles of holy water over the two beds.

"Pax huic domui . . ."

"Et omnibus habitantibus in ea."

"Asperges me, Domine, hyssopo, et mundabor . . ."

"Lavabis me, et super nivem dealababor."

"Miserere me, Deus . . ."

"Secundum misericordiam tuam."

With incense smoke filling the room and the aural onslaught of chanting, Rhys Michael noticed only as afterthought that all the principals of the previous night's debacle also were present, kneeling hard against the wall toward the foot of the beds: the four *Custodes* men who had conducted the interrogation—Lior, Magan, Stevanus, and Gallard—and Manfred and Rhun, nearest the door. Brother Polidorus, the infirmarian, was huddled against Paulin's bedside with his back to the king, mostly kneeling with his head jammed down over folded hands, but occasionally rising up to check his patient's pulse or peer hopefully under a slack eyelid.

"*Adjutorium nostrum in nomine Domine . . .*"

"*Qui fecit caelum et terram.*"

"*Deus huic domui . . .*"

"*Et omnibus habitantibus in ea.*"

"*Exorcizo te, immunde spiritus . . .*"

Rhun noticed the king's arrival just as Rhys Michael started to whisper a horrified comment to Cathan and shot him a sharp look. The abbot had turned to sprinkle holy water on the kneeling observers, but as soon as he turned his chanting back in Paulin's direction, Rhun crossed himself and quietly rose to come over to the doorway, drawing the king and his aides a few steps outside the room.

"I do not wish to hear your opinion of what is being done here," he said very quietly, keeping his eyes on the abbot but with his voice directed to the king. "Please accept that Abbot Kimball and Father Lior believe it prudent and efficacious."

"Are they *exorcising* Paulin and Albertus?" Rhys Michael whispered, incredulous.

"You will refrain from any comment or expression that might detract from the dignity of this occasion," Rhun murmured. "You heard Brother Polidorus' comment last night—wondering whether Dimitri's black magic had summoned evil spirits under this roof. They decided it was best to be safe, in case he did bring evil into the house."

"And that's why they're burning Dimitri's body," Rhys Michael said. "Just to be safe."

"To be safe, and to keep *us* safe," Rhun murmured. "That is why you and your aides will also submit yourselves for exorcism before we go to Mass." Rhys Michael looked up at him in quick rebellion. "Defiance in this matter would be most unwise, Sire, regardless of whatever personal distaste you might feel. This gesture costs little and retains the goodwill of the *Custodes*. You might even derive some benefit. We still do not know what the Deryni might have done to *you*, that you say you cannot remember."

All Rhys Michael's protests died in his throat. Dimitri had done nothing to him, of course—except to save his life—but if he hoped to maintain the illusion that something *might* have happened, and thereby reinforce his own innocence, then submitting to the abbot's ministrations must be a part of that illusion.

"They've begun the individual exorcisms," Rhun murmured, touching his elbow. "Come in and kneel with me and Manfred. Cathan, Fulk—go on in."

All wide-eyed obedience now, Rhys Michael went where he was bidden, dutifully kneeling beside Manfred and bowing his head over folded hands as the abbot came to stand before Father Magan. He had already done Lior, who was closest to the wall.

"Exorcizo te, omnis spiritus immunde, in nomine Dei Patris omnipotentis, et in nomine Jesu Christi Filii ejus, Domini et Judicus nostri, et in virtute Spiritus Sancti, ut discedas ab hoc famulo Dei, Maganus . . ." I exorcise you, every unclean spirit, in the name of God the Father almighty, and in the name of His Son, Jesus Christ, our Lord and Judge, and in the strength of the Holy Spirit, that you may depart from this servant of God, Magan . . .

Rhys Michael had never seen an exorcism before, much less been the object of one. In common with most laymen, who rarely delved beyond the externals of their religion, his performance of the obligations expected of him usually came more from a sense of duty than from devotion. Merely dutiful practice of one's faith generally did not require attendance at the casting out of demons. Certainly, his outward religious fervor in no way approached that of his father or his brother Javan; and in that, Rhun had been entirely correct in assuming that he might view the present circumstances with scepticism.

"Et hoc signum sanctae Crucis, quod nos fronti ejus damus, tu, maledicte diabole, numquam audeas violare . . ."

Cautiously Rhys Michael dared a glance at Abbot Kimball, who was tracing a cross on Magan's forehead with holy oil, forbidding accursed devils to violate that sign. The king's sparse liturgical Latin was not good enough to follow all that the abbot was saying, but to his surprise, he thought he could sense the faint stirrings of power being raised—which was somewhat startling, because he had not thought that religious ritual could do that, at least not when performed by mere humans.

As for casting out evil with it, the only evil possibly present in this room resided in the hearts of some of its occupants and was not likely to yield to any ritual motivated by hatred and fear. He felt certain that whatever taint of evil might linger with Paulin or Albertus had nothing to do with having been touched by Deryni magic.

"Per eundem Christum, Dominum nostrum, qui venturus est judicare vivos et mortuos et saeculum per ignem. Amen."

As Abbot Kimball moved on to Stevanus, the king could not deny that there was power in the words, even on the lips of a *Custodes* abbot whose blind intolerance surely prevented any understanding of what he did. Lacking the keener focus a Deryni might have given it, the power was merely brooding sluggishly in the room, as random and diffused as the incense smoke drifting over the heads of the men being exorcised. It did no harm, but Rhys Michael wondered whether Kimball could have put it to effective use even if there *had* been something evil in the room. Meanwhile, he would have found the present ritual almost ludicrous, were the abbot not so deadly serious in what he did.

Lest his misgivings show in his expression, Rhys Michael buried his face in his hands and affected to be moved by the ceremony, as Kimball moved on along the line of kneeling men and repeated his words, sprinkling each one with holy water, anointing each with oil. The ambient power level never rose above a certain level and never focused. Nor did anyone else in the room seem to be aware of it, even Cathan.

"Exorcizo te, immunde spiritus . . . et decedas ab hoc famulo Dei, Rhys Michaelis . . ."

He kept his head bowed as the abbot's words rolled over him, expecting to feel nothing, but he found that the focus of the anointing enabled him to draw a little of the random power to himself—very little, but enough that by the time the abbot moved on to minister to Fulk, he had managed to replenish at least a little of the energy depleted by last night's emotional workout and his lost sleep. He was considering the implications of this achievement as the abbot concluded the ritual with a general blessing.

". . . Per Dominum nostrum Jesum Christum Filium Tuum: Qui Tecum vivit et regnat in unitate Spiritus Sancti Deus, per omnia saecula saeculorum. Amen."

Immediately, the solemnity of the ceremony shifted to the bustle of the room clearing, the choir monks filing out, Lord Joshua's *Custodes* knights entering to convey Albertus' body to the church. Pressing back against the wall with Cathan and Fulk, Rhys Michael did his best to stay out of the way, resolving to pay closer attention to religious ritual in the future. He had no idea whether the others or Paulin or the dead Albertus had benefited, but he had to admit that *he* had derived something from it. He wondered whether power was raised every time and he simply had not noticed before.

He was feeling somewhat reassured as he fell into the procession to accompany the body back to the abbey church. They returned by a different route, along the east range of the cloister garth and into the church through a processional door in the south transept. He did not look toward the smoke still spiraling upward from the cellarer's yard.

Inside, he took the place reserved for him in choir and did what was expected of him, making all the appropriate responses and paying outward respect to the man laid before the altar, as he must.

But the prayers he offered up in his heart were for another, who went unshriven and unmourned to no grave at all, whose ashes would be scattered on the wind without ceremony or blessing when the flames died down.

CHAPTER FIFTEEN

And that we may be delivered from unreasonable men.

—II Thessalonians 3:2

It was nearing noon by the time they rode out of Saint Cassian's, after laying Albertus to rest in the crypt beneath the abbey church. In the absence of any higher-ranking *Custodes* priest, Father Lior had assumed leadership of the *Custodes* religious accompanying the royal forces, with Sir Joshua commanding the *Custodes* knights. Messengers had ridden out at dawn to notify the other *Custodes* Houses of the incapacitation of their vicar-general, so that an election could be held in due course. Further dispatches went to Rhemuth, to inform Hubert and the remaining great lords there.

Meanwhile Rhun of Horthness took up his duties as the new Earl Marshal of Gwynedd, riding at the king's right hand and directly under the Haldane banner as the cavalcade headed north out of Saint Cassian's at a brisk clip. The pace allowed no leisure for conversation or even serious cogitation, but it was not sufficient to divert Rhys Michael from the rumblings in his stomach. The promised travel fare had turned out to be a chunk of bread and a few sips of ale snatched before mounting up in the abbey yard, though at least the bread was fresh, direct from the abbey's bakehouse. Fulk's saddlebag produced some dubious-looking cheese during a brief rest stop at midafternoon, but Rhys Michael was ravenous by the time they began meeting outriders from Lochalyn Castle.

They approached Lochalyn just as dusk began settling over the foothills. The castle itself glowed golden in the failing light, just catching the last rays of the setting sun. The camps of the investing troops were sprawled tidily all around the base of the bluff on which it perched, slowly coming alight with scattered campfires. As Rhys Michael rode through the outskirts with his officers, under the dour inspection of rough-looking men in border tweeds and leathers, the delectable aroma of food in preparation mingled with the more earthy smells of wood smoke and damp earth and horse manure.

An informal guard of honor rode out to meet the king and his party as they approached the castle gates, bearing torches and led by Sighere of Marley, brother of the slain Hrorik. There was more grey in Sighere's red beard than when Rhys Michael last had seen him, but that had been nearly seven years ago, at Javan's coronation. Rhys Michael had plucked a grey hair from his own head only a few months ago and had remarked to Michaela that he was surprised that all his hair had not turned white, if worry was a cause.

"Well met, King o' Gwynedd," Sighere called, as he and his companions drew rein before the royal standard. "I bid ye welcome, in the name o' Sudrey of Eastmarch an' Stacia, her daughter." He gestured toward the senior of the two men flanking him, a darkly handsome young man with a close-clipped black beard and kind eyes. "This is Corban Howell, m'niece's husband. We pray that ye will acknowledge him as Earl of Eastmarch, alongside our beloved Stacia. This young sprat wi' the outrageous moustaches is m'son, Sean Coris," he added, indicating the redheaded youth at his other knee with a proud jut of his chin and a twinkle in his dark eyes.

Rhys Michael suppressed a smile, for young Sean's moustaches *were* impressive—as was the lad himself, sturdy as a young oak, though he could not be more than twenty.

"Lord Corban, Sir Sean," he acknowledged, and lifted a gloved hand toward Rhun, sitting beneath the Haldane banner at his right. "I believe the Earl of Marley will remember Lord Rhun, the Earl of Sheele," he went on carefully, for there was no love lost between Sighere and Rhun. "I am obliged to inform you that Lord Albertus has died, and Lord Rhun now serves as earl marshal."

"Albertus dead?" Sighere said, before the king could go on. "When? How?"

Rhun kneed his horse a few paces ahead. "I believe that would best be discussed in greater privacy, my lord," he said coolly. "Lord Manfred serves as my deputy, and Sir Joshua

Delacroix has assumed interim command of the *Custodes Fidei* forces. Perhaps you would be so good as to indicate the billeting arrangements, so our officers may see the men settled. We have ridden from as far as Saint Cassian's since noon, and men and horses are in need of rest and refreshment."

Watching and listening from the sidelines, swathed in border tweeds like most of the men around them, Ansel MacRorie and Jesse MacGregor exchanged glances, melting back from the cavalcade when the immediate royal party of about a score began to follow Sighere on toward the castle gates.

Well, that confirms the news from Joram, Ansel sent to Jesse, as Corban and Sean joined Joshua and several of his captains to confer briefly, and the new arrivals began dispersing to their designated campsites.

Jesse's eyes narrowed as he watched a party of *Custodes* clergy trot by, several of them following after the king and his officers.

Interesting, how the command structure seems to have shifted, he responded. *Quite a shake-up in the* Custodes, *that's for sure.*

Ansel glanced around, judged them sufficiently removed not to be overheard, and shifted to whispered speech.

"Not enough of a shake-up to suit me. That older priest who joined the royal party was Lior, the Inquisitor-General; I don't recognize the younger one. I think the battle surgeon with them was Stevanus—the one who patched up Rhys Michael after he was 'kidnapped,' six years ago."

"A thoroughly disreputable lot," Jesse agreed. "Methinks we shall have to make some discreet inquiries, once the camp starts settling down for the night."

"Aye. Meanwhile, this has to be a major topic of gossip among the men, to lose their earl marshal this close to a potential battle. They must know something about it. I'll have our folk see what they can pick up by more conventional means."

Lady Sudrey received the king's party in the castle's great hall, gowned and coifed in black, attended by her daughter, Stacia, and Graham, the twenty-year-old Duke of Claibourne, who was her nephew. Graham had grown from gangling boy to comely young man since Rhys Michael last had seen him—not so burly as Sighere or his cousin Sean; clean-shaven, but sporting a wiry border clout a good deal lighter than the rich shades of auburn that marked all the other male descendants of the first Sighere. Stacia's hair was a much darker red, full and wild where it escaped from the shawl of fine tweed over her head but otherwise confined only by a band of braided gold across the brow. She had her mother's dark eyes.

Sudrey gave the king profound obeisance as he entered the hall, sinking to both knees and kissing both his hands when he came to raise her up and express his condolences. Even in her grief, she was still a handsome woman—and with the air of brisk competence Rhys Michael would have expected of Hrorik's wife. She had several of her dead husband's senior captains ready to brief the king and his officers as soon as they had settled at table. The latest communication from Prince Miklos, received at midday, indicated a willingness to parley the next morning, but only with the king himself.

"That's out of the question," Rhun said, as they tucked into simple but hearty fare spread out on one of the hall's long trestle tables. "We've told you what happened last night. I couldn't possibly allow the king to be exposed to further Deryni treachery."

"How kin ye know what Miklos might be wantin' tae offer if ye dinnae at least receive his emissary?" Sighere wanted to know.

"Why should he be wanting to offer anything?" Manfred countered, around a mouthful of venison. "If your estimates of his strength are correct, we can push him out of Culliecairn in any military encounter. It might take a while, but we have the time. Does *he* have the time to spend the next months holed up in Culliecairn?"

"We dinnae want him holed up in Culliecairn, m'lord," young Graham replied. "We want him oot. But he certainly willnae go if ye willnae even treat with him."

Rhun scowled. "I thought I made it clear that I am not willing to deal with more Deryni treachery, especially not where the king is involved."

"Do you fear that the messenger might be Deryni?" Sudrey asked. "If so, simply specify that only a human is an acceptable courier. Tell Miklos that you'll test his man with *merasha*, and then do it."

" 'Tis common practice, here in Eastmarch," a captain named Murray volunteered. "Gi'e him a stirrup cup laced wi' *merasha*. It will only mak a human drowsy, but a Deryni cannae possibly hide the effects."

"We hae found it a safe way o' dealing with them," Graham

added, "an' far more civil than keepin' archers trained on them, the minute they approach. If ye agree, we can send a messenger tonight an' set up tomorrow's meeting."

"I suppose it does make sense to hear what they've got to say," Rhun agreed reluctantly. "Tell me more of how you go about this."

The discussion digressed into specifics, shifting to map briefings on the area where a meeting might take place, during which Corban and Sean Coris returned from the camp below to report that the royal troops were settled. After a little while, as Rhun and Manfred coordinated their plans with Sighere, Graham, and the others, Sudrey came to stand unobtrusively beside the king, who had joined little in the discussion.

"I cannot tell you how relieved I am to have you here, Sire," she said quietly. "My husband used to speak fondly of your brother Javan. He was a noble and honest liege. We were all shocked to hear of his death."

Rhys Michael glanced at her sidelong, wondering how much she knew of the true circumstances of Javan's death.

"I hope I may prove half so faithful a lord as Lord Hrorik was a subject, my lady," he murmured. "I was greatly saddened to hear of your husband's death."

She ducked her head. "That it came at the hands of my own kin made the anguish double, Sire. I—" She broke off and looked up at him hopefully. "Sire, might I beg a small favor of you this evening, while the others are occupied? I know your mind must be awhirl with weightier matters, but might I presume to ask that you accompany me to the chapel for a few minutes, to offer up a prayer for my husband's soul?"

He started to decline, knowing that Rhun would not approve of a solo foray, but she added, "Please, Sire. It would ease my grief greatly, to have my king come to pay respect to my dear husband. I ask only a few minutes of your time."

Though he could detect no menace in the request, neither did he think it motivated by simple piety. Sudrey had something on her mind that she did not wish to say in front of the others. Curious to see what it might be, he glanced aside at Fulk.

"Tell Cathan, very quietly, that I'm going to the chapel for a few minutes to pay my respects to the late Earl of Eastmarch," he murmured. "I shan't be long. We'll wait for you outside the door."

Not waiting to see the effect, as Fulk passed on the message and then rose to follow, Rhys Michael offered the Lady Sudrey his arm and escorted her from the hall. Since Fulk offered no comment when he shortly joined them, the king gathered that his explanation had been accepted. Bringing Fulk instead of Cathan probably had reassured Rhun as well, for the great lords believed Fulk's loyalty to be more certain than that of the king's brother-in-law. Now, so long as he did not linger too long out of Rhun's sight . . .

Sudrey said nothing as she led them out across the castle yard and up the chapel steps, but as she held back to let Fulk open the door, she briefly rested her free hand on one of his.

"Good Sir Fulk, please keep watch and see that our prayers are not disturbed," she murmured.

Somewhat to Rhys Michael's surprise, Fulk ducked his head in mute agreement, remaining outside the door as he closed it after them. Sudrey gave him a bleak glance as she led him through the tiny, dim-lit nave, directing his attention forward as they came to a halt before the altar rail.

"My Hrorik lies here, in the holy place before the altar," she murmured, crossing herself ponderously. "He would have scorned the presumption, but his chieftains insisted. When I die, I hope to lie there beside him. 'Tis no claim of sanctity on my part, I assure you, but my place is at his side. He was a bonnie man."

Choking back a sob, she buried her face in her hands and sank to her knees on the tapestried kneeler before the rail. Rhys Michael knelt down beside her a little awkwardly and dutifully crossed himself, intending to offer up at least a token *Pater Noster* in Hrorik's behalf, but something had struck him as odd about the exchange by the door. He found his gaze wandering across the carved stone of the screen behind the altar, lifting to the crimson gleam of the Presence Lamp suspended to one side. He would have expected some comment from Fulk, but there had been none.

"Do not react, in case we are observed," Sudrey's voice murmured low, close at his left side. "Are you aware that someone has been tampering with Sir Fulk's mind?"

The question startled him, though he managed not to make any physical reaction. He closed his eyes briefly, bowing his head over his folded hands, then dared to glance at her sidelong, ready to Truth-Read.

"What makes you say that?" he whispered. "If it were true, how could you know such a thing?"

She raised her face to the altar, but her glance darted sideways as she folded her hands piously before her.

"Now, that is a reaction I had not expected," she murmured. "You seem surprised that I know of this, but not surprised that the thing was done."

As she glanced at him again, he felt the faint quest of a probe against his shields, and he stiffened them in automatic reflex, brief panic surging up then as he realized she could sense it.

"Oh, my," she whispered. "Forgive me, Sire, but I had no idea. Or rather, I had heard rumors—about the Haldanes, not you in particular—but I paid them little mind. Sire, I swear to you that I would never do you harm. Can you Truth-Read that oath?"

He could only stare at her speechlessly, his mind whirling with the implications, still uncertain whether he dared trust her, even though he knew she spoke the truth.

"You do have the power of the Haldanes, don't you, Sire?" she whispered. "Dear God, this changes everything. I begin to have a little hope. Sire, though I share Miklos' bloodline, I have little power and am little trained. My allegiance I gave to my husband and his people many years ago, and that will always remain. I have not much to offer, but what I have is yours to command. Read me, I beseech you. We have little time, and there is so much I would have you know."

Trembling, she bowed her head and folded her arms along the altar rail, the left arm underneath, and turned that palm upward, her open fingers inviting his contact but hidden from sight from the door behind them.

"Read me, I beg you," she urged, pressing a little closer. "I will make you no resistance. God willing, I may be able to assist you in ways neither of us dreamed."

Her words were truth. He could sense no danger in what she asked. Adopting the mirror image of her pose, he laid the fingers of his right hand atop hers and used the link of flesh to forge a link of mind, extending cautious probes against erratic shields that wavered and rolled back immediately at the pressure. She had neither the strength nor the control of the other Deryni with whom he had had contact—except, perhaps, Mika and Cathan—but such support as she could give was there, and his for the asking.

Quickly he skimmed the bare details, as yet offering nothing of his own confidence. The question of Sudrey's fate had been the spark that reignited the old feud between Murdoch and the Kheldour lords at Javan's coronation festivities. Rhys Michael had been present, but paid less attention than he should have done, being young and never dreaming he would have to deal with the aftermath himself one day. Miklos himself had raised the question, claiming Sudrey of Rhorau as distant kin to the Torenthi Royal House, captured in the taking of Kheldour by Hrorik's father, Duke Sighere, and given as hostage with her brother into the keeping of Ewan, Sighere's eldest son.

The brother, Kennet, had become a squire and then a knight in Ewan's service, eventually dying with his lord at Murdoch's hands; Sudrey had married Hrorik, the middle of Sighere's sons, and set aside her powers and her links with Torenth out of love for him. When Hrorik finally had achieved his vengeance against Murdoch, for the murder of his brother Ewan, Sudrey had rejoiced with her lord and drunk the health of the king who had permitted justice to be done. And now, she was prepared to offer her loyalty and her powers, such as they were, to the brother of the man who had given justice to Eastmarch.

A rattling of the door latch behind brought Rhys Michael partially to awareness, ready to dismantle the contact.

"Nay, my lord, see for yourself," Fulk was saying, as the door creaked open. "He's only praying with the Lady Sudrey. She asked him to pay his respects at her husband's grave. It would have been an insult not to agree. There's no harm in it."

Rhys Michael all but stopped breathing, holding Sudrey passive in the link, straining to hear whether the would-be intruder would overrule Fulk, but then someone muttered a reply and the door closed again. Keeping the link suspended, Rhys Michael glanced back across the rear of the little chapel to confirm that no one had entered, then closed his fingers around Sudrey's and gave her a fuller account of Dimitri's capture and death, saving only such details of his own participation as might give clue to the identity of his other Deryni allies.

"What plan do you suppose Miklos had in mind?" he murmured, again reverting to whispered speech, lest he tire her. "Obviously, Dimitri had orders to eliminate certain individuals—and the ones he got rid of helped me as well. But what was he to have done, once we reached Culliecairn, if he'd still been alive? Given what I've just told you, does anything of Miklos' communications of the past week suggest anything? What do you advise?"

When she had given him her plan, again urging a mental link to speed the process, he let it settle for a few seconds, then slowly disengaged, releasing her hand as he rubbed his hands across his face and then looked up at the carved saints adorning the screen behind the altar. The light from the Presence Lamp was gilding them all with a ruddy, red-gold glow, all too reminiscent of blood.

"I grant that no one will question the motives you offer, but you put yourself at grave risk, if you do this for me," he said. "It will reawaken memories forgotten these twenty years and more. It may turn your own people against you."

"If other than military action is required against Miklos, they must not know it is you who have the powers, my liege," she whispered. "If they do gain some inkling, you must convince them it is a reflection of your sacred anointing as king. If I can divert even a portion of scrutiny, then it is worth being seen for what I am. And a widow can always retire to a convent and adopt a life of penance. Your *Custodes* would like that."

Rhys Michael snorted. "More likely, they'd think you'd contaminated the place. This morning, before we left Saint Cassian's, the abbot *exorcised* everyone who'd had contact with Dimitri last night—even Albertus' dead body. And they burned Dimitri's body."

"Sad men, indeed, so to fear us," she murmured. "But we shall try to ensure that they do not fear *you* for such reasons. Dimitri told you last night that he would die to protect you; well, I make you that same offer."

"I very much hope that it won't be necessary for anyone else to die for me," he said quietly, taking her hand again. "That's aside from a few more of my great lords, who are long overdue to pay for their crimes. But I thank you for your loyalty, more than words can say. Other than Cathan, I have none about me in whom I can place unqualified trust."

He raised her hand to his lips, then kept it in his and tucked it under his arm as he rose and helped her to her feet.

"We'd best go back now. That will have been Lord Rhun or one of my other keepers at the door."

"It's true, then—what they say," she murmured, looking into his eyes.

"And what do they say?" he asked.

"That the king is not wholly his own master, that the great lords rule Gwynedd."

"I intend to change that," he replied. "There's been nothing I could do, up until now; but they've finally made their big mistake, in letting me come here. I'm having my first taste of freedom in my entire life, and I don't intend to give it up again."

"They may kill you," she said, "especially if they find out what you are."

He inclined his head in agreement. "They may. But maybe they won't. And if my own people don't kill me, maybe Miklos will—or Marek. God knows they'll try. At least I'll have had a try at being a real king. And with support like yours, I might even come out of it alive *and* king."

She smiled and bent to kiss the back of his hand in homage, then turned her face toward the church door as they began walking in that direction.

So disarming was Sudrey's effusiveness over the king's kindness in joining her to pray beside her husband's grave that even Rhun could not take serious exception, at least in front of the lady. But after Manfred had briefed Rhys Michael on what had been discussed in his absence, Rhun drew him into an alcove of the castle hall to confront him. Manfred waited in the opening with his back to them, to ensure that they were not disturbed.

"Sire, I must insist that there be no repeat of tonight's little diversion," Rhun said quietly, though his eyes were blazing with anger. "What can you have been thinking? She's Deryni. I would think, after last night's events, that you would be well aware of the danger of such a contact."

Rhys Michael put on a look of injured innocence. "My lord, the lady is recently widowed, and in my behalf. It seemed a small enough courtesy, to offer up a prayer at her husband's grave."

"The sentiment is admirable, but the danger remains," Rhun said. "What if she had tried to take you over?"

"And why would she want to do that?"

"She is kin to Miklos."

"Rhun, he killed her husband. I hardly think—"

"*I* will tell you what to think!" Rhun muttered. "Do not presume to test your bonds, simply because you are temporarily free of the strictures at Court. Your heir is in our control, as are you. Must I elaborate on threats to keep you prudent?"

Rhys Michael felt himself blanch and had to remind himself

that he was not yet free. "I'm sorry, my lord," he made himself whisper. "I didn't mean to question. It's just that the Lady Sudrey—"

"I don't object to your concern for the lady," Rhun said. "What I do mind is that you went off on your own, without so much as a 'by your leave.' "

"I did have Fulk tell Cathan were I was going," Rhys Michael objected. "It was only to the chapel to pray."

"You're very fortunate that it didn't turn out to be anything else," Rhun said. "But it's done now. I trust that you now understand your error."

Rhys Michael's nod of meek contrition apparently satisfied Rhun at last, for he grunted acknowledgment and glanced out into the hall, where Fulk and Cathan were watching the royal knights bed down for the night alongside Eastmarch men. The castle had already been crowded when they arrived, but Lochalyn was prepared to offer what accommodation was possible—and it was preferable to the camp below.

"Very well, then. You'd best go and get some sleep," Rhun muttered. "We'll want to be out at our field headquarters early."

To Rhys Michael's astonishment, he was permitted to retire to the unexpected luxury of a room all to himself. Tucked into the thickness of the same wall that carried a straight stair behind the great hall, it was too small for more than a narrow bed, a washstand, and a chest at the foot of the bed, boasting neither fireplace nor garderobe, but it was the first true privacy he had been granted since leaving Rhemuth. Able to dismiss Fulk without suspicion, due to the size of the room, he let Cathan assist him out of his armor and took the opportunity to warn his brother-in-law about Rhun's reaction and pass on what he had learned of Sudrey. Cathan was amazed.

I remember now that there was talk about her being Deryni, years ago, but who would have thought she'd offer you her assistance? Cathan sent, as they piled the king's armor across the trunk at the foot of the bed. *I wish there were some way to let Joram and the others know.*

So do I, but there isn't. But maybe we can do this ourselves. We're just going to have to be alert.

Able to offer no further comment, Cathan sighed and turned away to unroll a pallet across the door to the little room while Rhys Michael finished shedding his riding leathers and climbed into bed. After pulling off his own armor and leathers,

Cathan laid his sword on the floor beside the pallet and stretched out, pulling his cloak over him for cover.

" 'Night, Rhysem," he murmured.

When the king did not reply, Cathan turned on his side with a contented sigh and gazed drowsily at the rushlight on the stand beside the bed, until the flame swam before his vision and he drifted into sleep.

Around another rushlight, in a tent in the encampment below Lochalyn Castle, three Deryni huddled together for whispered counsel, having exchanged the detailed results of their night's investigations by more arcane means.

"I'd love to get my hands on Lior or one of the others who was actually present," Ansel muttered. "It's clear that Dimitri was responsible, but it seems to have gone a bit beyond what *we* had in mind, at least."

Tieg nodded. "I'd rather both kills had been clean, though. From what I've been able to gather of Paulin's condition, it's clear that he managed to survive mind-ripping—which is either a testimony to Paulin's bullheaded stubbornness or an indicator that Dimitri wasn't as good as we thought."

"Or that Dimitri got interrupted before he could finish the job," Jesse replied. "My guess is that they found him out after he killed Albertus, they tried to take him, and Dimitri made a last-ditch attempt to take Paulin with him, knowing he wasn't going to get out of it alive anyway."

"For Paulin's sake, I wish he'd succeeded," Tieg said. "God knows how long he'll linger, with no hope of recovery—though I don't suppose he's aware what's happening to him."

"Well, at least *Custodes* influence is going to be at an ebb for a while, with both Paulin and Albertus out of the picture," Ansel observed. "More important right now is whether the king managed to come out of it without arousing suspicion. He didn't look particularly uneasy as he rode in this evening. It will be very interesting to see how balances shift, now that Rhun is in command."

CHAPTER SIXTEEN

With arrows and with bows shall men come thither.
                                    —Isaiah 7:24

A royal messenger was sent to Culliecairn with the dawn, bearing a white flag of truce and the demand that Miklos should send back his proposal with a human envoy prepared to be tested with *merasha* before he would be admitted to the king's presence. While the messenger was gone, the royal party and their Eastmarch allies moved down to the camp and established their joint headquarters in a command tent.

Two hours later the messenger returned with a second rider at his side: a tough-looking man of middle years clad in riding leathers with Miklos' badge on the shoulder, wearing a steel cap but no weapons of any kind. Archers covered his progress as soon as he and his escort came within bowshot, accompanying him into the heart of the Gwynedd camp and halting him some distance from where Rhun, Sighere, and Lior waited before the command tent with Stevanus and Gallard de Breffni.

The messenger was hurried off into custody, against the chance he might have suffered tampering at the hands of his Deryni hosts in Culliecairn; the envoy was ordered to stand fast and make no sudden moves. Rhys Michael watched from the shaded anonymity of the command tent as Stevanus and Gallard went out to meet the man. Stevanus had a cased Deryni pricker in his hand, but he kept it shielded.

"You are?" Gallard demanded.

The man's gaze flicked from him to Stevanus, noting the badge of a battle surgeon on Stevanus' shoulder.

"Hombard of Tarkent, special envoy of his Serene Highness, Prince Miklos of Torenth," he said. "And this is the surgeon charged to ensure that I am not Deryni?"

"Please remove your glove and give me your hand," Stevanus replied, unlimbering the Deryni pricker.

Hombard looked a little startled, but he complied, not resisting as Gallard seized the hand and held it steady so that Stevanus could jab the twin needles into the back of the wrist. A muscle ticked in one cheek, and he closed his eyes briefly, but he made no sound, only rubbing at the tiny punctures when Gallard released him.

"I had expected a cup," he said almost reproachfully, removing his other glove as well and tucking both into the front of his belt. "That must be one of the Deryni prickers we hear of occasionally."

"Do you not use them in Torenth?" Stevanus replied, closing the instrument but not putting it away, watching the man's eyes.

Hombard smiled without humor. "We know who our Deryni are, Master Surgeon, so *merasha* is little used. But I am quite human. May I be taken to the Haldane now, before I become too drowsy to convey my message?"

"When we are satisfied, you may be taken to the *king*," Gallard said coldly. "Even a human messenger should be careful to observe the courtesies due one prince to another."

The man shrugged and yawned.

"Then, may I be taken before your *lord*?" he amended.

Stevanus noted the dilated pupils and nodded to Gallard.

"Bring him."

Briskly the *Custodes* knight set a gauntleted hand under Hombard's arm and followed back toward Rhun and Lior, steadying his charge when he stumbled once or twice. Hombard yawned again as Stevanus brought him before Rhun, not objecting as Lior moved in to grasp his wrist, monitoring his pulse as he inspected the wide-dilated eyes.

"Your name, sir?" Rhun asked, while Lior made his own assessment.

"Hombard of Tarkent, special envoy of his Serene Highness, Prince Miklos of Torenth."

At Lior's nod, Rhun jutted his chin in the direction of the command tent.

"Come with me," he said, leaving Hombard to follow as he went inside, hands clasped behind his back.

Inside, they had made the command tent as imposing as possible. Rhys Michael had taken a seat in a camp chair with his shield hung behind it, the Haldane sword across his knees, and his commanders and aides ranged to either side of him, with Kheldish carpets underfoot. Like the rest of them, he wore full war harness, save for helmet and gauntlets and the Haldane lion bold on his scarlet surcoat. Manfred stood at his right hand, with Cathan and Fulk behind the chair. Sighere and Graham represented the Eastmarch alliance on his left. Gallard and Stevanus remained by the entrance with Lior, Gallard pulling the flap closed behind them when all had entered.

"Sire, this is Hombard of Tarkent," Rhun said.

Hombard inclined his head—a careful movement not intended to give offense, Rhys Michael sensed, but also indicative that he did not entirely trust his balance for a proper bow. Gesturing for a stool to be set behind the Torenthi messenger, the king returned the nod.

"Please be seated, my lord."

Hombard fought back a yawn as he settled on the stool, bracing his feet wide for better stability. The eyes that he turned to the king were all pupil.

"My lord, I bring certain propositions from my lord Prince Miklos of Torenth, under terms specified by yourself. Will you hear these propositions?"

"That's why you're here," Rhun said impatiently, coming to stand beside Manfred. "Out with it, man. We didn't bring you here to play games."

"Indeed not," the man agreed, setting his hands on his knees and drawing a steadying breath. "I am quite aware that this is no game. Sir, my lord desires you to know that he is graciously minded to reconsider his earlier plans for the castle and town of Culliecairn. Given certain assurances, he is minded to quit Culliecairn without further danger to lives—those of his men or yours. However, he requires that you treat with him directly, face-to-face, to resolve the terms."

"Prince Miklos expects me to agree to this?" Rhys Michael said, before Rhun could reply.

"Prince Miklos expects that you will wish to prevent further loss of life, my lord," Hombard said. "He deeply regrets the death of Lord Hrorik, for he was husband to the Lady Sudrey, who is distant kin to my lord. He suggests that the two of you approach a central, agreed meeting place under a flag of truce, within sight of both armies, each of you unarmed and accompanied by only one attendant. If you wish, he will stipulate that I shall be his, since you already have verified that I am but human."

As he paused to stifle another yawn, giving his head a slight shake, Sighere said stiffly, "Hrorik agreed tae parley under a flag o' truce, an' it cost him his life an' the lives o' many other braw men. An' the takin' o' Culliecairn was entirely unprovoked."

"An error was made," Hombard conceded. "Lord Hrorik was not to be touched, for the sake of the Lady Sudrey. My lord therefore proposes to quit Culliecairn."

"He was not proposing to quit Culliecairn when his herald delivered his demands in Rhemuth, a fortnight ago," Rhys Michael said. "Nor did he express any particular remorse over the death of the Earl Hrorik. Then, his talk was all bluster over the christening of his nephew, the son of a man who makes claim to my throne."

"It had the desired effect, did it not?" Hombard said.

"And what was that?" Rhun demanded.

"Why, attaining the homage of the Haldane, by his attendance at Culliecairn in honor of Prince Marek's son," Hombard replied, to a rumble of indignation from Rhys Michael's officers. "No further tribute is required at this time."

"No tribute has been given, nor shall be," Manfred said through clenched teeth. "Nor do I think Miklos ever intended that the King of Gwynedd should attend the christening of the Bastard's heir."

Hombard shrugged, not batting an eye at the insult. "It is not for me to speculate on my lord's intentions, sir. I can only tell you that my lord bade me say that his plans have changed. The young prince his nephew has taken ill. He was privately christened last night. He and his parents have already left to take him back to Tolan."

Rhys Michael sat back at that, wondering if it could be true. Hombard believed it to be true, but so would any messenger, repeating what he had been told to say.

"Why should we believe this?" Manfred demanded. "The fact remains that Prince Miklos is Deryni and has long and openly supported a pretender to the throne of Gwynedd. I do not think he would submit to *merasha* the way you have done, to ensure that we can treat with him without fear of treachery."

"I cannot refute that last, my lord," Hombard conceded. "I would point out, however, that even my lord Miklos can be

Truth-Read. My lord suggests that the Lady Sudrey might provide this service to your king, by accompanying him to the parley my lord requests. My lord reminds you that, as kin to the Torenthi Royal House, the lady bears Deryni blood—not sufficient to pose you any threat, but certainly sufficient to verify the truth of my lord's proposals from his own lips, as Gwynedd and Torenth discuss terms of a withdrawal."

"As Gwynedd and *Miklos* discuss such terms," Rhun said pointedly. "Unless, of course, it's King Arion who authorized this bit of mischief."

Hombard shrugged and yawned again. "I speak for Prince Miklos, my lord. I can tell you nothing more. I am sent only to treat for terms of a meeting."

After an instant's taut consideration, Rhun jerked his chin at Stevanus.

"Take the messenger somewhere and let him lie down while we sort this out," he said. "And stay with him."

When the two had gone out, Gallard accompanying them, Rhun came to sink down on the stool the messenger had vacated. Lior also approached, to stand with Manfred. Sighere looked uneasy, Graham dismayed. As Rhys Michael handed his sword back to Cathan to hold, he found himself wondering whether he could have misjudged Sudrey.

"This makes no sense," Rhun muttered. "Why this sudden change? Why would Miklos offer to withdraw? Unless, of course, he is aware of what happened to Dimitri."

As he cast an appraising look at those who had been present, Manfred glanced uneasily at the king.

"You think he was counting on Dimitri to shift the balance once he had lured the king here?" he asked.

As both he and Rhun looked at Lior, the *Custodes* priest shrugged. " 'Tis possible, my lord. With Deryni, anything is possible."

Rhun drummed his fingers on his knee, then turned his attention back to the king.

"Meeting Miklos under his terms is still out of the question, Sire. I can't allow you to see Miklos alone."

"I wouldn't be alone if Lady Sudrey accompanies me," Rhys Michael pointed out.

Manfred snorted. "That's hardly any more reassuring. If she's as little endowed with Deryni power as everyone has always insisted, then she'd be of little use to you against any tricks Miklos might try to pull. And if she's powerful enough to protect you against *him*, then she's powerful enough to be dangerous in her own right—especially if she should turn her ultimate loyalties back to her own blood."

Sighere folded his burly arms across his chest, anger smouldering in the dark eyes.

"If, by that, ye mean her Torenthi kin—have ye forgotten that those he calls her 'kin' are responsible for Hrorik's death? I assure ye, *she* hasnae forgotten."

"And *I* have not forgotten Hrorik's loyalty," Rhys Michael said, "or that of *his* kin. I certainly have no reason to doubt the Lady Sudrey's loyalty. It was Miklos who stirred this pot seven years ago, when he first inquired of my brother Javan concerning her fate. Her Torenthi kin don't seem to have cared much about her before that. She declined contact with them then, and I do not believe that recent events are likely to have produced a change of heart."

Manfred scowled. "Perhaps he hopes to change her mind, if he can contrive to meet her in person."

"I have no doubts about Lady Sudrey's loyalty," Rhys Michael repeated, hoping his faith was not misplaced.

"It still could be a trick," Rhun muttered.

"Well, if it is, it's one that's been hatching for about twenty years, which I doubt," the king replied. "Look. I'm not keen on the idea either. It's possible Miklos *will* try something, but he'll do more than try, if we have to fight it out in the field. Granted, we'd win eventually—but at what cost? And you can bet that Miklos and Marek will slip through our fingers before we can reach them. Marek already has, if you can believe what the messenger said. That only postpones the day of reckoning."

"If we simply let Miklos withdraw, it still postpones the day of reckoning," Rhun said. "And if he plans treachery, and you fall, it brings another day of reckoning immediately. Are you that eager for another regency?"

"Of course not. I'm no more eager to die than the next man. But we'd be gambling possible treachery against the certainty of many lives being lost, if we have to fight this out." Sighere was nodding as the king went on.

"I've been asking myself why Miklos would even offer to parley, much less withdraw," Rhys Michael said. "Up until this morning, he'd given no indication that he planned to make this anything other than a mortal insult, by taking my fortress and giving it to the heir of my chief rival—and a bloody confrontation, if I tried to make him back down."

"But now he's *offerin'* tae back down," Graham said. "Why?"

"A good question," Rhys Michael replied. "I can only suppose it's come of what happened the other night. Marek's son may well be ill, but I doubt it; I wonder if he was ever even in Culliecairn. No, I think that having Dimitri unmasked took Miklos totally by surprise—as it certainly did us. I don't delude myself by supposing that we came out of it as well as we did by anything other than blind luck—but he doesn't know that. And until he figures out what happened to Dimitri, he doesn't dare push us too far.

"That means at least talking about withdrawing from Culliecairn—and offering to let us bring the only other Deryni we've got is the best he can do to reassure us that he intends to operate in good faith."

"Sire, these are all well-reasoned arguments," Lior said thoughtfully, studying a thumbnail, "but has it occurred to you that we might not have come out of the Dimitri affair as well as we thought, and *that's* why Miklos wants this meeting?"

"What do you mean?"

"Well, we've been worrying about whether Lady Sudrey might betray you, if we allowed her to go with you to parley with Miklos. But another, even more insidious possibility is that Dimitri could have gotten to you after all—in which case, you could betray *yourself* into Miklos' hands."

While consternation whispered among them, Rhys Michael reflected that the possibility of betraying himself was not altogether farfetched—though not at all in the way Lior imagined. It occurred to him, however, that he might confirm that he had not misjudged Sudrey while simultaneously reassuring the great lords that Dimitri had not tampered with his mind.

"There *is* a way we could find out about that," he said tentatively.

"Find out about what?" Rhun said.

"The prospect is not personally reassuring," Rhys Michael went on, "and I don't even know whether she's capable of doing it, but you could ask Lady Sudrey to probe me, to find out whether or not Dimitri did any tampering."

"You suggest we *let* a Deryni touch you?" Rhun whispered.

"She isn't just any Deryni," Rhys Michael said carefully, "and I think we could stipulate safeguards to ensure that she didn't go beyond what was asked. Not that she would," he added, with a pleading glance at Sighere and Graham. "She has good reasons for remaining loyal to the House of Haldane, which has upheld her husband's family for many years—and even better reasons for hating Miklos, who killed her husband and whose line abandoned her when she was a young, frightened, forgotten hostage in a suddenly hostile land. Why should she turn against me, when Miklos is the enemy?"

Lior was nodding slowly as Rhys Michael finished. "If she is of such meager power as everyone insists, I would question whether she is capable of what is needed, but the idea does have merits," he said. "Father Magan could help me monitor the procedure. He's familiar with the outward characteristics of different kinds of workings."

Rhun snorted. "Both of you are familiar with what Dimitri wanted you to *think* were the usual characteristics, over the years."

"I fancy I do have some expertise in this area, my lord," Lior murmured, his pride now affronted. "If she tried anything, a Deryni pricker would put a stop to it very quickly."

"She wouldn't try anything," Rhys Michael said. "And don't drug her, or she can't go along to Truth-Read Miklos for me."

After some further discussion, Rhun sent Lior to fetch Sudrey, instructing him to bring Father Magan as well. Rhys Michael paced and fretted while they waited, sitting back down a little uncertainly as Lior and Magan brought Sudrey in. Both priests had Deryni prickers in their hands, though the instruments were not uncapped. Sudrey looked frightened, pale, almost betrayed.

"I apologize if these trappings cause you alarm, my lady," Rhys Michael said quietly. "I believe you are able to Truth-Read. Please do so, if you wish, and be assured that I bear you nothing but goodwill. You have been brought before me, but it is I who should be kneeling at your feet as a supplicant."

"Sire, I do not understand," she said carefully.

He nodded. "I hope to make everything plain. What was not revealed last night, when we told you of apprehending Prince Miklos' agent in our midst the night before, is that there is some chance he may have—interfered with me in some way. I have no memory of this—and, indeed, would have none, if he was as skilled as we believe. Nor does there seem to have been time for extensive tampering to have occurred—but again, his adjustments could account for my perception of the time involved. He could have had the opportunity for some degree of tampering, whether or not he used it."

Comprehension gradually had lit Sudrey's face as the story unfolded, and now she nodded, speaking up before the king could continue.

"Are you proposing that I probe you, Sire, to ascertain whether tampering occurred?"

"I am," he said. "If it did, it could affect my ability to treat with Miklos, if I agree to this parley he proposes. Father Lior and his colleagues are cognizant that, as a good daughter of the Church, you will have put aside your Deryni powers many years ago, but circumstances are such that we must know whether I have been compromised. Will you help me?"

She glanced aside at Lior, who was making no attempt to conceal the Deryni pricker in his hands.

"The law forbids me to use my powers, Sire, and the Church condemns them. These good fathers seem ready to intervene, in ways not at all pleasant to my kind. I have but little power, but either you wish me to try my meager abilities in your behalf, or you do not. If you do, I cannot help you with the threat of *merasha* hanging over my head."

"We are here to protect the king," Lior said under his breath. "There has been enough treachery from Deryni, over the years, that you cannot expect total trust on our part, while you lay the king helpless with your powers."

"What would reassure you that I act only in his interests, Father?" she said quietly. "I will swear on any holy relic you like, I will comply with any reasonable condition you wish to impose—but I cannot work with you hovering over me, threatening to stick me with *merasha* the first time your nervousness gets the better of you. What is it you fear? I have not much power, as such is reckoned among my people. With his consent, I can probe the king to look for alien traces, as you request, but subtle or powerful workings of my own, without my subject's knowledge, are quite beyond me."

"How can we believe that?" Magan asked.

She shrugged and allowed herself a wry smile. "It is for you to discover how you may believe anything, Father. Some folk call it faith. I can only give you my most solemn and sacred word—on the life of my daughter, on the soul of my beloved husband, who is dead because of Miklos of Torenth, on my hopes for my own salvation—that I am the king's loyal vassal and would do nothing to cause him harm, though it cost me mine own life."

She raised her right hand, touched her fingertips to her lips, then crossed herself slowly. Rhys Michael, glancing at the others, signed for her to come closer.

"I take you at your word, my lady," he said. "What must I do? How can I best aid you in your task?"

"He must not lose consciousness!" Lior said, seizing her shoulder and turning her before she could move from between him and Magan. "We must retain that control, to judge what you are doing."

Sudrey turned her gaze back to the king. "Can you rest easy under my touch, Sire?" she asked. "Conscious, you could be aware of my probe, which is apt to be clumsy, and your natural instinct will be to pull back, to deny me access. If I am to help you, you must not do that."

"I can only promise to try," Rhys Michael replied, watching her. "We had a Healer when I was a boy. I had learned to endure his touch."

"We shall do the best we can, then," she said, smiling slightly as she came around to stand behind him. "I shall work from here, so that the good fathers can see your face and reassure themselves that you are coming to no harm."

As she set her hands on his shoulders, drawing him back to lean against her waist, her thought flicked into his mind.

What is it you wish me to do, besides pretend to probe you?

Breathing out with a sigh, he made himself relax against her.

Set up this scenario first. I'll pretend to resist a little at first. Once we've convinced them Dimitri didn't tamper, I hope they'll let you go with me to treat with Miklos.

"That's fine," she murmured, thumbs moving up to massage at the base of his skull. "Try to relax. Look up at that spot on the ceiling, just above your head. Keep looking at it and let yourself float. Look only at that spot and let everything else drift out of focus . . . and drift . . ."

Making a show of compliance, he flexed his hands and consciously made them relax against the chair arms, allowing himself a heavy sigh then, as he let himself drift into trance of his own controlling. It was hard to keep his eyes open, but he knew it would alarm Lior and Magan if he appeared to lose consciousness, so he let his eyelids flutter but only close partway.

"That's very good," she murmured. "Just keep floating. You

needn't be afraid . . . Now, let yourself return to the night before last. It was frightening, I know, but the fear cannot touch you now. Picture the man called Dimitri. He Truth-Read you while questions were asked . . . Did he do anything else . . . ?"

As he felt her chin come to rest on the top of his head, he let the link form fully and himself took control of the working, apologetically sending forth his own probe, deeper than he had in the chapel, to confirm what he had read before—that Sudrey had long ago turned her back on her Torenthi kin and offered him her unqualified loyalty and service.

Forgive me, he set in her mind, *but Miklos wishes to parley, and has suggested that I bring you along to Truth-Read for me. I had to be absolutely certain you had no hidden agenda.*

More gently then, and all in the space of a few heartbeats, he sent her the essence of what Miklos proposed and the arguments Rhun and the others had raised against it. Acknowledging, she pulled back a little, again massaging at the tight muscles in his neck and shoulders.

"Well done, Sire," she breathed. "You can stretch now. You're perfectly fine—and so far as I can tell, this Dimitri did naught but Truth-Read you."

As Rhys Michael blinked and sighed, flexing his fingers and stretching his neck, flicking his gaze around the tent to reorient, Lior and Magan exchanged whispered counsel. Sighere and Graham looked noncommittal. Rhun was nodding reluctantly in response to something Manfred had muttered to him.

"You're sure," Lior said, "that Dimitri didn't tamper with him?"

She shook her head and came around to kneel before the king, taking one of his hands in hers to kiss it.

"He did not, Father. Nor shall his lord tamper with mine. Sire, I beg you, let me come with you to treat with Miklos. I have not much power compared to him, but he does not know that. Perhaps my mere presence will keep him on his best behavior. And if not, perhaps I can protect you at least well enough to get out of any trap."

To Rhys Michael's surprise, Manfred was nodding, and Lior, though he was scowling, offered no word of protest.

"Well, at least it appears Dimitri did no damage in this particular instance," Rhun said grudgingly. "I confess, I like not the idea of letting you treat directly with Miklos, Sire, but if you are willing to take the risk, it may well be our best option. Shall I send the messenger back to arrange the meeting?"

Raising Sudrey to her feet, Rhys Michael tucked her hand in the curve of his arm.

"Please do so, my lord marshal," he said. "My vassal and I are eager to end this confrontation, to ensure that no more good men fall to a folly that need not be. I shall treat with Miklos of Torenth and a single human companion at midafternoon, accompanied by this brave lady."

CHAPTER SEVENTEEN

Blessed be the Lord my strength, which teacheth my
hands to war, and my fingers to fight.
—Psalms 144:1

"Tell me about the Haldane," Miklos said to the man sitting
before him and Marek in a guardroom off the gate tower of
Culliecairn. "I wish your frank impressions."

Hombard of Tarkent contained a yawn and made himself sit
up a little straighter. The soporific effect of the *merasha* they
had given him in the Gwynedd camp had abated somewhat, but
he still would rather have been left alone to sleep it off.

"He is comely, fit, apparently competent," Hombard said,
delving back into memory. "He conveys an air of authority, yet
seems somewhat reluctantly dependent upon his lords—in particular, a man who, I believe, is his earl marshal. I would guess
there is some friction between the two, or at least an irritation."

"Most perceptive," Miklos murmured. "Who else was present?"

"Earl Sighere and the young Duke of Claibourne, as was expected; another senior military officer—by the device on his
brigandine, the Earl of Culdi, I believe. Also several men of the
Custodes Fidei—a knight, a battle surgeon, a priest—no names
were ever mentioned. And two aides."

"I see." Miklos glanced thoughtfully at the document
Hombard had brought back, then returned his attention to its
bearer. "Please continue. Perhaps you would summarize their
reaction to the proposal you presented, point by point."

"Aye, my lord. They doubt your promise to observe a truce
while you parley, knowing of Lord Hrorik's fate, and they

186

question your possible motives for seeking this parley. Knowing you are Deryni, they naturally fear your power. They resent that you have given aid to Prince Marek and seem aware that you act on your own in this matter—that the king your brother has not sanctioned your actions."

"Succinct and perceptive," Miklos murmured, nodding. "Anything else?"

"Very little, my lord. I was treated with civility and even kindness by the Haldane, who bade me sit when he observed that the *merasha* had made me unsteady on my feet. Incidentally, the drug was administered with one of their Deryni prickers, not by mouth; this made the onset much faster and more profound. When I had presented your proposals, I was taken to another place where, I confess, I dozed."

As he yawned again, Miklos glanced at Marek, who had been lounging against the sill of a window overlooking the yard below, wrapped in a dark cloak. Marek's most senior captain was with him, a seasoned veteran named Valentin who had taught both young men swordplay as boys. Also present was Miklos' personal physician, Cosim, a striking-looking man with piercing eyes and silver at his temples, wearing the high-collared dark green tunic of a military Healer.

"Do you still wish to try it?" Miklos asked quietly.

Marek nodded toward Hombard. "I think we ought to Read him first, despite the *merasha*."

Hombard looked neither surprised nor dismayed as Miklos bestirred himself to come and lay a hand across the man's forehead. The drooping eyelids closed and he exhaled with a sigh, his head lolling more heavily against Miklos' hand. After a few seconds, Miklos flicked a glance of summons in the direction of the Healer, who moved in behind Hombard to take control as his master stepped away.

"They did not permit him to see a great deal," Miklos said quietly, as he joined Marek. "He did gain a glimpse of our dear cousin, just before they released him to return, but it does not seem to have occurred to them that they could enlist her assistance. They even failed to use her to Truth-Read while they interviewed him."

"But they've apparently decided that she's sufficient balance to keep *you* honest," Marek said with a smirk. "Well, let's see what can be done. Cosim, is he ready?"

The Healer looked up, dark eyes veiled by his power.

"Ready, my lord. Valentin, bring another chair for his Highness."

As the captain brought the requested chair, setting it beside Hombard's, Marek threw off his cloak and came to sit. Underneath, he was wearing leathers and harness identical to Hombard's. In common with all the other men in the room, his long, dark hair was pulled back and braided and clouted in a soldier's knot. He grinned as he handed Miklos his signet ring.

"I'll ask you to take care of that for me," he said. "Have we candles?"

"Here, my lord," Valentin said, putting a slender, honey-colored taper into Marek's hands. "Blessed by the Patriarch."

"You don't approve, do you, Valentin?" Marek replied. "It isn't black magic, my old friend; just a simple deception. I have to be able to get to the Haldane if I'm going to kill him."

"It's too soon," Valentin muttered, handing a second candle to the Healer. "You should wait a few years, until you have more heirs."

"But the longer I wait, the more heirs *he'll* have," Marek pointed out. "Don't worry; if it isn't safe, I won't do anything."

"So you say," the old captain muttered.

Smiling indulgently, Marek patted his shoulder for the older man to come closer, then leaned back against him and settled with the candle clasped between his hands as Valentin rested both hands on his shoulders. The Healer had set the second candle between Hombard's hands and now came around to crouch between the two chairs, his left hand clasped around Hombard's. After passing his right hand over the candle to conjure flame, he clasped it around Marek's.

"Have you any questions, my lord, before I take you down?" the Healer asked, himself now the bridge between the two men.

Marek drew a deep breath and fixed his gaze on the candle flame in Hombard's hands, visibly relaxing as he exhaled.

"I'm ready," he murmured.

Standing before them, Miklos watched with detached interest as his cousin sank deep into trance at the Healer's bidding, noting as the signs of control deepened, the eyelids fluttered over the dark eyes, and Valentin eventually stepped back.

"Hand . . . to mind," Cosim breathed, himself very deep in trancing as he called forth the spell. "Mind . . . to flame. Bring forth the light . . . and then bring forth the glamour . . ."

Almost immediately, fire flared on Marek's candle, its light gilding the placid planes of his face—which then began to waver and change. Lines sank across the youthful brow, along jowls suddenly less firm; grey began to thread through hair no longer so dark or so glossy. Within seconds, two Hombards sat entranced before Miklos and the Healer Cosim.

A moment to orient himself, and Cosim raised his head to glance back at Miklos.

"Sufficient, my lord?" he murmured.

Miklos surveyed the two now-identical men seated before him and slowly nodded, smiling. "Well done, Master Cosim. Do release him now."

A flick of power, and Marek was stirring, drawing a deep breath and blinking several times as control was restored. His eyes, now gone from dark to blue, darted to the candle still burning between his clasped hands, and he blew it out with a grin as he glanced up at Miklos, also reaching across to pinch out Hombard's.

"Satisfactory?" he asked. The voice was several tones lower than Marek's usual light tenor.

Miklos chuckled and touched the Healer on the shoulder in congratulation. "*Very* well done, Master Cosim. Perhaps you and Valentin would take the real Lord Hombard off to a well-earned bed. Put Marek's cloak on him and pull up the hood. I would as soon it not become general knowledge what we do. We shall join you in the yard directly."

An hour later, two riders emerged from the line of Torenthi troops ranged across the mouth of the Cardosa Pass, heading slowly across the plain toward the Gwynedd line under a white flag of truce. Rhys Michael Haldane watched them from horseback atop a grassy knoll overlooking the plain, Sudrey at his side and Rhun and Manfred flanking them. He was armored but unarmed—as, presumably, were the men coming to meet him. Others of his officers and aides were also gathered round, with the forces of Gwynedd drawn up in orderly lines to either side and back, both Kheldour men and the ones he had brought.

"I still don't like this," Rhun muttered, his eyes never leaving the approaching pair. "Why does Miklos insist upon a face-to-face meeting?"

Sudrey, astride a bay palfrey at the king's left hand, turned her face toward the earl marshal. She had changed her widow's

weeds for the divided skirts and tweeds worn by most noble
ladies in these border highlands when they ventured forth on
horseback, though a black coif still bound her dark hair.

"Because you found out his agent and broke him," she said.
"He will have attributed at least a part of the credit to his
Highness, whether or not this is true. And there *are* the persis-
tent rumors that the Haldanes are divinely favored."

"What do you mean, 'divinely favored'?" Manfred rumbled.

"Why, that God protects the Haldanes," she replied. "Did
He not vanquish Imre, when Cinhil came to claim back his
throne? 'Tis the power of God that has ordained the survival of
Haldane's Royal House."

Rhun snorted. "Consorting with Deryni sorcerers hardly
constitutes divine aid, I think. Satanic, perhaps."

"Oh, do you still think that Deryni magic was responsible
for the Haldane restoration?" Sudrey asked, ignoring the jibe.
"Granted, Camber MacRorie and his kin convinced the Michaelines to provide military backing—but that was hardly
magic. I was only a girl when it happened, and far from
Valoret, but I remember that my uncle Termod was quite convinced that Cinhil Haldane had called up something far outside
our ability, to defeat Cousin Imre. 'Tis God who protects the
Haldanes, my lord, and He will not allow His anointed to
come to harm at the hands of a Deryni sorcerer."

As she rode down the knoll at Rhys Michael's side, heading
out across the plain, he glanced at her in some amazement, adjusting the golden circlet on his head with one gloved hand.

"Why did you tell them that? Do you want to get me
killed?"

She chuckled. "They have forgotten, Sire, but you are king
by Divine Right. I do not pretend to understand where your
powers have come from, but it is important that *they* believe
them come of God. Now, if it *should* become necessary to use
those powers against my kinsman, you have your own justification, even if, for some reason, I cannot cover for you."

"You expect treachery, then?" he asked.

"I do not expect it, no. But 'tis best to be prepared for such
things."

Nodding thoughtful agreement, he directed his gaze ahead
again, studying his adversary as he and Sudrey continued to
approach. Now halted in the central area designated for the
meeting, beneath the floating banner of white silk borne by
Hombard of Tarkent, Prince Miklos of Torenth waited astride

a fleet, desert-bred steed the color of a fox. The animal's flaxen mane and tail exactly echoed the shade of its rider's blond hair, which was braided and clubbed at the back of his head in a soldier's knot and bound across the forehead with a fillet of ruddy gold.

Other than some new lines around the dark eyes, Miklos looked scarcely older than when Rhys Michael last had seen him. Instead of the tawny, flowing silks he had worn at Javan's coronation, nearly seven years before, a close-fitting brigandine of russet leather encased his body, studded with roundels of polished brass that caught the sunlight like a galaxy of suns. Matching vambraces clasped his forearms above gauntleted gloves that flared at the wrists, and the thigh-high boots were cut and studded to incorporate greaves in their design. From what Rhys Michael could see, the prince bore no weapons.

Hombard bowed in the saddle as Rhys Michael and Sudrey drew rein, a proper courtier, but neither Miklos nor the king so much as flicked an eyelid downward.

"Well met, Haldane," Miklos said pleasantly enough. "You were but a lad when last we met. I see that time has at least enabled you to look like what you claim to be."

"I make no claim," Rhys Michael said carefully. "I am what I am—King of Gwynedd—and that is something that your kinsman, who calls himself Marek of Festil, can never hope to be."

"Indeed?" Smiling, Miklos leaned his crossed forearms casually against his saddle's high pommel. "That does remain to be seen, does it not?"

"Some other day, perhaps," Rhys Michael replied. "I believe possession of Culliecairn is the issue here. Your envoy indicated that you now intend to withdraw."

"In due course." Miklos nodded toward Sudrey. "Actually, I wished first to speak with my cousin. Thank you for obliging me by bringing her along."

Rhys Michael glanced at Sudrey, who had stiffened in the saddle.

"I have nothing to say to my husband's murderer," she said coldly. "I would not have come, except that my liege lord requested it. I am here to assist the King of Gwynedd, whose vassal I am."

"And that," Miklos said, "is precisely what I wished to discuss with you. Cousin, I have been trying for seven years to ascertain what became of you. I did not wish to believe that you would so far betray your blood as to marry against the interests of Torenth."

"And what is Torenth to me, except that a scion of Torenth has slain my lord?" she retorted. "Where was Torenth when my brother and I were abandoned, after the Festillic collapse? That I found kindness and love amidst my captors I count as one of God's great mercies."

"A dubious mercy, if it led you to betray your country, your race, and your kin," Miklos said mildly. "The royal blood of Torenth runs in your veins, Sudrey of Rhorau. Do you recall how we treat with traitors in Torenth?"

Without further preamble, he raised his right fist and thrust it toward her with a muttered Word, opening out his fingers with a snap. The gesture launched a fist-sized ball of fire that roared toward her like an inferno, growing as it came. Even as her shields went up, dismay and outrage flaring with her aura, Rhys Michael was interposing himself, his own shields blazing into being.

In a shower of sparks that scattered and fell like shooting stars, the sphere struck Rhys Michael's shields and dissipated harmlessly, much to the astonishment of both Miklos and Hombard.

What had begun as a casual, almost offhand accompaniment to Miklos' denunciation now shifted to more focused intent directed not only at Sudrey but also at Rhys Michael, who somehow had managed to avert Sudrey's just fate. As Hombard glanced uncertainly at his prince, increasingly fighting a now skittish mount, Miklos stabbed a gloved forefinger at the ground behind Rhys Michael. Sudrey screamed as flame leaped up from the very ground and began to trace a curved, fiery line around to the side and then behind Miklos, laying down a containing circle.

"No!"

Even as it began, Rhys Michael saw the danger—that if the circle closed, their escape was cut off. Instinctively he raised one hand in a gesture of forbidding. A Word of command conjured heavy cloud above the flames, weeping moisture that changed to steam as the fire below was quenched—to the dismay of the horses, who were growing increasingly difficult to control. The result was a smoking black line of burned turf outlining just over half of the circle Miklos had intended—now rendered impotent—and to underline his point, Rhys Michael sent a warning burst of energy against Miklos himself.

The Torenthi prince countered it easily, but his expression showed his shock. His horse began fighting the bit, white-eyed and on the verge of panic, and he had to turn some of his attention to bringing it back under control. Hombard was backing his horse away from Miklos, looking very alarmed, and Sudrey had turned her nervous steed, ready to flee at a word from the king.

"Don't try to interfere, Haldane!" Miklos shouted, again flinging fire behind them to prevent their escape. " 'Tis only Sudrey I want."

"Well, you shan't have her," Rhys Michael replied, as his own mount reared and fought him.

"No?"

For answer, Rhys Michael turned another, stronger burst of power at Miklos like a crimson wave of light, defense shifting to attack. The Torenthi prince repelled the attack and struck again, but at Sudrey—forked lightning that leaped from his hand to spear her horse through the chest and out one side. The animal squealed and went down under her, dead before it hit the ground, even as Rhys Michael spurred closer to snatch her from the saddle before she could be crushed. He had dragged her to a precarious perch before him and was wheeling his stallion back on its haunches, preparing to disengage, when Hombard's mount slammed into his and sent it and him and Sudrey tumbling.

He ended up flat on his back, wheezing for breath, but somehow he managed to keep hold of the reins. An exultant Hombard was pulling up his stallion a few paces beyond and yanking it around for another pass, gigging the animal into another charge. As Rhys Michael hauled himself around by the reins, scrambling on hands and knees to regain his footing, he managed to avoid being trampled, but one murderous, steel-shod hoof came slamming down on his right hand with crushing force.

He screamed and let go of the reins in reflex. The pain wrenched at his concentration, and he only just managed to deflect another blast of Miklos' magic as he rolled clear and finally staggered to his feet, the injured hand hugged to his breast.

Sudrey had caught his horse and was hanging on to the reins and one stirrup, trying to get back up. To Rhys Michael's shocked horror and surprise, a blast of magic from the "human" Hombard sent her reeling to her knees, with a little cry.

The horse bolted and took off for the Gwynedd line, where riders were already starting to thunder down the slope.

But Miklos was joining his attack to Hombard's, a clenched fist raised toward Sudrey, who was clutching at her chest. Through his own pain, Rhys Michael caught a wave of hers and dashed to her side, catching his arms around her from behind and launching another counterattack through the focus of his uninjured hand. The first bolt stopped Miklos' assault and nearly made him pull his mount over backward; the second all but bowled Hombard out of the saddle.

And how could Hombard be Deryni? They had tested him with *merasha*!

The air was atremble with lightning and the acrid smell of power gone rogue. Hombard was backing off, looking shaken and alarmed, but fury turned Miklos' face into a mask. As he readied another attack, this time against Rhys Michael, the king gathered up the power of the spell Dimitri had taught him—that Miklos had tried to use against Sudrey—thrusting outward through the focus of his good hand to punch his power through Miklos' shields and close a fiery hand around the Deryni prince's heart.

Rhys Michael had shaken Miklos' spell from Sudrey, but Miklos could not shake free of Rhys Michael's. And even as he clutched at his chest, doubling over with the pain, his horse betrayed him again, this time bucking him almost clear of the saddle—except for one spurred heel that caught in the stirrup and flipped him upside down to dangle amid the flashing, steel-shod hooves.

The beast bolted at this new outrage, continuing to buck and twist as it ran. Miklos' power flared erratically as he tried gamely to twist free, arms vainly upflung to protect his head, but he went limp after only a few strides. The power died away even as Hombard galloped in to seize the animal's reins and wrench it to a halt.

Except that Hombard no longer looked like Hombard. The pale eyes now were dark, the face of an age with Miklos, the hair escaping from its soldier's knot a rich chestnut, untouched by grey. Fury animated every line of the young man's body as he leaned down far enough to hook a gloved hand in Miklos' belt and drag him up across his saddle, and the look he cast Rhys Michael was murderous.

Sudrey caught Rhys Michael's good arm and raised it toward Miklos' rescuer with one of hers, power still bright around her.

"Help me warn him off, Sire," she gasped, summoning the spell and desperately willing him to augment her failing strength. "Quick, before your men reach us."

Obedient, Rhys Michael channeled a surge of energy into her directing. Fire lanced forth to score the earth before the burdened rider, and with a look of fury he turned and galloped off toward his own lines, Miklos' limp form before him. Rhun and Manfred and a party of mounted archers were approaching fast, galloping down the slope with arrows nocked to the archers' bows, and Sudrey fell back exhausted against the king's breast, encircled by his arms.

"We have not much time," she murmured. "Listen carefully. Say that it was my power that thwarted Miklos, but I drew upon your life-force to fuel it. I was able to do this because you are a Haldane, divinely appointed to rule Gwynedd. Find a way to suggest that the power within you has nothing to do with Deryni; it comes of God. Do not let my death be in vain."

"No! You aren't going to die!"

"Sire, I am wounded in ways you cannot see," she replied, grimacing. "Far better that I die now, in the manner of my own choosing, rather than face what your great lords might inflict upon me, for having sufficient power to defeat a mage of Miklos' stature. Promise you will not let them burn me."

"I promise," Rhys Michael whispered, putting from mind the image of Dimitri's dead body burning in the yard at Saint Cassian's. "But don't go. Don't give up. I can protect you."

She closed her eyes against a twinge of pain, then looked up at him again, as the hoofbeats thundered nearer.

"I make no judgment, Sire, but you will be fortunate if you can protect yourself. God be with you. Pray for me."

This time, when she closed her eyes, she did not open them again. There was one further, fluttering breath—and then, no more. As he laid his head against her still breast, knowing he would hear no heartbeat, his own men reached him.

"What the devil happened?" Rhun demanded, pulling up beside him and jumping down from his horse, as the mounted archers swept past and formed a line between them and the Torenthi line, where a party of rangers had broken and were spurring to meet Hombard.

Rhys Michael looked up dully, Sudrey's body still hugged to his chest.

"I think they were after Sudrey from the start," he murmured. "Miklos said she had betrayed her country and her race—and then he and the other man attacked her with magic."

"Are you saying that Hombard was Deryni, too?" Manfred said, jumping down to join Rhun. "But that's impossible. We tested him."

"I don't think it was the same man," Rhys Michael said uncertainly, as he started to ease her body to the ground. "His face changed, right at the end. He somehow looked familiar. She stood up to both of them, though, and I think she killed Miklos. The other man—aiie!"

He gasped as he jostled his injured hand while trying to put her down. He had managed not to move it much during the last little while, but now, as the rush of combat slowly faded, the pain set up a throbbing that coursed all the way to his elbow.

"Where are you hurt?" Rhun asked, as Manfred seized the injured right arm and turned it from the elbow, searching for signs of injury.

Rhys Michael sucked in his breath as Manfred prodded around a jagged gash in the leather gauntlet.

"Careful!" he snapped. "One of the horses stamped his great, bloody hoof down on the back of my hand, when I was on the ground. I'm sure there must be bones broken."

"Try to move your fingers," Manfred ordered.

Rhys Michael tried, but even the effort of trying made him nauseated from the pain. Lifting the trembling hand for closer inspection, he could see that blood and dirt crusted the gash in the glove and the wound inside, which looked to go well into sinews and bone. He fought down a wave of light-headedness as he whispered, "Damn!"

"Borg, come and take a look at this," Manfred called over his shoulder to one of the archers.

But Rhun was already pulling his horse around to mount again, glancing apprehensively toward the Torenthi line, which had opened to receive the fleeing Hombard and his burden.

"No time for that now," he said. "Mount up! We may have company very shortly, if we don't get out of here. Borg, give the king your horse, then lift Lady Sudrey's body up to Lord Manfred. Move!"

As Manfred helped Rhys Michael to his feet, the archer called Borg brought his horse over and gave Rhys Michael a leg up. Vaulting up into the saddle without using his right hand was difficult, and the hand throbbed with renewed pain when the archer jarred it in passing the reins to his good hand. He tried not to think about the hand as they moved out, instead fixing his gaze on the body of Sudrey, now cradled in Manfred's arms in the saddle before him. The pain accompanied him all the way back to the Gwynedd line and beyond.

Back in Culliecairn, Marek of Festil watched without expression as three of the patriarch's bearded and black-robed priests gently removed the last of Miklos' harness, starting to wash his body and prepare it for a lying-in-state later that night in the castle's chapel. The Healer Cosim stood at his elbow, but there had been nothing he could do for Miklos; it was not alone the injuries inflicted by his horse that had killed the Torenthi prince.

Marek had not wanted to believe that. Assisted by Cosim, he himself had conducted a Death-Reading on his dead cousin, before allowing the priests to take charge of the body. Afterward, he had erased what he read. Both he and the Healer now knew that magic had been the principal cause of Miklos' death—and that the power for the spell had come not from the Deryni Sudrey but from Rhys Michael Haldane.

"My worst nightmare, Cosim," Marek murmured, when he had drawn the Healer out of the little room where Miklos lay. "No, the very worst would be to fall to the Haldane myself—or even worse than that, for my son to perish as well. But for Miklos to fall—how could the Haldane do this? How is this possible?"

Cosim cocked a cynical eyebrow. "The allegations of Haldane power are hardly new, my lord—though, I confess, I thought them unlikely to be true, given the other tales we have heard these past six years of the impotence of this Haldane before his ministers of state."

"Well, it wasn't Cousin Sudrey who did that to Miklos," Marek muttered. "I'm still not certain how it happened. I *know* Miklos could have taken the Haldane in a proper duel arcane—or *I* could have done. This was meant to be a testing of the waters—though we were prepared to ambush him if that opportunity presented itself. Sudrey was the real target. Miklos had been obsessed with her defection since he found out about it at Javan Haldane's coronation. And I'd *swear* that this Rhys Haldane had no powers at that time—not even shields—though there was certainly something going on with his brother."

"Perhaps this odd Haldane power is somehow vested in Gwynedd's crown," Cosim ventured, after a short pause. "Perhaps that is why you detected nothing at the coronation, save in Javan."

Marek shrugged. "I was but young then, and we never managed to make physical contact with either Haldane brother. But how can the Haldane power be that strong? It did not save Javan Haldane from his great lords' treachery, and it has not enabled Rhys Haldane to be his own man, these six years of his reign."

"Yet it enabled him to kill my prince today," Cosim murmured.

Marek hung his head. "I must ask you not to reveal that, Cosim."

"I do not know how you can keep it a secret," the Healer replied, "or why you would wish to do so. Deryni who witnessed what took place, even from afar, are well aware that magic was afoot."

"Magic—aye. But they must believe it was Sudrey's magic that killed Miklos—an unfortunate accident. Surely his injuries would have killed him, if magic had not."

"Perhaps. But why should you wish them to believe this? Why perpetuate this uncertainty?"

"Because I do not wish his men to seek vengeance for his death at this time, riding out to fight a battle that was never intended to take place and that cannot be won under the present circumstances." Marek glanced down at his hands, then back at the Healer.

"Cosim, I hesitate to ask, but I find myself obliged to seek your further assistance. Those who can, will Truth-Read me as I speak to them."

Cosim turned his dark gaze on the younger man, searching the dark eyes. "Are you asking me to adjust your memory, my lord, so that your lies go undetected?"

"I am asking you to adjust my memory so that I can present a half truth without danger of contradiction—that it was not magic that killed Miklos. I would never attempt to claim that magic was not used. But left with the sad yet unprovocative conclusion that his death was largely due to misadventure, his men hopefully will withdraw in good order to fight another day—and for me."

Slowly Cosim nodded. "I understand what you are saying, my lord," he murmured. "Further, I believe my lord Miklos would have agreed." He glanced around to ensure that they were alone, then returned his gaze to Marek.

"I will set a fatigue-banishing spell as well, my lord," he murmured, lifting one hand to Marek's forehead. "Open to me . . ."

A quarter hour later, his energies somewhat restored by the Healer's ministrations, Marek was facing the decidedly uncomfortable duty of confirming the details of Miklos' death to his officers. In the back of his mind was the knowledge that Cosim wished to see him again after the court—the reason escaped him for the moment—but for now, Marek was content to leave the Healer alone with his grief, standing down among Miklos' other men.

He had summoned them to gather in the castle's great hall, but he did not presume to sit in the chair of state that stood at the center of the dais. Miklos had held court from there in the more carefree days, while they waited for the Haldane response, and now the patriarch himself stood beside the chair, glaring at Marek from beneath his black stovepipe headdress and veil.

Summoning Valentin to his side—who grieved, too, for the death of the young man he had loved like a son—Marek moved in front of the chair, though far enough in front to make it clear he had no intention of usurping the dead man's place. Not for the first time, he was glad he had sent Charis and the baby back to Tolan some days earlier; he did not relish telling his wife of her brother's death.

And telling King Arion was an even more daunting prospect. Though the late King Nimur, Arion's father, had given sanctuary to the infant son of Imre and Ariella of Festil following the Haldane Restoration, Arion's support for his exiled cousin's cause had never been more than lukewarm, especially since his becoming king ten years ago. Indeed, without Prince Miklos' friendship and patronage, Marek might never have survived to adulthood. Much less could he have mounted this expedition—which, unfortunately, had gone so badly awry.

Marek suspected that his sufferance by the Torenthi Royal House was about to become even more precarious than it had been all his young life. While neither illegitimacy nor incest were Marek's fault, the taint might only be truly removed by success—by taking back the crown his parents had borne. With Miklos gone, that now was not likely to occur for some time.

And it would never occur if Marek allowed himself to be stampeded into action prematurely.

"Gentlemen, you will have heard many rumors regarding the circumstances of the prince's death," Marek said to the assembled men, hardly daring to lift his eyes to them. "That incidental mishap should have cost my cousin his life is the supreme irony, when so much was at stake. It was not magic that killed him."

"Yet magic was used," one of the captains pointed out. "And it was you who instigated it, my lord."

"Prince Miklos instigated it against the traitor, Sudrey of Rhorau," Marek said. "And though she responded in kind, this was not unexpected. What *was* unexpected was the Haldane's response—though we have long believed that the Haldanes do have access to a kind of power akin to our Deryni powers. Unfortunately, I still am not certain how much of the power was Sudrey's and how much was the Haldane's. The question is academic, since ultimately it was my cousin's physical injuries that killed him, but the Haldane factor will bear further investigation."

"Not in conjunction with *this* campaign," another of the captains said. "It has already cost us our prince."

"I greatly regret that," Marek began.

"As we do, my lord," another said. "But we are not now prepared to follow you farther into Gwynedd. While our prince lived, we were obliged to go where he commanded. Our fealty returns now to the king his brother, who may not agree that Torenthi troops should lend their aid to your cause."

Marek bowed his head.

"I accept the reprimand you have not spoken, my lord," he murmured. "I count myself at least partially to blame for the death of Prince Miklos and remind you that he was my cousin and brother to my wife, as well as being brother to King Arion. I do not look forward to answering to either of these worthies when I must tell them of his death.

"As for venturing farther into Gwynedd at this time, I assure you that it was never Prince Miklos' intention, this time around, to commit Torenthi troops to any major incursion into Gwynedd. I will respect that intention and will not even suggest that you should go against it."

He waited for their sullen rumble of agreement to die down, sensing that the critical decision was past.

"Practicalities yet remain," he said, when he again had their attention. "With the concurrence of his Highness' senior officers, I intend that we shall begin withdrawal from Culliecairn at dawn, banners flying and drums beating. I shall have the appropriate notifications drawn up and sent to the Gwynedd camp within the hour. Meanwhile, I shall personally keep vigil beside my cousin's body through the night. Those who wish to do the same are invited to join me."

CHAPTER EIGHTEEN

For gold is tried in the fire, and acceptable men in
the furnace of adversity.

—Ecclesiasticus 2:5

The Kheldour commanders met the king's party as they rejoined the Gwynedd line, anxious and agitated to learn of
Sudrey's death. Corban was detailed to take her body back to
Lochalyn and her daughter; Sighere and Graham remained. It
was clear they did not blame Rhys Michael for what had
happened—Sudrey had known at least some of the danger—
but the king felt a grief akin to their own as he continued
numbly on toward the Gwynedd camp.

"Exactly what happened out there?" Rhun demanded, riding
at his knee. He kept glancing back over his shoulder at the distant Torenth line, now in obvious agitation, anxious lest the fall
of Miklos provoke a Torenthi attack. Manfred was on the
king's other side, Cathan and Fulk now following with Sighere
and Graham. A score of *Custodes* knights had replaced the
archers and rode close all around them.

"Miklos broke the truce, just as you said he would, but for
different reasons than we feared," Rhys Michael said. "I don't
think it's appropriate that I go into details right now. Let's see
if his men are going to respect the truce or attack us."

The reasoning seemed to satisfy Rhun for the moment—and
gave Rhys Michael a chance to think about what he was going
to tell the earl marshal when the inevitable reckoning came. He
cradled his injured hand to his breast as they rode, for the initial shock of the injury was wearing off, and the hand had begun to throb.

They drew up on a rise just outside the Gwynedd camp to await a Torenthi response. None came. After nearly an hour of watching and waiting and weighing the military factors, Rhun and his commanders decided that, with darkness coming on, an immediate attack was not likely. Leaving Joshua Delacroix in command at the perimeter, Rhun then escorted the king back to the command tent, accompanied by Manfred, Sighere, Graham, and the king's aides. Master Stevanus had been pacing back and forth before the tent, having been informed of the king's injury, and now came to take his royal patient in charge.

"Let's go inside and have a look at that," he said, as the king swung a leg over his horse and gently eased to the ground, trying not to jar his hand.

The king followed meekly into the command tent and sat where he was directed, on the edge of a camp bed. Father Lior was already there and waiting. As Stevanus came to crouch beside the king and began prodding at the gash in the red leather gauntlet, bidding Fulk to bring a rack of candles nearer, Rhun and Lior came to hover like two predatory vultures. Cathan knelt unobtrusively to unbuckle the king's spurs—and also stay close in case of need. Manfred remained near the entrance with Sighere and Graham, now anticipating a message instead of an attack from the Torenthi.

"Now, what the devil happened out there?" Rhun demanded. "You said Miklos broke the truce."

"He seemed ready to pull out—though we hadn't yet gotten to his terms," Rhys Michael said, wincing at Stevanus' ministrations. "Then he attacked Lady Sudrey with magic. In retrospect, I'm sure that's why he was so keen to have her come along. He felt she'd betrayed her family and her race by marrying Eastmarch. When some of the magic started spilling over to me, she interposed herself to protect me. She gave her life in my defense."

"I shouldn't have thought she was strong enough to stand against a Deryni like Miklos," Lior said. "You almost looked as if you were involved in it, too."

Rhys Michael gasped and tried to pull away as Stevanus attempted to straighten out his shattered fingers.

"I—don't remember that part very clearly," he managed to whisper. "I—think she somehow—pulled energy from me, to give her more power against him. He was still too much for her, though. If his horse hadn't exploded, he might well have—aiie!"

"Sorry," Stevanus murmured. "Lord Rhun, I'm going to have to ask you to continue this conversation after I've dealt with his hand. There's already a great deal of swelling. I'm going to have to cut away the gauntlet before I can even begin to assess the damage. Cathan, pour his Highness a double dose of syrup of poppies, would you? This isn't going to be pleasant."

Clearly unsatisfied, Rhun withdrew to the entrance of the command tent as Stevanus set to work, consulting in low tones with Manfred, Sighere, and Graham, though Lior remained to watch. Rhys Michael's first glimpse of the purpling flesh and the blood and dirt-caked laceration convinced him that he would rather have been almost anywhere than where he was, though he drank down only half the painkiller Cathan brought him.

"I'd rather not take too much of this until we know how Torenth is going to react," he said to Stevanus, as he handed back the cup, sucking in breath through clenched teeth as the surgeon's probing shifted broken bones.

"Very well, but don't say I didn't warn you. Once we get this clean, it's going to want suturing before I try to set it. How well it will ever hold a sword again remains to be seen."

"If I must, I'll learn to fight left-handed. Just get on with it."

Fulk went to fetch towels and a basin of warm water, and Stevanus set about assembling splints and bandages and other necessaries. Cathan helped the king shed his brigandine and the close-fitting leather tunic underneath, for it became clear that the narrow sleeves would not allow removal once the hand was bandaged. Even without bandages, the movement necessary to ease the hand through the sleeve was excruciating. Rhys Michael was shivering in after-reaction as he eased back against a stack of pillows and gladly let Cathan help shift his booted feet up onto the bed. Baring his torso had also revealed several substantial bruises forming, though he had not been aware of being struck at the time.

Very shortly, Fulk brought the warm water, setting the basin on a low table at Rhys Michael's side so he could immerse his hand. The warmth was somewhat soothing initially—but only until Stevanus began cleaning away the blood and dirt from his wound.

He tried to distance himself from the discomfort. Laying his good arm across his closed eyes, he attempted to set the pain aside and let himself float. As he gradually began to feel the effects of the painkiller and relax a little, he let his thoughts rove back over the events of the past several hours—and suddenly recalled where he had seen the face that replaced that of Hombard, out on the field. He wondered whether Rhun and the others had noticed the change.

"Rhun, the man we thought was Hombard was Deryni," he said, opening his eyes to search for the earl marshal, who turned at his words. "He may even have been Marek of Festil."

"That's impossible," Rhun said, coming over to him. "He was far too old. Besides, we tested him with *merasha*."

"No, we tested the *first* man," Rhys Michael pointed out. "The man who rode out with Miklos *looked* like the man we tested—and I had no reason, at the time, to doubt it—but his face changed while Miklos and Sudrey were throwing around all that magic, and he tried to join in. Things were happening very quickly, but I'd swear he was the same man who came to Javan's coronation as Miklos' aide. Is it possible that could have been Marek, in both instances?"

Rhun pulled a camp stool to the left side of the bed and sat, as the others also drew closer to listen.

"It can't have been Marek," Rhun murmured. "Not even Miklos would have had the audacity to bring the Festillic Pretender to the coronation of his chief rival."

"So one would think," Rhys Michael said, glad for the distraction as Stevanus removed his hand from the basin and laid it dripping on a clean towel. "But, how better to evaluate the opposition? And how would *we* have known? I should think that by now it's clear that Miklos had the audacity to try just about anything he chose. Has anyone ever *seen* Marek of Festil?"

"I once saw a portrait of his father, King Imre, at one of the Order's abbeys," Father Lior ventured. "One would expect at least a family resemblance, especially given the mother."

"Describe the man in the portrait," Rhun ordered, turning to look at the priest.

Lior frowned, casting back in memory. "Slender—not a very large man, I shouldn't think. Very fair skin, but dark hair to his shoulders. Fine features: a thin face, a straight, elegant nose, slightly protruding eyes—dark brown, they were. I would have to say that the expression was a bit insipid-looking, though."

Rhys Michael closed his eyes, trying to ignore the bite of Stevanus' needle as the surgeon began setting sutures, for the image Lior had conjured coincided very closely with the face he had glimpsed on the field—and the face of Miklos' aide at the coronation, neither of which Lior had ever seen. Could he really have come face-to-face with Marek of Festil and not known it—and not once but twice?

"You've certainly described the man who came to the coronation with Miklos," Rhun said to the priest, confirming at least that part of Rhys Michael's impression. "By God, I suppose he *could* have been Imre's son."

"He has also described the man I saw today," Rhys Michael said. He winced as Stevanus' needle bit again. "With both Marek and Miklos ranged against her, Lady Sudrey's defense is all the more remarkable. And we have Divine Providence to thank for—"

He broke off as Lord Joshua Delacroix came into the tent and handed a wax-sealed packet to Rhun.

"This just came in, my lord," Joshua said. "A herald brought it. I suspect they didn't think we'd believe a white flag."

Manfred came to look over Rhun's shoulder as the earl marshal hurriedly broke the seals and unfolded the single sheet of parchment.

" 'Prince Marek of Festil, rightful King of Gwynedd, unto the Haldane usurper,' " Rhun read aloud. " 'Know that I hold you personally responsible for the death of my well-beloved cousin and brother-in-law, the Prince Miklos of Torenth. Be assured that further communication will be forthcoming from the king his brother.

" 'In order to provide a fitting escort for my cousin's body, I shall begin an immediate withdrawal of the troops formerly under his command, commencing at dawn. No interference in this withdrawal will be tolerated. While the present circumstances have obliged me to decline further confrontation at this time, be assured that I shall continue to press my claim to what is mine. I now know your measure and will take appropriate steps to utterly destroy you.' Signed Marek *Princeps*."

"Insolent puppy," Manfred growled, reaching for the missive. "Let me see that letter."

Rhun shrugged and handed it over. "Yes, well. If he's pulling out of Culliecairn, slinking home with his tail between his legs, we've at least won this round. Later on, Arion may try to make life difficult, but we'll worry about that if it happens. At least we seem to have averted this particular battle. Joshua,

we'd better set patrols to keep an eye on things through the
night and to monitor the withdrawal. I'm sure my lords of
Claibourne and Marley will oblige by providing scouts with local expertise." Sighere and Graham nodded. "Manfred, what
do you think about pickets?"

As they withdrew to the other side of the tent to discuss logistic considerations, Stevanus finished his suturing and set
about the more delicate and painful task of easing shattered
bones back into place. Even with the thick piece of leather
Cathan gave him to bite down on, and Cathan himself to help
hold the arm steady for the surgeon's work, it was all Rhys
Michael could do to stay still and not cry out. He was exhausted and drenched with perspiration by the time Stevanus
finished, with bandages immobilizing his wrist along a flat
length of wood that extended down the forearm and into the
palm, curving the shattered fingers around its end and closing
the hand in an approximation of gripping a sword.

"I wish I could tell you that there won't be any impairment
of movement," Stevanus said, plucking the bit of leather from
between the king's teeth. "The hand has a lot of bones, most
of them fairly fragile, none of which are improved by having
a horse step on them. Don't be surprised if some bone splinters
work their way to the surface during the healing process. I've
done my best for you, but I'm not a Deryni Healer."

As the battle surgeon set about rigging a sling to support the
arm, Rhys Michael closed his eyes briefly and considered his
next move. He had not reckoned on becoming injured; it put
him far more at the mercy of the great lords and those who
served them. What he was contemplating carried some risks,
but there probably was not going to be a better time. The great
lords had left the tent during the process of setting the hand,
unsettled by his silent endurance, and only Cathan and Fulk remained in attendance with Stevanus.

"Maybe we'd be better off if we still had Healers around,"
the king murmured. "I'd certainly welcome one, right about
now."

Stevanus gave him a fleeting, uncomfortable smile as he
tucked the end of a bandage in place. "If we could trust one
not to do other things besides heal, so would I," he replied.
"But you saw today how the Deryni keep their word."

As Stevanus turned away to top up the dose of painkiller the
king had not finished earlier, Rhys Michael sent a quick summons to Cathan, who came to help him as he sat up and swung

his feet to the floor. At the same time, he advised Cathan of what he intended. Nodding, Cathan laid a mantle around his bare shoulders, then casually rejoined Fulk as Stevanus turned back, the little metal cup in his hand again.

"This should help you sleep through the night," Stevanus said. "The hand is going to throb for the first few days—maybe longer—but you should feel better after a good night's sleep. You look totally knackered right now, and small wonder."

Declining to take the cup himself, for even his good hand was none too steady, Rhys Michael nodded and set his hand on Stevanus', helping guide the cup to his lips. He drank deeply, but then he used the bond of flesh to seize control. The surgeon shuddered but could not resist, his eyes closing. Cathan had touched Fulk at the same moment and the aide stood likewise entranced.

"Stevanus, listen very carefully," Rhys Michael murmured, closing his good hand more securely around Stevanus' and drawing the surgeon nearer to crouch at his feet. "From this point on, regardless of what other orders you may receive, and from whom, my orders will take precedence. You will never reveal that I have given you these orders, but all your actions will be focused toward preserving me in life and health. Under no circumstances will you ever give me *merasha*; if you are ordered to do so by one of the great lords, you will pretend to comply, but will give me some other drug with a similar effect. Nod your head if you understand."

Stevanus' head nodded once in agreement.

"Good. Now, how long will the effects of this last, if I drink it all?"

"Only through the night, Sire, though it will be a heavy sleep."

Nodding, Rhys Michael drained the remainder of the cup, then brought the surgeon back to his feet and released his hand.

"That sounds just about right," he said, easing out of the link. "I don't know what will have happened by morning, but I need to be able to ride at the head of my troops, if necessary. It's important that the men see that I'm still alive and unharmed. Well, relatively unharmed." He jutted his chin toward his bandaged hand as he got shakily to his feet, leaning heavily on Stevanus' arm.

"Sometime tomorrow, I'll also need to pay a courtesy call

on Lady Stacia. She's now given both her parents in my service, and I owe her the respect of my presence at her mother's funeral; I expect it will be the day after tomorrow. Before I leave, I'll also confirm her and her husband in the Eastmarch titles, since I'm here. It makes no sense for them to come all the way back to Rhemuth, especially if this border area is apt to stay a bit unstable for a while."

"You'll have to take up the scheduling with Lord Rhun, Sire, but the physical demands don't sound too difficult," Stevanus agreed. "Jostling that hand won't be comfortable, but you'll find that out the first time you do it."

Rhys Michael stifled a yawn as he hugged the hand closer to his chest. "I'm already well aware of that, Stevanus. It is hardly one of the great mysteries of life."

Stevanus chuckled. "I'll come along to help see you settled in your own bed, Sire. It wouldn't do to have you fall on the way back to your tent and have the men think you're hurt worse than you are—or drunk."

In the gathering darkness outside the command tent, three men in the rough tweeds of the Eastmarch borders watched from the shadows as the king emerged on the arm of the battle surgeon called Stevanus, also accompanied by his aides. Though a mantle was thrown around the royal shoulders, mostly covering his naked torso, the right hand and forearm were bandaged almost to the elbow and supported by a sling. He kept the arm close to his body as he walked, his balance steadied against the surgeon's arm, face taut and pale in the torchlight brought by the pair of guards who fell into step around him.

That they were bound for the king's tent was almost certain. He did not appear to be in custody. Exchanging silent agreement, the watching three separated to skirt ahead along the route they expected the royal party to take, observing the royal progress, keeping their passage as unobtrusive as possible. As king, surgeon, and aides disappeared inside the tent that served as royal residence in the field, with the Haldane standard stirring lazily in the evening breeze before it, the three joined up again, staying well back from the clear area in front of the royal tent and the sentries guarding it.

The tent itself was altogether too well guarded, as it had been since the arrival of the royal troops, with torches set around it and *Custodes* knights detailed to walk its perimeter, always within sight of one another. When the surgeon alone emerged, a few minutes later, the three watched in silence until he had disappeared in the direction of the command tent with the soldiers who had escorted him, then melted away into the darkness themselves.

Later, in their own tent, where loyal retainers could ensure their privacy, the three huddled together to compare impressions regarding the events of the afternoon and evening.

"His injury may or may not be serious," Ansel murmured, as the other two bent to listen. "He didn't look too bad when he rode in."

"Speaking from a Healer's perspective, he looked shocky to me," Tieg whispered. "I don't know what happened to his hand, but Stevanus was a long time about whatever he had to do to it, even allowing for being human."

"I questioned one of the archers on that point, after I'd Read his account of all the magic flying around," Jesse said. "He thought a horse might have stepped on the hand. How seriously remains to be seen. The man didn't see much sign of bleeding, but that isn't necessarily good."

"True enough," Ansel agreed. "If he did get stepped on, then it could be anything from a bad bruise to badly broken bones. That's his sword hand, too."

Tieg snorted. "It doesn't much matter which hand it is, pain-wise. It's going to slow him down."

"Don't even think about trying to sneak in and help him," Ansel said, looking at him sharply. "At least right now, until we know more, we can't afford to risk losing you."

Tieg looked a little sullen, but could not disagree with the logic.

"Right, then," Ansel murmured. "I think we'd better let Joram know what's happened. This has all taken a turn that I don't think anyone expected—least of all, the king. I don't know how much of what went on out there was his doing, but Sudrey ended up dead, and probably Miklos as well. I also don't know what kinds of questions Rhun has already asked, but I hope to God that the king has answers."

Jesse nodded. "Well, I don't think he's going to be having answers to much of anything else tonight. If Stevanus had to set broken bones, he's probably given him a stiff sedative and painkiller—which would account for his somewhat unsteady movements. Do you want to notify Joram, or shall I?"

"I'll do it," Ansel said. "And let's do put a watch on his tent through the night, just in case. After that, you'd better turn

in—both of you. I think we've learned about all we can without interviewing some of the principals—which isn't going to
be possible—and it's getting too late to be out and about in the
camp without arousing suspicion."

"Agreed," Jesse murmured, and took his leave to go and set
up the desired surveillance. Tieg, though none too happy with
the arrangement, retired to the doorway of the tent to sit as
guardian while Ansel shifted over to his bedroll and stretched
out, starting to compose himself to reach out for the contact
with Joram.

CHAPTER NINETEEN

Who will bring me into the strong city?
—Psalms 60:9

Rhys Michael Haldane knew nothing of the efforts expended in his behalf that night. Soon oblivious, thanks to Stevanus' drug, he dreamed deep, disturbing dreams that he could not remember upon awakening—though at least he did sleep pain-free through the night, as the surgeon had promised.

The sounds of the awakening camp and the throb of his hand woke him a little after dawn, with a dull headache behind his eyes, a foul-tasting mouth, and a ferocious thirst. Cathan was asleep in a chair beside his camp bed, and Fulk had brought hot water for morning ablutions—and ale to quell the thirst. He felt a little better once he had drunk it down, but his whole body ached.

He was appalled to discover how helpless he was, with the use of only one hand, and found himself obliged to suffer the ministrations of both his aides to help him wash and dress. Since no one had come to tell him otherwise, he decided that armor might not be necessary, at least for the moment, and bade them help him don a full-sleeved linen tunic over leather breeches and boots. Stevanus came in just as Cathan was attempting to readjust the sling that supported his right arm, so the king enlisted his assistance. The hand was throbbing in time with his pulse beat, but Stevanus advised against another dose of the syrup of poppies until after he had eaten. The king had Cathan put a light cloak on him, fastening it at the shoulder with the Haldane brooch, and drew part of it over the sling before heading over to the command tent for the morning briefing.

Welcome news greeted him when he met his great lords over a substantial breakfast. No incidents had marred the night's peace, and true to Marek's missive of the night before, Torenthi troops had begun to ride out of Culliecairn at first light. The long column of them now stretched far up the Coldoire Pass to disappear into the steppes of Tolan. There had been no further Torenthi communication.

"Some of Sighere's scouts saw what they believed to have been Prince Miklos' funeral cortege leaving with the first outriders, just at dawn," Manfred told him. "There were several horse litters and an ecclesiastical contingent that probably was the patriarch's party. The last of the troops should clear by midafternoon, so that we can go and inspect the city."

Meanwhile, Marley and Eastmarch skirmish parties were observing the Torenthi line of retreat, dogging their heels, prepared to encourage stragglers. After breakfast, Rhun and Manfred rode out with Corban and another of the Eastmarch commanders to oversee, along with Lord Joshua and the principal *Custodes* captains. The king was left in the charge of Father Lior and Master Stevanus, with reluctant permission to ride to Lochalyn and pay his respects to the castle's new mistress. To his disgust, Lior insisted upon bringing along a *Custodes* escort, including the detested Gallard de Breffni.

On the short ride up to Lochalyn, with the pain of his hand throbbing up his arm with every jolting step, Rhys Michael racked his brain for an excuse to shake his keepers and speak privately with Stacia. A ghost of a plan was taking shape in his mind, but it would come to naught without the support of the Kheldour lords.

To his surprise and relief, he found the Duke of Claibourne's banner flying alongside that of Eastmarch as they rode beneath the gatehouse arch, with at least a dozen dour Claibourne men drawn up in a guard of honor outside the castle's chapel. Gallard de Breffni's brusque condescension proved to be his undoing—and Rhys Michael's salvation—for when Gallard attempted to send his *Custodes* in to supplant the duke's men, ordering the borderers aside for the king to pass, Rhys Michael had to intervene before indignation and verbal resistance escalated into armed conflict. Following on the heels of such evenhanded mediation, his courteous request to present his condolences privately to the bereaved countess enlisted the immediate support of the duke's men, who made it abundantly clear to Gallard, Lior, and their *Custodes* companions that the king might enter, but none other.

"I think it might be politic if you took your men up to the hall for some refreshment, my lord," he told the angry Gallard. "Perhaps some wine will cool hot tempers. I should hate to see our Kheldish hosts offended over so trifling an issue."

When Lior would have tried to stay behind, Rhys Michael put him in his place as well.

"Please go with Lord Gallard, Father. I may be some little while. Cathan and Fulk will wait here for me—and Master Stevanus, if you wish. Lady Stacia's mother gave her life in my service yesterday. The least I can do is to offer my condolences and spend a time in prayer with her."

It was the sort of pious justification to which even Lior could hardly take exception. Not giving the *Custodes* priest a chance to find one, Rhys Michael turned and went into the chapel.

The faint scent of incense and beeswax hung on the air as he quietly closed the door behind him and moved down the center of the tiny nave, accompanied by the faint jingle of his spurs. The open coffin was set on hurdles on a rich Kheldish carpet just before the altar, guarded by six thick, honey-colored candles on tall candlesticks. A proud, straight-backed figure gowned and coiffed in black sat at the coffin's head, her back to the door. Young Claibourne was kneeling at the altar rail directly left of the coffin, face in his hands and huddled down in a mantle of grey border tweed. He glanced back at the sound of the king's approach and would have risen in surprised respect, but Rhys Michael waved him back to his knees as he paused to bow to the altar and then passed to the coffin's right.

His unexpected presence elicited a tiny gasp from Stacia, who had her infant son on her lap. Her pretty face was pinched and pale against the black veil binding the fiery hair, all her vitality drained away in the wake of this new grief. Beyond her in the open coffin, her mother lay wrapped in a cocoon of fine blue border tweed, face lightly shrouded by a veil of white lawn.

Rhys Michael crossed himself awkwardly with his bandaged hand and sank to his knees beside the coffin, steadying himself against its edge with his good hand as he bowed his head. It was he who was responsible for Stacia's bereavement—both father and mother lost in the space of less than a fortnight, and in his service. When he had knelt here with Sudrey, not three days before, he had never dreamed that he would cause her so soon to lie at the side of the loyal Hrorik, whose body lay beneath the very floor where her coffin rested.

As he had on his ride from the Gwynedd encampment, he found himself reliving the events of the day before, well aware that he might not have survived without her help—and that *she* might still be alive, had it not been for him. He found himself wondering, not for the first time, whether she really would have died from her injuries, had she not chosen to hasten the process with her own magic—and whether he dared ask the help of her kin.

After offering a prayer for the soul of Sudrey of Eastmarch, and for divine mercy on Deryni in general, he got awkwardly to his feet and gently drew aside the veil of white lawn to press a respectful kiss to her forehead. He made himself draw a deep, steadying breath as he let the veil fall back in place and turned to face her daughter and her nephew. Young Claibourne had gotten to his feet as the king rose, and both his face and Stacia's were unreadable.

"Sudrey of Eastmarch was a very great lady," the king said softly. "Would that I had had the opportunity to know her better."

Claibourne glanced at his cousin a little uncertainly, then back at the king.

"If the King's Grace were more inclined to visit his northern provinces, he would hae had such opportunity," the duke said, though his tone conveyed no hint of disapproval. "E'en so, she kept faith with yer Royal House."

Rhys Michael cradled his aching arm in his good one, absently kneading at the stiff muscles along the forearm.

"Had it been wholly in my choice," he said quietly, "I would have come. Of all the great lords of Gwynedd, none have served my House half so well as the sons and grandsons of Sighere of Kheldour—and this daughter by marriage," he added, nodding toward Sudrey's coffin. "Claibourne, Eastmarch, and Marley—these are the brightest jewels in my crown."

"If they be yer brightest jewels, then why did ye no come?" Stacia asked. "Are ye no the king? Whose choice was't, if not yours?"

Rhys Michael glanced at her bleakly, wondering how much of the truth he dared to tell them—and set to Truth-Read them.

With Rhun and the others off on other business, this might be a unique opportunity to sound out the loyalties of Kheldour. Graham and Stacia were of an age with himself, of a younger generation than had spawned the great lords who ruled in Gwynedd, and Graham's father had been murdered through the great lords' treachery. Perhaps Kheldour could become the source of military strength Rhys Michael would need to take back control of his crown. But he would never know, if he did not ask.

He glanced back at the church door, still closed, then moved closer to the pair, drawing Graham with him to kneel at Stacia's feet.

"Please listen closely, because I may not have much time," he murmured. "If any of my men should enter besides my light-haired aide, we are praying together for Sudrey's soul. The great lords have gone to elaborate lengths to conceal it, but believe me when I tell you that I have been a prisoner for these six years of my reign, ever since they arranged for the murder of my brother and seized control of Rhemuth."

"The murder—" Graham began. "Ye mean, King Javan?"

Rhys Michael nodded.

"But, they said that renegade Michaelines—"

"It wasn't renegade Michaelines," Rhys Michael said softly. "His own great lords betrayed him. And that same day that Javan was killed, probably at the very same hour, Archbishop Hubert and others took me prisoner in Rhemuth Castle. They drugged me and forced me to watch while they slaughtered the few men still loyal to Javan. The shock made my wife miscarry of what would have been our firstborn son."

"Dear holy Mother," Stacia whispered, wide-eyed, clutching her own son more closely to her breast. "But, *why?*"

"To retain their power, of course. Javan was proving to be too powerful a king. They'd meant to pass over him in my favor. They'd hoped to keep him in the monastery and shunt him off into a harmless religious vocation. They didn't realize that he himself had sought out the monastery as a place to grow to manhood in safety, while he also gained the education he would need to rule. He never intended to be a monk. Weren't you surprised when you heard that Alroy was dead, and it was Javan to be crowned, not me?"

"Well, aye," Graham admitted. "But you didnae seem upset by it, when we came tae Rhemuth fer his coronation."

"Of course I wasn't. Javan was always supposed to be king

after Alroy. Knowing what befell your father, Graham, believe me when I tell you that the great lords have stopped at nothing to retain the power they seized after my father's death. All during my brother Alroy's reign, even once the legitimate regency had ended, he was kept drugged to ensure his compliance, and the great lords actually ruled."

"D'ye think my father found out, an' that's why they killed him?" Graham asked, horrified.

"If he didn't know, he would have found out, if he'd spent much time at Court," Rhys Michael replied. "And I'm convinced that the only reason you remained safe was because your uncles were quick enough to uphold your rights and then smart enough to pull back to the fastness of the borders and the Kheldour highlands, where the regents dared not come. As long as none of you tried to interfere in Rhemuth, they were content to let you remain unmolested in the north; but you saw how savagely Murdoch went after Hrorik, when you came to Javan's coronation."

"But, they all swore Javan allegiance, before God an' on holy relics," Graham murmured. "I was there; I heard them do it!"

"Aye, and they were forsworn within the year," Rhys Michael replied. "Javan saw the danger from the beginning and tried to warn me, but I didn't want to see. As he began gaining strength, they began trying to undermine him. They were very good at it. Both Hubert and Manfred secretly encouraged me to marry, even though Javan warned me of the danger, if there were minor heirs while the great lords still had such power. I didn't believe him—I didn't *want* to believe him, because I really do love Michaela—but I agreed to back off.

"When it became clear that I wasn't going to go against my brother, they had me kidnapped by 'Ansel MacRorie' and 'renegade Michaelines,' then had me 'rescued' by Manfred's men. They even arranged some convincing injuries in the process— and there I was, 'safe' in Manfred's castle to recover, and with Michaela conveniently there to nurse me back to health. She didn't know they were using her, of course. We both believed it was all real at the time, and we let the circumstances carry us right into marriage. Once Michaela was pregnant, it was only a matter of time before they set up Javan's murder."

Graham was still shaking his head slightly. "I cannae believe they would murder an anointed king," he whispered. "I mean, I dinnae doubt yer word, Sire, but—"

Rhys Michael glanced back at the door, then returned his gaze to Graham. "I understand," he said. "I didn't want to believe it either, at first. There's worse, too. Once Javan was dead, they kept me drugged until after my coronation, the way they'd done with Alroy. And once Michaela had recovered from her miscarriage, they—ordered us to start producing Haldane heirs."

"They ordered—" Stacia began. "But, ye cannae *order* someone tae do that."

Rhys Michael allowed himself a bitter smile. "To survive, and to ensure the survival of one's line, one learns to be far more flexible than you can possibly imagine, my lady," he said softly. "We delayed as long as we dared, but the ultimate threat was that if *I* didn't impregnate my wife, there were willing volunteers waiting in the wings to ensure that the job got done—and who would have known? Neither of us were ever allowed unsupervised contact with the outside world. From the time Alroy died, the eventual aim has been to secure the succession and then eliminate both Javan and me—which would give them another long regency in which to further entrench their power.

"They've got one heir now, and they'll have another after the first of the year. I expect I'm living on borrowed time. By the time my sons come of age, the authority of the crown will be so thoroughly bound up in the hands of Gwynedd's great lords that they won't even know it could be any other way. Unless . . . listen carefully," Rhys Michael said, drawing the two close. "I have a plan."

Stacia dared to lay a hand on his—cautious, tentative, sympathetic.

"Ye—dinnae sound like ye expect to get back to Rhemuth alive, Sire."

He shrugged. "Rhun probably would just as soon I'd died yesterday with Sudrey. It would have made life a great deal less complicated for him and the other great lords—though at least there're three fewer of them than when we rode out of Rhemuth."

Graham nodded, tight-jawed. "We'll no miss the likes o' Paulin an' Albertus," he muttered. "*Custodes* bastards! But—how can we help? Wha' can we do fer ye?"

Rhys Michael closed his eyes briefly in relief. "Do you mean that?" he whispered.

"Of course I do," Graham replied. "The Haldanes have al-

ways been friends o' my House. It wasnae Haldane treachery
that slew my father. I know my uncle Sighere would agree,
too. How can we help?"

Rhys Michael swallowed with difficulty and touched his
good hand to Graham's. "Now that you've offered, I'm—not
sure. I'd hoped for your support, but I haven't had much time
to work through the details. Eventually, I may need military
support, but for now—" He raised an eyebrow in sudden inspi-
ration. "Would you and Sighere agree to be appointed regents
for my son, if anything should happen to me before he comes
of age?"

"Regents? Aye, whate'er ye wish, Sire." Graham paused a
beat. "Are ye sure?"

. "Oh, I am. The more I think about it, the surer I am. I know
that neither of you could afford to neglect your own duties to
be at Court all the time, but maybe you could take turns in
Rhemuth. A regency council is already specified in my will;
they made me sign what they wanted, years ago. But now that
Paulin and Albertus are out of the running, they'll at least have
to draw up a codicil. Maybe I could draft a codicil of my own
before I leave; could you get me a local priest to witness it?
And I'd try to set it up so that the other regents couldn't boot
out either of you, the way they did with Duke Ewan and with
Bishop Alister. If both of them had remained regents, the way
my father wanted, Javan probably would still be alive and—"

He broke off as the door rattled behind them—Cathan's
warning that they might be about to lose their privacy—and
got to his feet.

"All right, we've got to make this quick," he murmured. "I
don't know how long Cathan can hold off whoever's out there.
Now, Rhun already knows I won't leave until after Lady
Sudrey's funeral; try to delay that as late in the day as possible,
so that by the time we've held court, he can't possibly try to
leave before the next morning. I'd also like to move back to
quarters here in the castle—tonight. There's no privacy at all in
the camp, and it's going to take Cathan most of a night to draw
up the document and make the necessary copies. Graham, I'll
ask you to brief your uncle and line up that priest." He drew
a breath and shifted his gaze to Stacia, who was hanging on
his every word.

"My lady, I haven't forgotten you. By statute, I can't appoint a woman as regent who isn't of the Royal Family, but I'll
be making a formal acknowledgment of you and your husband

as the new Earl and Countess of Eastmarch, and taking your oaths of fealty. It will fall upon the two of you to help keep the peace here in the north, when Graham or Sighere or both are needed for extended duty in the capital."

"I understand, Sire. Ye have my support nonetheless—an' that o' my lord."

"Thank you. One last thing. Graham, it won't be possible for all of us actually to sign the documents in one another's presence—that's why it's essential that we have a good man as witness. However, as a sign of your approval and support of Stacia and Corban here in Kheldour, it wouldn't be inappropriate for you and Sighere to offer me reaffirmation of the oaths you swore at my coronation, once they're invested. We could agree among us privately that this also serves as a public affirmation of taking on potential regents' duty, and so specify in the document."

Graham nodded, wide-eyed.

"And that," Rhys Michael said, kneeling down at the altar rail on her other side, "is about all we have time for today. I suggest we all pray."

He had time to bow his head into his good hand before the door rattled behind him again and then opened. It was the Earl of Kierney who had come to fetch him—Iver MacInnis, Manfred's son, fully harnessed and armed for the field as he came striding down the little nave.

"Culliecairn's vacant, Sire," he said, including Graham and Stacia in his nod of address, as Cathan also appeared in the doorway. "The last of the Torenthi troops disappeared up the Coldoire Pass about an hour ago. My father says that if your hand isn't giving you too much discomfort, you might want to ride up and have a look. Lord Corban has already begun investing the castle with Eastmarch troops. You could even stay in Culliecairn tonight, if you wish."

Relieved that Iver seemed to be offering a choice, Rhys Michael got to his feet. His hand was throbbing again, but he knew he must not let that slow him down.

"I'll concede that the thought of a proper bed is appealing, after camp last night," he said, "but I've already accepted Lady Stacia's kind invitation to stay here, as a mark of respect for her mother. It's also occurred to me that we'll need to arrange for a formal court tomorrow; immediately after the funeral would probably be best. I'll want to invest the new Earl and Countess of Eastmarch and take their oaths of fealty."

To his surprise, Iver agreed. "I believe Lord Rhun had already intended something of the sort, Sire. Did you wish to ride up anyway? We can be back before dusk."

Rhys Michael nodded, cradling the arm again. "The hand hurts, but I expected that it would. It's about time for more of Master Stevanus' painkiller. He tells me that tomorrow is apt to be the worst."

"My sympathies," Iver said, and actually meant it. "If you're ready, then, we ought to go."

After taking his leave of Stacia and Graham, Rhys Michael rode back to the Gwynedd camp with Iver and Lior and his *Custodes* escort. While Cathan and Fulk helped him arm—for he must look fit, even if he felt as if his whole body had been trampled, not just his hand—he managed to pass on to Cathan what was required in the way of documents. Since they had known of Hrorik's death before leaving Rhemuth, Cathan had been working en route to draw up the letters patent confirming Stacia and her husband as Earl and Countess of Eastmarch. Sudrey's death necessitated slight changes to the document—which provided perfect cover for Cathan to remain behind and also draft the codicil naming Graham and his uncle to any future regency.

"Consider the wording carefully," he murmured, as Cathan tightened down the buckles on the red brigandine. "It has to be unbreakable, and it has to stand up to the new will that I'll be forced to sign when we return. This may be the best hope yet, to at least help safeguard my sons, if anything happens to me."

He let Stevanus give him another half dose of the syrup of poppies before they rode out, and tried to set his mind against the pain that the drug could not control as he, Fulk, and Iver rode up to Culliecairn with a small escort to inspect the fruits of their past day's work.

In Rhemuth, while Rhys Michael rode toward Culliecairn, Queen Michaela gained her first inkling of some of those fruits as she strolled in the castle gardens with Rhysel. Earlier, they had taken advantage of the fine, sunny day to wash the queen's hair. Rather than remain cooped up in the solar with too many chattering ladies, Michaela decided to let it dry while she walked in the perfumed open air of the garden. She hummed snatches of a court tune as she paused to cut red roses climbing up a white-painted trellis, laying the blooms in a flat basket that Rhysel carried on her arm. The sun had kissed her face and hands with color, also lending highlights to her hair, which spilled past her hips in a fragrant cloud of wheaten glory.

After glancing around the garden with apparent indifference, Rhysel briefly closed her fingers round a handful of the tawny hair, then gestured toward a garden seat under the trellising.

"You're getting dry. Why don't you let me comb this again?"

Not thinking anything of the request, Michaela moved obediently under the trellising and sat down, closing her eyes as Rhysel set aside the basket and began gently combing through the damp tresses.

"Don't react, in case we're watched, but I heard from Joram last night," Rhysel murmured. "Culliecairn is resolved, and Prince Miklos is dead. So, unfortunately, is Sudrey of Eastmarch. She was Deryni, you know."

Michaela felt a cold claw clench at her insides, for Rhysel had not mentioned Rhysem, but she forced herself to keep her eyes closed as Rhysel kept combing, hoping nothing showed on her face.

"What about Rhysem?" she whispered.

"He's safe for the moment," Rhysel replied. "He had some kind of injury to his hand, but it doesn't appear to be too serious. What's potentially far more dangerous is that apparently there was a good deal of magic afoot when the king met Miklos. He'd taken Lady Sudrey with him, and most witnesses seem to think it was her magic that clashed with Miklos', but she wasn't thought to have that much power. Of course, no one really knew, because she put aside whatever she had when she took a human husband, and that's been twenty years ago."

"How—" Michaela had to pause to swallow before she could go on. "How did this meeting come to pass? I shouldn't have thought Rhun would let Rhysem meet Miklos face-to-face."

Rhysel shrugged and kept combing. "I can't tell you that. Joram had his information from Ansel, who isn't exactly in a position to ask the principals involved. All he's able to do right now is to observe—and be ready to step in, if that's possible and advisable. I hope to have more information after tonight. It's likely, though, that the army will be heading home in a few days. With any luck, you should have your Rhysem back within a fortnight."

Plucking one of the roses from the basket, Michaela brought it to her face and inhaled deeply of its perfume.

"Dear God, let it be so," she whispered.

She returned to her quarters to try to sleep after that, both heartened and uneasy about Rhysel's news—and obliged not to reveal, in any way, that her information was more current than what was in the letters she received almost daily from her husband.

The most recent had told of Albertus and the odd attack by bees, though she knew from Rhysel that Albertus now was dead, and Paulin as good as dead, and that the spy Dimitri had perished as well—and Rhysem had come through it all safely. She expected official confirmation of that news to arrive at any time. It would shake the despicable Archbishop Hubert to the very core of his substantial and sanctimonious self and leave the remaining great lords similarly discomfited, for it totally shifted the balance of power among those who continued to presume that they, and not the king, should govern Gwynedd.

Later that evening, as she paid her permitted visit to her young son, she hugged him close and kissed him before tucking him into bed, ruffling the thick, dark hair and reflecting that perhaps, if fate continued to smile on his father, young Owain might inherit a free kingdom after all.

CHAPTER TWENTY

Righteous lips are the delight of kings; and they love
him that speaketh right.

—Proverbs 16:13

It was not yet dark when the king's party returned to Lochalyn,
satisfied with the arrangements at Culliecairn, but Rhys Michael was exhausted. His hand had not ceased throbbing, and
he feared he was beginning to run a fever. After picking half-
heartedly at supper in the castle's hall, he asked Stevanus to
have a look.

"Maybe the bandages just need loosening," he said. "I expect it's more swollen than it was, but that's normal, isn't it?"

At Stacia's invitation, they retired to the lord's solar formerly shared by her parents, where his belongings had been
moved up from camp during his absence of the afternoon.
Though the new accommodation afforded greater comfort and
privacy, and a woman's touch gentled the process of baring the
hand for inspection, neither Stacia nor Stevanus looked particularly pleased. Most of the back of the hand was now a livid
purple, and the skin around the sutures in the laceration was
tight and shiny.

"There's certainly a good deal of swelling," Stevanus murmured, prodding at it gently, "but that isn't unexpected. I *am*
concerned about your fever. It could mean that an infection is
developing. I think I need not tell you that a horse's hoof
makes an incredibly filthy wound."

"But we cleaned it," Rhys Michael protested. He winced as
Stacia began applying a fresh dressing of sphagnum moss.

" 'Tis difficult tae clean sicht wounds properly," she murmured. "Ye shattered bones, too. That makes an injury like this especially dangerous."

"How dangerous?" Rhys Michael asked, turning his gaze on Stevanus.

The battle surgeon shrugged and began winding the bandages back over the splints. "I will not lie to you, Sire. Whenever bone is exposed to the air, there is danger. It could become necessary to take the hand. God knows, that would be a measure of last resort, for amputation carries its own dangers, but—"

"No," Rhys Michael whispered, hugging the wounded hand closer to his chest, remembering the Healer Tavis, who also had lost a hand. "Stevanus, I won't lose my hand. I won't!"

"We'll hope it doesn't come to that," Stevanus reassured him. "It's early on. A certain amount of fever is normal, with any wound. With luck, it will pass."

After Stacia had gone out, the surgeon prepared another draught of the syrup of poppies, watching the king drink it down before he left him to the ministrations of Cathan and Fulk for the night. When the drug had taken the edge from the pain but not yet made him too drowsy, Rhys Michael asked Cathan to show him the codicil he had drafted. Fulk had bedded down on a pallet near the door and, with a little encouragement from Cathan, was already fast asleep.

"I hope this is what you had in mind," Cathan said, perching on the edge of the bed beside the king. "If you approve, I'll make five copies during the night. I'm not sure exactly when we can arrange to get everybody to sign, but we'll manage something. At least Rhun has definitely agreed to stay through tomorrow night. Corban intends to host a supper after the funeral and court. I expect that will be our best opportunity, once the wine starts flowing."

He held a rushlight closer so that Rhys Michael could read through the text. It named Graham MacEwan, Duke of Claibourne, and Sighere of Marley as regents during any minority of the king's heir, to serve regardless of whatever other regents might be named in any present or future decretal or last will and testament of Rhys Michael Alister Haldane. The appointments could not be reversed save by the king himself or the resignation of the men themselves. In case Sighere died before a Haldane heir came of age, the document designated the twenty-year-old Sean Coris, Master of Marley, to serve as Sighere's replacement.

"You're sure you want to make this an irrevocable appointment?" Cathan said, when the king had read it through. "Rhysem, I know you trust Claibourne, because you had a chance to talk with him and Truth-Read him, but you hardly know Marley. You have only Claibourne's word that he'll even accept, under these terms and conditions, and you have no idea about Marley's son."

Rhys Michael closed his eyes. His medication was making him drowsy. "Sighere and his brothers have always been loyal to my line," he whispered. "Their father gave my father his unqualified loyalty and bound his three sons to my father as well. The blood runs true in the brothers' offspring; I must trust that it runs true in Sighere as well. Both Graham and Stacia trust him."

"Wouldn't it make more sense to appoint Stacia, then?" Cathan asked. "At least you know *she's* loyal. And she's got a few drops of Deryni blood, if that makes a difference."

"And I will cherish her for that, as well as for her loyalty today," he said, smiling as he glanced up at Cathan. "But I daren't appoint a woman as regent. The law forbids it and always has, except for members of the Royal Family. Besides that, I'm already treading on thin ice by trying to make this appointment at all. God alone knows whether it will stand up, if Graham has to exercise it. But at least he's a duke, so there's no one to outrank him."

Cathan allowed himself a sigh of exasperation, but he clearly could not argue his brother-in-law's point.

"I have to agree," he murmured. "Shall I make those copies, then? This is how you want it to read?"

Rhys Michael nodded, rubbing his upper arm above his bandages.

"I'd prefer to run it past more experienced legal minds, but we don't have that luxury. Make the five copies. Tomorrow we'll worry about how we're going to get them signed without Rhun or Manfred interfering."

Through the rest of the night he drifted fitfully in and out of sleep, unable to get comfortable, periodically aware of Cathan scratching away on his copies at a small table on the other side of the room, and that the rushlights burned nearly until dawn. On the occasions when he did dip deeper into sleep, his rest was marred by disturbing dreams that he could not remember on waking.

It was Fulk who came to rouse him, a few hours after dawn,

looking by far the freshest of the three of them for having had a full night's sleep. Rhys Michael himself was hardly more rested than when he had gone to bed. He suspected that his fever had worsened during the night—his whole right arm was hot, from shoulder to fingertips—but he made himself get up and wash and dress, for he *must* put in an appearance at Sudrey's funeral and the court and meal to follow.

Before the funeral, Rhun held an impromptu staff meeting in the castle's hall, to receive reports on the continued Torenthi withdrawal during the night and finalize plans for a departure on the morrow. Rhys Michael listened dutifully enough, brushing off Stevanus' attentions, for he did not want the surgeon to order him back to bed, but after drinking some ale he really did not want and eating a few mouthfuls of bread, he did accept another dose of painkiller.

The Requiem Mass for Sudrey of Eastmarch seemed to last forever, as he had feared. Being feverish, he bundled up in his crimson cloak with the Haldane brooch at the shoulder and alternated between shaking with chills and wanting to throw off all his clothes. The little chapel was packed, with people standing shoulder to shoulder, wall to wall, and even in the open doorway. Rhys Michael was feeling light-headed by the time it finished, but he could not even make an immediate escape, for Duke Graham had contrived to tell him, on the way into the chapel, that the priest, a Father Derfel, was utterly trustworthy and had agreed to witness the documents. But the king must make the final arrangements.

The priest disappeared into the little sacristy with his fresh-scrubbed altar servers, one of whom remained to extinguish the altar candles. The chapel quickly began to empty. Though Rhun and Manfred went out with the family, Graham gravely shepherding them as they headed toward the hall, where the court would follow, Rhys Michael kept back Cathan and Fulk—and Stevanus, lest there be any question, later on—and knelt near the front of the chapel in pretended prayer, waiting for the priest's servers to come out. Sudrey's closed coffin still lay before the altar, with four strong Eastmarch men waiting to lower it into its final resting place in the crypt once the mourners had gone.

Very shortly, the boys burst from the sacristy like exuberant puppies, their high spirits damping only momentarily as they saw him and made hurried bows before dashing on out the chapel door to the freedom of outdoors. Faintly smiling, Rhys

Michael glanced at his companions and got to his feet. He had liked what he Read of Father Derfel during the Mass. The man exuded an air of kindness—a quality he did not often see in the sour *Custodes* priests to whom he was accustomed.

"Wait here while I thank the good father for the Mass," he said. "I won't be but a few minutes. I know court will be waiting."

His smile dimmed as he passed close to Sudrey's coffin, where the Eastmarch men were starting to move the slabs away, opening the vault to receive her. Drawing a deep breath, he set his hand on the latch of the sacristy door and went in.

The priest was still in alb and stole, his back to the door, diligently shaking out the black chasuble he had worn. Gingerhaired and bearded, of indeterminate middle years, he looked around in some surprise as the king closed the door behind him.

"I hope I didn't startle you, Father," Rhys Michael said in a low voice. "I believe his Grace of Claibourne spoke to you earlier this morning—or perhaps last night."

The priest gave him a careful nod and laid the chasuble aside.

"He did that, Sire. If what he has told me is correct, ye tak a grave risk."

Rhys Michael allowed him a fleeting smile and rubbed at his aching arm. "I do, if my great lords find out what I've done while I'm still alive. For that reason, I must ask that you keep all knowledge of this under the Seal of the Confessional. Once I'm gone, of course, you're released from that Seal. Then I'll *want* the document to be broadcast as widely as possible."

"Ye have my word, Sire," the priest said, bowing slightly as he touched his right hand to the stole he still wore.

"Thank you." Rhys Michael pulled a much-folded copy of the draft of the text from inside his sling and passed it to the priest. "This is the draft version of the document I intend you to witness. Five copies have been drawn up in proper form. They'll need to be signed and sealed by the other principals before I sign. Do you mind if I sit while you read over it, Father? I'm feeling a bit light-headed. I fear my wound may be festering."

Quickly the priest procured a stool and shoved it under Rhys Michael as he sat, moving then to tilt the document by the better light from a lancet window beside the little vesting altar. He moved his lips as he read, his florid face going more and more pale, so that freckles stood out all across his tonsure and cheeks by the time he had finished.

"Sir, ye repose great trust in m'lords of Claibourne and Marley," he murmured. "Knowing both men, I believe such trust to be well placed, but ye *are* aware that if the document stands in law—that ye may appoint such regents—they cannae then be ousted?"

Rhys Michael sighed wearily and shook his head. "Father, if you're counseling caution, know that I must seize this opportunity while I may and trust that I have judged these men correctly. Once my great lords have me back in Rhemuth, there will be no further opportunity to adjust the terms of a future regency more to my liking and I cannot refuse to go back, or let my friends keep me here, for my wife and son and my unborn next heir lie totally in the great lords' power.

"As to whether the document will stand in law—that must be for others to determine, when and if it comes to that," he went on. "I can only do what best I may, while I yet live, to ensure that my sons have better regents than those with whom my brothers and I had to contend—if regents they must have. I pray, of course, that I shall live to see my sons' sons playing at my knee, serene in my old age, and free at last of the fetters of this past decade. But I harbour no illusions about my personal safety, once my queen is delivered of the child she now carries—especially if it is another prince, as I believe it to be."

He did not tell the priest that he already knew the child was another boy, for not even to a holy man dared he reveal that the Crown of Gwynedd again had Deryni connections. Even so, Father Derfel stared at him, mouth agape, then dropped to his knees at the king's feet.

"I am yer man, Sire," he whispered. "Earl Hrorik, God rest 'im, ever said yer line were brave and honorable, an' now I know it tae be true. But, how do ye mean to accomplish e'en this, if yer great lords watch ye so carefully?"

Rhys Michael rubbed his good hand over his face, trying to think. He was shivering with fever again, and even his good hand shook as he clasped it closer around the injured arm.

"After court, Sir Cathan will bring you the copies of the document. There are five: one each for Claibourne, Marley, and Lady Stacia, one for yourself, and one for me. The other principals will come to you individually during supper, in the place Lady Stacia shall designate, to sign and seal them in your presence. At some point I shall contrive to join you and add my own signature, such as it is." He slightly raised his bandaged hand. "That's another reason it's essential that I sign in your presence. I shall leave you my signet to seal the documents while I return to the hall, but you must get it back to me or to Sir Cathan as soon as possible, lest someone notice. I must also have my copy of the document before I leave tomorrow."

"I understand," the priest agreed. "But—Sire, are ye well enough to see this through? Ye look sommat feverish."

Rhys Michael touched the back of his good hand to his forehead and suppressed a shudder. "I *have* to be well enough, Father," he whispered. "I'm sure I'll be all right. Master Stevanus said I might expect a fever for the first few days." He indicated his bandaged hand and gave an ironic smile. "Did they tell you what happened? Somebody's damned horse *stepped* on me!"

Without invitation, the priest touched his hand to Rhys Michael's forehead and grimaced at the heat he felt. " 'Tis no matter fer jest, Sire," he murmured. "Are they giving ye sommat for the fever?"

The king shook his head. "Not that I know of. Just syrup of poppies for the pain. To be fair, the fever's only gotten bad in the last little while. But I have to make it through court."

"God willin', ye shall do, Sire," the priest replied. "May I tell Lady Stacia? Her dear mother taught her much o' the healing arts that is not widely known."

"She helped Stevanus change my dressing last night," Rhys Michael murmured. "I expect she's done all she can. But go ahead and tell her, if you think it might help."

A cautious rap at the door returned their attention to more immediate concerns.

"I'd better go," the king said, getting to his feet. "That will be Sir Cathan, warning me I'll be missed soon."

"Aye, Sire. May I offer ye t'drink before ye go? Ye should be havin' lots o' fluids, with that fever."

"If it isn't too much trouble, that would be very kind," the king replied.

Fetching a silver ewer from a credence table near the vesting altar, the priest set it beside the communion vessels he had brought in from Mass and swept the burse and pall and veil off the chalice.

"I noticed, by the way, that ye didnae come up for Communion," he said, as he poured wine into the chalice. "Was there a reason for that? Should ye be seeking me out for shriving?"

Rhys Michael snorted. "My great lords would never allow me to confess to a priest who isn't of the *Custodes* Order," he murmured. "Besides, I'd already eaten this morning. Master Stevanus wouldn't give me any more painkiller until I'd eaten something, and I thought that was more important than to keep the fast so that I could receive." He raised an eyebrow as the priest handed him the chalice, and asked, "Should I be drinking from this? I thought that holy vessels were reserved for holy things."

"What thing more holy than ministerin' tae one o' God's children who is ill?" Derfel replied with an arch smile. "Especially if that child be my anointed king. Would ye still be desirous o' receivin' Communion, Sire?"

Rhys Michael paused with the chalice halfway to his lips, suddenly aware that he did wish it. Somehow, the offer from this rustic priest meant more to him than all the bishops and other high-ranking clerics with whom he had ever come into contact.

"Yes, I would, Father. But only if you're sure it doesn't violate any rules."

"I keep the rules that serve His pleasure," Derfel said, gesturing toward the Presence Light burning atop the tabernacle on the little altar. "An' His pleasure is tae see His children come to Him in love an' prayerfulness. I dinnae think He cares o'ermuch for some o' the legalities imposed by the men who govern His Church on earth—not when those legalities would deny His solace to His children who are in need. Ye took food as part o' medicine." He gestured toward the chalice. "That's medicine as well. Drink up, Sire, an' then kneel in thanksgiving, while I bring ye the Body of our Lord."

Somehow imbued with new energy, just by the words, Rhys Michael drained the chalice to the dregs, welcoming the cool wine sliding down his dry throat, then eased to his knees, clutching the chalice to his breast. Father Derfel had turned to reverence the tabernacle on the little altar, and now swung wide its golden door to part a veil of green silk and take out a ciborium of hammered gold. Removing the cover, he set it aside and turned to face the king, carefully taking out a small Host, which he held above the cup.

"Ecce Agnus Dei: ecce qui tollit peccata mundi," he said. Behold the Lamb of God, behold Him Who taketh away the sins of the world.

Bowing his head, Rhys Michael murmured, *"Domine, non*

sum dignus, ut intres sub tectum meum: sed tantum dic verbo et sanabitur anima mea." Lord, I am not worthy that Thou shouldst come under my roof; speak but the word and my soul shall be healed . . .

He found himself gazing into the empty chalice as he recited the words, somehow visualizing light collecting in the golden bowl, and for the first time in many days he felt a sense of inner peace moving in his soul as he looked up again at Father Derfel, who now raised the Host a little higher.

"Corpus Domini nostri Jesu Christi custodiat animam tuam in vitam aeternam." The Body of our Lord Jesus Christ preserve thy soul unto everlasting life.

"Amen," Rhys Michael murmured, closing his eyes then as Father Derfel put the Host on his tongue.

He could not have said, later, that it tasted any different from Communion he had received a hundred times before, but it somehow meant more to him. He knew he dared not linger to savor the feeling, but when Father Derfel had covered the ciborium again and put it back into the tabernacle, he felt a greater sense of his own sacral station than he had ever felt before, even at his anointing as king. Despite the fever still mounting in his body, he felt profoundly at peace as he handed the chalice back to Father Derfel, and when the priest offered a hand to help him up, Rhys Michael bent instead to kiss it.

"Sire, ye shouldnae do that," Derfel murmured, gently shifting his other hand to caress the king's sable hair in blessing.

"But I wanted to," Rhys Michael murmured, looking up at him. "I give you this salute as a token of my gratitude. You've given me back my balance, so that I can go out and do what I must, as an anointed king. I'd almost lost that, after years of going through the motions with priests I detest, whose sins are in their hearts and on their lips, and whose hands are stained with innocent blood. Thank you for reminding me that it doesn't have to be that way."

"My dear, dear boy," Derfel murmured.

Another, more insistent rap at the door impelled him to draw the king to his feet again, this time urging him to go.

"Be off wi' ye now, Sire. I'll see to the arrangements. God be with ye."

Rhys Michael was blinking back tears as he made his way back to the door, and he had to pause for a few seconds to compose himself. Stevanus said nothing as he came out, obviously reassured by Cathan, but the king decided it was probably best to offer at least a partial explanation for his long absence. As soon as they had gotten clear of the chapel, where men were already closing the slabs above Sudrey's grave, he glanced at the surgeon.

"I was only going to thank him for the Mass, but he'd noticed that I didn't go forward for Communion," he told Stevanus, as they went into the courtyard to cross to the great hall steps. "I told him I'd already broken my fast, so I could take my painkiller, but he said that was medicinal, under the circumstances, so it didn't count. I didn't think you'd mind the short delay."

"That was very kind of him," Stevanus said. "I shouldn't think even Rhun will mind—but we do need to hurry." He reached out to touch the king's hand, then his forehead. "That fever doesn't seem to be abating, though. Are you up to this court? I could have Lord Rhun deputize for you."

"No, I want to do it," the king said. "After coming all this way and costing them their lord and lady, it's the least I can do for Eastmarch. I'm also very hungry, so don't try to send me off to bed until I've had a crack at the food they've been cooking for two days."

He was *not* hungry, but he knew he must establish from the start that he intended to perform his duties. He was feeling more and more light-headed, perhaps partially from the wine, but it was essential that he get through this, both for the reasons he had outlined to Stevanus and for the ones Stevanus must never know. He hoped he would feel better, once he had eaten. As it was, the smell of the food made him faintly nauseated as they approached the steps to the castle's hall.

The party to be invested were already assembled in the yard outside, Stacia and her husband waiting with half a dozen of their retainers. An adolescent girl in border tweeds held the infant Kennet, and two younger girls carried cushions bearing hammered silver circlets. Earl Sighere was husbanding a banner of the arms of Eastmarch in the crook of his arm, looking impatient, and his son Sean bore a sheathed broadsword with the sword belt wrapped around the scabbard—presumably the former property of Hrorik.

When Sighere saw the king approaching, he handed off the banner to his son and came over to greet the king.

" 'Tis glad I am tae see ye here, Sire," he murmured, inclining his head slightly. "Ye didnae look too well during Mass."

Rhys Michael gave him a wan smile. "I have some fever,"

he acknowledged, "but I could hardly allow it to interfere with so important an event. I tarried to thank Father Derfel for offering Mass in Lady Sudrey's behalf. Would that I had more such priests in my service."

Sighere nodded carefully. "Father Derfel is a braw priest, an' a credit to his callin'."

"That was my thought as well," Rhys Michael agreed.

"Aye." Sighere's glance flicked to Stevanus, to Cathan, then back to the king, betraying nothing. Fulk had gone ahead into the hall.

"They'll be waitin' fer ye, Sire. Ye'd best go ahead in. I do thank ye for coming to our aid, if ye were not thankit before. Kheldour stands ready tae serve, as we hae served yer Highness these past days. By yer leave, Sire."

So saying, he gave the king another nod of his head and withdrew to retrieve his banner. Stevanus watched him go, then turned to glance at the king, apparently suspecting nothing.

"You *are* looking peaked, Sire. Are you sure you're up to this?"

"I'm fine," Rhys Michael said.

They went on into the hall, which was already crowded. Rhys Michael had not thought about it before, but it was hardly half the size of the hall at Rhemuth. Mostly empty before, it had seemed larger.

With a supper to follow, the high table was set up across the dais as usual, with trestle tables and benches along both long sides of the hall. In the open space between the arms of the U thus formed, almost against the high table, they had positioned a high-backed chair to serve as a throne. Up to the right of it, an intense-looking Duke Graham was listening to instructions from Rhun and Manfred, looking none too happy, while Lord Joshua and Father Lior looked on.

The group dispersed as Rhys Michael approached, Rhun drawing Manfred aside in some private converse and Graham starting to marshal the retainers milling in the hall, urging them to approach the dais and leave a center aisle. Father Derfel had come in while the king spoke with Sighere, carrying a silver-cased Gospel book and wearing a white cope over his alb and stole. Father Lior looked none too pleased that the priest obviously expected to participate in the ceremony.

"Your offer of assistance is most generous, Father, but I believe we have things under control," Lior said.

"I've nae doubt that ye do, Father," Derfel said smoothly, as Rhys Michael passed, "but I am confessor tae Lady Stacia and Lord Corban. They hae begged leave tae swear their oaths on the Gospel book from which they hear the word o' God each day; an' who but their confessor can better remind them o' those oaths, when the king is far from Eastmarch?"

Even Lior could not gainsay that argument; and if he had tried, Rhys Michael was prepared to put in his own arguments for Derfel's presence. Fortunately, Rhun was approaching, gesturing for Fulk to bring the king's crown and sword.

"I think we should begin, Sire," he said, as Cathan took the crown from Fulk and put it on Rhys Michael's head.

You're burning up, Cathan sent, adjusting the crown on the king's clammy brow.

Rhys Michael could only shrug as he sat in the chair provided and Fulk laid the sheathed Haldane sword across its arms. As the others took their places around them and the retainers of Eastmarch and Claibourne and Marley crowded into the hall, he tried to summon up the strength to get through this ceremony. He was feeling worse and worse.

A muffled roll of drums demanded the attention of all present, then began beating out a slow cadence suitable for a stately procession. In happier times, border pipes would have accompanied the new earl and countess down the length of the crowded hall, but not with Sudrey buried hardly an hour before, and not with the late earl but a fortnight before her.

The two came before him and made their reverences, Stacia still garbed in the unremitting black she had worn to her mother's funeral, Corban in drab border tweeds. Sighere had unfurled the Eastmarch banner and footed it on the step of the dais, and Graham stood beside Rhys Michael's chair, bearing the letters patent. Father Derfel waited at the young duke's elbow, the Gospel book hugged to his breast.

Rhys Michael glanced at Rhun and Manfred, keeping attendance from the other side, then turned his gaze to his Eastmarch retainers and their new earl and countess.

"My lords and ladies, people of Eastmarch," he said, speaking quietly, but in a voice that carried to the far end of the hall. "Mere words cannot express the honor I feel to be here among you, and to know the loyalty that has surrounded me these past days, as we stood together against would-be invaders. You have paid a high price, for you have lost both your earl and his lady in my service. It is a price they were prepared to pay, but

I cannot but wish that payment could have been made in some other coin. I knew Lord Hrorik but slightly, from my boyhood days, and only met the Lady Sudrey on the night before she laid down her life in my defense, but both were brave and honorable. I can only hope and pray that our Lord in Heaven will richly reward those who, in life, served their earthly lord so well and so faithfully."

The hall had grown hushed and expectant as he went on, a murmur of approval whispering among his listeners. Rhun had an increasingly sour look on his face.

"But we have not come here today to speak more of Lord Hrorik and his lady, who are with us no more, but to acknowledge their daughter and heir, who comes before us to be invested as Countess of Eastmarch, and also her husband, Lord Corban Howell, who will rule as earl at her side. It is not often that so noble a title passes through the female line, but knowing what I do of the Lady Sudrey, I cannot think that her daughter will be any less noble as she assumes the office borne so faithfully by her late father. My lady? Lord Corban?"

At his gesture, the two came to kneel before him, Stacia directly at his knees, Corban a handspan back, for the two would give their oaths separately. As Stacia offered him her joined hands, he slipped his bandaged hand out of its sling to clasp her hands lightly against it with his good hand. Father Derfel had come forward with the Gospel and held it down beside their joined hands.

"Stacia, Countess of Eastmarch, I am prepared to hear your oath," the king said quietly.

Her dark eyes did not leave his as she spoke.

"I, Stacia, Countess of Eastmarch, do become yer vassal of life an' limb, an' enter yer fealty, an' do homage for all the lands of Eastmarch, formerly held by my father Hrorik, an' before him by my grandfather, Sighere, Warlord o' Kheldour an' first Duke o' Claibourne. Faith and truth will I bear unto ye, tae live an' tae die, against all manner o' folk, sae help me God."

Her hands were trembling between his, his injured hand throbbing to be so pressed, but he would not alter the symbolism merely for his own comfort. It struck him that this was the first time he had ever exchanged such oaths with any of his vassals with any sense that he actually had control over how the relationship was conducted. In truth, he had never been allowed an opportunity to interact with any of his vassals as king. The exhilaration made his blood sing through his veins and brought a faint flush to his cheeks that had nothing to do with fever.

"This do I hear, Stacia of Eastmarch, and I, for my part, pledge the protection of Gwynedd to you and all your people, to defend you from every creature with all my power, giving loyalty for loyalty and justice for honor. This is the word of Rhys Michael Alister Haldane, King of Gwynedd, Lord of Meara and Mooryn and the Purple March, and Overlord of Eastmarch. So help me God."

When both he and Stacia had laid their hands on the Gospel and kissed its silver-chased cover, Corban Howell likewise set his hands briefly between the king's and then kissed the book, though he was not required to repeat the oath—only to affirm it. Rhys Michael liked what he could Read of Corban and had no doubt that the new earl was well content. In all practical aspects, this younger son of an impoverished family of gentry was now Earl of Eastmarch for Stacia's lifetime, the title to pass to their son upon her death. If one could not himself be born to such titles, attaining such a title by marriage was an entirely honorable and satisfactory way to establish his own noble succession. Young Corban had done well for himself.

There followed the investiture with the emblems of rank, each with its own symbolism. Handing off the Haldane sword, the king stood to place the silver circlets upon their heads, first Stacia and then Corban. He was awkward with only one hand—he had slipped his injured one back into its sling—but Father Derfel assisted him.

The banner that Sighere brought forward was easier to manage one-handed. Declaring it a token of Stacia's authority to govern Eastmarch in his name, the king delivered it into Stacia's hands. She, in turn, passed it into the keeping of Murray, one of her captains, as Sighere's son Sean brought forward the sword that had belonged to Hrorik.

This the king also gave to Stacia, in token of her duty to defend her people. After kissing the holy relic on its hilt, Stacia presented it to Corban, who followed suit and then enlisted the assistance of Duke Graham to belt the weapon around his waist. When that was done, the new earl stood to draw it and salute the king before sheathing it again.

Finally Rhys Michael presented Stacia with a cauldron, symbolic of her duty to provide for her people. Stacia herself took charge of this, laying her hand upon it in acceptance before another of her captains took it aside. The ceremony completed, Rhys Michael at last raised her up and turned her to face those gathered in the crowded hall, also gathering Corban to her side.

"People of Eastmarch, I give you your new Earl and Countess of Eastmarch. Be ye loyal and true, as they shall be to you."

A lone piper struck up a jaunty march at that, as the men cheered and brandished their swords in support and a few of Stacia's men took her and Corban onto their shoulders and paraded them the length of the hall and back. Rhun and Manfred and some of the Gwynedd men looked a little dismayed at first, but it soon became clear that pride and high spirits prevailed, rather than any danger. While the demonstration continued, Rhys Michael sank back down on his chair, conserving his strength, trying not to look as if he were anticipating what, for him, would be the most important part of the afternoon's ceremony.

When the impromptu parade had returned, young Graham held up his hands for silence, then turned to face the king and bowed. Sighere also had moved closer.

"Sire, ane boon I would ask, before we adjourn tae tak refreshment," Graham said. "I assure ye that it is within yer power tae give, an' that it isnae to the detriment o' yer crown."

Rhun and Manfred drew closer, wary and suspicious, but Rhys Michael feigned ignorance of what Graham intended.

"Speak, my Lord Duke," he said. "The king listens."

Graham inclined his head, partially turning to address the court as well.

"Sire, as was my duty, I gave ye my homage and fealty at yer coronation. Neither of us were long come into our manhood at that time, an' it was said that yer Highness' health had suffered temporarily from the shock of yer brother's untimely death, both o' which perhaps lessened yer Highness' appreciation o' the oaths we then exchanged.

"Circumstances havenae brought me back tae Rhemuth since then, an' they didnae bring yer Highness tae Kheldour until a few days ago. But in these past days, I and mine hae seen ample evidence that the king to whom I swore allegiance out o' duty is also worthy o' that allegiance on his own merits. Accordingly, an' it please yer Highness, I beg yer leave tae renew my oath o' fealty at this time."

Even having known that Graham was going to do this, Rhys

Michael felt his pulse soar in excitement and pride and quickly swept his good hand before him in invitation for Graham to approach, before Rhun or Manfred could object. Paulin or Albertus would have forbidden it straightaway, as too public a display of personal support for the king, but Rhys Michael was gambling that neither Rhun nor Manfred was yet secure enough in his new office to make a public scene this far from home and on a point to which only those openly opposed to the king could possibly object.

As Graham came to kneel close before his chair, Rhys Michael sat forward and slipped his injured hand out of his sling again so he could clasp the young duke's joined hands between his own. As Graham's lips parted to speak the ritual words, Rhys Michael allowed himself to slip into the surface levels of the other's mind, reading the additional meanings already promised in their earlier conversation of the day before.

"Before God an' these assembled witnesses, I, Graham, Duke o' Claibourne, do affirm that I am yer man o' life and limb an' earthly worship. Faith and truth will I bear unto ye, tae live an' tae die, against all manner o' folk, sae help me God."

As he finished the oath, he dipped to press his forehead to their joined hands, first briefly touching his lips to the king's fingertips. Rhys Michael did not think Rhun or Manfred noticed, but he felt the fierce surge of the younger man's devotion, and held the joined hands more closely as Graham lifted his head, even though the pressure made his injured hand throb worse.

"Graham of Claibourne, this do I hear," he said, trying to keep his joy from showing but still convey his gratitude to the young duke. "As I swore at my sacring, so I pledge you anew—the protection of Gwynedd to defend you and all your people from every creature with all my power, giving loyalty for loyalty and justice for honor. This is the oath of Rhys Michael Alister Haldane, King of Gwynedd, Lord of Meara and Mooryn and the Purple March, and Overlord of Claibourne. So help me God."

As he released Graham's hands, the younger man crossed himself in affirmation of the oath and then got to his feet. Earl Sighere was already moving in to take his place, thumping to his knees to offer up his joined hands.

"Ye hae my pledge as well, Sire," he murmured, as Rhys Michael's hands enfolded his. "I am yer man—and do ye merely say *Amen* to affirm it, for there be many more who desire tae swear ye the same."

As he, too, ducked his head to kiss the royal hand and then press his forehead to their joined ones in homage, Rhys Michael whispered, "Amen." Several dozen more came forward after that, to his growing amazement and gratitude and to the consternation of Rhun and Manfred, who quickly figured out what the men were doing when they bent to touch their foreheads to the hands.

The two drew apart a little to murmur between themselves, and Rhys Michael knew he would have questions to answer when it was all over, but he hardly cared, in the soul-soaring exuberance of learning what support he actually had. He Truth-Read them as they came, knowing there was none to detect it and betray him, and plumbed the depth of loyalty that lay behind each murmured "I am yer man"—loyalty that was his to command, could he ever find a way to tap it to free his crown.

His hand was aching worse than ever by the time they finished, for he could not help but jostle it in performing the ritual gesture—but he would not have omitted it for all the world and disappoint such fervent devotion.

But other reckoning came almost immediately, as the court broke up and folk dispersed for the feast to be set up—and Rhun and Manfred shuffled him apart, into the relative privacy of a deep window embrasure.

CHAPTER TWENTY-ONE

And for this cause God shall send them strong delusion, that they should believe a lie.
—II Thessalonians 2:11

"What the devil was that all about?" Rhun demanded, drawing the king deeper into the window embrasure as Manfred took up a stance to block further entrance or departure. "They were kissing your hand—every single man jack of them."

"I suppose it's local custom," Rhys Michael murmured, cradling his aching arm. "They're a passionate people, these borderers. You've seen them in action."

"Yes, and I know what it means, when they seal an oath that way," Rhun said. "It makes the oath a personal one—to the man, not just to the crown."

"Does it?"

"It bloody well does, and you know it!" Rhun snapped, though he kept his voice low. "Don't play the innocent with me. Did you know Claibourne was going to do that?"

"Of course not," Rhys Michael lied. "If I had, I would have told you. But once they'd started doing it, what was I supposed to do? Jerk my hands away and insult them? Spurn the loyalty of a quarter of the kingdom? It may have escaped your notice, Rhun, but without the Kheldour lords—and in particular, without that lady we buried a few hours ago—we might not be having this discussion. And I might not be the only one dead."

Rhun breathed out in a perplexed sigh, obviously keeping his temper in check only with the greatest of effort.

"Well, it doesn't matter now; it's done," he muttered. "Just don't get any ideas in your head."

"Ideas? What ideas?" Rhys Michael retorted, as all the despair of the past six years came welling up, pulsing with the ache in his arm. "What the hell do you think I might do? What *could* I do?"

"I don't know!" Rhun retorted, then glanced around and lowered his voice as he continued in a more conciliatory tone. "Just don't push me, Sire. As you may have gathered, I'm still uneasy over this whole Eastmarch affair—the deaths en route, the resolution with Miklos, and now this little demonstration by Claibourne and Marley. And with Albertus and Paulin gone, the entire balance in Rhemuth will be shifting as well. If you were to become too inconvenient—well, I don't think I need to spell it out, do I?"

Rhys Michael blinked and swallowed with difficulty, tight-jawed, then shook his head.

"I thought not," Rhun murmured, glancing out into the hall again. "Now, I think no one would take it amiss if you were to retire early this evening. I'm a little concerned about your hand. You don't look at all well."

Rhys Michael looked away, hugging the injured arm to his chest. "I'll be all right," he muttered. "Why should you care? I should think it would be the ultimate 'convenience' if I died from it."

"Not really," Rhun said. "Actually, I should prefer to choose the time and place for *my* convenience." He gave the king a quick grimace that might have passed for a smile, though without a trace of mirth, then set his hand on the hilt of his sword.

"But I think we need not speak further of such things tonight, Sire. Shall I have Stevanus escort you to your quarters?"

Rhys Michael made himself stand more erect, setting his good hand on his belt and trying to strike the right balance between assertion and compliance. Were it only for his own comfort, he would have sought his bed some time ago, but one last duty remained to be done before he dared seek that comfort, and he must not allow Rhun to interfere.

"Not quite yet, if you don't mind," he said. "I really am feeling better than I probably look, and it would be insulting to our hosts not to make an appearance at least. Besides, I have to eat. If you prefer, though, I won't stay too late. I'll confess that bed sounds like an altogether tempting proposition."

"Very well," Rhun said, "if you're sure."

Rhys Michael could feel the earl marshal's gaze following him as he pressed past him and Manfred and went back into the hall. To his relief, neither man pressed the issue, though he knew, as he rejoined Cathan and Fulk, that they and probably Stevanus would be told to watch him. So long as it was just those three, the situation probably was surmountable. He prayed that it was, because the very future of the Haldane Crown perhaps depended upon it.

They were summoned to table very shortly. Rhys Michael was glad to escape to the less demanding small talk of a feast beginning, subdued though it was because of the castle's recent bereavement. He had Stacia seated on his right, in the place of honor, with her husband beyond and Graham and Sighere at that end of the table, though he could not speak freely because Lior was on his immediate left, followed by Joshua Delacroix. Rhun and Manfred sat beyond with several of their aides, where they might be free to observe and comment to one another in relative privacy.

Cathan and Fulk took turns serving the king, also giving instructions to the local squires assigned to wait table. Rhun had drawn the two aside early on, one at a time—to order them to accompany the king, if he even went out to use the privy—but later in the meal, Cathan was able to confirm that he had gotten the necessary documents to Father Derfel, who was waiting in a tiny chamber just beyond one of the garderobes.

After the pace of the previous few days, the meal seemed to drag, with the courses interspersed with interludes of sad harping and singing, some of it in a dialect Rhys Michael did not understand. He only picked at his food, but he managed to drink enough wine to further blunt the throbbing of his arm—though he took care lest it also blunt the edge of his wits for survival. Both Graham and Stacia had already disappeared briefly during the course of the meal, and Sighere had been in and out of the hall several times, ostensibly stewarding the flow of wine.

"All the others have signed," Cathan finally reported, as he bent close to refill the king's cup, "but it's worthless without your signature and seal. The way Rhun is watching you, though, it's going to be a near-run thing. You'll only get one chance."

The chance came a short time later, when Manfred had just returned from a trip to the privies and settled in beside Rhun again, in time for the serving of a new course; Rhun had disappeared briefly a short time before, so probably would not be inclined to disappear again for a while. Stevanus was talking to one of the men who had been wounded with Hrorik the week before.

Quietly excusing himself from the company of Stacia and Corban—Lior was deep in conversation with Joshua and one of Manfred's aides—Rhys Michael rose a trifle shakily on Cathan's arm and staggered from the hall, Fulk following a few seconds later. Sighere passed them en route to the exit, none too steady on his feet and with a goblet in his hand, but Rhys Michael suspected he was far more sober than he looked. The priest's chamber lay a few steps farther up the stairwell from which the curtained garderobe opened, just off the landing outside the hall. With a quick glance around, Rhys Michael simply continued up the stair to slip inside while Cathan took up a more leisurely stance outside the garderobe entrance, just as Fulk came out of the hall.

"Any problem?" he heard Fulk ask.

"No, but he may be a few minutes," Cathan replied. "Say, did you notice that pretty dark-haired lass who was sitting way at the end of the table on the left? She was watching you."

"Yes? Which one was that?"

Trusting Cathan to keep Fulk occupied and divert any suspicion, Rhys Michael closed the door the rest of the way and turned to the table where Father Derfel waited behind a rack of candles, a quill already in hand and extended to him. The faint perfume of melted sealing wax tickled at his nostrils as he removed his signet ring and gave it to the priest, then took the quill awkwardly in his left hand and bent to sign. It was difficult, but he did the best he could, scrawling a reasonably legible *Rhys R.* on each of the five copies. Derfel began sealing them as soon as Rhys Michael had finished the first one.

"Get the seal back to Sir Cathan as soon as you can," he whispered, after finishing the last one with a shaky flourish and then sticking the quill back in the inkwell. "They're really watching me. If anyone notices that I'm suddenly not wearing it, there could be questions."

"Gie me half a minute, an' ye can tak it now," Derfel replied, already applying wax to the third of the copies as the king moved to the door.

Nodding agreement, the king quietly eased the door open far enough to set his eye to the crack. To his horror, Rhun had just stepped into the landing and was looking either at Cathan and Fulk or at the garderobe entrance, a frown furrowing his narrow brow.

Rhys Michael drew back in momentary panic, heart pounding, then carefully set his eye to the crack again. Rhun did not look particularly suspicious or upset; but he was there. Fulk was nodding amiably to the earl marshal. Carefully Rhys Michael sent out a tendril of thought to Cathan, hoping he could reach him without physical contact.

Cathan?

Startlement came through, though Cathan showed no outward sign of it. Dismayed, Rhys Michael realized that his kinsman did not seem to have the power to send back more than impressions.

Don't waste energy trying to send back. Just do what I tell you. I know you can handle Fulk. I also want you to maneuver Rhun around so his back is to me.

From Cathan came a sense of query.

The only thing I can do; blank him for about five seconds, long enough for me to get into the garderobe. But you've got to get him up a few steps so I can reach him before he sees or hears me.

Agreement came through the link, even as Cathan turned toward Rhun. He was just opening his mouth to speak when Sighere came careening into the landing from the great hall, wine sloshing from a goblet in one big hand as he caught his balance against the door jamb.

"Weel, if it isnae Rhun the Ruthless," he said amiably, the words slurred and a little too loud, his gaze unfocused. "I rememmer you. What're ye doin' in Marley, Ruthless?"

As he lurched closer to Rhun and peered at him blearily, and Rhun drew back in distaste, Rhys Michael hoped desperately that Sighere was only trying to divert Rhun, not pick a serious fight. Of one thing he was certain; Rhun was not drunk. He was fairly certain Sighere was not really drunk either. There was bad blood between the two, though. If it came to blows, real blood might be shed—and at least one of the men was apt to die.

Not that he would mourn Rhun's loss. But if Sighere died, that would nullify half the document Rhys Michael had just gone to such pains to get signed—and sealed, he remembered, as the priest slipped in beside him to slide the signet ring back on his hand. And if it was Rhun who was killed, he would hate to have to bring Sighere up on charges of murder.

"You're drunk," Rhun said in disgust. "Why don't you go sleep it off?"

Sighere drew back in a theatrical posture of mock affront staggering a few steps away from Rhun and the garderobe entrance—and managed an exaggerated pout.

"Tha's no verra friendly. I hae sworn tae yer Haldane king. That makes us allies. Will ye no share a drink?" he asked.

As he held out his goblet, still weaving on his feet, Rhun was already summoning Fulk and Cathan—who would just about provide a convenient screen between Rhun and the garderobe, provided Sighere kept up the diversion. Already, Rhun had his back to the stairs.

"Fulk, get him out of here before I do something we'll both regret," Rhun muttered. "God, these borderers are all alike—"

"Wha's wrong wi' m'drink?" Sighere was muttering, looking into his goblet quizzically and sloshing a little as Fulk and Cathan swept in to take him in charge, also sweeping Rhun along. "Ish good wine. Ah, yer spillin' it. Careful!"

In those few seconds of confusion, as Sighere juggled his wine and the others tried to jolly him along, Rhys Michael was able to dash down the few steps and gain the shelter of the garderobe entrance, pushing the curtain aside even as he pivoted in the doorway, as if he had just come out.

"What the devil is going on out here?" he demanded, twitching the curtain closed behind him.

"Oh, *there* you are," Rhun said, straightening his tunic as Cathan and Fulk propelled Sighere back into the hall with a good-natured shove. "I wondered where you'd gotten to. Sorry, Sire, but your precious Earl of Marley is a sloppy drunk. The fool accosted me."

"What, outside the privy?" Rhys Michael said with a snort, unable to resist the gibe. "I shouldn't think he was serious."

Rhun stiffened and moved closer. "And just what is that supposed to mean?"

"Oh, never mind. If you're determined to take offense at some simple high spirits from men to whom we owe a great deal—Why were you lurking out here, anyway? You know Sighere doesn't bear you a great deal of goodwill."

"Actually, I was looking for you," Rhun said.

"Looking for me?"

"Yes."

"Whatever for? Can't I even go to the privy without you following me around? Isn't it bad enough that Fulk and Cathan are my faithful shadows?"

Rhun managed to look almost a little embarrassed. "You were in there for quite a while."

"What, having secret conferences?" Rhys Michael said, suddenly realizing that he had Rhun on the defensive and could skirt very close to the truth and make it seem outrageous. He gestured toward his injured arm.

"I don't suppose it occurred to you that this might have slowed me down just a little," he went on, letting the sarcasm bite with his words. "Or did you think I might have invited some secret supporter into the garderobe with me, so we could plot intrigues while he helped me take a piss? Your suspicion is getting out of hand, Rhun. Do you want to have a look and see if he's still in there?"

As he gestured scornfully toward the garderobe curtain, Rhun turned on his heel and stalked back into the hall. As soon as he had disappeared, Rhys Michael had to turn away briefly as he nearly convulsed in silent laughter, Cathan and Fulk also fighting to control wide grins as a bewildered-looking Claibourne retainer poked his head onto the landing, took one look at them, and went back into the great hall.

After a few seconds, Rhys Michael drew himself up more soberly, going nearly white as the throbbing in his arm recalled him to more immediate concerns.

"Well done, gentlemen," he said with a tight grimace. "And on that note, I believe I shall take my leave and retire. Fulk, would you please give my regrets to Lady Stacia and then ask Master Stevanus to attend me?"

He was shivering with fever again by the time he climbed into bed, and he curled onto his side under the sleeping furs until Stevanus came to him. With the surgeon were Stacia and an ample old woman dressed in the simple homespun and tweeds of the local folk, carrying a reed basket over her arm.

"Sire, I hae brought ye Mother Angelica," Stacia said, as Stevanus laid a hand across his forehead to gauge his fever, tight-lipped and grim as he then gave way to the woman. "She is midwife in the village, but her mother used to work wi' the Healer we had in those days. There is a remedy she uses fer childbed fevers. It might help this one."

Rhys Michael's hopes leaped, that the old woman might be a Healer herself, but as she, too, set a hand to his forehead, clucking her tongue and shaking her grizzled head, he knew she was not even Deryni.

"I would look a' the wound," she murmured, shifting her

hands to feel the strength of the pulse in the sides of his neck. The gnarled old hands were gentle; the nails were cut short and scrupulously clean.

He winced as Stacia began unwrapping his hand, keeping his gaze on Mother Angelica and seeking to Read her surface thoughts, though he did not probe lest she sense the touch, from working with the Healer long ago. When re-dressing his hand the night before, Stacia had positioned the bandages so that the dressing could be changed on the actual wound without loosing all the support that bound the broken bones into place. As the wound was bared, Mother Angelica peered at it critically, prodding around it and up his forearm, sniffed disapprovingly, then directed Lochalyn's chatelaine to clean it and bind it up again with fresh sphagnum moss. Rhys Michael thought it looked much the same as it had the night before.

"The wound is inflamed, but I dinnae see sign that the poison is spreading up his arm," the old woman said, rummaging in her basket. "This should help the fever."

She pulled out a small earthen jar corked with a wooden plug, opened it to insert a little finger and taste the contents, then nodded and turned to Stevanus.

"He should have as much o' this as will cover the bottom of a small cup, dissolved in water or wine, four times a day."

"What is it?" Stevanus asked.

"My mam called it tacil," the old woman replied. "This is the last of it. The Healer used to make it, but he died."

"A Deryni drug?" Stevanus said, frowning.

"A drug fer easin' fever," Stacia said briskly, taking a cup from the stand beside the bed and shaking in a layer of white, crystalline powder. "Do ye wish tae ease the king's fever or no?"

"The *king* wants to ease his fever," Rhys Michael said, sitting up and reaching for the cup. "And if there were a Healer available, I'd welcome his services, regardless of what Master Stevanus thinks of Deryni. I don't suppose there is one, though."

"Alas, not since I was a wee girl," Stacia said, and gave him an odd look. Cathan had come with a flask of wine, and she filled the cup halfway and gave it a quick swirl before handing it to the king. "Drink it doon, Sire."

He obeyed before Stevanus could decide whether or not to interfere, though he had to swallow three or four times to get it all down. The dregs were bitter, and he made a face as he handed back the cup and lay back on his pillows. The effort had exhausted him, though his hand seemed to be settling down to a lesser throb after the pain of being examined and rebandaged.

"Am I allowed to have more syrup of poppies, or will the tacil help with the pain, too?" he asked. "I need to get some sleep, if we're to ride out tomorrow."

"The poppy willnae interfere," Mother Angelica said, "but the hand doesnae want jostlin'. At best, ye will be sair uncomfortable."

"The earl marshal wants to get back to Rhemuth as soon as possible," Stevanus said, before the king could reply. "I don't think there's any appeal from that, Sire. We have surgeons aplenty in our train, and there are suitable halting sites all along the way."

"Well, we can discuss it with Rhun in the morning," Rhys Michael said. "If my fever is down, we should move out. The hospitality here at Lochalyn is impeccable, Lady Stacia, but I must get back to my wife and son. She's with child, you know, and she'll already be anxious when she hears I've been injured."

Stacia could not argue with that, and Mother Angelica merely shrugged. When Cathan had shown them out, Stevanus measured out another dose of syrup of poppies—and left convinced that Rhys Michael had drunk it down. In fact, as soon as he had gone, the king set Fulk to bedding down in the anteroom adjacent to the lord's solar and called Cathan to him.

"I do want to get home as quickly as possible, but I think it might be wise if we sent a copy of the codicil ahead to Mika, just in case."

"Just in case what?" Cathan murmured, leaning close as he sat on the edge of the bed.

"I'm not sure." Rhys Michael hugged his injured hand closer and rubbed at the arm above it. "It's a good week's ride back to Rhemuth with troops on the march, and a lot of things could happen. You don't die from having your hand stepped on by a horse, but I—I'd feel better if one of the copies was in her hands."

"Fair enough," Cathan agreed. "Do you have a messenger in mind, or would you like me to go?"

"Not you," Rhys Michael replied. "Trust-wise, I couldn't ask for better, but you'd be missed. Besides, I don't know that I could make it without you.

"But it's important that the copies be dispersed as quickly as possible. I don't think I've yet become too 'inconvenient' for Rhun to keep putting up with me, but if it looks as if he's losing patience, I intend to reveal that the codicil exists and that the only way to keep Graham and Sighere out of government is to keep me alive. I don't dare make that threat unless I'm sure he can't get at all of the copies."

"Sound reasoning. That doesn't answer the question of who goes, though."

"Who're our choices?" Rhys Michael said. "I'll want to set compulsions, in any case, but it's always better if I can start with someone who's loyal."

"How about one of the local men? Sighere's son, perhaps. He struck me as being levelheaded."

Rhys Michael shook his head. "Whoever goes, he has to be able to gain access to the queen; a borderer couldn't. One of our men—but he can't be someone who'd be readily missed."

"None of the *Custodes*, none of Rhun's men, or Manfred's," Cathan murmured, musing aloud. "That means someone in the service of one of the lesser lords, or—Yes. I know just the man. Lord Ainslie's son Robert—and I saw him in the hall earlier this evening. Do you remember him?"

"Of course. And he's perfect."

"I'll see if I can find him, then. I doubt he's gone down to the camp yet. I assume you'll want him to leave tonight?"

"Absolutely. And send Fulk in on your way out. I want to dictate another short document—something to provide for you, in case the other should need to be enforced. I'll want you to get it to Graham in the morning, before we leave."

Cathan looked at him sharply. "Rhysem, are you *sure* you're not keeping something from me? You're not going to die!"

"I'm certainly not planning on it," Rhys Michael said, forcing a grin as he tried again to ease his hand. "Just covering my options. Now, back to the codicils—have we got a copy, or does Father Derfel still have them?"

"Derfel's got them," Cathan replied, "but I'll fetch one before I bring young Ainslie. I'll be back as soon as I can."

Fulk came to him within a few minutes, moving the little writing table closer to the bed with a rack of candles and settling on a stool behind it. Reaching out with his mind, Rhys Michael confirmed that he was already controlled.

"You will take this down," Rhys Michael murmured, "but

afterward, you will not remember that you have written it. Head it with today's date and place.

" 'Unto Graham, Duke of Claibourne, and Sighere, Earl of Marley: In the event that you are successful in asserting your authority as regents after my death, as is my will and intention, I command and authorize you to confirm the appointment of Sir Cathan Cinhil Drummond as a fellow regent, as your first legal act following the assumption of your duties as regents . . .' "

When Fulk had finished taking the dictation, Rhys Michael read it over once, scrawled a reasonably legible signature at the foot, and had Fulk seal it. Fulk was just moving the table back from the bed when Cathan returned alone.

"Didn't you find him?" the king asked.

Cathan shook his head, coming to lay a hand on Fulk's shoulder.

"Go ahead to bed, Fulk. I'll take the first watch."

When Fulk had gone, closing the door behind him, Cathan came to crouch at the king's bedside.

"He's still drinking downstairs with the others, and I got the copy of the codicil, but it's going to be impossible to get him up here without anyone noticing. There are just too many people still about. If you want him to go tonight, the only thing I can suggest is to let me send him."

Rhys Michael closed his eyes briefly, hugging his injured hand and suppressing a shiver. "I really wanted to send him myself."

"I know that. What if we were to delay until tomorrow, catch him sometime during the day, and let him slip away?"

Rhys Michael shook his head. "Too chancy. Once we leave here, I'll have even less privacy. Besides that, we don't know what condition I'll be in. I could get worse instead of better, though the tacil does seem to be lessening my fever." A giant yawn took him, sufficient to make his jaws ache when he had finished.

"All right. I know you can't set the same kinds of compulsions I was going to use, but do the best you can. Come closer, and I'll give you some direction. I'm giving you my signet to give to him as well; that will be Mika's guarantee that it really does come from me."

He set his instructions in Cathan's mind, gave him the signet for Robert and the new document to deliver to Graham MacEwan, then bade him Godspeed and sent him on his way. When Cathan had gone, he took up the cup with the syrup of poppies that Stevanus had left, drank it down, rinsed the cup with a little water, and drank that down, too. His arm seemed to be throbbing worse than ever, even though the fever did seem to be diminishing. He was heavily asleep by the time Cathan returned, some hours later, and slept without moving until a bell ringing Prime roused him to the now familiar throbbing of his arm.

CHAPTER TWENTY-TWO

They gather themselves together against the soul of
the righteous, and condemn the innocent blood.
—Psalms 94:21

At least his fever seemed to have lessened. His head ached almost as much as his arm, from the aftereffects of the syrup of
poppies, and he knew he would have to take more to endure
the jolting of a day's ride, but neither his brow nor his arm felt
as hot as they had the night before. Stacia had left the tacil
with them, and Cathan handed the king another dose of it before letting him even stir from bed.

Rhys Michael made a face at the bitter taste but drank it
down. He groaned as he got out of bed and let Cathan help
him set about washing and dressing. His whole body ached,
and every movement was stiff.

"A lot of that is normal, considering what else you went
through, in the process of getting stepped on," Fulk said cheerily, as he packed up their belongings in saddlebags. "Do you
want Stevanus to see you before you go downstairs?"

"No, he won't give me any painkiller until I've eaten anyway. I'll see him in the hall after Mass."

"Very well. I'll take some of these down to the yard while
you finish, then, and meet you both in the chapel."

As soon as he was gone, Rhys Michael glanced at Cathan,
who was bringing the red brigandine to put on him. As on the
day before, he wore leather breeches and boots and a loose-
sleeved tunic, for he could not get the tunic of his riding leathers over his bandaged hand.

"I take it you got our friend away safely last night," he murmured.

Cathan settled the brigandine over the royal head and started doing up the side buckles. "Why don't you Read it direct while I do this? It's safer if we don't speak."

Closing his eyes, Rhys Michael set his good hand on Cathan's forearm and scanned for the memory, fetching out images of a slim but well-built young man with curly brown hair standing with his right hand clasped in Cathan's, the blue eyes all but veiled by long lashes, lightly entranced. Sir Robert Ainslie had fearlessly accepted the king's commission from Cathan, and offered no resistance when Cathan set such compulsions as he could.

"He was away before midnight," Cathan murmured, as Rhys Michael emerged from the probe. "Changing horses, and with minimal stops for rest, he should be in Rhemuth in about four days."

The king himself rode out of Lochalyn at midmorning, after hearing Mass with Lady Stacia, her family, and officers and eating rather more than he really wanted while standing in the castle's hall, after which Stevanus allowed him his pain medication. They were in the saddle soon after, with Graham, Sighere, and Corban riding with them for the first few miles as escort, accompanied by a score of fierce borderers. The men they had brought from Rhemuth went with them, but the levies from Caerrorie, Sheele, and Valoret would stay for another week or so, under the joint command of Joshua Delacroix and Iver MacInnis, in case the Torenthi withdrawal had been but a feint.

All too soon, time came for the three Kheldour lords to take personal leave of him, drawing rein to briefly touch gauntleted fists to armored breasts, proud heads inclining in wordless homage. Flanked by Rhun and Manfred, Rhys Michael could not go to them, but he read their fierce devotion as he bade them a formal farewell, wishing he could tell them what their loyalty meant to him, wishing he could stay.

As the mounted forms receded in a cloud of dust, heading back toward Lochalyn, Rhun and Manfred drew him on. The syrup of poppies was gradually lulling his pain to a dull ache, and soon his thoughts were less for regret of what he was leaving than minding that he did not doze and fall off his horse.

Meanwhile, from the slight disruption of the depleted Gwynedd camp, Ansel, Jesse, and Tieg had watched from the shade of a sprawling oak as the king rode past, noting the bandaged hand supported in a sling over his armor. He looked thinner than when he had arrived, pale and drawn. Tieg shook his head as the royal cavalcade receded, heading out across the plain of Iomaire.

"I certainly would like to have gotten a look at that hand," he murmured. "He looked as if he was in quite a bit of pain."

"I think you and I will pay a quick visit to Lady Stacia," Jesse said. "This may be our best chance, while the men are riding out with the king."

A quarter hour later, a servant was showing the two into the laird's solar at Lochalyn, where a slight, energetic girl-woman with a mane of dark red hair was sorting the contents of a pair of large chests. Several more women were sweeping and scrubbing, stripping the great bed, shaking out sleeping furs, bustling at the domestic chores involved in running a large household. A baby cooed contentedly in a nicely carved cradle, and a pair of shaggy grey wolfhounds lolled lethargically around it—ample reason why the servant had no qualms about bringing two strange young men to his lady's bower.

"These two men tae see ye, Lady Stacia."

The redheaded woman glanced at the two newcomers but continued folding a dull green tunic.

"Aye?"

Jesse inclined his head, reaching out to probe, but she was lightly shielded so he withdrew.

"We are friends of the king, my lady. May we speak with you in private?"

She flicked her gaze over them appraisingly.

"The king rode out an hour ago," she said.

"Aye, he did," Jesse replied.

The dark eyes flicked over them again; then she gestured toward a doorway in the corner of the room that led into a turret stair.

"Come ye this way," she said.

As they followed her, one of the wolfhounds bestirred itself to press past her up the spiral stair, waiting with tail-wagging impatience until she had opened the small door to the roof parapet and it could crowd through. The sun was warm and steady, gentled by a faint breeze. She dropped her hand to the wolfhound's head as she turned to face the two of them.

"Despite yer tweeds, I dinnae think ye be Kheldour men,"

she said. "I receive ye fer the sake o' the king, who is my liege. What is it ye wished tae say tae me?"

For answer, Jesse held out one cupped hand and conjured silvery handfire in it. The fire was pale in the direct sunlight, but she saw it, and her dark eyes widened. The wolfhound yawned.

"We came in hopes of helping the king, my lady," Jesse murmured, as he extinguished the fire. "Unfortunately, we were never able to get close enough to him to offer our assistance. My companion is a Healer. We hoped you might be able to tell us of the king's injury. It may be possible to gain access to him later, on the road."

Her gaze shifted over Tieg's lanky, gangling frame, then back to Jesse.

"He didnae mention that he had Deryni helpin' him," she said.

"The great lords must not know," Jesse replied. "Friendship with Deryni has already been the death of one Haldane king."

"It's true, then," she murmured. "He said they had killed his brother Javan an' others, that he has been spared only tae breed heirs."

"If he told you that, then it's clear he trusts you," Tieg said. "Will you trust us? We need to know about his injury."

Stacia bit at her lip, fondling at the dog's ears.

"Ye need tae know more'n that," she murmured. "The hand isnae good—a horse trod on it, an' bones were crushed—but I dinnae think 'tis only that wha' worries him. He had a document drawn, appointin' Uncle Sighere an' my cousin Graham as regents."

"A document?" Jesse breathed, exchanging a glance with Tieg.

Drawing careful breath, the young Healer moved a step closer to Stacia, the hazel eyes dark and serious in the boyish face.

"My lady, we have many questions and not much time. I think you know as well as we, how desperate is the king's plight. We know your mother was Deryni. Will you allow me to Read the details we need? I give you my word, on my Healer's oath, that I will do you no harm, nor Read past what concerns the king."

A faint smile tugged at her lips. "Yer voice is a man's, but can ye be old enou' tae have sworn the Healer's oath?" she said.

He grinned in return, looking a little sheepish. "My teachers tell me I am something of a prodigy. My father was a Healer called Rhys Thuryn. Perhaps you've heard of him."

"Och, aye." Her smile turned to a grin to match his own. "An' Rhys Thuryn an' his kin were e'er friends o' the Haldane line. Wha' will ye have me do?"

"Crouch down here beside me," he said, flicking a wary eye toward the wolfhound as he dropped to his knees, "and please reassure your friend that I mean you no harm."

"Conn? Och, he's but a big baby. He willnae hurt ye."

As she slipped to a sitting position with her back to the parapet wall, the wolfhound merely settled and laid its great head in her lap. Jesse had turned his gaze out over the wall, watching for the return of Stacia's kin, and glanced down at them as Stacia settled.

"Try to make this quick," he murmured.

"As quick as I can."

She closed her eyes before Tieg could even clasp her head between his hands. The shielding both he and Jesse had sensed melted away at the first touch of his probe, and she breathed out a tiny sigh as he gently took control. After blocking what little power she had, he drove deep, assimilating all her memories since Rhys Michael's arrival. The king's plan was brilliant, if it worked—and a dangerous gamble. But knowing of it, they perhaps could help facilitate its success, if the great lords called his bluff.

The condition of the king's injured hand was less encouraging, though Tieg decided that the "tacil" Stacia's midwife had given the king for fever probably was talicil, a mainstay of the Healer's pharmacopocia; it would have been his choice as well. He regretted that he had none with him to give her, to replace what had been sent with the king, for with the village Healer long dead, there would be no more until Deryni once more could walk freely in Gwynedd.

But he had learned what he needed to know. He restored Stacia's meager powers—a smattering of shields only, with perhaps a hint of Truth-Reading ability that would never come through as more than hunches—then gave her a brief assurance of the support that others of the king's friends might be expected to give in assisting the Kheldour regency, if it came to that. She blinked and peered at him as he brought her out of trance.

"My mother was better a' this than I am," she murmured,

one hand shifting to caress the wolfhound's ears. "I dinnae know what help I can be to the king."

"You can be his eyes and ears here in Eastmarch," Jesse replied. He had crouched down beside them, to read the spillover from Tieg while the Healer worked. "If Graham and Sighere can achieve the regency, if anything should happen to the king, at least there's a chance of eventually breaking the power of the great lords. With Albertus and Paulin already out of the picture, the process may already have started, if we can keep up the momentum."

"If the king dies," Stacia said, lifting her chin determinedly, "Graham an' Sighere will be at the gates o' Rhemuth with armed men at their backs, demandin' their rights, an' the rights o' the young prince. We willnae fail him, Master Healer. Tell him that, if ye can see him. An' tell the rest o' his Deryni friends."

"I will that, my lady," Tieg replied.

Since the king's arrival in Lochalyn, Joram had ordered that someone be on duty at all times in the domed chamber where the Camberian Council met, with a monitoring link ready for activation at any time Ansel or one of his party should attempt to open communication. When Tieg sought contact after his and Jesse's return from Lochalyn, it was Queron Kinevan on duty. Within half an hour of receiving Tieg's report, he had the other available members of the rebels' leadership gathered around the octagonal table and had shared Tieg's intelligence.

"The codicil idea is brilliant," Joram acknowledged, "but can he pull it off?"

Queron shrugged. "I certainly have the impression that Stacia and her menfolk will do whatever *they* can to enforce the decree, should that become necessary. Fortunately, their loyalty totally outweighs the fact that they'd stand to benefit if the king did die, so we don't need to worry about them helping him along."

"True enough," Niallan agreed, "and the very threat that the codicil exists should be sufficient to keep Rhun and Manfred in line, because they no longer stand to benefit from his death, if they have to share a regency with Kheldour. Once they know about it, I should think they'd do everything in their power to keep the king alive. It's a pity he couldn't have promulgated a second document as well, denouncing his great lords and calling upon his loyal Kheldour lords to free him and his family from their tyranny. They would have helped him, if he'd elected to stay; he's going home because of Michaela and the young prince."

"You're assuming," Dom Rickart said, "that the king will survive his injuries." He folded his pale Healer's hands before him as if in prayer, tapping his fingertips against his lips. "All our impressions are several times removed, of course, but the fever is worrisome. While we must bless that unknown Healer who left a legacy of talicil to the goodwoman Lady Stacia brought to the king, talicil may not be enough."

"Are you saying this injury may be life-threatening?" Joram asked.

Rickart shrugged. "That's impossible to say, without actually examining him. He has fever; he's in considerable pain. Quite aside from the fact that I mistrust the motives of any *Custodes* surgeon, I very much doubt that the good Master Stevanus was able to set the shattered bones correctly. If the hand heals that way, even if there are no other complications, movement is almost certain to be impaired. And as Queron will tell you—or Camlin, whose wrists will never be quite right—it is not always possible to effect full corrective Healing after the fact."

Camlin rubbed at one of his wrists, nodding, feeling for the king. "Couldn't we send a Healer to intercept the king's party?" he asked. "Perhaps in disguise—"

Joram shook his head. "The only likely outcome of that is of losing another good man—if not the Healer himself, apprehended before he could even reach the king, then perhaps the king himself, once it was discovered that he had been Healed."

"I thought we'd already agreed that the codicil would protect him," Niallan said.

"It *could* protect *him*, *if* they believe he's actually executed it and managed to get the copies dispersed; it wouldn't necessarily protect the Healer."

"There's some danger, I agree," Queron muttered. "I still feel that a Healer ought to see him."

Niallan raised a grey eyebrow. "You surely don't propose that we risk Tieg?"

"No, no, I had myself in mind," Queron replied. He held up a hand, shaking his head. "Now, don't all of you jump on me; I know what I'm proposing. I was looking at the map while I waited for all of you to arrive. They'll certainly overnight at Saint Cassian's tonight, but they're headed back the same way they came, toward Ebor and Sheele and Valoret. I'm the first to admit that using the Portals at any of those locations is too dangerous, but there's the secondary Portal at Caerrorie, which isn't that far off the line of march. I could disguise myself as an itinerant monk, a hospitaller of some sort, make my way from Caerrorie to Valoret, and then head north on the King's Road until I meet with the returning army."

"And then what?" Joram demanded. "Walk right up to Rhun and introduce yourself and demand to see the king?"

Queron rolled his eyes and sat back in his chair, drumming his fingertips on his chair arm.

"Of course not. But I can find out what the king's condition is by then. If it proves impossible for *me* to see him without subjecting myself to unreasonable risk, perhaps I can at least influence someone who does have access to him, if things can be done for him via conventional medicine that aren't being done."

"Those risks are acceptable," Rickart said, before Joram could disagree. "For that matter, it might be possible for Tieg to do much the same sort of thing, until Queron can get there to take over. We could ask him and Ansel and Jesse to shadow the army as they head south and watch for opportunities to find out more."

The creases in Niallan's brow had been deepening as Rickart spoke, and he cleared his throat uncomfortably. "I—ah—believe we may be losing sight of the fact that Tieg is not yet fourteen. I know he looks older, with all that gangly height and those big hands, but I'd be very surprised if he yet has the conventional training to do that kind of infiltration. Correct me if I'm wrong, but so far as I was aware, the bulk of his preparation to date has been centered around his vocation as a Healer."

"That's quite true," Queron replied, "and I'm not prepared to risk him, under any circumstances. But Ansel and Jesse do have the necessary skills to ferret out the kind of information Rickart was talking about. They could have collected a great deal of valuable information by the time I meet up with them. And if Tieg's assessments as a Healer are necessary, those can be done indirectly, without risking him overmuch.

"I really think this is the only reasonable approach we can take, just now," he went on. "The twin factors of the codicil and the king's injury make this both a more and less stable situation than it has been for the past six years. It may totally change what we were planning for year's end. I think we're going to have to be both flexible and conservative in our approach until we see how the current situation resolves."

They continued to discuss practicalities of the coming exercise for another hour, also agreeing that while Rhysel ought be alerted to what was happening, the queen should not be told.

"I fear for the poor lass, if the king doesn't make it through this," Queron told Joram, after the others had returned to the sanctuary. "This pregnancy still has a long way to go. If she should lose the king *and* this new baby, the way she lost the first one, I don't know that we'll ever be able to salvage the Haldane line—or if it's worth even trying anymore. One four-year-old prince isn't much on which to base a strong dynasty."

Joram only shook his head and dropped it to one hand. "Queron, I don't even want to *think* about that possibility," he murmured. "And I don't want to think about what I'll do if anything happens to *you*. Since we found out about the queen's new pregnancy, we've been focusing our preparations to make a major attempt at shifting the balance back in Rhys Michael's favor later in the year; but don't lose sight of what you and I have been doing for the last six years, in addition to monitoring the Haldane situation."

Queron smiled and reached out to pat Joram's hand. "You're a dutiful son and brother, Joram," he murmured. "For a man who didn't want to have anything to do with his father's sainthood, you keep displaying startling evidence of belief. I don't intend to do anything stupid, though. I'm well aware that, whether we succeed or fail with the Haldanes, Deryni fortunes will not be restored easily or quickly. Reestablishing a viable cult of Saint Camber may give our people hope for the long term, so that eventually we *can* resume a place of equal partnership again."

"I'd certainly appreciate a little assistance from Saint Camber in the present venture," Joram murmured. "Unfortunately, he seems to have a mind of his own regarding when and where he makes an appearance." He cocked an eyebrow. "Father always did have a mind of his own."

"As do you," Queron said, smiling. "As did your sister. We shall hope that her son has not inherited that aspect of his mother's stubbornness, when I give him his instructions. Perhaps I'll be able to reach Jesse or Ansel instead and urge them to keep a tight rein on young Tieg."

Joram finally allowed himself a hint of a grin. "I'll leave you to it, then, and start making what arrangements I can from sanctuary. Camlin will come to relieve you when you're ready."

* * *

Meanwhile, many miles south, Archbishop Hubert MacInnis was receiving news long known to Joram and his kin but just come to Rhemuth. A *Custodes* monk called Brother Fabius had arrived at the Gwynedd capital just at dusk, with news so dire that Hubert could barely believe what he was hearing. He and Father Secorim, who was *Custodes* abbot at the cathedral, had been visiting the ailing Archbishop Oriss when the exhausted monk was shown into the parlour near Oriss' sickroom.

"Dimitri killed Albertus?" Hubert murmured, when the man had gasped out the gist of his news. "And Paulin is not expected to survive?"

While Secorim questioned the man further, for he and Paulin had been friends since seminary days, Hubert quickly scanned over the written confirmations the man had brought—assessments from both Rhun and Lior—still unable to believe what he was reading.

"I must summon the council," Hubert said, folding the parchment pages and slipping them under his cincture. "Secorim, do you wish to come? I'd guess you're as likely as anyone to replace Paulin, if he doesn't recover. At very least, you can deputize for him for the present."

"I'll come," Secorim said. "Brother Fabius, please come along as well. The council may wish to question you further."

Half an hour later, they were seated around one end of the long table in the council chamber, now joined by Tammaron, Richard Murdoch, and the young Earl of Tarleton Bonner Sinclair, whose father had been Earl of Tarleton before he became Lord Albertus of the *Custodes Fidei*. Though Albertus and his eldest son had not been especially close, young Tarleton still looked stunned, as did the rest of them.

"I blame myself," Hubert murmured, when the messenger again had related the gist of his news and then Secorim had read aloud the texts sent by Rhun and Lior. "It was I who recruited Dimitri. And all these years—Dear God, have I sent them all into a trap? Was Dimitri working for Torenth all along and this all was a ruse to lure the king to a meeting on Torenth's terms?"

"If it was," Richard said coldly, "their strategy did not think far enough ahead. Even if the king perishes, we still have the heir and another on the way. Do you really think Marek of Festil is strong enough to assault the gates of Rhemuth to press his claim? No. We still hold the important cards."

"You're probably right," Tammaron said. "Nonetheless, I think it might be best if we pull additional troops from elsewhere to defend the city—just in case we've underestimated Marek. Richard, your lands are closest. How many men can you call up from Carthane?"

"How many would you like?" Richard replied. "A hundred? More than that? I should think we can also draw upon *Custodes* troops," he added, glancing at Secorim.

Secorim nodded. "I can secure perhaps a hundred overnight, from the garrison outside *Arx Fidei* Abbey. More, if I summon from farther afield, but a lot went north with the king."

Richard shook his head, busy jotting figures on a scrap of parchment. "No, an additional two hundred should be sufficient for now. If a messenger leaves at once, my men can be here within two days. Practically speaking, I don't think it's necessary to fortify any more than that until we hear further from Rhun. We do have to feed all those extra men if we bring them in, after all."

Hubert had begun to recover his equilibrium and nodded agreement.

"I quite agree. We should wait for further clarification of the situation before we let ourselves be stampeded into any sort of panic. Richard is perfectly correct in pointing out that we still hold the controlling factor, in young Prince Owain. To that end, however"—he glanced at Tammaron—"I believe it would be wise if we keep any knowledge of this latest development from the queen. It also may become necessary to confiscate future missives from the king, if he mentions anything to do with this latest development."

"Are you concerned about another miscarriage, if anything should happen to the king?" Richard asked.

Hubert nodded. "It may become necessary to confine the queen to her bed for the remainder of her pregnancy. Tammaron, I rely upon you to instruct the court physicians accordingly. No action is to be taken yet—I do not think that mere news and rumors of news would be sufficient to match the shock that brought on the first miscarriage—but we must hold ourselves in readiness. And it goes without saying that the safety of Prince Owain now becomes even more important than it long has been."

"I'll see about streamlining the running of the royal household," Tammaron said. "With reasonable care, things should be able to drift along as they have done, for at least another week or two, but appropriate precautions will be taken."

CHAPTER TWENTY-THREE

Keep thee far from the man that hath power to kill
. . . lest he take away thy life presently.
—Ecclesiasticus 9:13

While the great lords in Rhemuth pondered what had occurred at Saint Cassian's nearly a week before, the royal party was returning there en route home. For Rhys Michael, most of the day had passed in a merciful narcotic blur, though that had mostly worn off by the time they rode into the abbey yard, just at dusk. The first news to greet them was that Paulin of Ramos had died the night before and been buried that morning in the abbey crypt beside his brother.

Though hardly unexpected, the news elicited a wave of pious lamentation among the *Custodes* members of the king's party, with appropriate mouthings of regret from Rhun and Manfred and the junior officers in their immediate vicinity. Before quarters could even be assigned for those lodging within the abbey precincts, a joint summons came from Father Lior and the abbot for the king and his principal officers to join the *Custodes* clergy in the crypt beneath the church for special prayers beside Paulin's tomb. Rhys Michael tried to plead exhaustion to get out of it, for he could think of few actions more hypocritical on his part than pretending to pray for Paulin's soul, but Rhun made it clear that he must at least affect the appearance of regret.

Accordingly, the king knelt in the crypt with the rest of them and mouthed the prescribed prayers and tried not to think about his throbbing hand or the fever still simmering in his brow. He emerged into the evening coolness to find that gossip was spreading to the camp about Deryni involvement in Paulin's death. Clearly, the circumstances of his illness had not been forgotten by a week's absence. A little later, at table in the abbot's refectory, conversation inevitably turned to Paulin's death.

"In retrospect, I suppose it was folly to expect the outcome could have been any different," the abbot said, responding to a question by Manfred. "What chance had he against Deryni sorcery?"

"Surely you continued the exorcisms, the purifications," Lior murmured.

"And the prayers of the entire community," the abbot said, staring into his cup. "The taint remains, though, Father. I fear it shall take a prolonged period of fasting and prayer and mortification to cleanse this House of it."

Shaking his head, Manfred glanced at Rhun, who seemed to be biting back a caustic comment, then at Brother Polidorus, the abbey's infirmarian, who was sitting farther down the table next to Master Stevanus.

"I am no churchman," he said uneasily, "but it seems obvious to me that all was done that *could* be done, for his spiritual well-being. A pity nothing availed for his physical recovery."

Brother Polidorus raised an eyebrow and pushed his goblet away a little. .

"We did try, my lord, but as Father Abbot has said, the prognosis was poor from the start. He could not eat. He could not control his bodily functions. His heart remained strong and he continued to breathe, but my helpers and I were never able to elicit any kind of response.

"Except when he was bled," he amended, almost as an afterthought. "Several times, he seemed on the verge of stirring, and we hoped this might be evidence that the taint was leaving him." He shook his head. "But he never regained consciousness. At least I do not think he felt anything, there at the end. God grant him peace," he concluded, crossing himself piously.

Rhys Michael echoed the gesture along with the rest at table, but he could not find it in his heart to regret Paulin's fate. As he stifled a yawn and tried to find a more comfortable posture, he found himself wondering whether the bleeding that Polidorus had mentioned might have hastened Paulin to his reward, for the *Custodes* were known to use—and misuse—bloodletting as part of their internal discipline within the Order. He wondered whether they might view it as an alternative coup de grâce for one of their own with no hope of recovery, though the coup generally was limited to fatal battle injuries in the field, and the Church maintained only a precarious peace with the practice. He remembered hearing how a *Custodes* battle surgeon had given the coup thus to Murdoch of Carthane, the day after Javan's coronation—or rather, Rhun had done it under *Custodes* direction. More normally, the *Custodes* used bleeding as a means of discipline and intimidation, sometimes unto death. If Paulin had succumbed to loss of blood, Rhys Michael could not but think it fitting, to taste the fate he had inflicted on many others.

But his own fate was far more on his mind just now. After a while longer of listening to the *Custodes* mouth platitudes and make noises of regret, he excused himself and retired with Cathan and Fulk to the quarters the abbot had allocated him on his previous visit. He was dragging with exhaustion as they helped him out of his armor and into bed, and he lay there shivering under several sleeping furs until Cathan brought him another dose of the tacil. Though no one had summoned him, Stevanus came in very shortly with Brother Polidorus and another, younger monk carrying a small wooden chest and a two-branched candlestick for more light. Cathan had just set the empty cup and the little earthen flask of tacil on a small table beside the bed and tried to push them farther into shadow before the monk set the candlestick on the table.

"I want to change your dressing and see how you're faring after a day in the saddle, Sire," Stevanus said, setting down his medical satchel on the foot of the bed. "Brother Polidorus also thought to have a look at you. Brother Deiniol, could you fetch us a basin and some hot water, please?"

As the younger monk disappeared to obey, Rhys Michael reluctantly pulled his bandaged hand out from under the furs and let Stevanus begin unwrapping it, while Polidorus felt his forehead and made *tsk*ing sounds.

"Dear, dear me. These things are always so tiresome when broken bones *and* wounds are involved. The forearm looks clean enough. I see no red streaks."

"Aye, but there's fever in it," Stevanus said.

"Yes, I can feel that."

"And the laceration shows more inflammation than I would like. I also don't know what may be going on around the bones that were crushed. There's still too much swelling and bruising to see or feel much."

As he exposed the hand and the two started poking and prodding, Rhys Michael gasped and even cried out, trying not to squirm with the pain. At Stevanus' summons, Cathan and Fulk came to help hold the arm steady while the examination continued, and Brother Deiniol returned with towels, a basin, and a steaming pitcher, which he set beside the fireplace.

"I think perhaps those sutures should come out," Polidorus said, drawing back to wipe his hands on a clean towel. "The flesh is very swollen, the skin taut and shiny. I would say that the wound wants cautery to burn out the impurities. Have you bled him yet?"

"I didn't want to weaken him," Stevanus began.

"No! I won't be bled!" Rhys Michael whispered, sitting up in alarm. "And I don't want cautery. I'm making good progress. Just give me time."

"If you hope to keep the hand," Polidorus said coldly, "then you must allow us to do what we think best." He gave a curt nod to his assistant, who turned back to the fireplace and began taking things out of the chest he had brought. "The crushed bones may yet necessitate more aggressive treatment," he went on, returning his attention to Stevanus, "but we can postpone that for now, see how he looks in a day or two. What are you giving him for the pain, syrup of poppies?"

"Aye."

"But I can't stay here!" Rhys Michael protested. "I have to ride tomorrow—"

"Well, give him half again the dose you've been giving," Polidorus continued, paying the king no mind at all. "And you, sir—" He nodded to Fulk. "Fill that basin with very hot water, and we'll get his hand soaking. The heat will draw out some of the inflammation and also ease the removal of the sutures."

"I've told you, no," Rhys Michael said again. "Leave the sutures. I don't want cautery, and I won't be bled."

"Don't be foolish. You're in no condition to know what you want, or what's best for you," Polidorus muttered, turning away to supervise his assistant.

As Stevanus also withdrew, pulling his satchel from the end of the bed to measure out the painkiller Polidorus had ordered, Rhys Michael pulled Cathan closer with his good hand.

"Go and tell Rhun what they're doing," he whispered. And added, in Cathan's mind, *Tell him I refuse to stay here and that if I die, they're going to have a different regency than they bargained on. Tell him about the codicil—but you haven't got an*

original copy, and I've ordered you not to tell who does.
"Hurry."

Stevanus looked annoyed as Cathan nodded and turned
away to dash out the door, and he was shaking his head as he
brought a small metal medicine cup filled with syrup of poppies.

"Sire, Rhun isn't going to interfere in this," he said, holding
out the cup. "Drink this down now. You needn't make this any
more difficult than it has to be."

"I don't want the cautery," Rhys Michael said stubbornly,
ignoring the cup. "You can soak the hand if you want—I can
see how that might help—but the wound isn't bleeding. And I
won't be bled; I might be too weak to ride. I can't stay here.
I have to be able to keep traveling. I have to get back to
Michaela."

"Sire, are you trained as a surgeon?" Polidorus said pointedly.

"No, of course not."

"Then do not presume to tell me my business. Take this and
drink it. What must be done will be done, with or without this
help. Don't force me to have you held."

As he pressed the cup into Rhys Michael's good hand, Fulk
brought a steaming basin to the right side of the bed, looking
uneasy as Polidorus came to move the bedside table closer.
The earthen flask of tacil and the empty cup were still sitting
on the little table, and the monk had to move them before he
could spread the towel hung over Fulk's arm. He sniffed curiously at the cup as Fulk set the basin down.

"What is this?" he asked.

"It's something for the fever," Rhys Michael said, before
Fulk or Stevanus could reply. "It seems to be helping. The chatelaine at Lochalyn Castle gave it to me."

"Some folk remedy, eh? What is it called?" The monk
glanced at Stevanus as he opened the flask and then peered inside and sniffed again.

"The old midwife with her called it tacil," Stevanus replied.
"Lady Stacia said her mother used to get it from a Healer
who's since died."

"From a Healer? Then it's a Deryni drug!" Polidorus said,
holding it away from him with a grimace of distaste. "I'll have
none of that under *this* roof!"

"No, it's helping me!" Rhys Michael cried. Still encumbered
with the cup in his good hand, he made an inadvertent grab for

the monk with his injured one—and jarred it against the edge
of the basin with enough force to bring tears to his eyes, just
as Stevanus rescued the cup of painkiller.

"Don't be impertinent, Sire," Polidorus muttered, as Rhys
Michael curled defensively over the injured hand, gasping, and
Fulk moved in protectively. "Brother Deiniol, get rid of this.
Burn it or something."

"But, it *does* seem to be helping," Stevanus said uncertainly,
though he blocked Fulk from interfering with the younger
monk, who came and took the flask from Polidorus.

"Nonsense." Polidorus shook out another towel with a snap
and spread it on the bed beside the table. "If it's Deryni, it
can't possibly be helpful. Now, give me that hand, Sire, and
let's get it to soaking before the water gets cold. Stevanus, either persuade him to drink that or get some strong men in here
to hold him down."

As Rhys Michael heard the smash of pottery down the
garderobe shaft, he sank back against his pillows in dismay,
gasping but no longer resisting as Polidorus took his injured
hand and plunged it into the steaming water. The tacil *had*
helped—he was sure of it—but now there would be no more
relief from that quarter. And all because a Deryni had made
it . . .

Queasy and disheartened, jaws clenched against the heat
coiled around his hand, Rhys Michael anxiously watched the
younger monk return to the fireplace, where Polidorus had
gone to check the cautery instruments heating in the fire. As
Stevanus put the little cup of painkiller back in his good hand,
he reflected that his only hope was for Cathan to get Rhun
here before these *Custodes* butchers started doing really horri-
ble things to him.

It was not just the threat of pain that set terror in his heart.
He could have submitted to cautery with hardly a whimper if
convinced that it would be beneficial, but the thought of being
bled sent a cold chill of dread down his spine, especially since
he had heard of Paulin's treatment. He turned the little cup nervously in his fingers as his mind flashed back over his own reluctant acquaintance with the practice.

The first time, though he could not remember it, had been
after his "rescue" from his kidnappers, to make him think he
had lost more blood from his "wounds" than he actually had.
Stevanus himself probably had been responsible for that one.
They had bled him occasionally during those awful months af-

ter Javan's murder, to keep him weak; and he had been bled several times just before his coronation, so that he would display a paleness and lethargy appropriate to long illness.

There were legitimate medical reasons for bloodletting, of course. And he knew it was a common enough monastic discipline in some religious houses, sometimes permitted as a voluntary aid to preserving chastity, since lowering the blood also lowered inclinations to "passions of the flesh." *Minution*, they called it, from the Latin *minuere*, to lessen or diminish.

But the *Custodes* had a less benign use for it—not only a required test of the vow of obedience but also, in some cases, a vehicle of intimidation. Javan had told him how they bled an innocent priest called Faelan, trying to force him to reveal why Javan had requested his services as a confessor; they had even bled Javan himself, during his stay in the monastery, to demonstrate their absolute power over him.

Believe me, Javan had told him one night, *there are few more helpless feelings in the world than watching your lifeblood pump out of your veins and knowing that if it suits them, those in authority over you have the power to forbid a halt . . .*

Polidorus' return with a new pitcher of hot water brought an abrupt release from *that* image, though the monk's intent was hardly more reassuring as he bent to check the temperature of the water. Blessedly, and somewhat to Rhys Michael's surprise, the hot water actually was starting to ease the ache in his hand, after the initial shock. But when Polidorus began slowly pouring more hot water into the basin around the hand, increasing the temperature, the king remembered the cup in his good hand and gulped down about half the contents before handing it off to Stevanus.

"You ought to drink it all," the battle surgeon murmured, glancing into the cup. "That isn't enough to put you under."

"I don't *want* to be put under," Rhys Michael said stubbornly. "I have to be coherent when I talk to Rhun."

"That won't change anything," Stevanus replied. "At least lie back and let what you've drunk take effect. This first part won't be too bad."

"Sire, shall I go and see what's keeping Cathan?" Fulk asked a little nervously, from over nearer the door.

Rhys Michael shook his head and closed his eyes briefly, heartened that Fulk had offered that assistance on his own, belatedly wishing he had dared to set stronger compulsions in the young knight, who could not help the fact that his father was one of the men responsible for the king's servitude.

"I'm sure he'll be here soon," he whispered. "Just don't leave me alone."

"Just don't *interfere*," Brother Polidorus amended sharply, bending to peer more closely at his reluctant patient's hand.

For the moment, neither Rhys Michael nor Fulk had any choice but to comply. At least for now, in just the short time the king's hand had been submerged, either the heat or the drug or a combination of the two had eased the pain substantially. Some of that relief was canceled out when Polidorus began cleaning around the laceration, though it did not hurt as much as he had feared. At least the monk's touch was gentle.

What did hurt was when Stevanus started probing out the first of the sutures to be removed, for the stitches were deeply embedded. Resistance only made the surgeon's task more difficult and brought further sharp threats of physical restraint from Polidorus, who was steadying the hand, so Rhys Michael gave it up and lay back, turning his face away so he would not have to see his blood reddening the water in the bowl. Closing his eyes was not an option, because if he did, he could feel himself starting to float with the lethargy brought by the syrup of poppies. That was dangerous until after he had talked to Rhun. So long as he kept his eyes open—

"What the devil is going on?" an angry voice intruded suddenly—Rhun's—as Rhys Michael came alert with a start. "Stevanus, what are you doing?"

"It was my opinion," Brother Polidorus said, "that his Highness' wound should be cauterized to burn out the impurities. I believe he should be bled as well. For now, the hot water is drawing out the inflammation."

Rhun stalked over to look at the hand in its basin, flicked a glance to Rhys Michael's face—taut with discomfort and defiance, the grey eyes dilated from the painkiller—then swept a hand around the room.

"All right, everyone out of here. I'll speak to his Highness in private. Cathan, you may stay."

Stevanus set aside his instruments and hurriedly dried his hands, sketching Rhun a nervous bow before heading for the door, Fulk accompanying him. Polidorus let Cathan escort him and his assistant after them, but paused to murmur something to Cathan before the younger man closed him out of the room.

Cathan latched the door, then came to take the king's hand from the basin and set it on a clean towel.

"What are you doing?" Rhun demanded, as Cathan took the basin to dump it down the garderobe.

"Brother Polidorus said I should put the king's hand to soak in clean water while we talk," Cathan replied, returning to the fireplace to refill the basin with hot water. "That will prevent further contamination and continue drawing out the inflammation. I don't agree with the cautery, if the king doesn't want it, but I do agree with this."

As he brought the basin back to the king's bedside and eased the hand into the fresh water, watched suspiciously by Rhun, Rhys Michael allowed himself a tiny sigh and murmured his thanks, then turned his gaze to the earl marshal, who was staring at him from the foot of the bed.

"Thank you for coming," the king murmured, concerned that he had to concentrate to keep Rhun in focus.

"It doesn't appear that I had much choice," Rhun said. "What's this ridiculous story Cathan has been telling me about some codicil to your will that you had drawn up in East-march?"

"It isn't a story, and it isn't ridiculous," the king said quietly. "If I die before an heir of mine comes of age, the Duke of Claibourne and the Earl of Marley are irrevocably appointed as regents, regardless of whoever else you ramrod through the council. And before you even have a chance to kill them, they'll have appointed their own successors—and their successors will appoint successors. Kheldour will have a say in the next regency."

"Kheldour will be running the kingdom," Rhun said testily, "and the next thing you know, Kheldour will be providing the next king."

"I don't think so," Rhys Michael replied. "And if they did, they couldn't do much worse than your lot have done. You never gave Alroy a chance to be a real king, and you killed Javan when it looked as if he might be one. And you've only been keeping me alive until you were sure you had an heir and a spare to mold in exactly the image you wanted. If it isn't to be a free Haldane king on the throne of Gwynedd, Rhun, I think I might prefer one from Kheldour. The Duke of Claibourne would make an excellent king. Or maybe Kheldour can give my sons a free crown."

"I don't believe a word of this," Rhun said. "You're bluffing."

Rhys Michael laid his head back on his pillows and glanced at the ceiling.

"Show him the draft copy, Cathan." And as Cathan went to the king's saddlebag to get it, Rhys Michael added, "And don't think that you can simply destroy all the copies and pretend they never existed. There are a number of them—I won't tell you how many—and at least one is bound to reach the hands of those best equipped to make proper use of it. I'll tell you right now that none of them are in my hands anymore."

As Cathan brought the draft copy over to Rhun, the earl marshal snatched it out of his hand and took it over by the fire to read it. His face was white as he looked up at the king, and he slowly refolded the piece of parchment as he returned to the foot of the bed. Cathan had gone to stand with his back against the door.

"What is it you want?" Rhun asked, creasing the parchment between nervous fingers as he stared appraisingly at the king.

Closing his eyes briefly, Rhys Michael allowed himself to breathe a faint sigh of relief, trying not to drift as he sank deeper into the thrall of the syrup of poppies.

"First of all, I want to get home," he whispered. "I want to see my wife and son. I don't want cautery, I don't want to be bled, and I don't want anyone to cut off my hand. If we still had Healers—if your colleagues hadn't shot Oriel down like an animal, six years ago—he would have been with me at Culliecairn, and this probably never would have gotten to this state. Without one—well, I simply have to hope I'll be lucky. If I'm not, you can blame it on your precious *Custodes*. The ever-pious Brother Polidorus threw out the 'Deryni' drug that Lady Stacia gave me to take my fever down. It was helping, but that didn't matter; a Healer had made it. Therefore, it was evil."

Whatever Rhun was thinking, his lean face revealed none of it. After a taut pause, he said, "I somehow expected the Deryni sympathy."

"It isn't Deryni sympathy; it's acknowledgment that Healers were a good thing," Rhys Michael said. "I'd give a great deal to have one here right now. But that isn't going to happen, because by going after the Deryni, you've lost us the Healers as well."

Rhun shrugged, still toying with the folded piece of parchment, but his eyes had gone hooded and dangerous. "It's pointless to argue about this. You've given me a list of things you *don't* want done to your hand, and you've said you want to go home. What happens then?"

"Once I'm home and well?" Rhys Michael allowed himself a faint smile. "You'd like to know that, wouldn't you? For now, if I were you, I'd worry about keeping me alive. And it's also in your best interests to keep Cathan alive," he added, improvising to protect his brother-in-law but not revealing the conditional appointment as regent, which would spell his death. "If anything happens to him, you are personally named as the one responsible, Rhun. If you kill the queen's brother, you'll hang. I drew documents to protect him, too."

Rhun nodded, anger now smouldering openly in the pale eyes. "That's what all that little dance outside the privies was about, isn't it?" he said. "You *told* me to look inside, and I didn't."

Rhys Michael chuckled weakly. "I didn't sign the documents in the privy, Rhun. There was a tiny room off the stair, just a few steps up. Sighere helped create the diversion so I could dart back down and make you think I'd come out of the garderobe."

"I suppose Fulk was a part of it, too? Cathan I can understand—he's kin. But Fulk—"

"No, he was a dupe," Rhys Michael replied. "He hadn't a clue what was going on. He'd have gone straight to his father."

"Tammaron will still kill him," Rhun muttered.

"I hope not. He's a good man, and he'll be as appalled as you to learn how he was used."

Rhun let out an explosive snort and set his hands on his hips, glancing at the floor, then cocked his head at the king.

"All right. I'm a practical man, Sire, so let's get down to practicalities. What shall we do about your hand? If you should die from it because you won't accept sound medical advice, that isn't *my* fault."

"You'd better hope I *don't* die from it," Rhys Michael replied. "Have a look. You've ample field experience. What do you think?"

He lifted it slightly from the basin, to the sound of dripping water, glanced at it, then looked away queasily as he let it back down. As he had hoped, Rhun came over to inspect it more dispassionately, lifting it slightly out of the water with two fingers from under the palm and then shifting his gaze to the grey

Haldane eyes—and was snared in them, as Rhys Michael had intended, though the king drew in his controls gently, so Rhun would not realize what was happening.

"It looks as if Stevanus started removing the sutures," Rhun said.

Rhys Michael nodded. "I couldn't stop him."

Rhun blinked. "It will let the wound drain, if you won't let him cauterize."

"If it were your hand, would you let him cauterize it?" Rhys Michael asked. "Tell me truly."

Rhun looked at him and blinked again, sinking deeper into the spell. "I—don't know. There's fever here and local infection, but no sign of poisoning going up the arm. Still, if you really intend to keep traveling with this—"

"I *must* be able to travel, Rhun," he said softly. "I want to get home. I'll do it flat on my back in a horse-litter, if I must, but I have to keep moving. I don't know what's going to happen with this, but I—want to see my wife and son."

He set his good hand on Rhun's wrist at that, clasping his fingers around and using the closer contact to press deeper. Rhun's eyes closed, and he started to sway on his feet, but Cathan came to support him from behind, though he held back from any further involvement as Rhys Michael drove deeper still.

It was difficult to stay focused, with the syrup of poppies dulling his concentration, but he feared he might never have another chance like this. Skimming over the filth and guilt and hatred he knew was there, not touching their earlier conversation about the documents, he set a succession of irresistible commands—some of which he would probably regret, when called to final judgment, but which would serve what must be done, to secure a Haldane future. It took a while, but he had been thinking about what he needed to do while he waited for Rhun to show up.

When he was finished, he blocked all memory or access to what he had done, released Rhun's wrist, then released Rhun himself to the new instructions set deep in his mind. Cathan very quietly returned to his place against the door.

"I'm very tired now," Rhys Michael murmured, as Rhun blinked. Rhys Michael let the injured hand back into the water—cooler now than when they had begun—then looked up at Rhun again. "Could we please ask Master Stevanus to come back and rebandage my hand? And it's understood that there isn't going to be any cautery or bleeding?"

Straightening, Rhun picked up one of the towels and dried his hands, his jaw set, the anger back in his eyes.

"You're a very stubborn man, Sire. You always have been. If you're determined to continue on tomorrow, though—"

The king allowed himself a yawn that was not at all feigned. "I really don't care to discuss this further, my lord. I've had a fairly stiff dose of painkiller, so I'm afraid I'm starting to drift. Please fetch Master Stevanus."

"I'll call him, Sire," Cathan said.

Rhun left as Stevanus came in with Fulk, but Polidorus was not allowed to enter. Rhys Michael could hear voices raised in anger receding down the corridor as Stevanus came over to him.

"No cautery and no bleeding," Rhys Michael told him, extending his dripping hand. "Just dry it and dress it and wrap it up again. I want to be out of here early in the morning."

He had drifted into sleep by the time Stevanus finished wrapping up his hand, as certain as he could be that Cathan and Fulk would ensure that his wishes were respected, and slept deep and dreamlessly for what remained of the night. He would have been heartened to know that the Healer Queron once more was on the move, riding to rendezvous with him, bringing hope of relief from his pain; but he did not know.

CHAPTER TWENTY-FOUR

Traitors, heady, high-minded, lovers of pleasures
more than lovers of God.

—II Timothy 3:4

The news of the king's injury and the outcome in Eastmarch
reached Rhemuth in the early morning hours as Rhys Michael
slept uneasily at Saint Cassian's. Though troops were already
on the way to the capital from *Arx Fidei* and Carthane, the
former expected to arrive by midmorning, the great lords resident in the capital breathed a collective sigh of relief as they
gathered in the council chamber by torch and candlelight to
hear one of Hubert's scribes read out Rhun's account of the
resolution at Culliecairn. That the king had survived, apparently by the grace of Sudrey of Eastmarch, was received as almost miraculous, especially when they learned that Sudrey had
stood against not only Prince Miklos, but almost certainly the
disguised Marek of Festil.

"What do you suppose they were trying to accomplish?" Father Secorim asked, rubbing sleep from his eyes, for like the
rest of them, he had been summoned from his bed when the
messenger arrived—a knight called Henry of Rutherford.

Hubert rolled his eyes heavenward, trusting the candlelit
darkness to cloak his impatience; Secorim had much to learn
before he could hope to be Paulin's match.

"If they could have done it, I'm sure they would have slain
the king then and there," he replied. "However, I very much
doubt that was their expectation. What they apparently intended in the short term was the slaying of Sudrey of
Eastmarch, née Rhorau, whom they considered to have be-

trayed her House and her race by marrying Eastmarch. In truth, *I* would have said that *Eastmarch* betrayed his lineage and his race by marrying Deryni." He sighed. "But we were hardly in a position to pursue the point, when we only learned of it fifteen years after the fact. At least the bitch is dead now."

Tammaron raised an eyebrow at that, but Richard only smiled, cunning as his father had been, and even more pitiless.

"So Miklos is dead, and Marek has gone slinking home to lick his wounds and answer to Miklos' brother," Richard said. His smile became wolfish. "That means the king will be coming home after all."

"Until the queen is safely delivered," Tammaron said archly, "you'd best hope the king does come home. And best not to count on *that* until we see him riding through the gates. Personally, I shall not even begin to rest easily until we are certain that Marek has, indeed, gone home, and that Culliecairn is well and truly in the hands of Eastmarch again."

Richard yawned and stood, affecting the uttermost bored indifference. "Gentlemen, you may continue this discussion until dawn, if you wish, but I'm going back to bed for what few hours remain of the night. Until the king does return, I still have a city to protect and troops arriving in the morning."

As Richard left and the others began to disperse, Hubert took Rhun's letter and read over it again for himself, weighing each turn of phrase, for Rhun was not given to choosing his words lightly. The apparent treachery of Miklos of Torenth, while amply repaid, underlined the complexity of the deception in which Dimitri must have been involved and made Hubert worry about how much farther the tendrils of deceit might extend.

That Marek himself had managed to gain access to the king was particularly disturbing, though it was Rhun's opinion that the bulk of his and Miklos' effort seemed to have been focused on eliminating the Lady Sudrey. But given the past history of the Haldanes, Hubert had to wonder whether it had been only Sudrey's resistance that had prevented Marek from launching an attack to utterly crush his Haldane rival. It did not occur to him to worry about the injury Rhun had reported to the king's hand.

Marek himself was about to face the wrath of his brother-in-law, the King of Torenth, in whose torchlit audience chamber he and his two companions nervously waited; he had already weathered his wife's tearful anger in Tolan. Cosim had warned him to send a written message first, knowing King Arion's temper, and Valentin had been reluctant to go at all, but Marek had insisted he must bring the news in person. After they arrived at the Royal Portal in Beldour, the gist of their mission evident by their stark attire and the absence of Miklos, a stony-faced chamberlain had whisked them to the most austere of Arion's private reception rooms, there to languish without refreshment or even seating as the taut minutes gradually stretched nearly to an hour.

The door opened at last. Unattended, looking recently roused from sleep, King Arion swept into the room in a dark shimmer of black silk robe, his feet unshod, the long hair loose around his shoulders, fairer than Miklos' had been. Cosim, who had long been King Arion's vassal, took one look at the rage seething in his sovereign's eyes and sank to his knees, bowing his forehead to the floor and not daring to rise from that position. Old Valentin gave the young king a precise and respectful military salute but kept his gaze averted, staying well behind Marek. Marek himself, well aware of his potential danger, ventured close enough to kneel humbly at the king's feet and reached for the hem of his robe to kiss it.

"How dare you show your face here?" Arion whispered, yanking the silk from Marek's grasp and moving back a pace, the nimbus of his power crackling around his head, his eyes almost colorless in the torchlight. "Did I not warn you that the time was not yet right to pursue this mad cause of yours?"

"Sire, it was not entirely Prince Marek's fault," old Valentin began.

"*Silence!*" Arion commanded. "*I* will decide what is and is not Marek's fault!"

In the stunned hush that followed, Marek cautiously dared to lift his eyes about to the level of Arion's belt, though he stayed on his knees, his hands crossed tight under his chin in an attitude of deference. The king was only five years older than Marek, but he had the presence of a man of far more years—and had far more mastery of his power than Marek expected he would ever wield. Miklos had been powerful, but casual in his use of his magic; Arion was all focus and steely will. Though Arion terrified Marek when he was in such a mood, the younger man knew he had but one hope of winning back even a chance at the other's goodwill or even tolerance.

"Sire, I throw myself on your mercy," he whispered, cautiously lifting his gaze to the king's. "If the negligence is entirely mine, I will accept whatever discipline you choose to impose, whatever penalty—even my death, if you deem it fitting. I loved Miklos as the brother I never had and never shall have again. We encouraged one another in the dream we pursued, but our miscalculation was mutual. Though we sought to test the Haldane for the future, our true objective was to put an end to the traitor Sudrey of Rhorau. Neither she nor the Haldane responded as we expected. She—"

"Do you dare to tell me that *Sudrey* bested my brother?" the king demanded. "That cannot be."

"I *know* that," Marek said miserably. "Yet her power played a part. She seemed to lend power, or knowledge, or focus, or *something* to whatever the Haldane has. Read the truth of what I say, Arion! I don't *know* how it happened! You know I cannot lie to you!"

Arion's eyes seemed to glow like pools of quicksilver, impaling Marek's will, the tall, lean form towering above him like an avenging angel. Not bothering with mere words, the king flicked a silent command at Cosim, who had fearfully lifted his head to observe the exchange between the two. Quickly the Healer moved to do the king's bidding, coming to kneel behind Marek and brace him for the king's touch, ready to assist when Arion took up Marek's offer.

"I give you fair warning, Marek. If you resist at all, I am apt to cause permanent damage," Arion said, the strong fingers sliding into Marek's dark hair as the thumbs pressed to his temples. "This angry, I cannot promise to go softly."

Numbly resigned to accept what he had invited, whatever might be the cost, Marek closed his eyes and eased back on his hunkers, leaning into Cosim's enfolding, letting his hands fall loosely to his sides in token of utter submission. As he yielded up his shields, he felt the deft soothing of the Healer's touch first, relaxing his body and taking his consciousness gently enough down the first few levels into passive readiness. But then Arion's cold probe was knifing into his mind and soul with surgical precision, laying bare every particle of memory that had to do with Miklos over the last two weeks, every perception and intuition about Rhys Michael Alister Haldane, about Sudrey of Eastmarch, née Rhorau, who had betrayed her kind and helped bring about Miklos' death—and all the dark memory and anguish of Miklos' passing and its aftermath.

As Arion thrust ever deeper, touching now on Dimitri and

his mysterious demise, Marek's growing discomfort began verging into real pain; but having given over control to Cosim, he could only let the Healer take him through and beyond the pain to unconsciousness rather than the oblivion of mind-ripping, for Arion would not relent until satisfied that his subject had yielded everything of consequence.

When next Marek became aware of anything besides a dull throbbing behind his eyes, he was lying in Valentin's arms and struggling to breathe. Cosim was kneeling beside them, one hand still touching Marek but himself still reverberating to the memory of the Death-Reading the two of them had done on Miklos, also given over for the angry examination of Miklos' bereaved brother. Marek heard Arion before he saw him—a stifled sobbing that he soon tracked to the dim recess of a nearby window embrasure, where a darker shadow hunched amid the flickering shadow play from the torches in the room.

"Arion?" he whispered, struggling to sit up despite the warning murmur from Valentin.

The sudden movement caused a lancing pain behind his eyes, which abated not at all as the king turned to glare at him, the swollen eyes still angry.

Say nothing, Cosim warned, stirring enough to try to wrap his healing around the pain in Marek's head. *He knows it was not entirely your fault, but that does not cancel out the loss.*

"We shall not discuss this further at this time," Arion said quietly, without any inflection whatsoever. The temperate tone was far more frightening than any outburst of further anger might have been. "Go back to my sister's capital in Torenth. Give her what comfort you may. Bring my brother's body back here for burial, but do *not* come by Portal. By land, with a fitting escort, the journey should take at least a week. Perhaps by then I shall be able to speak to you civilly."

With that he was gone, out the door in a swirl of black silk and blacker mood. Not for several seconds did Marek dare to stir, only then turning his gaze uncertainly to the men the king had left him.

"Cosim, will he ever forgive me?" he asked.

The Healer bowed his silver head.

"Do not count on his support for a very long time, my friend," he said softly. "I have never seen him so angry. Just now, he is angry with you. When his anger turns to Miklos and the Haldane as well, perhaps he will be able to at least accept what has happened. I think it now clear that the Haldane is something we had not anticipated, even if he did not directly kill Miklos."

"One day I will take him, Cosim," Marek said. "But even though I best him with magic, I will need troops to secure what I have won. And I can only get them through Arion's good graces."

"In time, you may regain Arion's favor," the Healer replied. "But for now, be thankful that he has spared your life and sanity. Are you able to stand?"

"I think so," Marek said, letting Valentin help him shakily to his feet.

"Then let us obey the king's command, and go back to the Princess Charis."

"Aye," Marek whispered, passing a trembling hand across his eyes. "And pray a curse upon the man who calls himself King of Gwynedd."

The bells of Prime startled the king awake as they had on his previous visit to Saint Cassian's, and he dragged himself from bed to ready for the day's journey, not looking forward to the jarring of the ride, but eager to be quit of the place. His hand seemed marginally less swollen, perhaps because of its hot soak the night before, but all his body still ached. He could feel the tension in his neck and shoulders and the warmth of fever in his brow.

He skipped Mass that morning, for he could not bear the thought of having a *Custodes* priest minister to him, after the simple sanctity of Father Derfel. Deliberately ignoring Stevanus' advice, for the battle surgeon was a lay member of the *Custodes Fidei*, he took his morning dose of painkiller before going into the refectory to break his fast. It made him slightly nauseated on an empty stomach, as Stevanus had warned; but again, eating seemed entirely too much effort, and he only managed to get down some ale and a little bread before pushing away from the table and heading out to the yard, where Rhun and Manfred sullenly awaited orders. He gathered Rhun had shared the previous night's revelation about the codicil with the older man, for Manfred gave him a hard, cold look before mounting up. Father Lior's sour countenance suggested that he knew, too; and Brother Polidorus now had joined the other *Custodes* men riding at the Inquisitor-General's side.

The second day's travel was much like the first, except that

Rhys Michael felt worse as the day wore on. As they forged on across the rest of the Iomaire plain, he tried to make himself eat a little whenever they stopped to rest—or at least drink some wine to fortify himself, for he knew he must keep up his strength—but he could feel his fever mounting without the tacil to control it. Rhun and Manfred were never far from his side, and the *Custodes* bodyguards who rode before and behind him seemed unusually attentive. Gallard de Breffni was prominent among them. When they camped for the night, Cathan reported that there seemed to be more guards around the royal tent than usual, no doubt to prevent the export of any more unauthorized codicils.

He ate sparingly in his tent with Cathan and Fulk, for he could not stomach the prospect of his enemies' cold-eyed speculation if he dined in the command tent. After supper, despite his exhaustion, he had Cathan take down a letter to Michaela, for there had been no opportunity to write to her the night before. Writing was less than satisfactory, for other eyes would read his words before they reached the queen, but he knew that having the letters would bring her some comfort. Before they were finished, Stevanus came to dress his hand, accompanied by Brother Polidorus, Father Lior, and even Rhun and Manfred, but no one said much, Stevanus only commenting that his fever seemed to have worsened since morning. Rhys Michael decided it was pointless to remind them that the drug Polidorus had taken away from him might have prevented that.

When they had gone out, he lay back on his camp bed and brooded on developments as Cathan finished the letter by lantern-light, and Fulk spread his pallet before the tent entrance, preparing for sleep. Stevanus had left the usual dose of painkiller, but Rhys Michael had not yet touched it.

Outside, the bustle of the camp gradually settled down to the usual night sounds, with Fulk's gentle snoring soon providing a reassuring background drone. By the time Cathan had brought ink and quill for the king to sign Mika's letter, Rhys Michael had conceived a further measure he might take, to the comfort of his family, for he was coming to worry that either his weakening condition or the growing enmity of Rhun and Manfred might conspire to prevent him from ever reaching home.

"Before you take that to Rhun for dispatch, I need you to fetch me the Haldane brooch from my cloak," he murmured to Cathan, as he scrawled his awkward signature. "And when you come back, please don't disturb me until I indicate that it's all right. I'll tell you then, what this is all about."

"Very well."

When Cathan had gone, Rhys Michael lay back with the Haldane brooch cupped under his good hand, resting on his chest, his thumb lightly caressing the sleek gold of the clasp as he set the Haldane lion in his inner sight like a battle banner. He gathered his intent as he drove himself deep into trance then, shutting out the pain, shutting out the fever coursing through his body, coiling his design around the core of his Haldane potential, knowing exactly what must be done. He could not and would not impose the full weight of the Haldane legacy on his son at so young an age, but he knew beyond questioning that the potential must be set, both in Owain and in the second son Rhysel claimed Michaela carried. And it might be that Michaela herself would have to do it, if he could not.

Using the brooch as a focus for this new purpose, as he and Michaela had long used it as a focus for their aspirations to free his crown, he set the requisite spells and bound them with his power, also setting instructions for Michaela on a more superficial level. It took a great deal of energy.

He was sweating and trembling with chills by the time he had finished. To seal the intent and bind it to his will, he turned the brooch over and braced it against his chest, the clasp now pointed upward, gleaming in the lantern-light. Even his good hand was shaking, and he had to steady the body of the brooch against his bandaged hand so that he could rest the other atop the clasp.

For strongest binding, he would have preferred to thrust it through his palm, as he had at his empowering; but he knew he did not have the strength, and also dared not risk debilitating injury to his one good hand, with no Healer to attend to it. Considering, he lightly tried the point against the join of thumb and forefinger, then shifted it to the web of skin and muscle and sinew between his middle and ring fingers and closed his eyes—and shoved hard.

The pain was sharp but brief, and as nothing beside the pulsing throb of his other hand. He drew a deep breath, and another, to disengage from the spell. When he opened his eyes, Cathan was sitting quietly on the edge of the bed beside him, eyes wide. The king managed a shaky smile as he glanced down at the sliver of gold protruding from between his fingers.

"You can pull that out now, if you will," he whispered, wincing as he turned his hand slightly to accommodate Cathan. "It's done. Just make certain that Michaela gets the brooch, if anything happens to me. And the Eye of Rom."

Cathan had picked up the hand and was poised to pull out the clasp, but he faltered at the king's words, blue eyes flicking first to the great ruby in the king's right earlobe, then to the grey Haldane eyes.

"Do you know something I don't?"

Rhys Michael swallowed audibly and glanced at the brooch, jutting his chin at it for Cathan to proceed, breathing a little sigh of relief as the clasp slid free.

"Thank you," he whispered. "No, I don't have any particular prescience of disaster; I'm just taking precautions. I'm mostly worried about the hand." He swallowed again as Cathan laid the brooch aside and then inspected the two small puncture wounds. There was very little blood, and Cathan squeezed the hand to make them bleed.

"You'd better let me clean that for you," he murmured, going to dampen a clean towel in the pitcher left from Stevanus' earlier ministrations.

When he had done that, also wiping the damp towel over the king's perspiring forehead and neck, he knelt down and took the newly wounded hand again, pressing it to his forehead, tears in his eyes.

"You don't think you're going to make it, do you, Rhysem?" he whispered. "Dear God, what's to become of us?"

"I don't know," Rhys Michael murmured. "Humour me, though, and put the brooch in your saddlebag right now. I hope it's my fever that's making me fearful, but I want to be sure you have it, if anything does happen."

When Cathan had obeyed, he came back to the king, who nodded his thanks and managed a faint smile.

"Thank you. Now, there's one more thing I want to do tonight. If I shouldn't make it through this, I want Michaela to know that my last thoughts were and are of her and our sons. I don't want to write it, because I can't be sure she'd get it, but I *can* set the message in you, to deliver if—if that becomes appropriate. Will you let me do that?"

"Of course. What do you want me to do?"

"First give me the painkiller Stevanus left, so I can drift off to sleep when I'm done, then sit here beside the bed so that I can rest my hand on your head. You won't even remember unless it becomes necessary. I'm taking precautions, because it's wise to have contingency plans, but it isn't my intention to die."

Other contingency plans were also being set into place, though the king did not know it. In the very campsite where he shortly slipped into drugged, exhausted sleep, Ansel, Jesse, Tieg, and a much depleted band of quondam "borderers" gathered by turns in Ansel's tent, there to compare what they had learned since joining the royal party late in the afternoon.

What little information could be had suggested that the king's fever was giving cause for alarm. Further, he had quarreled with his commanders, and the *Custodes* clergy were even more out of favor than previously. No one seemed to know specific causes, but some put it down to differences of opinion over the king's medical treatment. A *Custodes* battle surgeon called Master Stevanus was still the king's principal physician, but another man, the infirmarian from Saint Cassian's, had been added to the king's household when they left the *Custodes* establishment that morning. Brother Polidorus seemed an officious individual, and even other *Custodes* seemed not to have much complimentary to say about him. The medical implications troubled Tieg, in particular, and made him glad to know that Dom Queron was on his way at all speed to try to intervene.

That same Queron even then was emerging from an underground passage in a village at the foot of Caerrorie Castle, some miles eastward, disguised as a common monk, his Gabrilite braid once again sacrificed in the interests of less distinctive tonsuring. Skirting past the village church, he slipped silently into a neatly kept barn where he saddled a quiet brown mare and led her outside, leaving behind a gold coin and a slip of parchment sealed with the arms of old Culdi. Its finder would take the latter to the village priest in the morning, who would read, *A friend of Father Joram had need of this horse and will return it if at all possible.*

Queron pushed the mare hard, all through the night. Approaching dawn found him far along the road to Valoret and striking off northward and overland toward the King's Road, to gain a few more hours' progress before daylight forced him into hiding. His brown robes marked him as a brother of the Order of Saint Jarlath, whose House lay in the direction he was riding, but his blooded steed was no monk's mount.

Not that both he and the mare would not benefit from a few hours' rest, but he resented the delay, when every hour might make the difference for the king's survival. At least they were headed toward one another. According to Ansel, whose report had been relayed via Camlin before he left sanctuary, Queron could expect the king's party to reach as far south as Ebor or even Sheele by the end of this third day out of Lochalyn; but Queron still had many miles to cover.

CHAPTER TWENTY-FIVE

And as troops of robbers wait for a man, so the company of priests murder in the way by consent.

—Hosea 6:9

Rhys Michael's condition had not improved by morning, but at least it seemed no worse. Though still feverish, he insisted upon pushing on. He still had little appetite and had to force himself to eat what little he did.

Despite increasing doses of his pain medication, his hand throbbed almost unbearably, and he continued to shiver and burn by turns as the morning wore on. Just past midday, not long after the column had passed a tiny convent perched jewel-like on a distant hill, his condition took a dramatic turn for the worse.

He had been riding along in a sort of stupor for several hours, head bowed over his injured hand and his hood pulled up to shield him from the sun, when a bout of shivering shifted into something very like a mild convulsion. Already hunched down in cloak and hood, his good hand clinging to the pommel of his saddle, he managed to weather the first attack without anyone noticing. But an hour later it happened again, more violently, and he had to pull up, teeth tightly clenched as the spasms bowed his spine and threw his head back, nearly wrenching him out of the saddle.

"Rhysem, what's wrong!" Cathan cried, pulling up beside him and catching at his reins as Fulk set a steadying hand on his good shoulder.

The spasms eased but little as Stevanus crowded close alongside to take Fulk's place, reaching out to clasp his wrist, and Rhun and Manfred halted the column, trotting back to find out what was happening.

"Jesus, he's burning up!" Stevanus muttered.

"What's wrong with him?" Rhun demanded. "Sire, can you speak?"

Rhys Michael could hear them, but he could not seem to get any words out. The spasms were easing, but his vision was blurred, and his ears were ringing, and it took all his strength of will to keep from falling off.

"We've got to get him to shelter and knock down this fever," Stevanus said, glancing around urgently. "What's in the vicinity?"

"We're still about an hour's ride from Ebor," Manfred said, consulting a sergeant at his stirrup. "Can he stay on a horse that long?"

"I doubt it," Stevanus said. "Wasn't there a convent a mile or two back?" Releasing the king's wrist, he pulled his medical satchel over his shoulder and started rummaging in it. "Cathan, get up behind him and make sure he doesn't fall off, or we may not get him back up. Fulk or somebody—fetch me something liquid in a cup—water, wine—it doesn't matter. Just something to dissolve a sedative. No, that's not it," he muttered, discarding several small parchment packets.

"C-cold," Rhys Michael managed to whisper through clenched teeth, eyes tightly closed, using almost all his strength to get the word out. "B-burning up." But Cathan was scrambling to a seat behind him, bracing him with his arms around him, and no one heard.

While Stevanus continued to search his satchel, hampered by the restless shuffling of his mount, Fulk had swung down and dashed back along the column. Very shortly he returned with a small horn cup.

"I've got wine!" he shouted, as he made his way back toward Stevanus.

Two *Custodes* knights meanwhile had dismounted and come to stand on either side of the king's horse, holding his legs steady in the stirrups and keeping the animal quiet, casting alarmed glances at Rhun and Manfred as the king started shaking again. Father Lior and Father Magan were urging their horses forward from farther back to see what was wrong, followed by Brother Polidorus. As Fulk presented his cup, Stevanus passed down two of the parchment packets.

"Dump those in the wine and swirl it round," he ordered, returning his attention to the king as he set a steadying hand on the royal shoulder. "Sire, I want you to drink this sedative. It will put you to sleep, but it will help control the spasms. Cathan, help him!"

As Fulk held the cup up, Rhys Michael managed to take it, assisted by Cathan, but a new spasm closed his hand around the cup with such force that it shattered, spattering him with wine as his head jerked back. They got him onto the ground before he could fall, amid a milling confusion of grasping hands and anxious voices shouting conflicting orders, and the next thing he knew was a sharp jab of pain in the side of his neck, a second, and then waves of nausea and psychic disruption joining with the spasms and the unrelenting throb of his injured hand.

"Goddammit, Lior, I didn't want to give him *merasha*," he dimly heard Stevanus muttering, as the wave of darkness came welling up. "I don't know how it will react with what's already in him!"

Just before he passed out, he found himself wondering whether they would figure out that he was reacting like a Deryni. But the spasms already racking his body prevented that, and the double dose of *merasha* added to his earlier medication took him quickly beyond being able to care.

How long he remained unconscious he did not know; only that the room in which he briefly surfaced was dim and cool and presided over by several dark-clad women of indeterminate age, with gentle hands and kindly faces. Two of them were sponging his naked body with cool water while a third, younger one applied cold compresses to his burning forehead. At chest and hips, wide bands of cloth bound him to the bed. Dimly he realized that his arms and legs were likewise restrained. Every muscle and joint in his entire body seemed to ache.

He managed a painful croak, yearning for something cool to drink, something to still the pounding pain behind his eyes.

"So, you've come back among the living," a cheery female voice said, owned by a fourth black-clad figure who joined the others at this sign of life and bent to feel his forehead under the compress. "Don't try to move. Your physicians had you restrained because of the convulsions. Now that you're conscious, though, we must do something more about that fever besides just sponging you down. Sister Regina, release that chest band, please, so we can raise him up. We don't want him to choke on this."

Another woman came and put a wooden cup in the speaker's hand. The women sponging him set aside their basins and drew a sheet up to his waist, then released the band that bound his chest. Through the dull lethargy and pounding in his head, a muzzy part of Rhys Michael's brain dimly registered that his ministering angels must be religious of some sort. The disjointedness of this conclusion reminded him that at least part of the cause for his wretchedness was *merasha*, never mind the fever and the hand.

"Where's Cathan?" he managed to whisper, letting out an inadvertent groan as one of the sisters raised him up with a gentle arm behind his shoulders. "Cathan?"

"That's one of your men, isn't it, Sire?" the cup-bearer murmured. "Drink this first, and I'll call him."

"What is it?" he asked.

"It's a tea we brew from white willow bark, very good for fever. Believe me, it will help."

"My head hurts," he protested weakly, as the cup pressed to his lips.

"That's from the fever. Just drink this down. It will help that, too."

He had little choice but to obey, though he could only get it down in tiny sips, almost a trickle past dry lips. The effort exhausted him enough to slide him back into darkness.

His head was a little clearer when he woke again, but his body still ached, as did his hand. He could feel the chest restraint back in place with the others, and someone was prodding none too gently at his abdomen.

A tentative try at reading the prodder's identity with his powers produced a stabbing pain behind his eyes and a new wave of nausea and vertigo, confirming that *merasha* aftereffects continued to disrupt his abilities. A poke in the bladder made him gasp and open his eyes, to discover that his tormentor was a sour-faced Brother Polidorus. Stevanus stood beside him, looking underslept and far too anxious.

"Did that hurt?" the battle surgeon asked, almost hopefully, as Polidorus continued to poke and prod.

Rhys Michael had to swallow before he could summon the energy to shake his head. "Bladder's full."

When the appropriate receptacle had been brought, utilized, and taken away, Stevanus took Polidorus' place, still looking grim as he laid his hand across his patient's forehead. Cathan and Fulk had come into the room, accompanied by Manfred and Rhun. The latter two looked angry. The room was dim, as before, but now Rhys Michael sensed light beyond the heavy curtains to his right. He wondered what day it was.

"How do you feel?" Stevanus asked, very quietly.

"Am I supposed to feel better?" the king replied.

Stevanus quirked him a faint smile as he took his hand away.

"One keeps hoping. Your fever is a bit diminished, but you've had convulsions off and on, all through the night and morning. The hand is draining, but that's to be expected."

Rhys Michael flexed at his bonds and closed his eyes briefly. "Do I have to be restrained?"

"When you go into convulsions, you're pretty spectacular. You could break bones. I'm afraid the restraints have to stay."

"How long?"

"Until the convulsions ease up."

"No, how long until *that* happens? Stevanus, could I die from this?" he asked, trying to catch the battle surgeon's gaze.

Stevanus glanced away. "I—don't think you're going to die from this, Sire," he whispered. "But here, I've got some more of the sisters' willow-bark tea for you. And a bit of sedative. It seems to help the spasms a bit. Cathan, just lift his head a little."

Whether the sedative would have helped was a moot point, because the draught had not been in his stomach long enough to take effect before his body was again racked by wave upon wave of violent, cramping convulsions that arched his spine and choked off his breath and eventually left him unconscious. When he came around, he knew not how much later, angry voices were being raised in argument all around his bed, and he could feel his body tensing for another set of convulsions even as he opened his eyes to look around him.

"Medically, that's precisely what is called for!" Brother Polidorus was saying, as Lior laid a restraining hand on an angry Stevanus' shoulder. "I wanted it done days ago and look what's happened."

Manfred was standing in the background, looking determined, and Sir Rondel, his aide, had the furiously struggling Rhun in a hammerlock, two *Custodes* knights pulling his arms outstretched while Father Magan bared one burly forearm and angled for a clean jab with a Deryni pricker. Cathan was nearby, but Gallard de Breffni had *him* in custody, with a dagger held to his throat rather than a Deryni pricker. Fulk was over by the door flanked by two more *Custodes* knights, not actively in custody but looking defeated and sick at heart.

"But he's too weak already!" Stevanus was protesting. "If you bleed him, he may not even survive *that*, much less the longer-term effects."

Through the red haze that was creeping over the king's vision as convulsions claimed him again, wrenching him once more toward oblivion, the sense of Stevanus' words sent cold dread flooding through his mind. They meant to bleed him after all! He had forbidden Stevanus or Rhun to allow it, but Lior and Polidorus apparently had prevailed against even Rhun's orders. By an exhausting act of will, for the residual effects of the *merasha* continued to cloud his access to his powers, Rhys Michael managed not to succumb to this latest set of convulsions, but as they receded and he could again turn his perceptions outward, he was not certain he would not have been happier not to know.

For they were not arguing over him anymore. Cathan was kneeling at the right side of the bed, one hand gently stroking his forehead, weeping bitterly into his other hand. And on the left, as a sudden, burning pain in his arm made him flinch and turn his head in dismay, he saw Polidorus lifting a bloody lancet.

"No!" he cried weakly, instinctively trying to jerk away, even as Polidorus released the ligature that had kept his blood from flowing. "Noooooo!" he groaned, as the hot blood began to stream around his arm and collect in a basin set beneath his elbow.

But a *Custodes* knight had one hand set firmly against his shoulder and the other on his upper arm, and Father Magan had that forearm in an unrelenting grip, to ensure that their unwilling patient did not twist against the padded wrist restraint that held the arm outstretched. Another *Custodes* knight had moved in beside Cathan at the king's first sign of movement and restrained his right arm and shoulder. Stevanus was nowhere to be seen.

The horror and the helplessness of it all swept through him in less than a blink of an eye, along with the anger and betrayal and the utter futility of continuing to resist. Even so, he did try, wrenching at his bonds with a moan of outrage but then forced to succumb as Gallard de Breffni pressed across his body to pin him helpless, crushing the breath from his lungs, and his other captors tightened their holds on his twitching limbs. The exertion made the blood flow even faster, a still-rational part of him dimly realized, briefly spilling over the edge of the bowl until Polidorus could steady it. As the king gave up his struggling, Gallard eased off on crushing his chest, and the *Custodes* men pinning his shoulders let up slightly.

"Rhysem, forgive me, I couldn't stop them," Cathan whispered, urgently turning his kinsman's face from what was being done. "They won't kill me, for Mika's sake, but they would have made me leave you, if I hadn't stopped fighting them. I couldn't bear the thought of you suffering this alone."

"But, why?" Rhys Michael managed to croak, his voice quavering. "Is this how they're going to kill me?"

"Now, Sire, you mustn't get such ideas in your head," Polidorus purred, calmly milking at his upper arm to keep the blood flowing, the bloody lancet still in his hand. "You're a very stubborn patient. You don't know what's best for you. Bleeding will let out the evil humours that are causing your illness. Believe me, we know what we're doing."

Unable to argue such illogic, Rhys Michael cast his gaze helplessly around the room and saw that Rhun had subsided onto a stool over nearer the door, eyes closed, his head leaned back against the wall. Manfred was standing beside him, one hand on his shoulder, glancing down at him occasionally. Lior was on his other side. And Rhys Michael's blood continued to run around his elbow and into the basin, more and more of it, just as Javan had described when the *Custodes* bled him, what seemed like a lifetime ago.

"Rhun, listen to me," Rhys Michael called, with as much strength as he could muster. "Rhun, if they kill me, I've told you what will happen. Don't let them do this—for your own sake, if not for mine."

Manfred's hand tightened on Rhun's shoulder, and he quirked an uneasy smile at the king. "I'm not certain he can hear you, Sire. In any case, I am not as gullible as Lord Rhun. I don't believe you."

"Shall I have Cathan show you the document?" the king asked.

"Anyone can draw up any document in their fantasies," Manfred replied. "I think you're bluffing."

"And if I'm not?"

Manfred shrugged. "Sire, it is regrettable that sometimes, despite the best of medical care, even the most illustrious patients do not survive illnesses as serious as yours. There will be ample witness that all was done that could be done and that your Highness refused sound medical advice on more than one occasion, until it was too late to save you."

"But, it's murder," Rhys Michael murmured, despair curling in his gut like a slithering snake. "What's more, it's sacrilege. But then, you've killed a king before, haven't you? At least Javan was able to die in the field, with his sword in his hand!"

Smiling a terrible little smile, Manfred walked over to the bed and glanced dispassionately at the basin collecting the king's blood, now nearly filled.

"I am not a vindictive man, Sire. I give you my faithful promise that when the time comes, you may die with your sword in your hand, if you wish—with the very sword that Javan held in *his* hand, in *his* last moments. But it will not be today."

At his nod, Brother Polidorus set aside his lancet and pressed a pad of clean towel to the wound in the king's arm, lifting it clear so that Father Magan could remove the bowl of royal blood. When they had washed the arm clean, Polidorus applied a new dressing and bound it up, then directed Cathan to press his fingers against the dressing to be sure the wound was stanched, for they did not loose the restraints.

"Thank you, Brother Polidorus," Manfred murmured. "Your services may be required again during the night, if our patient shows no sign of improvement, but for now, you may go. Sire, I'll send Master Stevanus and Lord Fulk back to you after Father Lior has had a word with you."

Polidorus made Manfred a slight bow and retreated with him, the *Custodes* knights following with the groggy Rhun stumbling between them. When they had gone, Lior came over to the bed to sniff disdainfully at the bowl of blood still set on the table beside it. Father Magan was quietly gathering up the bloodied towels and instruments, collecting them on a wooden tray.

"A pity your Deryni friends could not be here, Sire," Lior said softly. "No doubt they would find royal blood highly desirable for their rites of abomination. As it is, the custom in religious houses is to fertilize the gardens with the products of bloodletting. Perhaps in a year or two, the good sisters will be able to tell us whether royal blood is superior to merely mortal blood for that purpose."

Increasingly light-headed, either from the loss of blood or the sedative earlier, Rhys Michael could hardly believe what he had just heard. But it was Cathan who challenged the *Custodes* priest, blue eyes wide with horror and indignation.

"Just what is that supposed to mean?" he demanded. "That's a lie, about the Deryni!"

"Oh, had you not heard of their blood rites?" Lior asked. "Of course, you mostly escaped their taint. I remember testing you. But 'tis well known that the Deryni consort with demons, who demand blood of their devotees. My sources inform me that royal blood is considered to be only slightly less efficacious than that of virgins or infants. In some cases, it is more useful. Be thankful that they do not have access to your body, Sire, much less to your soul."

Cathan had blanched, unable to reply, and Rhys Michael could only turn his face away in loathing. His breathing had become more labored, and his thinking was not as clear as it had been.

"Speaking of which," Lior went on, "I shall have a priest come to you in a little while. I am sure you will wish to make confession and receive Extreme Unction, being in mortal peril. I would offer my services, but somehow I doubt you would find me acceptable. Or Father Magan, I expect." Rhys Michael could only shake his head numbly. "Well, I shall find someone. Good evening, Sire."

When he and Magan had gone out, taking the tray and the blood with them, Stevanus was allowed to return, Fulk also coming to stand uneasily by the king's bed.

"I am truly sorry, Sire," the battle surgeon murmured, looking distraught. "I tried to stop them. Sir Fulk tried as well, but we could only insist so far."

Rhys Michael closed his eyes, tensing for a new set of convulsions he could feel coming on.

"I know," he whispered. "You're none of you to blame. Cathan—"

Cathan's hand closed around his good one, and he hung on for his life as the spasms racked him again and Stevanus and Fulk tried to still his thrashing. Thereafter he slipped into troubled sleep, given respite at last by his sedation, his three guardians keeping watch by turns, as day slipped into evening and to night.

CHAPTER TWENTY-SIX

For I am now ready to be offered, and the time of my departure is at hand.

—II Timothy 4:6

Queron caught up with the Gwynedd army late in the morning of the next day. He had expected to find them much farther south, and caught intimations of a royal pause only a little after dawn, when he paused at a farmer's steading to beg food and drink.

"Aye, Father, they're camped round about the convent up the road," the goodwife told him, as she poured him fresh milk from a crockery jar. "They say the king fell ill, an' they took him there for the good sisters to care for him."

Queron soon found opportunity to probe the woman more closely, but she had already told all she knew. Begging a slab of cheese and a hunk of bread, he left the brown mare in exchange for the farmer's more suitable grey donkey and set off up the road, wolfing down the food for sustenance and planning how he might gain access to the king.

The cover he had chosen was an excellent start. Not only did his obviously advanced years present no physical threat to whatever laymen might be responsible for the king's safety, but his monastic habit virtually guaranteed the hospitality of just about any religious house. An itinerant cleric could always be prevailed upon to share the latest news of the outside world in exchange for his supper and a bed, while also enabling his hosts to exercise Christian charity. A visiting priest also might be asked to hear the odd confession and perhaps celebrate Mass, if the community did not have its own resident chaplain.

Begging a noonday meal was perhaps not as satisfactory an entrée as requesting travelers' fare and lodgings at day's end, but Queron reflected that he could always make the donkey limp temporarily, if no other ruse seemed likely to gain him entrance.

He did not have to resort to such tactics. Though he could see the vast sprawl of the army's encampment across the fields as he approached, and there was much evidence of horsemen riding to and fro on the road as he neared the convent gates, no one gave him a second glance as he guided the little donkey under the entrance arch. Across the cobbled courtyard, several armed men were tending horses outside what he presumed must be the guesthouse, and more horses stood tied beside what appeared to be the entrance to the stable yard. As he drew rein, a smiling young sister in a black wimple and habit came to greet him, setting work-roughened hands on the donkey's bridle as he slid to the ground.

"God's greeting to you, good brother. Welcome to Saint Ostrythe's. How may we serve you?"

"God's greeting to you, Sister. Might I trouble you for a bite to eat and fodder for my four-legged friend? 'Tis a long ride yet to Saint Jarlath's, and I do not know where the evening will find me. My name is Father Donatus."

"And I am Sister Winifred," she said, bobbing him a curtsey. "Of course you may find hospitality in this house, Father. I fear the fare may be less ample than our usual wont, for we guest the king and his party, but you are welcome to share what we have. Come and I'll show you where to put your beast."

Following her into the stable yard, Queron took in as much as he could of the layout of the place, alert for any sign of the king's presence nearby; but he could find no trace.

"Tell me, what brings the king to these parts?" he asked, as she led him past several soldiers into a well-built barn.

The little nun gave a sad shrug, stroking the donkey's neck as she guided it into a spacious box stall strewn with sweet-smelling hay.

"I fear he is very ill, Father. They brought him here yesterday, all but unconscious, and 'tis said that even bleeding has not eased him. Mother Prioress instructed us to pray for him, both last night and this morning."

Stunned, Queron laid a hand on her shoulder, gently taking control as he turned her to face him and then probed deep. Sister Winifred's discretion was what might be expected of a religious, but her knowledge of the king's condition was not confined to a mere glimpse or convent gossip. She was only a very junior member of the community, but she had been one of several sisters to tend the king immediately after his arrival.

From her he read the king's condition at that time and what had been done for him in her presence. The injured hand had not been dealt with, for it was fever and convulsions that had interrupted his journey. Queron would have preferred talicil for the fever and could have prescribed several specific Deryni drugs that might have eased the very alarming spasms, but the tea brewed from white willow bark conveyed some of the same benefits as talicil, and sedation, in general, usually helped to ease convulsions.

Unfortunately, Sister Winifred had no direct knowledge about the bloodletting, though it was understood that the king almost certainly had been bled more than once since his arrival and possibly as many as three or four times. That was alarming enough, but earlier this morning, one of the king's officers had made inquiries concerning the availability of the convent's chaplain—which seemed odd to young Winifred, since the king's immediate party certainly had several priests among their number. One had celebrated Mass for them this morning, for the convent's resident priest was away.

This additional piece of information struck a dread chill in Queron's heart. That a priest was being sought was ill news, indeed, for it bespoke the very real possibility that the king was in danger of death. And how like Rhys Michael to refuse the services of his *Custodes* priests. Queron recalled being told that the dying Alroy had done precisely the same thing, only finally receiving his last Communion from his brother Javan's hands.

But herein lay a possible way to gain access to the king, not as an itinerant hospitaller but as a disinterested and neutral priest who might be acceptable to a man who knew the failings of his own priests far too well to entrust his soul to them as he approached death. It was not what Queron had hoped to accomplish, and he tried not to let himself expect that he was in time to make a difference as a Healer; but at least if Queron was too late to save the king's life, perhaps he might help ease that life to a more peaceful close, with the solace of a friend beside him, even in the midst of his enemies . . .

"It grieves me to hear that the king is so ill, Sister," Queron murmured, shaking his head, smoothly releasing her without memory of any passage of time. "Far from home and kin, it must give him comfort to receive the loving care of this House. And for his soul's cure, I should imagine he has the ministrations of many good priests."

She dropped her gaze and folded her hands in the wide sleeves of her habit, biting at her lower lip. "I—am not certain he has yet received the sacraments, Father. Earlier this morning, one of his young officers was inquiring for a priest; alas, ours is away. Later, the senior of the king's priests said Mass for us—a Father Lior—but he seemed preoccupied and almost angry. I—wonder whether he and his brother priests may be out of favor with the king. I can think of no other reason to ask for ours."

Queron raised an eyebrow. "You think he would not see his own priests? But—oh, dear. Sister, I can hardly claim to be the sort of courtly, sophisticated priest to which the king must be accustomed, but do you suppose he still needs one? I would be honored to offer what solace I may, if he would think it no impertinence from a humble country cleric."

Sister Winifred smiled hopefully.

"You're very generous, Father. I can take you to the king's men. It may be that his Highness would be well content to confess himself to a priest who knows him not at all. Perhaps there lies the problem."

"Perhaps," Queron agreed.

Leaving the stable with Sister Winifred, Queron followed her back across the central courtyard and through into the cloister garth, heading for the Chapter House. It appeared the king's officers had appropriated the building for a temporary command headquarters. Several *Custodes* guards were posted outside the open doorway, some of them looking grim, indeed, but they gave only casual interest to the aged, brown-robed cleric who followed silently at the heels of the pretty Sister Winifred, hands folded piously in the sleeves of his habit and head ducked down in his cowl. Fortunately, Queron had never had a face-to-face meeting with any of the men likely to be inside, though he knew most of them by others' mental recall and description.

"Beg pardon, my lords," Sister Winifred said, peering timidly into the open doorway and bobbing a nervous curtsey as several of the men looked up. "One of the young officers was inquiring earlier this morning about a priest. This is Father

Donatus, on his way to Saint Jarlath's. Could he be of any assistance?"

An intense, black-eyed priest in *Custodes* habit detached himself from a knot of *Custodes* officers and came over to the doorway—Father Lior, Queron realized.

"What was that name again, Father?" Lior asked.

"Donatus," Queron said, making the obviously grander Lior a deferential bow, eyes averted. "I do beg your pardon, Father, but perhaps Sister was mistaken. I was told a priest was required, but I see several priests among you."

Behind Lior, Manfred gave a snort. Rhun of Horthness stood beside him, sullenly nursing a large goblet.

"Well, Lior, your prayers are answered," Manfred said. "I doubt it will make much difference to *him*, but I'm sure you priestly types will feel better about all of this if the proprieties are observed."

Biting back whatever retort had come to mind, Lior merely folded his hands behind his back and curtly gestured to Queron with his chin as he headed out the door.

"Come with me, please, Father. Thank you, Sister."

A few minutes later, Lior was leading Queron past a pair of *Custodes* guards and into a dim, close room tinged with the sweetness of incense and beeswax and the underscent of blood. Two motionless figures in leather and shirtsleeves knelt to either side of a white-covered bed, and a third in the black tunic of a *Custodes* battle surgeon turned a compress on the forehead of the bed's occupant. Though Queron had never met any of the three, he recognized all of them as they looked up— Cathan, Fulk, and Stevanus—and he sent a quick burst of thought to Cathan, who alone might guess what he was.

Say nothing. I am sent by Joram.

"This is Father Donatus," Lior said, gesturing toward Queron. "How is his Highness?"

"Quiet," Stevanus said, setting his compress aside, not meeting Lior's eyes as he got to his feet. "It—cannot be much longer."

Lior's lips tightened, and he shook his head, piously folding his hands at his waist. "These are sad times, indeed, Father. I gave his Highness holy anointing early this morning, when his condition became grave, but he would not speak to me, he would not make last confession, nor would he receive Viaticum. If you can reach him, if you can persuade him to make his peace with God, I would count it a personal favor."

"I am honored to offer that comfort to any soul in need, Father," Queron said quietly, somewhat surprised to find that Lior's regret seemed genuine—though he was also aware that Lior took little personal risk by asking another priest to hear the king's last confession, since any accusations against Lior or the others would be sealed by the confidentiality of that sacrament. "If we may have some privacy, please?"

"Of course."

With a pointed glance at the others, Lior began making shooing motions to urge them out of the room. Cathan rose obediently enough, though clearly on the brink of tears, but he lingered near the foot of the bed as Fulk, Stevanus, and then Lior passed outside.

"Might I stay in the room, please, Father?" he whispered. "Maybe over in the corner? He has been like a brother to me. The queen is my sister."

"Not just now, son," Queron said, setting his hands on Cathan's shoulders to guide him to the door—and in those seconds Reading all he could of what had been done to the king. "Why don't you wait outside with the others? I promise I'll call you before the end."

Cathan choked back a sob but gave a nod as well, for Queron had sent explicit instructions during the brief contact. When he had passed outside, Queron gently closed the door and then came back to gaze down at the king.

Rhys Michael's eyes were closed, and his labored breathing barely stirred the stark white sheet pulled up to midchest. He was no longer restrained. Both arms lay outside the sheeting, the right hand heavily bandaged and splinted and lesser bandages binding both arms at the elbows, evidence of the repeated bleedings. Cathan had witnessed four, though the king probably had not been aware of the last of these. He still had lucid moments, but they were becoming fewer and shorter.

Crossing himself with weary resignation, Queron knelt at the king's left and took the slack hand in one of his, chafing it gently as his other hand came to rest on Rhys Michael's forehead, Reading deep as a Healer Reads and knowing, as only a Healer can know, that all his powers could not reverse what had been set in motion. The physical damage to the hand could still be Healed—and Queron would have been willing to risk personal discovery, if such Healing might save the king's life—but nothing could be done to replace the vast quantities of blood the king had lost, or to quell the fever burning away what little strength remained to him.

The pain Queron blocked, for that, at least, he could do; but nothing more for the body that housed Rhys Michael Haldane's soul. The king stirred slightly at this respite, though his breathing still was labored, and he did not open his eyes.

"Rhysem, I know you can hear me," Queron whispered softly, very near the king's ear. "It's Dom Queron. Joram has sent me. I deeply regret that I cannot Heal you, but is there anything else I can offer you? Don't try to speak aloud; just give me your thoughts. Rest in the Mercy and let me help you find your peace."

The hope that had stirred faintly in Rhys Michael's soul fluttered back and was stilled, yielding once more to resigned acceptance, for he had given up any real hope of surviving this when they bled him the second time. Before the third time, Manfred had even laid the Haldane sword under his hand, in confirmation of their intentions, though he already had been too weak to hold it. Still, this final acceptance of what soon must be his fate enabled him to send his thought to Queron strong and focused.

Dom Queron . . . sweet comfort come at last . . . Please hear my confession, Father. I would not go to God unshriven, but I could not confess to Lior . . .

Dear son . . .

Their thoughts merged and blended then, beyond all need for mere words as the king offered up all his fears and failings for the examination of his spiritual physician, humbly acknowledging the Healer's assessments, letting Queron guide him in making his contrition. Withholding nothing, he also revealed to Queron how he had made provision for passing the Haldane potential to his son—not the full empowering, for Owain was only four, but the means for the ground to be prepared and the seeds sown.

And Cathan must be his agent in this and cautioned not to do or say anything after the king's death that might prevent his return to Michaela, for whom he also bore a last, loving farewell from her Rhysem. It was all the king could offer, in the end—one final bequest to the kingdom he had never really ruled. Having discharged this ultimate obligation, he was content to rest, mind intertwined to mind as hand to hand, even as Queron softly pronounced the ritual words of absolution and signed him in blessing.

"Ego te absolvo, in nomine Patris, et Filii, et Spiritus Sancti, Amen."

"Amen," Rhys Michael whispered, opening his eyes at last, the light blazing in them, fierce and strong and nearly burned out.

"Rhysem, I have brought you the Blessed Sacrament," Queron murmured, touching a hand to his breast, where the little pyx rested under his habit in its soft leather pouch, suspended from a cord. "Will you receive Viaticum now? It is heavenly bread, the Body of our Lord, to speed you on your way."

Almost too weak to speak, Rhys Michael nodded, tears welling in his eyes as he remembered the passing of his brother Alroy and how Javan had called him to the dying Alroy's side to share Communion together one last time.

"Call Cathan?" he managed to whisper. "And Fulk and Stevanus, if they wish. They have served—as best they could. In another little while, I think I could have won them truly . . . but no time."

"Perhaps you have won them better than you knew," Queron murmured. "I'll call them."

He did. Cathan slipped past him anxiously, almost as soon as Queron opened the door, Fulk and then Stevanus following gratefully at the priest's beckoning gesture. Lior had been joined by Manfred, Rhun, and several more *Custodes* clerics, and would have followed the three the king had asked for, but Queron laid a hand on his wrist to stay him, his stern glance also halting the others.

"He wishes only these three, my lords."

"But I should be there," Lior protested, looking quite ashen-faced in his *Custodes* black, for he knew that Queron must be aware of his duplicity. "I have offended him, and I would seek his forgiveness."

"I think it best if you remain here and pray for him, Father—and for yourself," Queron said, neutral of tone but with the force of compulsion behind his words. "He forgives, but he does not wish your presence."

Queron did not wait to see the effect of his order, only closing the door and returning to Rhys Michael's bed. Cathan and Fulk had gone to the other side, Cathan kneeling nearest the king's head to pull the Haldane sword quietly from underneath the bed and lay its shining length atop its owner's body with the cross-hilt at the breast, gently bringing the king's good hand to rest upon it, sign both of faith and of kingship. Queron bade Stevanus come beside him, on the king's left, pulling the leather pouch from inside the neck of his habit as he knelt.

The little pyx inside the pouch was silver-gilt, plain, but it blazed like a sun in Queron's psychic sight as he opened it and took out a small consecrated Host. Holding it before the king's burning gaze, the Healer-priest spoke the words that proclaimed their faith, speaking them in the common tongue, that none might mistake his meaning:

"Beloved son, behold the Lamb of God, Who taketh away the sins of the world. Receive this food for thy journey: the Bread of Heaven, containing in itself all delight; the Body of Christ, to keep thee in life everlasting."

Rhys Michael's breathless "Amen" barely stirred his lips, and tears were trembling on the closing lashes like jewels as Queron laid the Host on his tongue. Leaving the king to commune with his God, the priest returned his gaze to the vessel of sunlight glowing in his hand and carefully took out another Host, breaking it in quarters and giving one to Cathan, another to Fulk, the third to Stevanus. The fourth he himself reverently consumed after murmuring the accompanying words in Latin:

"Corpus Domini nostri Jesu Christi custodiat animam meam in vitam aeternam. Amen."

But he had gently caught the minds of all the others as he touched them, and when he had given thanks for his own Communion, he gathered together their several strands of focused meditation to weave another, silent exhortation, this time calling unseen Powers to witness the passage of the one who shortly would enter their realms. Those Powers were the same Rhys Michael had seen come to speed Alroy on his way, who had witnessed Rhys Michael's coming into his heritage, the same whose presence Queron himself had sought so many times, to bless so many purposes—Guardians and Protectors and Teachers.

And now, Conveyers at last of the soul's passage into— Other. Queron's sorrow was tempered with joy as he bade them welcome, lifting up his heart in glad summoning, offering up wordless greeting by names that caught but a hint of their bearers' puissance and beauty.

Raphael of the winds, serene and gentle, ethereal as a dawn mist but powerful as a raging storm, transparent wings trailing beams of golden sunlight.

Michael of the flames—better known to Joram and his warrior kin than to a Healer like Queron, but a steady and faithful protector of those who must live by the sword—or by the fire of their wits.

Gabriel, Queron's own especial patron, glad herald of the Blessed Virgin, powerful but compassionate, quicksilver-subtle, changing as the tides and as deep as the sea.

And finally Uriel, whose specific commission it was to usher souls across the Great Abyss; Uriel, rock-steady, whose earth would claim the earthly bodies of all, in time, but who now waited to receive a soul. The rainbow shiver of unseen wings rustled the very air around Queron as he gave the Four thanks for their coming and brought the king into their presence.

Rhys Michael did not rouse, but his hand contracted slightly on the hilt of the Haldane sword. As he gave a little shudder, his breath rasping in his chest, Queron used his thumb to sign a cross on the king's forehead in blessing, then gently laid his hand over the king's, with the sword beneath, bowing his head in homage both to him and to the Ones who waited.

Dearest son, be free to go, he whispered in the king's mind. *Your body can no longer serve you. You have fought a noble fight against powerful adversaries, and you have won a chance for your sons. Others will take up the fight now. Be at peace, and go when you are ready.*

The king did not go immediately. A little while longer he lingered, inward-focused and scarcely breathing, perhaps gathering his resolve for that final leap into the Unknown. But Queron sensed that moment when Rhys Michael Alister Haldane finally cast loose the last of the ties binding him to earthly life.

The labored breathing faltered once and then ceased. The hand under Queron's went slack. Lifting his gaze to search the too-pale face, at peace now, Queron fancied he saw the king restored, the king Rhys Michael should have been, crimson-mantled and crowned with the great state crown, clear-eyed and brimming with health, his grey gaze fixed steadfastly on something beyond Queron's head as he rose up out of his abandoned body to join another young man who looked very much like him, with the same grey eyes and jet black hair and a crown of running lions on his head, who also pointed where Rhys Michael was looking.

Queron turned his gaze to follow and beheld another figure cloaked and hooded in grey, extending something in both its

hands toward the raptly staring Cathan. Neither Fulk nor
Stevanus seemed aware, both with their faces buried in their
hands. And as the greyling figured turned, lowering the hands
almost enough to reveal what he held, Queron caught just a
glimpse of the face deep inside the hood—a face he had
sought to know for many years.

Camber!

He almost spoke the name aloud, but even as his lips parted,
that portion of the vision was gone—and all the spirit hosts
that had surrounded it, receding at dizzying speed to a single
point of brilliant light directly above Rhys Michael's head, that
suddenly was not! Queron gasped as it winked away, the spell
broken, then let out a slow sigh, for he had not remembered to
breathe for many seconds. Cathan was staring at the king's
face, blinded by tears, slowly nodding. The others remained
unmoving, with heads bowed.

"May Christ—Who has called thee—now receive thee, beloved son," Queron managed to whisper, almost by rote,
slowly crossing himself, willing the pounding of his heart to
slow. *"Requiem aeternam dona ei, Domine "*

"Et lux perpetua luceat ei," Cathan murmured, the other
two joining in raggedly.

"Kyrie eleison."

"Christe eleison, kyrie eleison . . ."

CHAPTER TWENTY-SEVEN

I have seen the wicked in great power.

—Psalms 37:35

A short while later, kneeling at the back of the convent church, Queron did his best to help Cathan regain some measure of equilibrium before leaving him. The younger man had done with weeping for the moment and now knelt merely trembling beside the brown-robed old priest, though his face remained buried in his hands.

Queron still did not know what Camber had shown to the boy, though he suspected it might have had something to do with Cathan's final commission from the king. There had been no time to ask at the king's bedside. Further prayers beyond the *Kyrie* seemed superfluous after the holy simplicity of Rhys Michael's passing, and Queron knew he must be away from here as soon as possible.

So after Cathan had tearfully slipped the Haldane sword back under the bed and removed the Eye of Rom, secreting it in his belt pouch for Michaela, Queron had left Fulk and Stevanus to grieve at the king's bedside and silently instructed Cathan to indulge his own grief in as dramatic a fashion as he could, as cover to get the two of them out of the death chamber.

"The king is at peace," Queron informed Lior and the others waiting outside, as he led the sobbing Cathan out of the room. "His passing was very gentle. I shall take this young man outside to compose himself now. Father, perhaps you would lead the appropriate litanies here at the king's bedside."

Lior and the others had surged into the room to see for themselves with hardly a second look at Queron and Cathan, each with his own priorities, now that the king was dead—Lior coldly practical, Polidorus sharp-eyed and intent, Manfred apparently unable to believe they had actually done it, Rhun all too well aware what they had done. Cathan had been reluctant to leave his beloved Rhysem in such hands, but knew with his reason that the king was no longer there to be hurt by them.

"I've given you what guidance I can, as quickly as I can," Queron murmured, shifting back to speech as he prepared to leave Cathan in the chapel. "I have to ask, though, before I go, just what you saw, there at the end. I shan't intrude, but I have to ask."

Cathan lifted his head, not looking at Queron, still a little caught up in what he had witnessed, both sacred and profane.

"It was a reminder of something I have to do for Owain," he whispered. "Rhysem wanted me to see that he gets the Haldane brooch. I know the earring is somehow important—the Eye of Rom—but there's something about the brooch as well." He shook his head. "I can't tell you any more."

"There's no need," Queron said gently, for Rhys Michael had told him of Cathan's mission.

Cathan swallowed, then looked up at Queron searchingly. "Can you see that Mika knows Owain is meant to have it, Father? It isn't a state jewel, so no one may think of it. If—something happens to me, before I can get back to her, they'll still give her Rhysem's things, won't they? They've killed him; surely they wouldn't deny her a few keepsakes." He swallowed hard and looked away, shaking his head. "God, widowed at twenty!"

"Steady, son. I'll see that she knows. But you must do your part to see that you get back. Don't give them any excuse to kill you."

Cathan nodded, sniffling back the last of his tears, and stiffened as Fulk came into the church, looked around, and headed right for them.

"Father, they're looking for you," he whispered, leaning between them. "You'd best go while you can. You know too much about the king's death."

Nodding, Queron murmured, "Thank you," and sent the young man to kneel at the back of the church in the shadow of a clerestory pillar.

"At least we've won that one," he murmured, as he set his

hand on Cathan's arm and prepared to leave. "If he survives this, keep track of him and don't underestimate his usefulness."

"What do you mean, 'if he survives this'?"

"Well, being Tammaron's son may save him, but he still knows too much. So does Stevanus. So do you. Be very careful."

"I plan to be," Cathan agreed. "And you?"

Queron gave him a grim smile. "Your Rhysem really did strike the regents what could be a deathblow, son, by issuing that codicil. But it will all be for naught if it can't be implemented. I'll inform our people as soon as I've left here, and they'll notify the Kheldour lords. From here out, we've all got to play our parts, to make certain all our sacrifices haven't been in vain."

Nodding bleakly, Cathan looked up again at the Deryni priest. "I'll do the best I can, Father. And thank you for coming. I know what you risked."

Queron smiled gently. "I only wish I could have reached him in time to bring healing to his body as well as his soul. The Haldanes have not been lucky in this generation. God grant that his sons will fare better."

As Cathan nodded again, wistful, dispirited, Queron gently laid his right hand on his head in blessing, sending across a burst of further information Cathan might need, even as his lips moved in the traditional words.

"Benedicat te omnipotens Deus, Pater, et Filius, et Spiritus Sanctus. Amen."

Cathan managed to repeat the *Amen*, reeling a little on his knees, unable to see for a few seconds for the emotion whirling through his mind; but even as he recovered his senses, Queron was gone. Cathan remained where he was for a few minutes, head bowed in his hands, gathering his composure, then rose to follow, pausing to lay a hand lightly on Fulk's shoulder.

"Come, we have duties to the king," he said softly. "If it's permitted, I intend to keep watch by him tonight. Will you join me?"

Fulk nodded slowly and got to his feet, a kindred spirit in his grief, his face a mask of stunned disbelief and loss.

"It will be my honor," he said quietly.

Still shaking off the numbness of his sorrow, Cathan tried to make his mind turn toward practicalities of survival as he and Fulk crossed the courtyard, heading for the cloister garth. He saw no sign of Queron, but there seemed to be a great deal of activity over by the stables. He hoped it was not an indication that Queron had been taken, but as he watched several mounted patrols ride out, he guessed that the elusive Father Donatus was still being sought. He thought the wily old Deryni would be hard to corner.

Thankful for that, at least, he continued on into the cloister garth and headed toward the infirmary and the room where the king's body lay. Somewhat to his surprise, he saw no outward sign that anything had changed within. When he and Fulk entered the room, he found out why.

It apparently had not occurred to the guards outside that the king's aides should not be admitted. Close beside the deathbed, their faces starkly lit by the torches held by two *Custodes* monks, Manfred and a tight-jawed Rhun looked on while Polidorus stitched at the bloody stump of the king's right hand, assisted by Father Magan. Master Stevanus was present but not participating in this desecration of the royal corpse, head bowed where he stood between Lior and Gallard de Breffni. The king's severed hand lay in a bloodied basin, purpled and almost obscene, hardly recognizable for what it was.

All eyes shifted toward the door as Cathan and Fulk came into the room, and Lior was gesturing urgently to Gallard even as Cathan gasped, "What are you doing?" and started forward, and Fulk tried to hold him back.

"Lord Cathan, I must ask you not to make this any more difficult than it already is," Lior said mildly, as Gallard restrained the younger man, then controlled him with a choke hold when he tried to twist free. "Your loyalty to the king cannot be faulted, but it won't help him now. I shall tell you the official story just once. If you forget it, it could cost you your life. Lord Fulk, I advise you to listen carefully as well. I don't intend to repeat myself."

Fulk had started to go to Cathan's aid, but halted at Lior's warning, stiffening as Manfred came around to lay a heavy hand on his shoulder.

"Remember who you are, son," Manfred murmured. "None of this is your affair."

Fulk darted an affronted, helpless look at Cathan but subsided, as had Cathan. Physical resistance clearly was useless. As Cathan carefully shuffled to get his feet back under him, bracing against Gallard's leather-clad arm, the pressure eased across his throat, but the *Custodes* knight did not release him even then.

"That's much more sensible," Lior purred, casting his glance back to where Polidorus and Magan continued to work, ignoring Stevanus. "Now, as you know, the king has had the very best of medical attention, but his illness became far more serious than initially supposed. Despite the most zealous of care, his hand became gangrenous and had to be amputated. Most unfortunately, his Highness did not survive the shock of the procedure."

"It isn't true," Cathan whispered. "You bled him to death!"

"Not at all," Polidorus interjected, blithely continuing to suture the dead flesh. "While it's true that his Highness was bled several times, to relieve the evil humours causing his fever, numerous witnesses saw him alive this morning after the last of the bloodlettings."

"That's still what killed him," Cathan said stubbornly.

Scowling, Rhun bestirred himself to come and stand directly in front of Cathan, his pale eyes cold and even more pitiless than usual. Whatever differences had existed between him and Manfred earlier, the two apparently had resolved them and now were in one accord.

"If you say that outside this room, you may well suffer the same fate, brother of the queen or no," he said quietly. "The king's injured hand had become badly infected and had to be amputated. Weakened by his fever, he sadly did not survive the surgery. Anyone who says otherwise will be dealt with most unpleasantly. *Anyone.*"

Cathan could only close his eyes briefly in dismay, swallowing with difficulty. Fulk had gone pale with disbelief, shrinking back a little under Manfred's hand. Stevanus only shook his head, eyes closed, swaying so alarmingly that Lior caught a hand under his elbow.

"I trust that everyone now understands the rules of engagement," the *Custodes* priest said quietly. "Lord Fulk, I believe that neither you nor Lord Cathan got very much sleep last night. Perhaps Master Stevanus would be so good as to provide a suitable sleeping potion for each of you—and for himself as well. A rather strong one, I should think. See to it, Stevanus," he said sharply, releasing the battle surgeon's arm. "None of you will be required until tomorrow, when we leave for Rhemuth, and I do not wish to see any of you stirring before that time."

Outraged, Cathan started struggling again, hardly caring when Gallard's choke hold took him swooping into unconsciousness. As he started to come around, gasping for breath and with his heartbeat pounding in his ears, he found himself flat on his back on the floor, with Stevanus lifting his head and setting a little metal cup to his lips.

"Just drink it," the battle surgeon murmured urgently, as Cathan pressed his lips together stubbornly and tried to shake his head. "If you won't, I'll have to stick you with *merasha*. I'll have no choice."

Cathan made himself gag it down, tears of impotence welling in his eyes, laying back then to catch his breath as the queasy disorientation of returning consciousness began to give way to the drifting, woolly-headed sensation of the sedative taking hold. After a minute or two, Gallard and another *Custodes* knight came and took him and Fulk into custody, escorting them civilly enough to another room; but Cathan never remembered his head hitting the pillow.

Meanwhile, Queron had made good his escape from Saint Ostrythe's, blocking memories of his passage and slipping through the convent gate on his little donkey before any serious effort could be organized to detain him. As soon as he could gain shelter in the next village, hiding the donkey in a farmer's barn while he secreted himself in the hayloft, he put himself in trance and sent out an urgent call to Jesse or Ansel or Tieg, all of whom should be nearby.

It was Jesse who caught the summons, though full contact was delayed until he also found a safe place in which to open to rapport. That done, Queron passed on a full account of what he had learned and witnessed at Saint Ostrythe's, saving only the content of Rhys Michael's final confession. Jesse was stunned, but agreed to make certain the news was passed on to the Kheldour lords.

They must not come until they've received the news by conventional means, Queron reiterated, *but this time can be used to plan their strategy. None of us thought it would be this soon.*

Shall we send them to Rhemuth, then? Jesse asked.

Aye, as quickly as possible. I have no doubt the regents will wish to crown the young king as soon as possible—they may even try to do it privately—but it will take a little while to sort out the new regency, with Albertus and Paulin out of the picture. I'm also not sure how long Cathan will be safe there. It's essential that he go back, for reasons I'll convey to Joram in detail, but his position will become more and more precarious as the queen's pregnancy progresses. Be thinking on this. Meanwhile, I shall be heading back to Sanctuary.

When he had ended the contact, he lay there in the straw for perhaps a quarter hour more, first running through a fatigue-banishing spell and then considering whether he ought to attempt a second contact now with Joram or whoever was on duty in the council chamber. After reflection, sensing that he was not yet fully restored, he decided that it was wisest first to put more distance between himself and whatever soldiers might be out looking for an aged priest named Donatus, who had heard the king's last confession.

Descending from the hayloft, he retrieved the little donkey and made his way without incident back to the farmer's barn where he had left the brown mare. This time, besides exchanging mounts again, he left a gold coin in compensation for a set of the farmer's clothes and another quick meal, and by dusk was riding at speed through the forest tracts that would lead him back to Caerrorie in a few days' time.

He would stop again in a few hours, to attempt the call to Joram, but for now he could only ride, focused on his intent that the day's events should bring success in the end, praying that their efforts would be enough, praying for the young king who lay dead at Saint Ostrythe's, and praying for the far younger little king who lay somewhere in Rhemuth, as yet oblivious to the weight of the crown which this day had passed to him all unknowing.

Chapter Twenty-eight

A wicked messenger falleth into mischief; but a faithful ambassador is health.

—Proverbs 13:17

While the new king of Gwynedd slept in Rhemuth Castle, as unaware as those around him that his destiny was upon him—and in four-year-old innocence, unlikely to comprehend his new estate, even had he known—one set as a guardian of his welfare moved unobtrusively among the men dining noisily in the castle's great hall, filling wine goblets when needed and looking for a young knight she had never seen before.

Rhysel had received word that he was coming two days before, passed from Jesse to Joram and then to her. His name was Sir Robert Ainslie, and what he carried was of inestimable value to the future of the Haldane line. That the king had managed not only to draw up a codicil to his will, naming regents of his own choosing, but also to smuggle it out from under the great lords' noses, was no mean feat. It was already common gossip around the castle that Lord Albertus had been killed while on the campaign in Eastmarch, with Father Paulin so badly injured that he was not expected to live.

What was not common gossip was the way Albertus and Paulin had met their fates. Rhysel knew, because Joram had passed on what was picked up from the link they had set in Dimitri. She was sure that Hubert and the other great lords also knew—or thought they did. Rhysel still could hardly believe that the king really had emerged unscathed and unsuspected from the incident. She had told the queen of none of this, just as she had kept back the extent of the king's recent injury,

315

though she now feared the latter to be rather more severe than first thought.

Neither had she yet told the queen of the messenger she now awaited, nor of what the man carried. There was time enough for that, once Rhysel had it in her hands. As she had last night and the previous one, as the officers protecting Rhemuth gathered at the long trestle tables for the evening meal, she lightly scanned each new man who came into the hall whose face was not already familiar to her. Though she knew the messenger's name and that he must be reasonably young, her sources had been able to tell her nothing of his physical appearance. She hoped his arrival would not cause someone to wonder why he had returned prematurely from the campaign with the king.

When she finally caught his trace, she realized she need not have worried. His appearance would never turn heads, even in court attire. He was not unattractive; simply not memorable. He was stocky and nearly a head shorter than most of the other men in the hall, soberly clad in nondescript brown riding leathers, and only his gilded spurs and the dingy white belt supporting a good but plain sword declared his knightly rank—yet another anonymous young knight perhaps come to Court to seek royal service. He had halted uncertainly just inside the doorway, looking tired and a little irritable as he pulled off a leather cap and swept a watery blue gaze across the hall, obviously looking for someone, one hand riffling idly through curly brown hair that was starting to thin on top.

Changing her pitcher for a fuller one, Rhysel took up an empty goblet and began casually working her way toward him, changing direction as he started to make his way slowly along the row of window embrasures that overlooked the gardens. By the time she drew near to him, he had found a place at the end of one of the long tables and had sunk down wearily on one of the benches. She gave him a friendly smile as she filled the goblet and set it before him with a curtsey and managed to brush his hand with hers as she withdrew, confirming that he was, indeed, Sir Robert Ainslie.

"You look thirsty, my lord," she said coyly, refilling the cups of several of the other men seated around him. "Have you ridden far today?"

"Not so far as I would ride tonight," he said with a grin, taking appreciative measure of her with his eyes as he lifted his cup in salute and then took a healthy quaff.

Ribald hoots of approval surrounded them as he set it down,

still grinning, and swept her onto his knee to bend her in a lusty kiss. Giving only token struggle, she let him enjoy it—for she had put the notion in his mind—and used the opportunity to probe him. The missive was inside his tunic. That confirmed, she set instructions for a later rendezvous and a present withdrawal. Young Robert surfaced from the kiss flushed and ardent, blue eyes smouldering, but he let her go without protest as she disentangled herself good-naturedly from his embrace and reclaimed her pitcher.

"A notable introduction, sir knight, but you needs must feed your weary body before indulging other appetites," she said, lightly laughing as she beckoned to a serving squire with a full platter of roast pork. "At least Rhemuth can sleep easy, knowing she has such lusty knights defending her."

He grinned and made another grab in her direction, kissing his hand to her when she deftly avoided him, and was grinning still as he helped himself to food and began wolfing it down, interspersed with banter with his fellows.

She slipped out of the hall as soon after that as she could and made her way to the chapel royal to wait for him. It was one of the few public places in the castle where both of them might be seen without causing comment and where some degree of privacy might be hoped for or at least arranged. An old soldier and one of the elderly laundresses were praying in the chapel, so after lighting a votive candle and kneeling for a brief prayer of her own, Rhysel went back outside to lurk in the shadows.

He came half an hour later, a trifle less steady on his feet than he had been, but alert and purposeful as he spotted her beckoning gesture and came to join her in the little vestibule past the chapel doors. His blue eyes were boyish-wide and mystified, and she decided he was somewhat younger than she had first supposed, perhaps hardly older than herself.

"You have something for me?" she whispered, as he took her hands.

"Aye, for the queen," he replied. "But how came it that you spoke to me so openly in the hall? I was told to be most wary."

It was not open at all, she whispered in his mind, catching control before he could tense and start to draw back in alarm. *I am Deryni in service to the king. You're in no danger. Give me what you carry.*

Without will to resist, he reached into the front of his tunic and produced the document, folded to palm size and sealed on the outside with the king's seal. Even as her fingers touched it, the door to the chapel opened from the inside.

By the time the old soldier had emerged, limping and leaning heavily on a stick, Rhysel had drawn her dazed accomplice into an embrace to rival the one in the hall, the incriminating document pressed between their bodies as their lips pressed together, his body shielding her face from the soldier's gaze as she again linked her mind deeply with his and bade him assist in the illusion they were creating for the old man's benefit. Robert was only human, but he adapted to her instruction without hesitation or question, bending her back in the curve of one arm in a passionate kiss while the other hand probed deep into her bodice—and also secreted his document there.

A part of her mind remained detached, keeping track of the bemused soldier who limped past smiling, but she found her body responding to the young knight's kiss, as he to hers, and a part of her mind as well. Her heart was pounding as she withdrew from him, the danger now past, and she relaxed her controls as she glanced up at him.

"Forgive me for that," she whispered. "I hope you understand why I had to let it happen."

He took a deep breath and suppressed a little shudder as he nodded and reached into a pouch at his belt, producing the king's signet ring, which he pressed into her hand with a lopsided grin.

"I would give a great deal to be the man you really love," he murmured. "You were in my mind, weren't you?"

As she arched an eyebrow at him, slipping the king's ring onto her finger with the seal turned inward, he ventured a cautious nod.

"I'm not afraid," he whispered. "Lord Cathan taught me that there's nothing to fear. Did you Read all that you need to know?"

"There wasn't time or focus," she admitted. "May I do it now?"

He smiled with just a touch of irony. "Have I a choice?"

"I prefer to have permission," she replied. "I'm sorry I had to use you the way I did, but I would do far more than that to serve the king and his House. If it's any consolation to your manhood, I rather enjoyed it, despite the sheer terror that the man was going to interfere."

The irony of his smile turned slightly more wistful. "That's something, then. I—suppose you must block my memory when you're done. I know you have to protect yourself."

"I do," she said softly, taking his face between her hands. "But I can leave you the pleasure—and keep my own."

Her kiss took him gently into the promised forgetfulness, as she delved deep and Read as much as she could of Cathan's briefing when he handed over the document and of Robert's own observations throughout the campaign. She found him an honorable young man, both clever and kind, loyal to his pledged word and faithful to his friends. Regarding his possible continuing usefulness to the king's cause, she noted that his loyalty had been freely given, even before Cathan set the mild compulsions of which he was capable.

She had no right to recruit him to active conspiracy when in this vulnerable state, but further probing confirmed that he gladly would choose to serve, if given the chance. She resolved to give him that chance, well aware that she made her decision on personal grounds, as well as those of expediency for the Haldane cause, trusting her instincts. Leaving intact his memories of what he had done, both by choice and by constraint, she forbade him only the forced disclosure of information that might be harmful to the king; no torture might wrest it out of him.

She gave him then some knowledge of herself and her mission, though of that he could not speak or even write—the protection he himself had expected. But concerning what had passed between the two of them, she made no adjustments at all—and allowed herself to drink deeply of his pleasure as she withdrew from control but not from the kiss, letting him slowly bring it to an end in his own good time and pull back, gazing wonderingly into her hazel eyes.

"I have a thousand questions that I know there isn't time to ask or answer now," he whispered, stroking trembling fingertips down her cheek and across her lips. "When may I see you again?"

She swallowed noisily, her head tipped back to meet his gaze.

"You should return to the king when you've slept," she whispered. "He needs friends nearby, and 'tis best the great lords never learn that you were the bearer of this document." She lightly touched her hand to her bodice, under which it rested. "The sooner you go, the less chance of being missed by those with the king."

"For *his* sake, I will do it," Robert agreed. "But may I not see you again before I go, even briefly?"

"Arrange to be walking in the garden tomorrow at mid-morning," she replied. "Over near the rose arbors. I often walk there with the queen in the afternoons, but I will try to contrive a reason for an earlier walk tomorrow. I will say that her High-ness wishes some roses for her hair. But if, by some chance, I have not come by noon, you must go anyway."

He nodded, lifting her hands to his lips. "I will be there. God keep you."

"And you," she whispered.

He kissed her palms, then her lips, briefly and gently, then turned away and set out along the corridor toward the great hall, too prudent to risk further danger, now that their farewells had been said. She watched until he had disappeared around a turn in the corridor, not once looking back, then retreated to the little cubby she shared with one of the other maids.

Elspeth was already asleep, but Rhysel deepened that sleep before striking a light to the little rushlight set on the tiny table on her side of the bed. It was too late to go to the queen with-out arousing suspicion, but she could at least confirm what the packet was alleged to contain, before hiding it away. The sig-net she would give to the queen in the morning, as confirma-tion that the document had arrived.

Taking the packet from her bodice, she undressed down to her shift, extinguished the rushlight, then lay down beside Elspeth and clasped the packet between her two hands, closing her eyes and drawing a deep breath to begin settling into trance. As she exhaled, she visualized the staring pattern known as *An Suil-Dia*, the Eye of God, and let her conscious-ness be drawn toward the center of its mazelike convolutions, deepening her trance. When the centering was focused, she reached out a tendril of questing to the message between her two hands and slowly read the words.

We, Rhys Michael Alister Haldane, by the Grace of God King of Gwynedd, Lord of Meara, Mooryn, and the Purple March, and Overlord of all the lands of Kheldour, being of sound mind and body, do declare this to be an irrevocable Codicil to Our Last Will and Testament, and hereby re-nounce all previous arrangements that may conflict with this Codicil, and hereby set in place the following Provisions, which may not be changed or set aside save by unanimous assent of the parties herein named or their legal heirs, they being of age and legal majority.

In the event of Our death before the coming of age of Our Son and Heir, the Prince Owain Javan Cinhil, or the coming of age of the Child now carried by Our Queen, should the said Owain die before Our second Child's majority, We do hereby appoint as Regents for the Kingdom of Gwynedd His Grace the Duke of Claibourne, also known as Graham MacEwan, and the Right Honourable the Earl of Marley, Sighere son of Sighere, to serve jointly or separately, as may seem to them most expedient for the welfare of Our Kingdom, regardless of whatever other Regents may be appointed by Instruments signed by Us or said to be signed by Us. These appointments shall be effective until such time as our Heirs shall come of age or until said Lords are replaced by their heirs of legal age, whether by resignation or death.

In that We repose full and unequivocal trust in the said Lords of Claibourne and Marley, We hereby authorize and pardon any military action deemed necessary by the said Lords to secure and exercise their lawful authority as Regents for Our Heirs.

Given under Our Hand and Seal this twenty-fourth day of June, being the Feast of Saint John the Baptist, in the Year of Our Lord Nine Hundred Twenty-Eight at our Castle of Lochalyn in the Earldom of Eastmarch, Kheldour Province, wherefore the undersigned have this day publicly reaffirmed their Oaths of Fealty to Us, in further witness of their Fidelity to this Our Solemn Decree.

(signed) Rhys R. (his seal)
Agreed: Claibourne (his seal)
Agreed: Marley (his seal)
Attest: Stacia, Countess of Eastmarch (her seal)
Attest: Fr. Derfel (+).

Rhysel let herself drift for a moment when she had finished scanning, allowing the import to sink in. As Joram had told her, it was a brilliant document—no guarantee that the great lords would not try to kill off Claibourne and Marley and thus eliminate the opposition, but certainly a good incentive for them to keep the king alive as long as possible, to avoid having to deal with the problem.

For to deny the Kheldour lords their just due was to risk civil war—a thing she did not think the great lords would dare, given that their ranks had recently been reduced by the loss of Udaut, Albertus, and Paulin. The great lords probably would allow Richard Murdoch to continue in the constable's post left vacant by Udaut's death, since Richard had married Udaut's daughter; but until the *Custodes* question was sorted out and stabilized and replacements for Albertus and Paulin had been confirmed on the royal council, she suspected the great lords would tread very carefully, indeed. And the document in her hands was a way of ensuring that they did.

Still hovering between trance and wakefulness, Rhysel cupped her hands over it on her breast, considering the hiding place she had already devised for it, then decided that before surfacing she would first send through confirmation to Joram that the document had arrived. It was the hour when they might expect her sending, but to her surprise, a link not only was open but seeking, with Joram himself pushing at the other end.

With both parties stretching for the contact, Joram's amplified probe swept into her mind like an avalanche, imparting his grim news with a force that nearly made her cry out. Her confirmation of the codicil's arrival was overwhelmed by the devastating news that it was already in effect, that young Prince Owain had already been king for nearly half a day. The king had died at an obscure convent called Saint Ostrythe's, somewhere between Sheele and Ebor, already weakened from his hand injury and then bled unto death by order of the *Custodes Fidei*, despite the fact that Rhun, at least, had known of the codicil's existence and of the crisis that would loom for him and his fellow regents as soon as the king's death became known.

It changed everything. Despite Rhys Michael's heroic effort to safeguard what he could for his sons, his effort now would be tested in the forge of internal strife and possible civil war; and if the shock of his death cost the queen the child she carried, young King Owain Haldane might well be the last Haldane king.

Rhysel kept herself focused for Joram's instructions, but her mind was numb, the fragile delight of her brief flirtation with Robert Ainslie all but blotted out in the greater urgency of what she must do for the queen. When Joram had withdrawn from his contact, leaving her stunned and bereft, she lay there for nearly an hour with tears running silently from her eyes and into her hair, hugging the now priceless codicil for comfort and caressing the king's signet between her fingers, mourning this new failure of their hopes and dreams.

Eventually she rose by the light of cautious handfire to secrete the document and the king's signet underneath one of the floorboards, with a charm set to dispel any curiosity about the possible hiding place. She lay back down in darkness then, though it was a long time before she drifted into troubled sleep.

CHAPTER TWENTY-NINE

For she is privy to the mysteries of the knowledge of
God, and a lover of his works.
—Wisdom of Solomon 8:4

Rhysel went to the queen the next morning with some reluctance, for she did not relish the charade she must play, the deception she must maintain. She had awakened to the leaden knell of the cathedral bells tolling down in the city, soon picked up and carried by the closer bells of Saint Hilary's-Within-the-Walls and other lesser bells throughout the city. Though she knew that news of the king's death could not have reached Rhemuth yet, apprehension was a choking lump in her throat until she could make inquiries.

She was somewhat dismayed to learn that it was Archbishop Oriss who had died, sometime during the early morning hours, for he had been the sole moderate sitting on the Royal Council and the only one of its members not to have been actively involved in the murder of King Javan six years before. In theory, he would be replaced by a formal vote of the assembled bishops, but in fact it was Hubert, the Archbishop-Primate, who would determine Oriss' successor—and to Hubert's advantage, rather than the advantage of the House of Haldane. The one positive aspect to the entire matter was that the mere turnover of the office would further destabilize the existing Council, already weakened by the loss of Udaut, Albertus, and Paulin.

But for now, as a dutiful member of the queen's household, she must feign respectful regret for the archbishop's passing, just as she must pretend that she did not know of a far more devastating loss farther north of here. She presented herself in the royal boudoir to find Michaela oddly pensive, wistfully fingering a little gold cross around her neck while Eithne, one of her maids, laced her into a gown of dull purple. Lady Estellan had chosen the gown as a mark of respect for Archbishop Oriss, also laying out a seemly black veil and the simplest of the queen's gold circlets; but as Rhysel set about the usual morning ritual of brushing and arranging the royal tresses, she realized that the queen's subdued mood was caused not by regret over an archbishop's passing but by growing concern for her husband's safety.

And Rhysel dared do nothing to reassure her on that account, for the truth must be avoided for yet a little while, and offering any false hope would be cruel. To lighten the immediate atmosphere, and also to set the stage for covering any outward reaction to the more welcome news she brought, Rhysel gradually shifted their casual chitchat to a shyly offered description of the young knight who had paid her court in the great hall the night before. It soon focused the attention of all the ladies in the room, eager for the gossip of little Liesel's new romance, but it also provided ready cover for the queen's real relief when Rhysel silently confirmed that the knight had delivered the codicil as well as a kiss. Supposed shyness about imparting too much detail about so delicate and new a flirtation also saved Rhysel from possibly letting slip hints of the more dread news that had arrived later in the night.

Protocol demanded the attendance of the entire household at Mass that morning, out of respect for the archbishop. En route to the Chapel Royal, Rhysel contrived to press the king's ring into Michaela's hand, biting her lip at the glad surge of happiness that swelled the queen's breast as she slipped it on her hand with the seal turned inward and clasped her hands prayerfully around it.

The Mass itself provided focus for Rhysel to set about the next of the tasks Joram had set her the night before. Kneeling beside the queen, who soon lost herself in renewed prayers for her husband's safe return, his ring clasped between her hands, Rhysel offered up her own prayer for the repose of the king's soul, then used the remainder of the service to gently insinuate new controls in Michaela's mind, set to damp her grief when the inevitable word came that her beloved Rhysem was dead— for nothing must interfere with the child she carried, now become Heir Presumptive of Gwynedd, even before his birth.

Afterward, when the queen returned to her solar for the

morning's unvarying session of needlework with her ladies, all
unaware what her Deryni confidante had done, Rhysel betook
herself to the castle gardens, far toward the end by the great
hall. There she set herself to cutting flowers for the queen's
bower, taking her time, laying them one by one in a flat basket, being careful to move slowly and openly among the garden's wide paths. She had carried her basket into a rose arbor
and was admiring a perfect bloom of blood-crimson when
Robert joined her, slipping his arms around her waist from behind and leaning down to nuzzle the side of her neck.

She stiffened and averted her face, ready to muffle his reaction if he could not, as she whispered, "Please, you mustn't. I
have ill news. The king is dead."

She felt him go rigid as well and sensed the dull grief
welling from deep inside him even as he held her more tightly,
burying his face against her neck for comfort now rather than
passion.

"His hand?" he asked.

"His physicians," she replied, turning in the circle of his
arms to face him. "Or rather, I should say his *Custodes* physicians. They bled him, Robert. Four times in less than a day
and a night, and far too much. Even once or twice would have
been perilous, as weak as he had become. One of our people
got to him before the end—a Healer, even—but it was too late.
He died yesterday afternoon."

Robert swallowed hard and held her to him. She could feel
his heart beating next to hers, but she steeled her own will and
made herself extend light controls as she slid her arms around
his waist.

"You must go back as quickly as you can," she whispered.
"The little king is safe enough for now, but Lord Cathan must
be protected. He will be one of the queen's few sources of
comfort when she learns of the king's death—but only if he
can stay alive to do it. He knows this, but his grief could make
him rash. It also may not have occurred to him how important
his help will be in aiding the Kheldour lords to assert their
rights as regents. You must go to him and be his voice of reason, if you can. I'll set a message for him. You will not know
what you carry until he Reads it from you. Are you bold
enough to invite his touch?"

"To use his powers on me?" Robert asked. "He did before,
and you have done. If I was going to be afraid of *that*, it's a
little late, isn't it?"

She drew back and smiled sadly, setting her fingertips lightly on his cheeks. "My bold, brave knight," she whispered. "How I wish we had met in less dangerous times. I like it not, to impose my will on one I would liefer have offer his aid."

"Dear lady, I gladly offer all I have and am," he breathed, "whether you are Deryni or no, whether or not you must impose your will to help me do what will help our new young king. Do you think I would scorn such assistance, knowing it will make me stronger in his service? I am not so proud as to think I cannot be the more effective tool, simply because the aid you give me is beyond my ability to do alone. If it is humanly possible, I will bring Lord Cathan back safely to the queen. Tell her she may depend upon it." He frowned. "She doesn't know yet, does she?"

Rhysel shook her head. "No, and she must not, until official word comes, lest I be discovered. It will also give me time to prepare her. I've begun that already. Nothing must be allowed to endanger the child she carries."

"Aye, God forbid," he murmured, bending to gently kiss her forehead.

She used the contact to implant the message for Cathan, sent and set in the blink of an eye, even as Robert pulled back to look at her in question.

"You must get to him somehow and give him opportunity to Read you," she murmured. "I hope he will know to attempt it when he sees you have returned. There will be at least one other among that company who can help you; he will make himself known to you. Once Cathan has my instructions, simply do as he and the other bid you and try to bring both of you back safely. Both the queen and I shall be waiting."

She kissed him then, this time with no subterfuge or mental augmentation, simply letting herself melt into his arms, feeling the sweet pleasure flooding through her body and his. It was he who pulled back at last, trembling with passion yet unleashed, to draw apart and only hold her hands, looking searchingly into the golden eyes and drawing shaky breath.

"When I come back, Rhysel Thuryn, I intend to ask for your hand in marriage," he whispered. "Don't answer now; just think on it until I return. I don't care what you are; perhaps I love you more because of it. I do know that I love you, as God is my witness. May He keep you safe."

With that, he was bending to kiss both her hands, then catching up the perfect red rose she had laid in her basket just when he arrived. He took it with him as he receded down the path, not looking back, and Rhysel sank to her knees to weep over her basket of roses, unable to watch him go, wondering whether all their efforts would come to naught. The codicil was even now in force, but could the Kheldour lords execute it?

The codicil to the king's will was about to become of great interest to others in Rhemuth, though they would not learn for some days that it was already in force. As Sir Robert Ainslie galloped northward out of the city, a sedate ecclesiastical procession under *Custodes* escort was winding its way back up to the castle after a noon Requiem Mass for the departed Archbishop Oriss, whose body now would lie beneath the cathedral transept until his state funeral, two days hence. Archbishop Hubert had presided alongside Rhemuth's Auxiliary Bishop, Alfred of Woodbourne, and now gave blessings from the scarlet-upholstered sedan chair that had become his habitual mode of transport in the last few years, as his bulk increased beyond the ability of any single horse to carry him securely.

Six burly gentlemen bore him this afternoon, all but engulfed by the vast black cope that swept from beneath a jeweled golden mitre. His crozier was in his left hand, set in a socket along the side of the sedan chair. A crucifer and two priests swinging thuribles walked before him, and Lord Tammaron and Richard Murdoch rode to either side, both soberly clad in mourning like the rest. The two pressed on ahead as the litter negotiated the last ascent through the castle gate, and as Hubert alighted from the chair before the steps of the castle's great hall, he was surprised to see Tammaron already reading a missive just handed over by a weary-looking courier in Rhun's livery.

"I think we'd better go inside to discuss this," Tammaron said, giving Hubert an odd, strained look as he folded the letter and slipped it into his gown. "It's from Rhun. It appears the king may have taken the bit in his teeth in a totally different manner than we feared. Oh, and Paulin has died."

When they were closeted in Tammaron's private study and Hubert had read the letter for the third time, he tossed it onto the table and shook his head, anger lighting the china-blue eyes. He had shed his mitre and cope and loomed in the sober purple of his episcopal robes.

"It has to be a bluff," he said. "There's no way he could

have executed a codicil to his will. And even if he did, it wouldn't stand up in court. Not one of *our* courts."

"You've read Rhun's letter," Tammaron said blandly. "He saw the draft copy. If it isn't a bluff—if enough originals were executed and witnessed by enough people—even one of our courts would at least have to give the matter consideration. And there's no doubt that the Kheldour lords would certainly push it as hard as they could. I've always said it was a mistake to eliminate Duke Ewan from the last regency, and now it's come back to haunt us. Sorry, Richard, but your father was occasionally overzealous."

Richard picked up the letter and scanned it again, ignoring the reference to his father.

"We can force him to write a new will when he gets back," he said. "We'd already begun drafting the provisions to replace Albertus and Paulin in the list of future regents. We'll simply make certain the wording is ironclad, superseding anything else he's ever signed."

Tammaron waved a hand dismissively. "That's understood. It still won't stop Claibourne and Marley from producing their documents and trying to assert their rights."

As he sighed, Hubert was pulling a fresh piece of parchment toward him and taking pen in hand.

"I'm sending for Father Secorim," he said, over the scratching of the pen on parchment. "Oriss' death leaves another gap on the Council that I want to fill as quickly as possible, certainly before the king returns. I trust neither of you will object if I name Secorim as archbishop-designate? He'll have to be ratified by the bishops, of course, but they'll do as I command. That will put another man I can trust back on the Council right away."

Tammaron cocked his head quizzically. "Didn't you have him in mind for Paulin's replacement?"

"Yes, but if he were only vicar-general of the *Custodes*, he could be ousted; the Archbishop of Rhemuth can't. I'll find another vicar-general: Lior, perhaps, or maybe Hallex, out at *Arx Fidei*. Meanwhile, this will give us another strong voice on the Council, to put pressure on the king when he returns. Richard, give this to a courier, please."

As Richard disappeared with the summons, Tammaron gave Hubert an uneasy glance.

"He's pulled a very shrewd move, has our clever young king," he murmured. "Even the threat of such a document's existence ensures that we'll do our utmost to keep him alive. It cancels out all our old threats until Owain comes of age."

Hubert picked up the offending letter once again and hefted it in his hand, the rosebud lips pursed in sour indignation.

"It's a clever enough challenge, I'll grant you. But I think he'll find it isn't clever enough by half. He thinks he's found the ideal threat, but it's worthless, so long as he's alive. And while he's alive, he *can* be manipulated. There are worse threats than death, for a king."

But the king had already passed beyond the threat of death. The military cavalcade that had borne him ailing to Saint Ostrythe's Convent two days before left it that morning as a funeral cortege, silent save for the creak of leather and the jingle of harness and the quiet whuffling of fresh steeds eager for the day's journey. *Custodes* monks mounted on black horses led the procession, one bearing a processional cross and the other the king's banner, the latter drabbed by black streamers drooping from its staff.

The king's body, now coffined in oak and covered with a rich funeral pall, traveled in a litter borne by two black horses and escorted by a score of black-clad *Custodes* knights. Atop the black damask and velvet of the pall had been fastened the king's sword and the golden circlet he had worn upon his helmet. The king's earl marshal and vice-marshal rode to either side of the coffin as a particular guard of honor, both in borrowed black *Custodes* mantles despite the rising heat of the day.

Sir Cathan Drummond, the dead king's brother-in-law, rode farther back in the cortege, hollow-eyed and looking very pale. There was reason for that besides his grief, for he had clawed his way from drugged sleep that morning to find that he had been bled during the night—probably not enough to endanger health, for they preferred to keep him alive for Mika's sake, but certainly enough to weaken him appreciably. The other bed in the tiny room had been slept in—by Fulk, he supposed— and a dried smear of blood on the sheet suggested that he, too, had been bled.

The threat did not need further elucidation. Clearly, even the possibility of resistance was not to be allowed. Even as Cathan had considered this grim development, fingering the bandage on his bare arm and trying to shake off a beastly headache, Stevanus had come into the little room with a monk Cathan did not recognize, who silently examined the arm and then remained until the patient had drunk down every drop of the cup he had brought. It looked and smelled like ordinary morning ale, perhaps a bit better than most, but there was an undertaste to it that Cathan did not dare to question. Once the monk had left, he rounded on Stevanus in near panic.

"What was that?" he demanded. "What does this mean?" He indicated his bandaged arm. "And where is Fulk?"

"You'd better dress while we talk," Stevanus said quietly, drawing the pile of Cathan's discarded clothes to him and sitting on the edge of the bed.

Wearily he related how Fulk had already been removed from the temptation to speak of what he had witnessed in the king's death chamber—rousted from bed at daybreak and posted off to Cassan without so much as a by-your-leave, in custody of two *Custodes* officers and half a dozen Culdi archers, to enter house arrest at his brother's court until it was certain he could hold his tongue.

"As for you," he went on, "that was your new physician, Brother Embert. The ale he gave you was laced with rather a stronger dose of what the regents used to give Alroy to keep him tractable. I'm afraid you can expect the same every morning. Embert's also the one who bled you, on Manfred's orders. I don't think they'll do it again soon—they've made their point abundantly clear—but you'd better be very, very careful. Rhun didn't try to stop it. I hardly need remind you that he's wanted to see you dead for a very long time. The only thing saving you for now is that he and Manfred both know they'll have to answer to Archbishop Hubert if you die and then the queen loses the new baby. If Hubert had been along on this expedition, things might have gone very differently. He's a very pragmatic individual."

"He's a murderer like the rest of them," Cathan murmured, pulling on his boots, though he kept his voice low.

Stevanus heaved a disconsolate sigh. "I've come to see that. I can't but think the entire *Custodes* Order must be tainted as well, though I didn't want to believe it at first. I thought I had a true vocation, that the Order had important work to do. I even thought I was doing the right thing when I helped stage the king's 'abduction' while he was still prince. And I was very good at what I did.

"But it was all a lie," he continued, handing Cathan the tunic to his riding leathers. "The entire focus of the *Custodes*

Fidei is and always has been a cover for gaining secular power. I lay most of the blame for that on Paulin and Albertus, but I have little hope that their successors will be any better."

Cathan pulled on the leather tunic over his head, wincing at the twinge on his sore arm, and began doing up the front laces.

"You said this Brother Embert is to be my new physician. Does that mean you're being sent away, too, like Fulk?"

Stevanus glanced at his feet, nodding dismally. "Would that it were so benign. No one will dare to slay Earl Tammaron's son. I'm—ordered to go to the abbey at Ramos tomorrow, when we pass nearby. Father Lior has called it a 'retreat,' to refocus myself after the strain of what I've been through. He's my superior in the Order, so I have no choice but to go. But it's the harshest of the *Custodes* houses. God alone knows whether I shall ever leave there, save in a coffin like the king." He looked up uncertainly. "Can you forgive me for what they made me do to him?"

"You were never like them," Cathan assured him, bending uncomfortably to buckle on his spurs. "And you tried to serve him faithfully, in the end."

"Aye, but too little and too late."

"For him, perhaps, but not for the Haldane line, pray God."

"I do—and shall," Stevanus whispered. "And for you, my lord."

Saying nothing, Cathan tried to put on a brave face for Stevanus as he stood to buckle on his sword, a little surprised that he had been allowed to retain his weapons—though what harm he could do with them now, with the king already dead, God alone knew. To his dismay, his knees went weak and his vision blurred, and he had to catch his balance on the battle surgeon's arm until a wave of vertigo had passed.

"Light-headed," he murmured. "Is that from the drug or the bloodletting?"

"A little of both, I expect. If you can exaggerate the effects, pretend to be more affected than you are, there's a chance they'll decrease the medication after a day or two. I wish there were something I could do to help, but—" He shrugged and sighed, apparently resigned to his fate. "Do you think you'll be able to manage a horse?"

Cathan gave a weak snort. "I'm sure I'll have minders to keep an eye on me. You don't really think they'd let me fall off, do you?" His tone made it no question at all.

One of his minders turned out to be Gallard de Breffni,

though he hardly cared who rode to either side of him that first morning. Merely staying on his horse occupied the greater part of his conscious effort until well past noon, and he had no need to exaggerate anything. It was not until late afternoon that his brain had cleared sufficiently for him to string together more than two thoughts without getting lost in his own chains of logic, and by then he was too physically exhausted to do more than fall into bed after picking wearily at an ill-cooked meal.

His observations over the next few days were not reassuring. Though his minders became less attentive, once convinced of his disinclination to do anything besides try to stay mounted, Gallard de Breffni's presence at his side was a constant reminder of the story Rhysem had told him of his kidnapping, a few months before Javan's murder, when the treacherous Gallard had posed as one of the prince's captors and Rhysem himself had been swept along similarly helpless and drug-blurred and weakened. He thought they did ease back on his medication after the first day, but he continued to feign greater weakness than he actually felt, in hopes that he might begin to regain some degree of control.

But always with him was the awareness that any untoward initiative on his part might bring a dose of *merasha* with a Deryni pricker rather than the gentler sedative Embert had been giving him. He nearly wept that second morning when, just before midday, he saw Stevanus and half a dozen *Custodes* set off on another road, headed eastward toward Ramos. He found himself hating the *Custodes Fidei* more with every passing hour.

And ever before him was the fear, the uncertainty, both for his personal safety and for the greater goal. He wondered whether Robert Ainslie had made it safely to Rhemuth and prayed that Mika's copy of the codicil was now in safe hands.

For that matter, what of the even more important copies in Kheldour? Did the holders even know yet that the document must already be exercised? Dom Queron had promised to get word to their allies at Lochalyn Castle, but could Claibourne and Marley act quickly enough?

Even as Cathan pondered these questions, Ansel and Tieg and an escort of four armed men rode under the gate arch of Lochalyn Castle and asked for urgent audience with the highest-ranking person in charge. It was just on noon, and the castle yard seemed mostly deserted, though a blacksmith was hammering away in his forge, over by the stable yard, alongside several armorers repairing weapons. Stacia came down to see them presently, a wolfhound pressing against her apron and tweed skirts, the glorious red hair bound under a linen kerchief. She blanched as she recognized young Tieg.

"May we speak with you in private, lady?" Ansel murmured.

She summoned Father Derfel as soon as she heard the bare gist of their news, and by midafternoon they had been joined in the solar by Graham, Sighere, and Corban, recalled from their patrolling of the surrounding area.

"Damn the bluidy lot o' them!" Sighere blurted, slamming a beefy hand against the table when Ansel had given them a sketchy account of the king's death and touched anew on the implications. "That puir lad. An' they're apt tae cut us right out if we dinnae act quickly."

"*Can* you act this quickly?" Ansel asked. "Is the border secure enough to pull troops just now?"

"Och, aye," Graham replied. "There hasnae been a peep fra Torenth this week gone, nae sign o' Marek. Besides, we willnae need ta tak many. No more'n a score, or we cannae travel fast enou'. Corban, kin ye spare us those?"

Corban nodded. "Aye, the fewer gone, the fewer missed. It's coverin' yer and Sighere's absence I'm thinking will be chancy. Ye dinnae want the bluidy *Custodes* houndin' ye back tae Rhemuth tae mak life more difficult."

"God forbid!" Tieg breathed. "Can you create some kind of diversion?"

"Aye, it can be done," Sighere said. "We'll send the *Custodes* north wi' Delacroix, tae check out the pass through the Arranal, an' the levies fra Caerrorie an' Sheele can be dispersed locally tae guard the pass here."

Corban nodded his agreement. "Just ane favor I'd ask: Could ye mebbe figure a way tae clap the Caerrorie commander in irons? He's Manfred MacInnis' son, ye know. I wouldnae feel safe wi' one o' *that* tribe left in any position of authority while ye hare off tae Rhemuth."

"I think something can be arranged," Ansel said grimly. "I'd also suggest that you try to keep news of the king's death from leaking out until we're well away. I suspect that official notification will be delayed for some time, since Rhun and Manfred know about the codicil, but it *will* reach here eventually. What are MacInnis' officers like? Anyone who can be trusted?"

Sighere shrugged. "I couldnae say. He's keen on discipline, though. 'Tis probably best tae pretend he's goin' with us, an' mebbe forge some orders tae cover his absence."

Tieg chuckled. "No need to forge anything, my lord. If you'll get him here, I believe I can safely assure you that Lord Iver MacInnis will write a brilliant set of orders to cover whatever we'd like. I don't ordinarily condone tampering with a person's free will, but in this case, I'll be pleased to make an exception."

"I think I can improve on that idea," Ansel said. "We'll send Iver MacInnis *and* the *Custodes* commander north to do some reconnoitering—after both commanders have written impeccable orders to cover their maneuvers. That will also delay them finding out about the king, and give us a few more days' lead time. If we succeed in Rhemuth, it will be right away or not at all."

"About Rhemuth," Graham ventured. "D'ye really think we can pull this off wi' only twenty men?"

Ansel smiled. "We'll be more than twenty by the time we reach Rhemuth."

As he outlined the rest of their plan, hastily reworked from the original scenario for year's end, Sighere laughed aloud in sheer delight, his bristling red hair and beard giving him a look of vulpine cunning. Stacia, too, was smiling and nodding, as Ansel started drafting the brief sets of orders that would be necessary to get Iver and Joshua out of Lochalyn.

By nightfall, following a flurry of activity in the several hours preceding, Lord Iver MacInnis and Lord Joshua Delacroix led out fully half the royal troops still based at Lochalyn, heading northward on a special recce to scout the next pass northward. The remaining royal troops were left in Corban Howell's capable hands.

Shortly after their departure, a rather smaller, more lightly mounted band headed south, led by the Duke of Claibourne and the Earl of Marley and including two new-come borderers and a middle-aged priest mounted somewhat precariously on a smooth-gaited rouncy. The new Earl of Eastmarch rode with them as far as the camp, his lady watching from the castle ramparts. When the riders had disappeared into the dusk, the countess retired to the castle chapel to offer prayers for the success of their mission, and a special mother's prayer for the little boy in Rhemuth who now was king.

CHAPTER THIRTY

And through covetousness shall they with feigned
words make merchandise of you.

—II Peter 2:3

It was on the morning of the next day, the royal party's third
day out from Saint Ostrythe's and the fourth since the king's
death, that Cathan Drummond at last was able to seize some
small hope concerning his situation. The army had camped the
previous night in a field half a day's ride south and west of
Ramos, close along the banks of the Eirian. Wispy fog still
clung to the ground, risen up from the river during the night,
as his minders escorted him to his mount. Just as Gallard was
giving him a leg up, Cathan spotted Robert Ainslie not far
away, leading up a saddled horse for his father.

The exertion required to mount made Cathan light-headed,
so that he had to hold tight to his horse's mane for a few seconds until his vision steadied. When he could look around
again, Robert was gone.

Though he knew his mind was at its muzziest early in the
morning, right after taking Brother Embert's potion, he was
sure it was Robert he had seen. But Embert's drug also made
him uncertain whether the young knight had returned from his
mission or simply had betrayed Cathan and the king and never
gone. He put but little stock in the compulsions he had tried to
set, for he knew his own shortcomings as a Deryni, but he
hoped he had not misjudged Robert that badly. Beyond thinking was the possibility that Robert had gone right to Rhun and
Manfred and given them the codicil—though he could not

imagine his own life would have been spared, if that had been the case.

All day, as they rode along, he tried to figure out a way to speak with Robert. The prospects seemed slim, for Gallard or the other man, a knight named Cloyce de Clarendon, were always beside him, maintaining the illusion of benign regard but ready to intervene if he put one foot wrong.

It must be something subtle, then—or as subtle as Cathan could manage, with his thinking fogged and his physical reflexes slowed, though at least they had not bled him again. He decided that if Robert *had* been to Rhemuth and returned—as was most likely, when Cathan was not feeling paranoid—he probably had delivered the missive through Rhysel. And if the Deryni Rhysel had been the contact, there was a fair chance that she had set some return message in Robert's mind for Cathan's reading—perhaps instructions and guidance, though she probably would not have known yet of Rhysem's death.

But how to gain access to the young knight? Since Robert was not Deryni, and Cathan only a very weak one, even when in full command of his faculties, he could only Read such a message through physical contact. But how was Robert going to get past Cathan's ever-vigilant minders?

Cathan decided he was going to have to create his own opportunity and trust that Robert would recognize it and follow through. He watched for his chance all through the afternoon, the while continuing to feign listlessness and fatigue and even nodding off in the saddle, but he did not once even see Robert again. Not until they were splashing through the sandy shallows of a wide ford across the Eirian, approaching the *Custodes* House that was their destination for the night, did a ghost of a chance present itself.

It was not much of an opportunity, and if Robert was not trying to get to *him*, it was not going to work, but it was worth a try. The day was warm; a dunking would do no harm.

For Robert and another young knight were spurring casually forward along the line to make some inquiry of an officer just beyond Cathan, who was already turning in his saddle in response to Robert's hail. Cathan waited until the two were nearly abreast of him and his minders, slumped heavy-lidded in his saddle—and let himself topple soundlessly over the side closer to the pair, which was also the side away from Gallard, who was more likely to be alert than Cloyce.

Gallard gave a shout as Cathan tumbled, but it was too late

for Cloyce de Clarendon to catch him. The startled *Custodes* knight caught enough of a handful of tunic to slow his charge's fall, but keeping hold would have dragged him off, too, and Cathan was already hitting the water.

Cathan started flailing weakly as he briefly sank beneath the surface, glad he was only wearing riding leathers and the water was only knee-deep on the horses. To his relief, Robert Ainslie was off his horse and dragging his head above the water before he could even worry about being stepped on or kicked or possibly drowned.

"Easy, my lord," Robert murmured, as Cathan struggled to a sitting position with his help and started coughing, affecting grogginess and disorientation. In that same instant, Cathan had almost the impression that Robert himself, who was not Deryni, had willed him to Read. The message came through in a burst of crystal clarity—reassurance from Rhysel and tight-focused instructions that he would have to examine later, when Gallard de Breffni stopped yanking him out of Robert's grasp.

"I've got him!" Gallard snapped, as Cathan murmured, "Sorry, I nodded off." "Leave him to me. He hasn't been sleeping well since the king's death. Just help get him back on his horse."

Apparently taking Gallard at his word, as Cathan continued to murmur embarrassed protestations of apology, Robert gave a hand getting the queen's brother back up onto his mount. The further contact gave Cathan opportunity to send the gist of what had been done to him while Robert was away. Both compassion and determination showed on the young knight's face as he handed up the reins, but he turned away and sprang back onto his own horse without a word as Gallard also remounted.

Despite the mildness of the summer evening, Cathan could feel himself starting to shiver, as much from after-reaction as from any real chill, and he gratefully drew close the dry cloak Cloyce laid around his shoulders. His leathers were already getting clammy. As they carried on toward the abbey gates ahead, he wondered whether he could get out of the usual vigil beside Rhysem's coffin that night. He thought Rhysem would not mind; and with his medication mostly worn off, he was not certain he could contain his relief at the news Robert had given him.

That the codicil was delivered was greatly reassuring; that the Kheldour lords were on their way was news more welcome yet. And that at least one further ally was already with the royal party was most personally reassuring of all.

Later that evening, when duties at last released him, Sir Robert Ainslie casually made his way to the tent of a handful of borderers who had joined his father's party a few days before his arrival. Their leader had sought him out that morning and given him new instructions.

"I was wondering when you'd get here," Jesse MacGregor said, beckoning Robert across the bodies of several sleeping men to a space beside the stool where he was sitting, cleaning a boot by lantern-light. "I'm glad it wasn't cold. I take it you did make contact?"

"Aye."

"All right, sit yourself down and let's see whether he was able to send anything back. The others won't stir."

He set the boot aside as Robert settled gingerly, patting his knee to invite the younger man to lean against it. As strong hands drew Robert back, thumbs slipping upward into the curly brown hair, time seemed to pause. When Robert next became aware of anything, the Deryni was breathing out a long sigh, his hands kneading gently once at his tight shoulder muscles and then releasing him. Robert felt revitalized, though he knew he would sleep heavily when he shortly sought his bedroll.

"You did that very well," Jesse murmured. "He did *his* part very well, despite what he's been through."

Robert nodded. "I was surprised at that myself."

"He's alive, though, and that's what's most important for now," Jesse whispered, shifting his gaze into the lantern flame. "We'll be in Rhemuth in a few more days, and God willing, the Kheldour lords will be there shortly after that. Once that happens, I have a feeling things are going to move very quickly indeed, for better or for worse." He glanced at Robert. "Are you afraid?"

"I'd be mad not to be," Robert admitted, nodding. "But that isn't going to stop me from doing what must be done."

Jesse smiled. "Good man. You've been more help than you know. For now, stay close and watch for any chance to gain some kind of regular access to Cathan. I'll let you know what happens next. You'd better go and sleep now, though."

When the younger man had gone, Jesse extinguished the lantern and lay back on his pallet, soon imparting his night's report to Joram, who was waiting to add this most current piece of the puzzle to the master picture building in a Michaeline war room, deep within the stronghold that had housed him and his renegade band of Deryni for nearly a decade now.

You can't get to Cathan yourself? Joram asked.

I don't see how. But at least I think we'll get him to Rhemuth alive. What's the word on the Kheldour lords?

On their way, came the answer. *They shouldn't be more than two or three days behind you.*

In Rhemuth, at that same hour, what remained of Gwynedd's royal council was about to receive the latest news to arrive from the returning expeditionary force. Archbishop Hubert had been dining privately with Tammaron, Richard, and Secorim in the withdrawing room behind the dais of the great hall. Earlier, Hubert had presided at Archbishop Oriss' funeral rites, with all the Court in attendance—an affair that stretched well into the afternoon, by the time they laid Oriss' body to rest with his predecessors' in the episcopal crypt beneath the high altar.

As they lingered over wine and sweetmeats, rehashing the significance of the day's events, Tammaron and Richard still wore the deep mourning of earlier in the day; Secorim was always clad in funereal *Custodes* black, and Hubert had put aside the usual robes of his rank in favor of a plain black cassock, retaining episcopal purple only in the broad cincture bound around his ample girth—and in the episcopal ring and the amethysts studding the jeweled pectoral cross suspended at his breast.

One pudgy hand darted to that cross as a guard admitted a haggard-looking messenger wearing Culdi livery—Sir Rondel, Lord Manfred's own principal aide. Rondel pulled off his gloves as he came to kneel and kiss Hubert's ring and remained kneeling and with head bowed until the door had closed behind him. Hubert saw that his hands were shaking.

"Is my brother dead?" Hubert asked quietly.

Rondel shook his head, only then daring to look up.

"No, your Grace. Lord Manfred is well. I—regret to inform you that the king has died—"

"What?"

"When? Where?"

"Let him finish!" Hubert snapped, holding up a hand for their silence. "Out with it, man. How came this to be?"

"At—at Saint Ostrythe's Convent, near Ebor, some three days ago," Rondel stammered, daring to look up. "He took a raging fever. His—hand became badly infected and had to be amputated. Unfortunately, he did not survive the surgery."

The stunned buzz of their comment died away as Hubert slowly crossed himself, his rosy face gone ashen, the tiny lips trembling.

"You—have further details of this?" he whispered, after a few seconds.

"I do, your Grace." He got to his feet, his composure returning. "Might I suggest, however, that this company first retire to the council chamber?" He touched a hand to his breast. "I have further information to convey to your Lordships, but my Lord Manfred suggested that its sensitive nature recommends the utmost in discretion."

Stunned to silence by his implications and the stark unexpectedness of his news, they retired immediately to the more secure council chamber, ordered by Hubert to say nothing en route. Secorim set *Custodes* guards outside the double doors as servants lit candles and torches in the room and then departed. As they took their customary places around the long table, Hubert and Secorim on one side, Tammaron and Richard on the other, Hubert reflected that there were not nearly enough of them—especially not if, as the king had threatened, there really was a codicil that broke his most recent will and named Kheldour appointees to what had just become a council of regency.

But not everyone at the table knew about the codicil—Secorim did not—and until Hubert knew the circumstances of the king's death, he was not going to raise the issue. By the light of a candelabrum set at the end of the table where they huddled, he held out his hand to Sir Rondel, seated in Manfred's customary spot three places to the right. Impassive and silent, Rondel passed a sealed packet across Father Secorim, directly to Hubert. Hubert broke the seals and scanned over the text—written in Manfred's crabbed hand but also signed and sealed by Rhun—then passed it over to Tammaron, who pulled the candelabrum closer and began to read aloud.

" 'Manfred MacInnis unto his brother and Father in God, Hubert, Archbishop of Valoret and Primate of All Gwynedd; and also unto Earl Tammaron Fitz-Arthur, Chancellor of

Gwynedd, and Richard Murdoch, Acting Constable, Greetings.' "

Not having read Secorim's name among the addressees, Tammaron glanced at Hubert, who gestured with a hand for him to continue.

" 'I regret to report the death this afternoon of our sovereign lord, King Rhys Michael Alister Haldane, who succumbed to his injuries at about the hour of three after an illness bravely fought. His Highness had received the final sacraments and died peacefully, his weakened body being unable to survive necessary surgery.

" 'His Highness' body will be brought back to Rhemuth by stages, departing Saint Ostrythe's Convent tomorrow morning. We estimate arrival in Rhemuth on or about the third of July. Owing to the season, I recommend a short lying-in-state, with funeral to follow on the fifth of July.

" 'Given at Saint Ostrythe's Convent, this twenty-eighth day of June, in the Year of Our Lord Nine Hundred Twenty-Eight, under our hands and seals: Manfred, Vice-Marshal and Regent; Rhun, Earl Marshal and Regent.' "

Tammaron looked up when he had finished reading, glancing at Hubert and then back at Rondel.

"I had hoped for more detail," he said a little pettishly. "Sir Rondel, would you be so good as to elucidate?"

Rondel lowered his eyes. "I have been told to be brutally frank, my lords. You are aware of the alleged codicil to the king's will?"

As Tammaron and Richard nodded, Hubert said to Secorim, "The king claims to have written a codicil to his will while in Eastmarch, appointing the Duke of Claibourne and the Earl of Marley as regents in the event of his death. Several copies, duly signed and witnessed, are said to exist. Sir Rondel, am I to take it from your comment that you do not believe there ever was a codicil?"

Rondel met Hubert's gaze coolly, not flinching.

"I do not, your Grace. What is more, my Lord Manfred does not believe it exists."

"But Rhun believes it exists," Tammaron said.

"That's as may be." Rondel looked decidedly uncomfortable. "My lord, I am bound to tell you this, because my Lord Rhun will tell you anyway, when he and Lord Manfred reach Rhemuth. There was a—difference of opinion in the choice of treatment for the king's injury. Before even leaving Lochalyn

Castle, he developed a heavy fever. Master Stevanus, the battle surgeon attending the king, had allowed the use of a Deryni drug to reduce it, given by the chatelaine of Lochalyn, but the infirmarian at Saint Cassian's withdrew the Deryni drug and recommended cautery and bleeding to release the evil humours, both of which the king refused. That was when he informed Lord Rhun of the existence of the so-called codicil."

"Are you suggesting that the king invented this story to avoid receiving unpleasant but necessary treatment?" Hubert asked.

Rondel inclined his head. "So your brother believed, your Grace. He was also furious that the king would dare to use the threat of a codicil to defy himself and Lord Rhun. When the king's condition continued to deteriorate, Lord Manfred decided to allow the bloodletting recommended by Brother Polidorus. The official story—which will be borne out by the condition of the body—is that the king's hand had to be amputated, and he did not survive this surgery."

"And what is the *true* story?" Tammaron whispered, suddenly gone white.

Rondel swallowed and looked very uneasy. "If you later confront me on this, my lord, I will deny I ever said it. The king's fever had worsened to the point that convulsions halted our journey. Brother Polidorus again recommended bleeding to release the ill humours, and this time Lord Manfred allowed it."

"And did the king agree to this kind of treatment?" Hubert asked sharply.

"It was for his own good—"

"*Did he agree?*" Hubert repeated. "More specifically, was force employed?"

Rondel flicked his gaze to his hands, clasped rigid on the table before him.

"It was only really necessary the first time," he whispered. "The *Custodes* men held him."

"I see." Hubert studied the knight without blinking, glanced casually at the ashen-faced Secorim, then returned his gaze to Rondel.

"Father Secorim is a priest of the *Ordo Custodum Fidei*, Sir Rondel. Are you aware of a *Custodes* discipline called minution?"

Rondel swallowed. "I am, your Grace."

"Then you are also aware that it is a very specialized form

of bloodletting, with both physical and spiritual benefits. Occasionally, in very special cases, a form of minution is administered in lieu of the coup de grâce. Isn't that right, Richard? Please tell Sir Rondel how your father received the coup."

"Lord Rhun and a *Custodes* surgeon opened his veins," Richard whispered, his eyes wide and frightened.

"Rondel, is that what happened to the king?" Hubert asked.

"It wasn't the coup," Rondel whispered. "They meant to release the ill humours causing the fever."

"And how many times was the king bled?" Hubert persisted. "Do you know?"

"I was only present the first time, your Grace."

"How many times?"

"F-four, I think."

"And over what period of time?" Hubert said more gently.

"Less than a day."

"I see. And after he eventually succumbed to this entirely benevolent treatment, his hand was cut off to support a more acceptable medical explanation."

"He was already very weak!" Rondel blurted. "Even if he hadn't been bled, he might not have survived the surgery. It little matters now."

"It matters if the story of the codicil is true!" Hubert snapped. "And my dear, impulsive brother dared to wager that it is not! Dear God, Manfred, you always were pigheaded!"

"Your Grace, the king's defiance could not be tolerated!" Rondel said. "What matters it if a fatal blood loss came *before* the amputation of his hand rather than because of it? 'Twill be a new regency now."

"Pray God it will not be far newer than any of us bargained for," Tammaron muttered. "Why did Rhun do nothing to stop this? He surely realized what Manfred really intended. From his earlier letter, I'd have sworn he was convinced the codicil was real."

Rondel drew a deep breath and let it out. "The—ah—two gentlemen quarreled on this point, my lord. After the king's collapse, the *Custodes* physician again pressed for bleeding as the best course of treatment, and Lord Manfred finally agreed. Lord Rhun was—under the influence of *merasha* when the order was given to proceed. I believe he later conceded that Manfred had acted correctly."

"For all our sakes, I hope he did," Hubert said, folding his hands before him to tap his thumbs against rosebud lips. "In this case, however, I would have been inclined to let nature take its course. But it's done now. How many know the particulars in this matter?"

Rondel's gaze flicked nervously to the table. "Other than those in this room—Lords Manfred and Rhun, Sir Cathan, Sir Fulk. The rest were *Custodes* men, lay and vowed, including Brother Polidorus, the physician who carried out the treatment, and the battle surgeon Stevanus, who refused to have any part of it. Those considered to be risks have been dealt with."

"Where is my son?" Tammaron said evenly.

"Oh, safe, my lord, never fear," Rondel assured him. "He was sent next morning to Cassan, under heavy guard. Lord Manfred trusts you'll put in a word to make certain he holds his tongue. The battle surgeon Stevanus and those *Custodes* men deemed less than trustworthy in this regard were to be sent on to the *Custodes* abbey at Ramos, whence I believe it's intended they shall not depart. Out of deference to your Grace's regard for Lord Cathan and his calming influence on the queen, he travels well sedated with the king's funeral cortege, having himself been weakened by bleeding, to make it clear what must be his fate if he does not cooperate. I trust these arrangements meet with your satisfaction, your Grace? My lords?"

Hubert nodded slowly, already adjusting to the new parameters his brother had placed on the situation by his rash action.

"Yes, they do," he murmured. "If, indeed, the codicil does not exist, Manfred has done what probably ought to have been done some time ago. The story will hold, I think." He glanced at Secorim, who was the newest member of their conspiracy. "Are you able to deal with this, Secorim? If not, just say the word, and I shall post you off to some remote abbey where you can live out your life in peace, so long as you keep *your* peace."

It was a lie, of course, for he would have Secorim killed here and now if he showed any sign of wavering; but though obviously shaken by what he had just heard, the *Custodes* archbishop-designate did not flicker an eyelash as he gravely nodded.

"I have given you my vow of obedience, your Grace," he murmured. "I am greatly saddened to hear of the king's unfortunate demise. Clearly, he had the best of care."

Hubert allowed himself a faint, sly smile. "I think my new Archbishop of Rhemuth and I shall get on very well," he said.

"But enough of this. We now are regents for a very young new king. It's late to roust him from his bed, but the mother should be told, I think—gently, lest her grief dislodge the babe she carries—and with a physician there to give her a soothing potion. After a night's sleep, she should be past the worst of the shock and reasonably able to accompany us to the boy's chamber in the morning. Meanwhile, I shall post extra guards outside his apartments, but the news of the king's death is to be suppressed until tomorrow. Are we all agreed?"

At their nods, he rose.

"Very well, then. Tammaron, please fetch Master James and have him prepare a sleeping draught for her Highness."

A short while later, as Rhysel brushed out the queen's hair in preparation for retiring, Archbishop Hubert came with one of the Court physicians to inform the queen that her husband was dead. Rhysel guessed their mission as they came into the room and held tightly to the queen's hand as she rose to receive them—and knew that the queen guessed, even before Hubert opened his mouth. Michaela blanched and sat back down again, covering her face with the hand Rhysel was not holding, and Rhysel damped the pain as the inexorable words conveyed their dread message.

"It is not believed that he suffered greatly, my lady," Hubert said quietly. "He simply was not strong enough to survive the surgery. I am very sorry. I've had Master James prepare you a sleeping draught. I strongly recommend that you drink it—for the sake of the child you carry, if not for your own. In the morning, if you wish, I—shall allow you to inform young Owain. He is king now, of course, and there are proclamations to be drafted, ceremonies to be performed, but I believe there is no need to wake him at this hour."

As Michaela managed a jerky nod, saying nothing, Rhysel took the cup from the court physician and set it in the queen's hand, urging her to drink. The queen obeyed without demur and numbly allowed herself to be put to bed. A quarter hour later she had escaped into sleep. The tears would come with the morning.

CHAPTER THIRTY-ONE

His sons come to honour, and he knoweth it not.
—Job 14:21

Michaela woke to the slow, leaden tolling of church bells and a dull ache of heart that knew for whom they tolled. Rhysel lay beside her, fully clothed, faithful guardian through the night. The younger woman sat up as Michaela stirred, gently setting a hand on her wrist.

"Mika, you must be strong," she whispered.

Michaela drew a deep breath and let it out in a heavy sigh, grateful for the human intimacy of the other's mere presence at such a time.

"I feel numb inside," she replied. "I know he's gone, but I can hardly feel it. Is that your doing?"

Gravely Rhysel nodded.

"You have a child on the way and another who will need you today, especially. I have never lost a husband, but I was seven when my father died." She gave a wan smile. "When I learned of it, I had only my grief to contend with, devastating though that was. I did not become a king as well."

Michaela could feel tears welling in her eyes, but she blinked them back and sniffled resolutely, wiping her free hand across her eyes as she sat up.

"I'll be all right," she whispered. "You'd better help me dress. I want to be ready when they let me go to Owain. You don't think he'll have guessed, from the bells?"

Rhysel shook her head. "He's very young, and there have been ample bells these past few days."

347

Half an hour later, dressed in deepest mourning, Michaela sat waiting among her black-clad ladies in the shade of the solar, eyes downcast, turning Rhysem's marriage ring on her finger. She would have preferred to go to her son informally, with her hair tumbled loose and free the way he liked it, but protocol required otherwise of queens, especially on such a day. Under Lady Estellan's tight-lipped direction, Rhysel had been obliged to scrape back the queen's wheaten mane in a tight knot before covering it with the mandatory widow's coif and veil. Michaela made no protest to this, but stubbornly declined the prescribed jeweled diadem in favor of a light circlet of gold and silver roses—because that was Owain's favorite.

The waiting now began. While Michaela's women sat murmuring prayers all around her, Rhysel settled quietly at her feet, her head resting lightly against the queen's knee as she continued to urge calm and serenity—for she would not be allowed to accompany the queen to the new little king's apartments.

A knock at an outer door brought Rhysel to her feet and set Lady Estellan hurrying to answer it. Shortly she returned with the queen's two visitors of the night before, plus Tammaron, Richard Murdoch, and Father Secorim. As the archbishop and Secorim bowed, somber and correct in their ecclesiastical robes, the physician hung back to study his royal patient. Tammaron and Richard came to kneel and kiss the queen's hand.

"Your Highness, our condolences this morning come on behalf of the Regency Council," Hubert said. "Did your Highness spend a quiet night?"

"I am well enough, your Grace," she said, not meeting his gaze. "May I see my son now?"

"If Master James feels you are strong enough."

Michaela sighed as the physician silently came to clasp her wrist. After a moment he released her and lightly felt her forehead.

"Her pulse is steady, your Grace. She seems composed enough, but this will be a difficult day. Your Highness, may I recommend something to ease you? Nothing as strong as last night. I know you would have your wits about you when you speak to the King's Grace."

"I thank you, no, Master James," she said, rising purposefully. "Your Grace, I would go now to my son."

Only Tammaron's wife, Lady Nieve, was allowed to accompany her as the regents escorted her to the nursery apartments occupied by the young prince. All of them remained in an adjoining anteroom as the queen went on into the prince's solar, where he had been lining up toy knights on the floor of a window embrasure. His little tunic of Haldane crimson was a bright splash of color against the whitewashed stone. A sad-eyed governess had been supervising his play, but withdrew immediately at Michaela's appearance, only pausing to bob her a sympathetic curtsey.

"Good morning, my love," Michaela called, smiling and holding her arms out to Owain as he scrambled to his feet with a crow of delight and ran to embrace her around the knees.

"Mummy! Come and see my knights! There's one that looks like Papa. He's going to fight the bad prince who wants to take away his crown."

Fighting back her grief, smiling despite it as she bent to kiss him, she let him lead her back to the window embrasure, where she sank down on the step to let him point out his favorites. There was, indeed, a knight on a white horse that looked something like Rhysem, with a tiny gold lion painted on his crimson shield and a little crown on his helm. Cathan had made them for Owain the previous winter, and they were rather larger than the usual sort, standing halfway to the boy's knees. Another knight on a grey carried a miniature Haldane banner.

"That's Uncle Cathan," Owain said, pointing him out, "and there's the bad prince. He keeps falling down."

She looked beyond the royal forces at a motley array of smaller figures painted in the tawny and black and white of Torenth, one of which had fallen over. Stiffening her resolve, Michaela held out her arms to Owain again.

"Darling, come and sit on Mummy's lap, would you? I have something to tell you."

Owain looked at her curiously and picked up the figures of his father and Cathan before coming to climb down a step and then ease onto her lap, settling a little uneasily as he twisted around to watch her. She hugged him close for a moment, pressing a kiss to the tousle of black, sweet-smelling hair, then reached around him to gently stroke a fingertip across the crown on the figure of the king.

"Darling, something very sad has happened to your papa. He hurt his hand, and it made him very sick. His doctors tried very hard to make him better, but he—"

"Papa's sick?" Owain whispered, his little face going still and anxious.

Michaela shook her head, blinking back tears. "Not anymore, my darling," she whispered. "Your papa is with the angels now. His hurt hand made him very, very, ill, so—the angels have taken him to be with God."

"With—God?" the boy repeated, bewildered.

"Your papa has died, my love. He's gone to Heaven, to be with God."

"No!" Owain said flatly. "My papa can't be dead."

"Oh, darling, I wish it weren't true—you know I do. But it is. It's very, very sad, but—"

"Who hurted my papa's hand?" Owain demanded, anger flashing in the grey Haldane eyes as tears began to well. "Did the bad prince hurt my papa?"

"I—don't know exactly, darling," she heard herself saying. "We'll know more when . . ."

She let her voice trail away as he collapsed weeping in her arms, sobbing his little heart out, the toy knights still clutched in both hands. She wept with him, letting fall the tears she had denied herself the night before but aware, in some deep recess of dispassionate logic, that her grief was tempered still by the discipline Rhysel had imposed, lest the shock do harm to the other life she carried. She felt it as a profound sadness that might well persist until her dying day, but not a life-shattering sorrow that might keep her from her duty.

As Owain gradually subsided to hiccoughs and moist sniffling, huddled down in her lap, Michaela also mastered her tears. Pulling a handkerchief from her sleeve, she wiped her eyes and composed herself, then produced another one to blot away her son's tears.

"Can you blow for me?" she whispered.

He complied, but he would not let go of the toy knights in his hands. Still sniffling, he squirmed around to turn tear-reddened eyes to hers.

"Mummy, I have a question," he said tremulously.

"Yes, darling?"

"Did the bad prince take away my papa's crown?"

She smiled gently and brushed the hair off his forehead as she shook her head. "No, my darling, he did not. Your papa left his crown for you. And no one shall ever, *ever* take it away from you—I promise."

Owain looked doubtful. "But I'm only little, Mummy. What if the bad prince comes?"

"The bad prince is dead, my love," she whispered, wishing the other "bad prince" were dead as well. "He can't come and take your crown. And you shall grow up to be a very brave and wise and powerful king, the way your papa wanted."

"I'll be king like Papa?"

"You will, my darling. And until you're big like Papa, there will be wise men to help you learn how to be a king."

Owain sighed. "More lessons."

"I'm afraid so," Michaela said with an amused chuckle. "For many, many years. But for now, I think you should have your first lesson today in being a proper king. The archbishop and some of the other great lords are waiting outside to see you. Now that you're king, there are some things they have to do and some words they have to say. Do you think you could be a very brave boy for me and make Papa proud in Heaven?"

"What I have to do?" he asked suspiciously.

"Just be very polite and answer when you're spoken to. There will be quite a lot of bowing, and after they've said some words, they'll want to come and kiss your hand, the way you've seen them do for me and for Papa. That's their way of showing you that they know you're the king now. Would that be all right?"

He nodded thoughtfully. "Can I take my knights?"

"Well—how about just the one of Papa? And you must hold him like this, with your left hand, so they can kiss the other one. We'll let Uncle Cathan stay here to see that the other ones behave—all right?"

"All right."

"Now, hold out your hand the way you've seen Papa do, so that I can rest my hand on yours while we go into the next room. That's right." She rose and laid her left hand on his right. "Now, you are the king, and I am your lady, and we must be very dignified as we go to meet your great lords."

She could tell that Hubert was pleased, when it was over. Little Owain escorted her into the next room with four-year-old dignity, accepting their bows as his due, and waited for another chair to be brought for his mother before he would sit on the one they had provided for him. After that, while Earl Tammaron read out the proclamation of accession, Owain sat quietly, tightly hugging his toy knight, then gravely allowed each of them to kiss his hand. He came close to tears when

Hubert briefly slipped his father's Ring of Fire on his left hand, bewildered and a bit distressed because it was far too big, but he brightened when Lady Nieve produced a sturdy gold chain from which to suspend it around his neck.

His exemplary behavior earned his mother the privilege of taking him back to her own apartments for the rest of the day. Secorim was dubious at first, being but recently apprised of the nature of the late king's tense relationship with his great lords, but Tammaron argued as the father of four sons that a child's place at a time like this was with his mother, king or no king. Even the usually hard-hearted Richard, whose son was a year older than Owain, had to agree that the young king ought not to be kept from his mother, at least until after the two very emotion-laden events still to come—the return of the late king's body to Rhemuth, with its reception on the cathedral steps, and the state funeral to follow. Hubert concurred.

Thanking God for this small mercy, Michaela let them escort her and Owain back to the royal apartments, herself bringing the Uncle Cathan knight so that Owain could carry the Papa knight and still cling tightly to her hand. As soon as she and Owain had reached the sanctuary of her solar, she divested herself of coronet and veils and bade Rhysel loose her hair, letting it tumble around her shoulders the way Owain liked it as she bent to give him another hug.

As they retreated to the bedchamber beyond, she found that Lady Estellan and the other ladies had set out a light lunch—much appreciated, for Michaela had not had the stomach to eat anything earlier. She still could not bring herself to eat very much, but young Owain tucked in with surprisingly good appetite, making sure that Papa, Uncle Cathan, and their horses all had portions of bread and cheese set before them. After he had eaten his fill, Rhysel helped his mother pull off the crimson tunic and shoes and bed down the little king for an afternoon nap. When the other ladies had gone out, all solicitude and sympathetic tongue-cluckings for the brave little prince, Rhysel bade the queen lie down, too.

"You need the rest as much as he does," she whispered, as she helped the queen remove her outer robe and lie down in her shift. "And don't worry about telling me anything; I'll Read it while you sleep and then see how the king fares as well, underneath his show of bravery."

The respite into sleep was welcome and left several fewer hours of the afternoon to be endured, when she awoke.

Owain's governess and a page had brought the rest of his beloved knights and a very small black tunic while they napped, and Michaela sat silently watching him until suppertime, as he took the knights out of their wicker basket and improvised an ambush for the bad prince from behind a hillock made of her shoes. Both his concentration and the black tunic were all too sober for so young a child, but she knew they were but the least of things he would have to bear all too young.

A bath was brought after supper, and Michaela gladly bent to the task of bathing him herself—something she had not been allowed to do for some time. Afterward, when he was asleep, tucked clean and sweet-smelling into the bed she lately had shared with his father, she knelt beside him and stroked the raven hair and prayed for his life. There was another child beneath her heart, but this one was the one who would have to bear up under whatever the regents tried in the days and weeks and years to come. Far too soon, he would be asked to follow in his father's footsteps and take up at least the promise of his Haldane heritage.

And tomorrow, he must watch his father's body brought back to Rhemuth in a coffin. Hubert had come after supper to tell her that the cortege would arrive sometime after noon. The news set a further blight on what remained of the evening, and she was glad to retire early and let Rhysel take her deep into undreaming sleep.

An update the next morning, after breakfast, indicated that the procession probably would not reach the cathedral much before three. Already dressed in her widow's weeds but with hair still flowing loose for Owain's sake, Michaela spent the morning gazing out the window at the gardens below, while Owain played at her feet with his knights, the Ring of Fire and its golden chain a bright contrast against his funereal black. After lunch, she let Rhysel do up her hair and donned her widow's veil and the State Crown, with its crosses and leaves intertwined.

Tammaron and Richard came to fetch them at two—an easy enough escort as far as the great hall, for Owain knew both of them. But as the royal party emerged on the great hall steps, great lords and bereaved queen and wide-eyed boy clutching a toy knight under one arm, a *Custodes* guard of honor came to attention with such clashing of weapons and stamping of feet that young Owain faltered, burying his face in his mother's skirts.

"There, now, my darling," Michaela whispered, bending down to comfort him as Earl Tammaron indicated they should proceed to the canopied sedan-chair waiting at the bottom of the steps. "Those men are doing you honor. Many men will do you honor today. Do you remember how the great lords kissed your hand yesterday?"

He nodded tremulously.

"Well, soldiers show their respect by clashing their weapons like that, because that is how they serve you—with their strength of arms. Now, hold your head up and take Mummy's hand the way you did yesterday. Why, I do believe we're meant to ride in one of the archbishop's rather splendid sedan-chairs. Have you ever wondered what it would be like to travel in one of those? I know I have."

Thus reassured, he did as she bade, gravely taking her down the steps and handing her into the sedan-chair with the aplomb of a courtier many times his age. He was rather less dignified as Tammaron lifted him up beside her, once she had settled her skirts and made space for him.

"It's high," he whispered, as he settled the Papa knight more securely under his arm and held on with his other hand.

"A little," she conceded. "But think how well you'll be able to see."

The ride down to the cathedral started out bumpy, but it gradually settled to a gentle side-to-side motion as the horses fell into step. As constable of the castle, Richard rode before them with a mounted guard of his own men in Carthane livery. Tammaron rode on Owain's side, with Sir Rondel on Michaela's; *Custodes* knights followed behind. All along the way, silent crowds had gathered to watch their passage, the men doffing their hats as the little king passed by, many of the women weeping to see him come so young to his throne.

When they alighted at the cathedral steps, Archbishop Hubert was there to receive them, along with Bishop Alfred, who should have been the next Archbishop of Rhemuth, and Abbot Secorim, who would actually have the position. A bevy of additional clergy and choristers also waited with torches and incense and a huge, jeweled processional cross, but Hubert came and led the two of them inside, out of the sun, to wait in the cool of the baptistery near the rear doors until the expected cortege should actually come into sight. The cathedral was well filled with richly dressed men and women, and Owain peered out at them with interest through the brass-latticed baptistery gate when Hubert had gone back out.

"Mummy, have all these people come to honor Papa?" he whispered.

"I do believe they have," she replied. *And also to see this child who will be their new king,* she thought to herself, pitying him anew—and herself. "Why don't you sit here very quietly beside me while we wait for the archbishop to come back? Shall we say a prayer for Papa?"

They had finished several prayers, and Owain had taken to prancing his knight along the edge of the fount, when Lord Tammaron came to fetch them.

"It's time, your Highness," he murmured, as the *Custodes* guards outside the gate clashed to attention. "Sire, will you come this way, please?"

A little stiffly, Owain lifted his chin and held out his arm for his mother's hand, gravely conveying her after Tammaron, who had to bite at his lip to keep from showing his emotion. The choristers had begun intoning a Latin hymn, and as Michaela and her son emerged into the sunlight, she could see the procession approaching the cathedral steps. Her brother Cathan was among the lead riders, Rhun and Manfred to either side; and beyond them, escorted by *Custodes* knights and preceded by a processional cross and Rhysem's banner, was the horse-borne bier that bore his black-draped coffin. She could see the sunlight glinting off the sword and crown fastened atop it, and tears blurred her vision as she held tightly to her son's hand and watched it draw near.

The lead riders were dismounting, Rhun and Manfred coming up the steps with Cathan and a pair of *Custodes* knights behind them. Her brother looked dreadful, pale and much thinner than when he had left, but at least he had come back.

She shifted her gaze to Rhun and Manfred, armored and full of their own self-importance as they came to kneel at Owain's feet and kiss his small hand, rising then to give Tammaron quiet greeting before withdrawing to either side for Cathan to make his salute. Cathan managed a reassuring smile for his young nephew as he bent over the boy's hand, but as he rose to embrace his sister lightly and kiss her on both cheeks, she saw that his eyes were dilated even in the bright sunlight.

Drugged, then; that explained his appearance and the lethargy that blurred his grace as he moved around to her other side, one hand lightly keeping balance against Owain's shoulder. She knew the signs well, from those years ago with Rhysem. She slipped her arm into his for reassurance and comfort, but he did not admit her to his thoughts, only gazing numbly at Rhysem's coffin as the horse-litter came to a halt and strong men began lifting it down.

Tears welling in her eyes, Michaela watched the priests begin to cense her husband's coffin and sprinkle it with holy water and heard the words that Hubert sang as he invoked the saints of God and the angels of the Lord to come to Rhysem's aid, presenting his soul before the sight of the Most High.

"Suscipiat te Christus, qui vocavit te . . ." Hubert sang. May you be received by Christ, Who has called you: and may the angels bring you into the bosom of Abraham.

They did, you know, came Cathan's thought in her mind, as he shifted her hand into his hand for comfort. *The angels came—archangels, actually—the same as came the night he received his power. Dom Queron called them. I know he's at peace, Mika.*

"Requiem aeternam dona ei, Domine," Hubert sang, *"et lux perpetua luceat ei."*

"Offerentes eam in conspectu Altissimi . . ."

Both stunned and cheered by his message, her vision blurred by tears, Michaela somehow managed to get through the rest of the ceremony, numbly following her husband's coffin into the hushed cathedral, Owain clinging to her left hand and Cathan supporting her on her right. The great lords served as his pallbearers: Tammaron, Manfred, Rhun, Richard—and Lord Ainslie and Sir Rondel to round out the numbers, since Hubert and Secorim were otherwise occupied. Clouds of incense followed them down an aisle that seemed far, far longer than it had the many other times Michaela had walked it. The most joyful had been to repeat her marriage vows to the man whose coffin she now followed; the most difficult, before now, to follow him to his coronation, knowing that he must make vows before God that they would never allow him to keep.

The choir offered up a hymn promising resurrection and salvation as the great lords gently set the coffin on the catafalque prepared for it and then moved the funeral candles into place: thick, bright-burning yellow brands set in six tall silver candlesticks, three on a side. Hubert offered more prayers as the pallbearers came to kneel behind the queen and the little king, and he sprinkled and censed the coffin again, sending up more clouds of sweet-smelling smoke that made Owain sneeze. At some point, Tammaron and Rhun brought the State Crown and sceptre from the altar, Rhun laying the wand of gold-embellished ivory close beside the Haldane sword and Tammaron exchanging the state crown for the simpler circlet that had traveled with the king from Eastmarch. The latter he brought to the queen, presenting it on bended knee.

She thanked him softly as she clasped it to her breast, kneeling dutifully with Owain and Cathan at the head of the coffin while the prayers droned on and on, the pious responses murmuring from the congregation kneeling behind them. Only with Rhysem's circlet in her hands, the one she once had set in place on his helm, did she truly begin to accept that he was dead. Not the eternal part of him, of course, which Cathan assured her had been taken up to God by archangels; but she still could mourn the human part of him, that lay in that oaken box, that nevermore would take her in his arms—and that other part, so recently glimpsed, that might have made of him so truly magnificent a king.

She was weeping quietly by the time it was over at last, but it was a sadness rather than an anguish. Tammaron approached her as the procession was forming up to go out, accompanied by a concerned Master James, but she assured both that she would be fine and let Cathan escort her and her son back up the aisle with the rest of the royal household. Blessedly, the curtains had been let down on the sedan-chair, so she and Owain were screened from prying eyes for the return to the castle. The curtains also muffled the sounds from outside, the hollow clip-clop of hooves on cobblestones and the faint murmur of the crowds still lining the streets.

"Mummy," Owain whispered a little later, as they lurched along and he snuggled close in the circle of her arms, hugging the Papa knight close. "Mummy, Papa wasn't really in that box—was he?"

She bit back a smile, wondering whether he could have caught some hint of her own soul-searching, back in the cathedral.

"No, my darling. His body was in there, but it's only an empty house now. His soul, the most important part of him, has gone to God."

He pulled back to glance down at his chest, then looked back up at her. "Is this my house, Mummy?"

"Yes."

"When—when I go to sleep, does my soul come out of my house?"

She closed her eyes briefly, trying to think of imagery that a four-year-old could understand and that would not frighten him.

"Some people say it can—but you mustn't be afraid of sleeping, darling. We always come back to our bodies until it's time for God to call us home. Some people think every person has a silver cord connecting the soul to the body. It's a magical cord that can stretch to the very ends of the earth—but it always brings us back when we're ready. When people get old, the cord starts to wear out, it starts to ravel. And eventually it goes all unraveled and lets the person go back to God."

"Papa wasn't old. What happened to his silver cord?"

"Well, sometimes, when we're very sick, or very badly hurt, the cord breaks. When that happens, angels come to carry the person to God. That's what happened to Papa. You can ask Uncle Cathan. He says he saw the angels."

"He did?" Owain's eyes got very wide and round. "He saw angels take away my papa?"

"You mustn't think they did it to be mean," she said hastily. "It's the angels' job to guard us and keep us safe. But Papa's cord was already broken. His body had been very sick. That's why the angels came to take him to God."

"Oh."

Owain's momentary anger at marauding angels died away at that reassurance, and he subsided against her arm, apparently satisfied with the explanation, cradling the Papa knight close. He was asleep by the time the sedan-chair drew up before the great hall steps, and it was Cathan who drew back the curtains to gather the sleeping boy into his arms.

"Let him sleep," Cathan murmured, when Michaela would have protested that he himself was too weak for the exertion. "I can carry him. He isn't very heavy."

He was allowed this privilege, though clearly no privacy would accompany it. Manfred followed them up to the royal apartments, Tammaron trailing after. As soon as Cathan had deposited the boy in his mother's bed, Manfred crooked his finger at him from the doorway.

"May I have just a moment with my sister—please?" Cathan begged.

"That will have to wait. We're expected downstairs."

"Just a few seconds. I only want to give her a few of her husband's keepsakes."

"What keepsakes?" Manfred demanded, barging into the room with an uncomfortable-looking Tammaron following.

Trembling, for he feared he might not have another chance at this, Cathan hastily pulled a folded handkerchief from the pouch at his belt and fumbled out the Eye of Rom.

"This is part of the regalia of Gwynedd," he said, placing it in her hand. "You'll have to pierce his ear so he can wear it." *And do it, as soon as possible,* he managed to send, while he briefly had contact with her.

She nodded numb agreement as she closed it in her hand and Manfred set a heavy hand on Cathan's sleeve.

"The Council requires your presence, Sir Cathan. Don't make me ask again."

Shrinking from the thought of what they might want him for, he pressed the Haldane brooch into his sister's hand, still partially wrapped in the handkerchief.

"He also wanted you to have—my lord, this is a private piece!" he added sharply, his hand blocking when Manfred would have reached for it. "It's only his cloak clasp. She had it made for him after the birth of Prince Owain! May she not keep this one remembrance of their love?"

"Manfred, leave it be," Tammaron said wearily. "Your Highness, I apologize for Lord Manfred. His manners obviously have worn thin from his journey. Manfred, the Council has certain questions it would like to put to you, as well as to Sir Cathan. Will you both please come with me, or must I call a guard?"

"Don't *you* push me," Manfred muttered, as he turned on his heel to go. "Drummond, come along, or you haven't heard the last of this."

Head meekly dipping, Cathan let himself be herded toward the door. "If they'll let me, I'll try to come and have supper with you, Mika. God keep you, sweet sister."

"And you, dear brother," she whispered, as the door closed behind all three of them.

CHAPTER THIRTY-TWO

Then the chief captain came near, and took him, and
commanded him to be bound with two chains.

—Acts 21:33

The reckoning that awaited Cathan in the council chamber was
both more and less than he had feared. Not unexpectedly,
Richard was waiting just inside the door to demand his sword.
Cathan could feel the hostile eyes upon him from the table beyond as he slowly unbuckled the belt and wrapped it around
the scabbard before handing it over, using the time to assess
his chances, wishing his head were a little clearer, trying to
keep his hands from shaking.

Hubert was already seated in his customary place at the left
side of the table, nearest the king's empty chair, with Lior to
his right and Rhun next. After indicating that Cathan should sit
at the foot of the table, where the queen normally would sit,
Richard escorted Tammaron to the chair opposite Hubert and
sat beside him, casually laying Cathan's sword on the table before him. Abbot Secorim was directly to Cathan's right, and
Manfred huffed himself down in the empty place between Lior
and Rhun.

"Manfred, we shall speak with you privately later about certain aspects of your actions during your absence," Hubert said
without further preamble, shuffling a stack of papers in front of
him, the amethyst on his hand glinting in the sunlight. "For
now, I am far more concerned with the report that Lord Rhun
sent us some days ago, stating that the late king claimed to
have written an unauthorized codicil to his will, naming additional regents not sanctioned by this council. Father Lior be-

lieves this to be the draft of the codicil that the king showed to Rhun to substantiate his claim." He indicated the page before him. "Sir Cathan, I believe the hand is yours. Perhaps you would be so good as to shed some light on this subject."

Cathan bowed his head, aware that every word he said from here was likely to bring him that much closer to a death sentence. He supposed Lior had found the draft copy in the king's saddlebags, to which Cathan himself had not had access since the king's death.

Denying anything was pointless. The draft *was* in his hand, as were all the executed copies—as they would discover, when the Kheldour lords arrived to try to enforce the codicil. He could not and would not change the truth about his part in helping the king produce and execute it; but if the great lords became too angry with him, too soon, he was a dead man.

"The codicil exists," he said quietly. "It was executed at Lochalyn Castle, before valid witnesses. The king was unable to write out the text with his injured hand, so he dictated it to me, and I made copies, as was my duty to him—to do as he commanded."

"And what about your duty to this council?" Hubert said sharply. "I seem to recall that the terms of your appointment to the king's household were such that your first loyalty was to your superiors on this council. You swore an oath on holy relics."

"And I swore another, more binding oath to my king," Cathan said boldly. "With my hands between his sacred hands, made holy at his anointing, I swore him faith and truth before all men, saving only my allegiance to God. In obeying his command, I kept that faith. I am not sorry."

"That has been clear for some time now," Manfred said. "How many copies of the codicil were executed?"

"Enough," Cathan dared to retort.

"Don't you play cheeky with me!" Manfred said. "How many?"

"One each for those named in the codicil, one for Lady Stacia, one for the priest who witnessed it, and one for the king," Cathan said evenly, for it could make no difference now whether they knew or not—and they would torture it out of him anyway, if he did not tell.

Lior cleared his throat. "Your Grace, we found no copy among the king's effects, other than the draft."

"What happened to the king's copy, Cathan?" Tammaron asked.

Cathan looked him in the eye. He was the most decent of the men seated at this table, but he was still one of them.

"The king had it sent ahead to Rhemuth, I don't know by whom or to whom." The first part was true, the rest a blatant lie—but plausible enough that they probably would not torture him to get another answer.

"That's impossible," Rhun muttered. "You must have known. *We* would have known. Not that many of our men moved freely about the castle."

"With all due respect, my lord, it was not *your* castle," Cathan said quietly, seizing on an ironclad explanation that would not implicate him. "Having just entrusted the regency of his young son to the Duke of Claibourne and the Earl of Marley, do you not think he could have enlisted their aid to smuggle out his copy of the document?"

As Rhun and Manfred stared at him dumbfounded, Hubert snorted and pulled the draft codicil back into his stack of papers, jogging the edges self-importantly as his hard blue gaze flitted briefly among the others—resentful and agitated, but willing to let him take responsibility.

"Cathan, I have no more time for playing games with you," Hubert said. His voice had the exasperated tone of a parent finally pushed too far by a wayward child. "Your sister carries the next heir. Clearly, I cannot risk killing you until after she is safely delivered. I promise you, however, that you shall not enjoy these last months of your life."

Cathan kept his eyes averted, hands clasped tightly in his lap.

"I'm sure you are aware of the constraints that were placed on the late king in the months following the death of King Javan," Hubert went on blandly. "Well, your constraints shall be far more rigid, and the worse for knowing, beyond hope of reprieve, that the day the queen is delivered, you shall die—with merciful quickness, if the child lives.

"But if she loses the child—well, you cannot begin to imagine the pain that the human body can endure before death finally releases it. Or perhaps you can—but no, you did not witness the fate of one Declan Carmody, who betrayed our trust some years ago. You were too young. It happened the same day that Richard's father rid us of an earlier Kheldour lord—the father of the present Duke of Claibourne, if I'm not mistaken. Did Murdoch tell you of it, Richard?"

Rhysem had told Cathan of it; and obviously Murdoch had told, too, for Richard went very pale as he gave the archbishop a curt nod.

"I thought he might have done," Hubert said with a cold smile. He drew a deep breath and let it out before going on. "But, enough of these pleasant digressions. As for the immediate future, dear Cathan, your docile presence will be required at the king's funeral two days hence. You will make one more public appearance at the young king's coronation in a few months' time. Father Lior, if I entrust him to the *Custodes'* tender care, can I be assured that he will be sufficiently biddable to meet his remaining obligations?"

Lior inclined his head. "You have my word on it, your Grace, by the obedience I owe you."

"Then take him out of here," Hubert said coldly. "I don't wish to look at him any more."

As Lior summoned guards, and Cathan suffered himself to be bound and hustled from the council chamber, he thanked God for his temporary reprieve and resigned himself to at least his immediate fate—though he allowed himself a breath of hope that the Kheldour lords might arrive in time to save him from everything that Hubert had planned. He could endure the next few days, unpleasant though they would be.

And after that—after that, if the Kheldour lords were not successful, it really hardly mattered . . .

When supper time had come and gone and Cathan still had not appeared or sent word, Michaela's anxiety began to mount. Increasingly worried inquiries to the guards outside her door revealed nothing until a sympathetic captain finally informed her that Sir Cathan was indisposed and would not be able to join her that evening. Her tearful persistence eventually elicited the opinion that the queen's brother was exhausted from his journey and was expected to catch up on his sleep in the next day or two.

Rhysel fared little better in her efforts to gain information. She found excuse to go abroad several times during the early evening hours, first to fetch her belongings from her former room and then making foray to the kitchen for a cup of warm milk for Owain, the while trying to pick up some hint of what had happened behind the Council's closed doors. She learned only that the Council was still in session, supper having been sent in. No one seemed to know if Cathan was still among them.

She returned to the royal apartments with Owain's milk to find the queen just finishing his bath, pulling a clean white nightshirt over the tousled raven head. Later, when they had tucked the boy into the big state bed, his Papa and Uncle Cathan knights propped against the lion headboard to guard him while he slept, she and the queen withdrew to sit in the window embrasure. With Rhysel's promotion to the queen's household, she now slept on a pallet at the foot of her mistress' bed, but with both women in their night shifts, and fair hair caught in fat braids down their backs, they looked like sisters or two errant schoolgirls rather than queen and maid.

"What did you find out?" Michaela asked, huddling over the rushlight set between them. "Is he all right?"

Rhysel shrugged and shook her head. "I don't know. The Council was still in session. That first story we got, of him being 'indisposed,' suggests that he isn't going to be able to see you for a while."

"Maybe he *is* catching up on his sleep," Michaela said hopefully. "He did look awfully tired."

"He also said he'd try to come back for supper—if they'd let him," Rhysel replied. "But I don't think they'll dare to do anything to him at least until after the funeral," she added, at the queen's look of panic. "By then, the Kheldour lords should be here, and I hope everything will be all right."

"What if it isn't?" Michaela whispered.

"We aren't going to think about that right now," Rhysel said sternly. "In the meanwhile, the great lords think you're in far more precarious health than you are, and they're terrified you'll lose the child. You don't want to push that fear to the point that Master James comes poking around, wanting to keep you in bed or sedated, but it wouldn't hurt to keep asking about Cathan and demand to be allowed to see him and make it clear that you're pining for your brother, especially now that—the king is gone."

Michaela bowed her head, fighting back her grief—for both men—then remembered the brooch Cathan had been at such pains to get to her. Returning to her dressing table, as Rhysel leaned out to watch in some curiosity, Michaela picked up the Eye of Rom and the Haldane brooch and brought them back to the window embrasure.

"I wonder why he made such a point of giving this back to me," she said, laying the great ruby aside and taking the brooch between the fingers of both hands. "I can understand about the Eye of Rom; it's part of the Haldane regalia. And certainly, the brooch was important to the two of us, as a symbol of—"

She broke off as Rhysel laid a hand on hers.

"May I see that?"

Wordlessly Michaela gave it to her, watching as the Deryni woman closed her hands around it briefly, then laid the enameled side of it against her forehead, eyes closed. After a moment she took the brooch away and looked up, grinning a little as she fingered the red-enameled gold.

"You have a very brave man for a brother, and your Rhysem was far wiser than I ever gave him credit for. I can't Read it, because it isn't meant for me, but there's something locked into this brooch, Mika—something your Rhysem set there, just beginning to learn to use the powers we loosed in him, here in this very room. I shouldn't be at all surprised if he's left you the key to setting the Haldane potential in his son."

"In Owain?" Michaela breathed. "Rhysel, he's too young!"

"Too young to wield the power, but not too young to have it set upon him, so he can grow into it, guided by wise men who'll gladly come to teach him, if we can ever get him truly crowned. That's why Cathan brought you the Eye of Rom as well. You know it's always been more than just a physical part of the Haldane legacy. What did Cathan say when he gave it to you?"

"Why, only that I'd have to pierce Owain's ear so he could wear it—*and that I should do it, as soon as possible,*" she added, suddenly remembering that silent exhortation he had sent her, temporarily forgotten in her concern for his safety.

She picked up the Eye of Rom and looked at it, the great cabochon ruby the size of a man's thumbnail, set in gold as an earring, with a golden wire to secure it.

"Rhysel, I don't know how to do this," she whispered, her eyes going round. "Oh, not how to pierce his ear—I remember when my mother did mine. But the rest—the ritual. I can only vaguely remember what we did for Rhysem, and *I* didn't really do it; I only said and did as I was told."

Smiling, Rhysel took away the Eye of Rom and replaced it with the brooch, closing the queen's fingers around it.

"See what he's left you, Mika," she whispered. "Close your

eyes and let yourself relax. Draw a deep breath and let it out . . . and now think of Rhysem, lying in some darkened room, not very long ago, with the brooch clasped in his hand, thinking of you and of Owain . . . And when you're ready, press the brooch to your forehead, the way you saw me do . . . and open to Rhysem's message . . . an ultimate message of love and strength that can sustain you and Owain and even the other son you carry, even beyond Rhysem's mortality . . . When you're ready . . ."

Michaela could feel the lethargy stealing over her, the power of Rhysel's magic taking her deep and centered, and gradually she came to know that she could do as Rhysel asked. She could feel all her concentration focusing on the brooch in her hand, the resolve that she and Rhysem together had forged in this symbol of Haldane freedom. And as the other woman's hand fell away from hers, she was aware of her own hand slowly lifting, seemingly of its own volition, the brooch cupped in its palm; and her head nodding lower and lower until it touched the cool enamel.

Knowledge came complete and crystal-clear, of how he had wanted it done. He had simplified and refined what had been done for him, both the night she had been witness and another night, when his own father had done secret things to his own three sons. It was the nature of the Haldane power that a father might not see his son fully empowered, but it was also its nature that each holder of the power sensed, by instinct, how its potential was to be transmitted. Owain *was* young for what was asked; but Rhysem had trusted in the wisdom of the new regency he had tried to create. And if Michaela trusted in *him*, subjecting their son to what was required, and Rhysem had, indeed, judged the Kheldour lords with wisdom, the Haldane crown might yet be free.

Tears were spilling from her lashes when she at last looked up, but she also was smiling. Still lightly in trance, she offered Rhysel her hand, to share what she had learned. Rhysel, too, was crying after she had Read it and moved closer to hug the queen in comfort until they both had spent their tears.

"Should we try to do it tonight," Michaela whispered, drying her eyes on the sleeve of her shift, "or do you think we ought to wait until tomorrow night? Cathan might be able to help, if we wait."

"We maybe ought to do it while we have the chance," Rhysel replied. "The situation could get worse. For one thing, the new regents could decide that you need closer observation, what with fears about your pregnancy and the threat of the Kheldour lords coming to challenge them." She raised an eyebrow in faint amusement. "This is going to be interesting: no medication, no Healer, no priest—"

"And nobody who really knows what she's doing," Michaela said, returning a brave smile. "But Rhysem thought we could do it; he thought *I* could do it, just in case you weren't available to help me out. With both of us, how far wrong could we go?"

"Now *that*," Rhysel said with a grin, "is a question you must never ask."

It took them most of an hour to prepare, assembling and improvising materials and waiting for activity to settle down in the outer rooms of the apartments and in the corridors outside. After they heard the guards change, Rhysel slipped into the solar where Nieve and Lirin were sleeping on daybeds—the ladies on duty, should the queen need them during the night—and deepened their sleep so that only a commotion in the corridor outside would rouse them. She could do nothing about the guards, but intrusion was unlikely at this hour, given the queen's delicate condition.

She tiptoed back into the bedchamber to find Michaela sitting cross-legged in the middle of the great bed with a sewing basket on her lap, the sleeping Owain close beside her. In Rhysel's absence, she had unreeled a skein of silken thread to define a circle around the bed—Haldane crimson, almost invisible against the dark floorboards. Included in the circle was the small nightstand hard by the left-hand side of the bed, which held a towel and basin and a single rushlight. As instructed, she had left a gap in the northeast quadrant, as had been done in another circle in that room only a few weeks before.

"I'll confess before we start that this is as primitive as *I've* ever worked," Rhysel whispered, as she came through the gap in the circle, closed and loosely tied the ends of silk behind her, and climbed up onto the bed beside the queen. "My mother would have loved it—experimental ritual. My father would have been appalled. But then, Healers are often quite conservative. Look at my brother: you'd think he was thirty, not thirteen." She smiled and glanced down at the sleeping Owain.

"On the very positive side of things, if anyone walks in on us, unless they catch us at *exactly* the wrong moment, there isn't any physical evidence to get us into trouble. I'll try to keep the necessary formality to a minimum. Are you ready to begin?"

"I am."

And she was. As Rhysel smiled and held out her hands, Michaela took them and bowed her head, closing her eyes as they lowered the circle of their arms around the sleeping Owain.

"Thou shalt sprinkle me with hyssop, O Lord, and I shall be clean," Rhysel murmured, taking this simple verse as symbol of the more formal purification they dared not enact, with incense and aspergillum. "Wash me, and I shall be whiter than snow. The Lord is my Shepherd, I shall not want. He maketh me to lie down in green pastures."

"He leadeth me beside the still waters, He restoreth my soul," Michaela continued softly, whispering the words with Rhysel until they had finished the Psalm. After repeating the Lord's Prayer, she crossed herself in the protection of the Holy Trinity, also signing Owain's forehead with the sacred symbol, then watched as Rhysel slowly stood in the center of the bed and faced the east.

Her head nearly touched the canopy above them, pale yellow Forcinn silk shot with gold, nearly the color of her hair. After clasping her hands before her for a moment, lips pressed against her fingertips, Rhysel lifted her arms in a silent gesture of orison, sweeping them up and wide to either side and back to cross on her breast, after which she bowed. Then, with left hand still pressed lightly to her breast, she pointed the first two fingers of her right hand at the floor in a gesture of command, just where the silk thread lay. Michaela could almost see the ghostly, steel-bright blade of her focused will shoot out to touch and ignite the silk with an unseen fire that did not burn.

Rhysel spoke no words aloud as she began turning slowly to her right, her two fingers following the line of the silken thread, but Michaela could feel the power pouring through the focus of that hand and sensed the invisible light that followed the hand like snagged silk caught and dragged behind it, a gossamer veil that billowed wider as she turned, rising up and over the canopy of the bed in a softly shimmering dome of not-light by the time Rhysel had come full-turn to her starting point.

She clasped her hands before her again at that, bowing slightly to the east, then cocked her head to listen to the outside sounds before turning her palms upward, just at her breast, and beginning a whispered invocation.

"O Lord, Thou art holy, indeed: the fountain of all holiness. In the name of Light arising do we summon Thy holy Raphael, Heavenly Physician, Guardian of Air, to witness this rite and bring healing of minds and souls and bodies."

She brought her hands together and bowed, then turned a quarter circle to lift her palms southward.

"O Lord, Thou art holy, indeed: the fountain of all holiness. In the name of Light increasing do we summon Thy holy Michael, Protector, Wielder of the Fiery Sword, to witness this rite and protect us in our hour of need."

Again the bow, the turning, the lifting up.

"O Lord, Thou art holy, indeed: the fountain of all holiness. In the name of Light descending do we summon Thy holy Gabriel, Thy Herald of the Heavens and Lord of Water, to witness this rite and carry our supplications to Our Merciful Lady."

And finally to the north.

"O Lord, Thou art holy, indeed: the fountain of all holiness. In the name of Light returning do we summon Thy holy Uriel, Lord of the Earth and Conveyer of Souls, to witness this rite but to take only fear from this place. All this, if it be Thy will."

When she had turned back to the east, she bowed again, then spread her arms again, throwing back her head to whisper, "Now do we stand outside time, in a place not of earth. As our ancestors before us bade, we join together and are one. Amen. Selah. So be it."

"So be it," Michaela repeated, bowing her head to cross herself again.

In the silence that followed, as Rhysel turned with a soft sigh to sink to her knees opposite the queen, the sleeping Owain between them, Michaela pulled her sewing basket closer and took out a needle threaded with scarlet silk, bidding Rhysel bring the rushlight closer.

"Your father had a distinct advantage when he did this to Rhysem and his brothers," Michaela said softly, holding the needle in the flame, glancing at the sleeping Owain. "Deryni potions to cleanse the wounds, and Deryni talent to heal them."

Smiling, Rhysel handed Michaela the rushlight and leaned over to fetch the basin, which was partially filled with water.

"I can't help you on the healing, but it doesn't take Deryni talent to know that boiling things helps to clean them." She plucked the Haldane brooch and the Eye of Rom from the sewing basket and slipped them into the basin. "Put your needle in, too, but leave a bit of the thread hanging out. Now draw back a little. It *does* take Deryni talents to boil water this way."

Wide-eyed, Michaela watched as Rhysel held her hand close above the water's surface and closed her eyes. After a moment, tiny bubbles began to form along the surface of the water, deeper; then steam began to rise.

"My father taught me how to do this shortly before he died," Rhysel finally murmured, as she took her hand away and the bubbling stopped. "It's an old Healer's trick, but it doesn't take a Healer to do it; just Deryni concentration. I later learned a variation for cleaning off magical residues, but this was just for physical cleansing. We wouldn't want to cancel out whatever the king left on these. Hand me that towel, and we'll give our young man's earlobe a good wipe before you go poking your hole."

In the flat silence while they waited for the water to cool a little, Michaela listened to the sound of her own heart beating and the occasional, muffled sound of a guard stirring far outside. At length, Rhysel dipped a corner of the towel in the hot water and used it to clean Owain's ear, also bidding the queen to wipe off her hands. Then, while Rhysel held the boy's head steady, also keeping him asleep and free from pain, Michaela used her sterile needle to pierce her son's right earlobe. He did not stir, and there was very little blood.

"I have another earring of twisted gold wire in my jewel casket, that Rhysem used to wear before he became king," she whispered, as she inserted the Eye of Rom in Owain's ear. "It's lighter and will be more comfortable while the ear is healing, but he's supposed to wear this one for what we're doing now."

Rhysel nodded. "It's heavy for such a wee lad. Special occasions, until he comes of age. It's the power that's important."

"Aye. Now we'll see about *that*."

Together she and Rhysel shifted the sleeping Owain round so that his shoulders lay in her lap, head cradled against her stomach. Rhysel let him stir as Michaela began washing his left hand, though she kept loose controls with a hand on one bare foot.

"Mummy—why you washing my hand? Is it morning already?"

"Not yet, darling. There's something Papa asked us to do,

but you must be very, very quiet. It might be a little scary, but you'll be very brave, won't you?"

"For Papa?" Owain murmured, rubbing at his eyes with his free hand, which he then offered her. "Wash other hand, too?"

"All right, we'll wash both hands," Michaela murmured, glancing at Rhysel, who was only barely containing a smile. "Can you sit up a little better for me now? That's right. Let me put my arms around you and hug you. Mmmmm, I do love you!" she declared, kissing the top of his head.

He grinned and wriggled contentedly in her arms. "An' I love you, Mummy. What we do for Papa?"

"Well, Uncle Cathan brought us something that Papa very much wanted you to have. It's a very special present."

"Papa's Lion," Owain breathed, as she took it out of the basin, not touching the clasp, and shook off the excess water.

"It is, indeed. Soon after you were born, I asked a man to make this for your papa, to remind us of the crown Papa wore—the crown that you're going to wear." She set the curved body of the brooch in Owain's small right hand with the gold clasp opened at right angles, cupping her own hand around his to steady brooch and clasp, glancing at Rhysel.

"Now, here's the part that's very special. You can't see the lion right now, can you?"

"No."

"Well, something else that you can't see is a special kind of magic that Papa left you, that will help you be a proper king some day, like him." She gently sought his left hand with hers and opened the little fingers. "I can't explain how or why right now—you'll find out when you're bigger—but I promise you that Papa wanted us to do this. You might think it's a little scary, so you must be brave, but I promise I won't hurt you. Will you be brave for Papa?"

Frowning a little, he twisted his face around slightly to look at her, grey Haldane eyes searching hers.

"Brave for Papa?" he murmured.

Before he could change his mind—or she could change hers—she braced his hand against hers and set the point of the brooch's clasp lightly against his flesh—flesh of *her* flesh. Not against the palm, as his father had done the night of his empowering, but just against the tender web of skin stretched between thumb and forefinger—and thrust the sliver of gold home.

With Rhysel controlling, *he* felt no pain, though he gasped with surprise, but the passage of the gold through her own flesh as well sent a hot chill up her entire arm as the power began to flow.

That he felt, though Rhysel damped his ability to make any sound as energy began to shift within the circle, swirling and then focusing through the Haldane brooch transfixing the hands of mother and son. Most of it flowed into Owain, sending tendrils of potential power probing into the deepest recesses of his being, long after he ceased to be aware of any of it; but some of it cycled through the mother and then back into Owain.

And some of it, and then more of it, flowed into the mother and, finding Haldane flesh, flowed into the child she carried, beginning to quicken the heritage of his blood before ever his tiny body quickened, stirring the Haldane potential in him as well.

She felt it in herself as the power channeled through her and stirred her own Deryni blood to new potency—a tingling and a quickening—and as its wonder registered, she dared to raise her eyes to the glorious light all around her and Owain, to the gossamer forms of winged Others who moved within that light and lifted exquisite, transparent hands to touch their faces in benison.

Tears of gladness welled in her eyes as she held her son close, their hands joined by love as well as gold, and just as she thought her heart could contain no more wonder, she caught just a scarlet glimpse of another among those glorious creatures—surely her own Rhysem, come back to her for just this instant, his form radiant with the perfection of health restored and the beauty of eternity, his face shining beneath a golden crown as he pressed his fingertips lightly, tenderly to his lips, smiling as he offered her his kiss on outstretched hands.

And behind him was another, with quicksilver eyes and quicksilver hair, and a wise, knowing face that smiled, just as the light and the love overwhelmed her.

When Michaela awoke, perhaps an hour later, she wondered a little fuzzily whether she had dreamed it all. The rushlight still was burning on the little table beside the bed, and Owain was snuggled down beside her, his Papa knight loosely clasped under one arm and one thumb but recently slipped from his perfect rosy lips. She smiled and eased the toy from his grasp, leaning it against the headboard beside its companion to take up watch again, then absently smoothed a lock of black hair back from her son's face—and brushed the little hoop of twisted gold wire in his right earlobe.

"He'll be fine," Rhysel's voice said softly from behind her, at the same time setting a hand on her shoulder to soothe her startled response as she rolled onto her back to stare. "I changed the earring—blooded the Eye of Rom and the Ring of Fire before I put them away in your jewel chest—then I cleaned up the two of you and put everything back the way it was supposed to be. It's a good thing you didn't try this on your own."

Michaela swallowed and blinked at the Deryni woman, amazed that she could be so calm and matter-of-fact after what had happened.

"Did you—*see* anything?" she asked.

Rhysel nodded slowly. "I felt quite a lot, too. Now I know why no one's supposed to touch the subject during such a working. No harm done to any of the parties involved"—she held up a hand to stay Michaela's concern—"I was prepared. But it was—intense." She cocked her head. "I never met Cinhil or Javan, but I'd have to say that your Rhysem probably was the finest Haldane to date, when it comes to figuring out how the Haldane power is supposed to be used. If his sons are half as good, they'll be something very special."

"Did you—see Rhysem?" Michaela asked.

"Aye. And my grandfather, I think." She sighed. "I wish I'd known him. Uncle Joram says he really is a saint—or at least he seems to do a lot of things that saints do. One thing is certain: he didn't just die, all those years ago."

Michaela nodded slowly, fighting back a heavy yawn, then went ahead and indulged it.

"You'd better get some sleep," Rhysel said softly, laying her hand gently on the queen's. "I can't explain it, but I think your own power may have increased from the spillover. I do advise rest, though. The next few days are apt to be rough. Please don't fight me."

Fighting sleep was the last thing on Michaela's mind as she let her eyelids close. And the last thing she thought, as she drifted into sleep, was to wonder what Rhysem had done to her, from beyond the grave—or from the cathedral, it occurred to her, as she yawned again and then sank. Because Rhysem wasn't even buried yet . . .

CHAPTER THIRTY-THREE

I speak of the things which I have made touching the king.

—Psalms 45:1

When Rhysel reported the results of the queen's work to Joram, a short while later, his elation could scarcely be contained. Almost, she fancied she could hear him laughing aloud in the room with her, as she had not heard him laugh in years.

The new king confirmed in his potential and Michaela somehow boosted to higher ability? This is welcome news. I begin to think we may actually pull this off. I've never heard of such a secondary effect, but who really knows anything about the Haldane potential? Ansel and Queron and the others will be delighted.

After giving her an update on their progress and estimated arrival time, he offered further instructions.

Just be certain that nothing prevents the queen from making the usual appearances in the next few days, and the young king with her. We wouldn't want the regents to decide, for example, that attending the funeral would be too much strain on her and the baby. On the other hand, if she seems too strong, they may decide that they don't need Cathan any longer. You've not been able to discover a clue as to what's become of him?

The official word is that he's "indisposed." Someone tried to tell us that he was simply catching up on his sleep, but I didn't like the tone when Tammaron and Manfred took him off to the first meeting of the Regency Council. I'll try to find out more in the course of tomorrow.

Do that, he responded. *And in the meantime, if it can be managed at all, try to give Michaela an intensive course in using what she's acquired. You know the specific skills to concentrate on.*

I'll do the best I can, she agreed. *Tomorrow is the lying-in-state, but I don't expect they'll allow her to go to that, since they let her be there to receive the body this afternoon. Even if they did, they wouldn't let Owain go—and she wouldn't leave him. Nor would I wish her to. But the great lords will go—or else remain closeted in the council chamber, trying to decide what to do about Kheldour. In either case, I'll try to find out more about Cathan. It would be bitter irony if he got this far, only to perish before we can bring our plan to fruition.*

Cathan had not yet perished, though he could almost wish he had. He had guessed they might bleed him again, so was not surprised when Lior and his *Custodes* guards took him to a bleak cell in the bowels of the castle where Brother Polidorus soon appeared, armed with basin, ligature, and lancet. The guards had held him while Polidorus performed the operation, and Cathan had fought it despite the futility, sickeningly aware how his strength ebbed as the volume of his blood in the china basin grew.

Lior had stopped it short of seriously endangering him, of course, for they still needed him for a few more days at least. It was done purely to intimidate him further; their drugs would have been sufficient to keep him docile. But the medication Polidorus gave him afterward, though enough to blur his vision and render him incapable of standing unassisted, was not enough to force him into the mercy of sleep, where he could forget his plight for a few hours; and merely dozing brought nightmares. At midnight, left alone in only shirt and breeches, his bandaged arm still smarting, he lay awake by choice in his close prison cell, staring at the barrel-vaulted ceiling and praying for deliverance, one bare ankle shackled to an iron ring in the wall at the foot of the wooden bedstead.

And at midnight, the torches and candles were still burning in the council chamber, as the newly reunited Regency Council continued to consider strategies to protect what they had stolen.

"It doesn't seem likely, then, that any serious force from Eastmarch can reach here in less than two or three days," Tammaron was saying, as he rubbed wearily at his eyes.

"We're probably safe until after the funeral. By then, we'll have our troops in place and the city secure. Also, the more men they try to bring, the slower they'll be. What's the earliest that a messenger could have reached them with the news?"

"Well, it would have been a solid two days' ride to Lochalyn Castle," Manfred said. "Obviously, we made no attempt to send word north, but it's possible, I suppose, that they might have had agents among our returning forces, who could have carried the news. But our own men didn't know of the king's death until the next morning, other than the officers billeted at the convent. The sisters at the convent knew, of course, but we closed it down for the night, and no one left."

"Except that priest who heard the king's final confession," Rhun murmured. "You wouldn't have thought such an old man could disappear that quickly, without someone seeing him."

"What priest was that?" Hubert inquired, looking sharply at Lior.

"Just—an itinerant father who showed up at the convent, your Grace," Lior answered uncomfortably. "Some priest of Saint Jarlath—a Father Donatus. I'd given the king the last anointing during the night, but he'd refused confession and Holy Communion. By then, he was—not kindly disposed toward *Custodes* clergy." He blanched as he caught Hubert's simmering look of resentment, only then remembering how the king's brother, King Alroy, had similarly refused Hubert's ministrations when *he* lay dying.

"I'd been trying to locate someone not of my Order," Lior offered. "I couldn't let him die without full benefit of the Sacraments."

"A salve to your conscience, after you'd set about his death," Rhun muttered, subsiding at Manfred's sharp glance.

"The convent's own priest was away, but one of the sisters produced this Father Donatus just after noon," Lior went on cautiously. "He looked harmless enough—he was quite old— and he wasn't in *Custodes* habit. I took him to the king immediately. Apparently his Highness found him acceptable. The priest was with him when he died, and he comforted Sir Cathan afterward."

"And disappeared before he could be interrogated," Hubert said coldly, "being well aware of the circumstances of the king's death, having heard his last confession."

Secorim frowned, daring to come to Lior's defense. "With

all due respect, your Grace, the priest *is* bound by the seal of—"

"You apparently assume far more conscience in the Order of Saint Jarlath than exists in your own Order, Secorim," Hubert said coldly. "How many times have you and I—and Paulin, in his time—broken the seal when it suited our convenience? Donatus, Donatus—the name means 'a gift,' doesn't it? Lior, what did he look like?"

"Just an aging country priest, your Grace. Not a large man," he elaborated, at Hubert's sharp look. "Sparse of flesh—wiry, I would say—dark eyes, white hair, neatly tonsured."

"And wearing the robes of the Order of Saint Jarlath." Hubert shook his head, still looking annoyed. "Secorim, send to the Abbot of Saint Jarlath's and find out whether he has a priest meeting that description. I know it will take some time, but I want to know. In the meantime—" He leaned back in his chair, smiling dangerously. "I wonder what else Sir Cathan can tell us about the man."

A quarter hour later, Cathan was again seated in the chair at the end of the council table, barefooted and restrained by manacles and fetters, his prisoner status now undeniable. Again he wished they had given him the mercy of heavier medication, so he could have escaped this interrogation. Instead, he fought to keep his head up and follow the line of Hubert's questioning.

"I've told you, I never saw the man before that day," he said, which was true enough. "Surely you don't expect me to recognize every priest in every little religious order in Gwynedd. Besides, I was hardly in any condition to notice details. He was a priest that the king was willing to see. That was the only thing on my mind."

"And what did he say to you, after he took you out of the death chamber? Where did you go? Where did *he* go?"

"I don't remember exactly what he said. Words intended to comfort, I'm sure. I'm afraid I wasn't in any condition to appreciate them."

"And you went—where?" Hubert repeated.

"To—to the chapel." Cathan shook his head bleakly. "We prayed, I think. Yes, I'm sure we must have done. And then he—left. And Fulk and I went back to the king."

"Did you see him leave? Did he take a horse?"

"I don't remember seeing either," Cathan whispered, which was true. "I wanted to get back to Rhysem's body. I wanted to—attend him, to serve him one last time. But they were—cutting off his hand ..."

The memory was suddenly before him again, far too vividly, loosed and intensified by the drugs in his body. He felt the bleak horror rising in his throat as he buried his face in manacled hands and started sobbing, a still coherent and logical part of him daring to hope that his interrogators would find it difficult to cope with emotions loosed by the medication they themselves had given him.

Even drug-fuzzed, his logic turned out to be correct. When they concluded that he could tell them nothing more, they let the guards take him back to his cell.

This time, he did sleep from sheer exhaustion; but in his dreams, stirred by emotion and unfettered by his medication, he relived those terrible last hours over and over again.

He saw no one but his *Custodes* jailers the next day. He dozed uneasily through most of it. The meal they brought him at midday was drugged, but he ate it anyway, for starving himself would only make him weaker, and they would only drug him some other way if he refused to eat; the sting of a Deryni pricker would utterly betray him. His only consolation was that they would have to bring him out for the funeral the next day, for they dared not risk his sister's hysteria, if he was not at her side to help her through the emotions of the day.

Michaela, too, dozed through much of the day, though her sleep was that of deep trance, interspersed by the usual constraints imposed on a captive queen. Archbishop Hubert invited her to attend Mass that morning in the chapel royal, but she did not wish to subject Owain to the strain of another public appearance and would not leave him while she went. In any case, she could not bear the thought of receiving the Sacrament from Hubert when it was not required. Tomorrow would be more than sufficient for that.

At least Owain seemed fine when he woke, chirpy and eager for breakfast, apparently unaffected by what had happened the night before, if he even remembered any of it. Rhysel assured the queen that he would not.

"He Reads very much like a Deryni child," Rhysel told her, as she braided her hair after their leisurely breakfast, still cloistered in the queen's bedchamber. Owain had retreated to the window embrasure with the Papa knight and the Uncle Cathan knight and was setting up the others his governess had brought the day before, taking them out of their wicker basket and lining them up for royal inspection.

"If he grows into his powers in a similar way," Rhysel continued, "he won't have much access until he approaches puberty—but that's as it should be, because you wouldn't want a child wielding the kind of power he'll have until some discretion is acquired. After all, he still has to survive among humans who are basically afraid of us."

"Which means a benign regency, to protect him until he's grown," Michaela murmured. "Oh, Rhysel, do you think they'll be able to do it? Will the Kheldour lords reach here in time?"

"God willing," Rhysel whispered. "God knows they will try."

The Kheldour lords, meanwhile, were galloping southward from Valoret on blooded horses from the archbishop's stables, striking out across country rather than sticking to the better-traveled route that skirted the Eirian. The going was harder, but the distance was considerably shorter—and the only way they had a chance of reaching Rhemuth before the king's funeral on the morrow. The great lords would not be expecting them so soon, certain they could not have received the news and responded so quickly.

They would stop at Mollingford in a few hours to change horses again. They had made the three-day ride to Valoret in two, where Queron had already paved the way with Bishop Ailin MacGregor, Valoret's long-suffering auxiliary bishop.

Ailin was and long had been one of the keys to their plan. Singled out early in his career by no less a churchman than the saintly Archbishop Jaffray, to whom he had been devoted, Ailin had been hardly a year in his incumbency as Jaffray's auxiliary when the archbishop's death necessitated the election of a new successor—and Ailin had not supported the man who eventually won and held the See of Valoret. Not only had he supported the candidacy of Alister Cullen over Hubert as Primate of Gwynedd, but he dared to abstain in the election that made Hubert the ousted Alister's replacement, a few days later.

It was not an offense for which Hubert could remove him from office—and Ailin dutifully gave his new superior the vow of obedience demanded at his enthronement—but Hubert soon had made it clear that Ailin might forget about ever being promoted to a see of his own, so long as Hubert lived. Nor might he even expect escape as an itinerant bishop, for they enjoyed too much freedom. In Valoret, as a functionary in Hubert's episcopal machine, Ailin would remain closeted away where he could do no harm, under close observation by Hubert's spies—who increasingly wore the habit of the *Custodes Fidei*, whose Mother House was nearby. Resigned to his fate, Ailin continued to honor his vow to his office, for he was a conscientious man and a dutiful son of the Church, but he harboured a smouldering resentment against the man who had stymied his career out of spite and now proceeded to abuse the office of primate and archbishop to extend his secular power.

This resentment did not go unmarked, though Ailin had kept it carefully private in Valoret. The exiled Bishop Dermot—and through him, the coalition led by Joram and the Deryni Bishop Niallan—had been courting Ailin for several years, against the eventual military ouster of the great lords. Ailin had been hesitant about supporting an armed undertaking that could be construed as rebellion against the king he had sworn to uphold; but supplanting Hubert and his cronies in favor of the king's duly chosen and appointed regency appealed to Ailin. He had inspected the codicils produced by the Duke of Claibourne and the Earl of Marley, duly witnessed by the queen's brother and a priest who was *not* a member of the despicable *Custodes Fidei*, and he had smiled as he lodged one of the copies in the archives of Valoret Cathedral. And he was ready to back up his approval with horses, men, and his own person.

Now, as they pressed on toward Mollingford, pulling back to a walk after a long stretch of cantering, Bishop Ailin drew rein alongside Ansel. Like the rest of them, he wore riding leathers and a leather brigandine, his tonsure covered by a leather cap and with no other sign of his calling visible. Unlike the rest of them, he was unaccustomed to such long hours in the saddle— fit enough, for a man in his mid-fifties, but they had ridden through the night, with only brief stops to water the horses and snatch rations on the go.

"Could we stop for a few minutes?" he said breathlessly.

"Legs still bothering you?" Ansel replied.

At Ailin's pained nod, Ansel surveyed ahead and behind, catching Sighere's glance backward, and signaled a halt. They were passing through a broad meadow studded with tiny lakelets, with a clear view for miles in either direction.

"A quarter hour to rest the horses," he called, as he pulled up. "Tieg, see if anyone has a problem. Dom Queron, could you join us, please?"

As he swung down, giving his horse to one of the Kheldour men and then going to help Ailin dismount, Queron kneed his mount closer and also slid from his saddle. He was at least a decade older than Ailin, but the past week in the pursuit of the king had reaccustomed him to the rigors of long-distance riding, and he knew exactly what the bishop must be feeling.

"I thoroughly sympathize, your Grace," the Healer said easily, as Ansel helped Ailin ease down on a rotten log. "From very recent experience, I can imagine that your legs must feel like jelly. I can give you something to dull the pain, or I can do something more direct. It's your decision."

Ailin grimaced and stretched out first one leg, then the other, leaning against Ansel for support, his face grey with fatigue and discomfort:

"Well, I don't suppose I ought to take anything, as tired as I am," he said, massaging at his inner thighs, "so that leaves something more direct. I won't deny I'm a little apprehensive, but I've trusted you with my life and office and maybe my soul; I might as well trust you with my body."

Smiling, Queron knelt down in front of Ailin, glancing up at Ansel in quick instruction. "My Healer's vows are as holy as my priestly ones, to do no harm," he said gently. "Your Grace may rest easy."

So saying, he set his hands on Ailin's knees, even as Ansel took control from behind Ailin, pulling his head back to rest against his waist. Ailin's pale eyes closed, his whole body going limp against Ansel's. In Healing trance, Queron worked his magic very quickly, easing the cramped muscles in knees and thighs as best he could, then setting a fatigue-banishing spell on the human bishop. It would need renewal before they rode into Rhemuth, but the rest of the journey would be easier for it.

He left Ailin sleeping for a few minutes while he moved among the others, but everyone seemed reasonably fit. The Kheldour men had slept for a few hours in Valoret, while Graham and Sighere and their Deryni allies talked to the bishop, and the Valoret troops, some thirty of them, were still reasonably fresh. They watched him curiously as he moved among them, for most were young enough never to have known a time when Healers were regarded for their worth and not for their "tainted" blood, but Ailin had chosen his men well. He sensed no hostility or fear.

Tieg was talking to one now, his hands clasped around the fetlock of the man's mount in healing concentration and carrying on a conversation at the same time, with the young Duke Graham crouching to look on. The lad was good. Queron gave him an appreciative nod before heading back to Ailin and Ansel. Sighere had come over to look at the bishop while he slept, taking a swig from a leather flask, but he stoppered it and hung it back on his saddle as Queron approached.

"Is he going to make it?" he asked quietly.

"Oh, yes—especially now that he's let me give him a hand. I wasn't sure about that, but I didn't want to force anything. He's got to be a totally willing ally, or it won't work."

"Well, it willnae work if we dinnae get there, either," Sighere muttered, glancing over where Graham was talking to Tieg and the Valoret man. "Mebbe when we change horses at Mollingford, I'll ask ye fer a jolt o' whate'er ye gave him. Graham, let's awa!"

The order brought an immediate flurry of activity, as men and horses reunited and began falling into place. As Queron knelt by Ailin again, Ansel brought him out of sleep, himself abandoning the light trance he had entered to refocus his own energies.

"Better?" Queron asked, as Ailin's eyes fluttered open with a start.

Ansel's hands helped him straighten more upright, and the bishop rubbed tentative hands along his thighs, letting out a sigh as he looked up at Queron.

"That's miraculous," he murmured. "How can anyone say that's evil?"

Queron cocked his head and shrugged. "I'm sure *I* don't know. Something to think about, when you get back up on that horse."

A few minutes later, they were on their way again, settling into the ground-eating pace that would take them to their next stop, that much closer to Rhemuth.

And in Rhemuth, as dusk began to settle over the city, the self-proclaimed regents of Gwynedd met once more in the castle's council chamber—Hubert and Rhun and Manfred and Tammaron.

"So we simply shut the gates to Claibourne and Marley,"

Tammaron said. "We don't let them into the city. It isn't as if they won't be recognized."

"True enough," Manfred agreed, "but a great deal depends on how many men they bring. We can shut the gates, but eventually we'll have to answer them. And once word gets out of this codicil, it's going to be difficult to deny them entrance."

"Richard has a force ready to take north to intercept them," Rhun said. "Do you want them dispatched tonight?"

"How many?" Hubert said, drumming his pudgy fingers on the chair arm.

"About two hundred," Rhun said. "A joint command of Carthane lancers and *Custodes* knights. I should think that more than adequate to deal with however many Claibourne and Marley have been able to scare up. Borderers!" He sneered. "Richard will chase them right into the river."

"Manfred, do you agree?" Hubert said.

Manfred nodded. "I've briefed Richard. We can depend on him."

"Let's dispatch him, then," Hubert said, nodding. "What about the eastern approach to the city? Is it possible they could come that way?"

"Unlikely," Manfred said. "It's slightly shorter, but not a route for moving lots of men in a hurry. The roads are poor, with very rough going in some spots. For speed, I think they'll come along the river—and Richard will be ready for them. And if they should come from the east—well, no one is going to let border levies into the city. In any case, I can't imagine anything will happen tomorrow."

"Very well," Hubert said. "In that instance, I suggest we all get some sleep."

CHAPTER THIRTY-FOUR

Their bodies are buried in peace; but their name
liveth for evermore.

—Ecclesiasticus 44:14

The morning of the king's funeral, Great George was slowly
tolling in the cathedral tower below the castle as Gallard de
Breffni came with *Custodes* guards to take Cathan from his
prison cell. An hour later, bathed, shaved, and dressed in unre-
lieved black, still under guard, Cathan received a not-
unexpected visit from Manfred MacInnis, accompanied by the
Custodes monk called Brother Embert.

"I hear that it's a fine day for a funeral," Manfred said
coldly, as Gallard set heavy hands on Cathan's shoulders to
prevent him rising. The earl was carrying Cathan's sword, its
white belt wrapped around the scabbard, and Embert had a cup
in his hand. "I trust you aren't going to cause any problems for
us today. I shouldn't want the queen to be upset."

Cathan shook his head, tight-lipped, well aware what
Embert had in the cup.

"Good. I'm glad that's understood. You will now be so good
as to drink down the little potion that Brother Embert has
brought you. You know the drill."

Cathan took the cup that Embert put into his hand, but his
eyes flashed his hatred as he glanced up at Manfred, his hand
tightening around it.

"What would you do," he said softly, "if I tipped this onto
the floor?"

Manfred's face went even colder, the light eyes narrowing.
"I would make you lap it up like a dog, and then I would have

384

Brother Embert bleed you again, to compensate for what had been lost."

Raising an eyebrow, Cathan lifted the cup slightly in salute—he could feel Gallard's hands tensing—then tossed off the contents in a single draught, grimacing as he swallowed and handed the cup back to Embert.

"Bad ale but a good threat, Manfred. It's far more original than I expected. Come now, you didn't really think I'd be stupid enough to deny my sister what little comfort I can, today of all days, just to spite you? Gallard, take your hands off me. I'm hardly in any position to defy anyone. I've taken my medicine; I'll be lucky to stay on my feet today."

"You'll be lucky to stay alive, if you keep that up," Manfred muttered, thrusting Cathan's sword into his hands. "Put that on."

"Of course."

With Gallard's hands still on him he stood, unwrapping the sword belt and passing it around his waist, noting that someone had cleaned the white leather. In addition, though this hardly surprised him, a thin piece of wire had been bound around the quillons and through the rings of the scabbard, to prevent the weapon being drawn. They were taking no chances with him.

When he had finished buckling the belt, passing the tongue behind and through the loop and pulling it taut, he reached aside for the black cap they had provided, setting it squarely on his fair head as he looked back at Manfred.

"I am yours to command, my lord."

"Yes, you are," Manfred said, the pale eyes dangerous. "And still shall be, when this day is over. I suggest you remember that, before taking any action that I might find objectionable. Bring him," he added to Gallard.

They took him downstairs then, to await the arrival of his sister and the young king. The drug started to hit him on the way, the familiar fogging of his senses and faint dizziness, and he had to catch his balance on Gallard's arm as he came out of the stairwell.

By the time he reached the yard and mounted up on the white charger they had provided—for the little king would ride with his uncle on the way to and from the cathedral—he knew it would take all his concentration to keep him and Owain on the horse and not disgrace them both. It was hot in the sun, especially dressed all in black, and he let himself doze in the saddle as they waited for the royal party to come out.

The royal party, meanwhile, was making final preparations for departure. While the queen's ladies fluttered nervously in the solar like so many blackbirds, waiting for their mistress, the queen and Rhysel were nearly finished dressing Owain. The process was being overseen by both the Papa knight and the Uncle Cathan knight, whom the boy had set on his mother's dressing table beside the jewel casket.

"Just hold still," Michaela murmured, fumbling at his ear, "and then Liesel will hold a mirror so you can see."

She finished fastening the Eye of Rom in place, setting the other earring of twisted gold back into her jewel box, then gave the black hair a quick swipe with an ivory comb. She wore the Haldane brooch at the throat of her gown, her only adornment save for the State Crown and her marriage ring.

"That's fine," she said, turning him to where the black-clad Rhysel stood with the mirror. "It doesn't pull too much, does it? It's a little heavier than the other one."

He fingered at it uncertainly as he turned, his little face screwed up in concentration—and froze as he caught sight of his reflection in the mirror, his mouth gaping in wonder. After two days of wearing plain black tunics, he had paid little attention when she pulled this one over his head a little earlier, but now he smoothed an almost reverent hand over the crimson and gold of the Haldane shield embroidered full across the chest of the black velvet. The Ring of Fire hung almost to his waist on a substantial gold chain, but he ignored that to stroke the embroidered lion again.

"Oh, Mummy, it's beautiful!" he whispered.

"Yes, it is, darling. I thought you'd like it," she heard herself saying, as she took up the small black velvet cap of maintenance, with its gold coronet nestled behind the ermine of the turn-up. His rosy lips made an awed O as she set it on his head, and Michaela felt her own breath catch in a pang of memory almost too dear to be borne.

"Mummy, I almost look like Papa," he whispered, reaching up to touch the coronet. "Mummy, do you think Papa looked like this when he was a little boy?"

Most assuredly, Rhysem had never looked like this at this age, as the third son of the king, but Michaela recalled that he had looked a great deal like this at Javan's funeral, the only time she had ever seen him in mourning. She blinked back the tears and forced herself to put the image from her mind as she dropped to her knees to hug him to her.

"Oh, my darling, you look very much like Papa," she murmured against his shoulder, choking back the tears. "Your papa would be so proud . . ."

"Don't cry, Mummy," he whispered, patting her cheeks with his little hands. "You said we must be brave for Papa."

"Yes, darling, I know."

"Mummy smile, then? Mummy be brave?"

"Yes, darling, Mummy will be brave," she said, and pressed firm kisses to both his hands before getting shakily back to her feet.

Help me, Rhysel, she sent, as the younger woman steadied her. *I don't know if I can get through this.*

"Your Highness must be strong," Rhysel murmured, for the benefit of the other ladies now beginning to peer in from the solar, impatient to depart. "Let me fix your veil." And with her mind she reached out for the soothing controls, blurring the grief, instilling calm, urging courage and hope.

Michaela had recovered her composure by the time she must pass through the solar to where Tammaron was waiting to escort her and Owain. Obliged by protocol to take his arm, she had Rhysel walk before her with Owain, the other ladies going ahead and behind, fluttering sympathetically and making much of their privilege of being in the queen's entourage. At the last minute, Owain again had insisted on bringing the Papa knight, but Rhysel was carrying it and had gotten him to agree that it might ride to the cathedral in the sedan-chair with his mother, for he was to go on horseback with his Uncle Cathan.

As they came out onto the great hall steps, foot soldiers lined up along either side clashed to attention and an honor guard of twenty mounted *Custodes* knights dipped their lances in salute, already dressed in mourning in the sweeping black mantles over their black armor. This time understanding the honor they did him, Owain did not flinch, holding his little head high as he followed Tammaron and his mother to the waiting sedan-chair and watched her handed into it, checking to see that Rhysel installed the Papa knight safely at her feet. He waved good-bye to Rhysel as she followed the other ladies to the palfreys provided for them, only then allowing Tammaron to lead him down into the yard, where Cathan sat watching him on a white horse with red leather harness. Rhun and Manfred waited behind Cathan, mounted on black horses, and Gallard de Breffni was on his left.

"Uncle Cathan!" the boy cried, breaking free of Tammaron to dart between Cathan's horse and a sorrel waiting for Tammaron, catching at Cathan's off-side stirrup.

Bending carefully, for sudden movements made him dizzy, Cathan leaned down to take the boy's hand and press it to his lips.

"Good morning, my prince," he murmured, as Tammaron caught up with the boy and picked him up, boosting him to sit in the saddle in front of Cathan.

"Just mind your manners, Drummond," the earl murmured, as they helped the boy settle.

The look he gave Cathan before backing off to bow gave similar warning, but Cathan only held the boy close in his arms, gathering up the red leather reins as the groom released them, and Tammaron mounted his own horse. He was somewhat heartened to see that Owain wore the Eye of Rom and hoped that meant that Mika had followed his instructions; he thought he had caught a glimpse of the Haldane brooch at her throat as she got into the sedan-chair.

"It's good to see you, Owain," he murmured, desperately wishing his head was clearer, wondering whether help would come today. "You look very fine this morning. Your papa would be proud."

"Mummy said we must be brave for Papa," Owain whispered. "You be brave, too, Uncle Cathan?"

Cathan nodded, bending to kiss the boy's neck. "We'll all be very brave, my prince. God help us, we all must be very brave."

The royal procession rode slowly out the castle gates and through the streets of Rhemuth—no true funeral cortege, since the late king's body had been taken directly to the cathedral on arrival in the city. Still the crowds lined the streets to glimpse their new young king and his brave, widowed mother, many remarking how fine the boy looked, sitting there straight and proper with his handsome uncle, many bowing as he passed, some of them weeping.

Again Archbishop Hubert was waiting on the cathedral steps with his clergy, ready to follow the royal party inside for the Requiem Mass that would lay Rhys Michael Alister Haldane to rest with his father and brothers. When Cathan had let Owain down into Tammaron's arms, he carefully swung down himself, forced to steady himself for a moment against the earl's shoulder, for his medication was at its peak.

"You'd better pull yourself together," Tammaron whispered sharply.

The moment of dizziness had already passed, but Cathan kept his voice carefully low as he whispered back, "If I fall flat on my face, blame your blessed archbishop. It won't be because *I* wished it."

So saying, he drew himself carefully erect and took Owain's hand, leading him over to the sedan-chair where Michaela was alighting with the assistance of Manfred and Rhun—obviously with little enthusiasm. But when Owain made to retrieve the Papa knight, Manfred tried to keep him from it.

"Papa—" Owain whimpered, reaching for it.

"You can't take it into the cathedral," Manfred said, lifting it away, as Owain trembled on the brink of tears. "It isn't fitting."

"For God's sake, my lord, let him have it!" Michaela begged. "It gives him comfort. He's only a baby."

"He's the king."

"He's four years old," Cathan said softly, locking his hand around Manfred's wrist.

"Drummond, you push too far," Manfred whispered, his face but a handspan from Cathan's, though his hand began to lower.

"Just give the boy his toy."

Snorting, Manfred jerked his hand away, but he did thrust the wooden knight into Owain's hands before stalking over to Rhun, muttering under his breath. Cathan saw Rhun glance at him murderously, but he put it out of mind as he bent to comfort Owain, who was hugging the Papa knight and tightly clutching his mother's hand, lower lip still trembling.

"Here now, what's this?" he murmured, chucking the boy lightly under the chin. "I promised your papa we'd all be brave. Can you hold your head up like a king while we go inside? It would make your papa very proud."

Sniffling away the last of his tears, Owain lifted his head and nodded, almost managing a smile. At that, Cathan adjusted the boy's cap and coronet, then carefully straightened to join Michaela on her other side.

"Thank you," she whispered, not daring to meet his eyes as he slipped his arm through hers—and had to steady his weight against her until he caught his balance. "Cathan, what's wrong?"

"It's nothing," he whispered. "Just a little dizzy." *I'll tell you later,* he added in her mind.

He had to wait until the procession began moving into the cathedral, to clouds of incense and the chant of monkish voices and the distraction of Hubert's ecclesiastical splendor, before he dared the concentration to answer her.

Remember what they did to Rhysem, right after Javan died? Well, they haven't forgotten how, in six years. Since Rhysem died, I've been bled twice and kept drugged almost continuously. I'm all right for now, he added, at her start of fear. *Just weak and a bit groggy. But I don't give myself very good chances if the Kheldour lords don't get here fairly quickly.*

Might they reach here today? she dared to ask.

It's possible, he replied. *I pray God they do.*

The Kheldour lords even then were approaching the city, though they had taken pains at their last stop to disguise their origins. Bishop Ailin now led the company, a scarlet cope sweeping from his shoulders and his pectoral cross hanging outside his black leather brigandine where it might be seen. A steel cap covered with purple leather also proclaimed his rank.

The episcopal knights he had brought from Valoret backed him, wearing blue and gold surcoats with the device of the See of Valoret on their chests. Tieg rode at his knee dressed as a squire, bearing the banner of Ailin's episcopal arms; Queron had resumed the brown Saint Jarlath's habit he wore at Saint Ostrythe's and rode as Ailin's chaplain. Graham and Sighere and their twenty bordermen rode after the episcopal knights in plain harness, telltale tweeds now hidden away in saddlebags and bedrolls, with Father Derfel and Ansel and his few ex-Michaelines interspersed among them. In all they were perhaps fifty strong; not a great many, but with a bishop at their head and Deryni power to back him—though magic must remain a last resort.

Ailin's authority got them into the city by the east gate.

"I'm Ailin MacGregor, Auxiliary Bishop of Valoret," he told the sergeant who challenged them at the gate. "Why is this gate closed? I've been summoned for the conclave to elect the new Archbishop of Rhemuth, and we heard en route that the king has died."

"Aye, that's true, your Grace. They're burying him right

about now," the man replied, giving smart salute and signaling for the gates to be opened. "What you maybe hadn't heard is that some kind of rebellion has broken out in Kheldour; that's where the king died. There's some talk that the Kheldour lords had a hand in his death, and that now they're heading south."

"You don't say!" Ailin gasped.

"Oh, I doubt they'll get this far. The Earl of Carthane has taken a couple of hundred crack troops north along the main road to head them off, if they do come. And even if they did, it wouldn't be for several days."

"It sounds as if we're just in time to be useful," Ailin said aside to his "chaplain." "Thank you, Sergeant. *Dominus vobiscum.*"

He lifted his hand in blessing, then kneed his horse forward through the gate as he signaled his men to follow. At his nod, his "chaplain" fell back to pass the word among the men, remaining at the rear as they penetrated deeper into the city.

The city streets were mostly deserted, approaching the cathedral from this direction, for many folk had gone to the cathedral square to catch a glimpse of their new young king. As the bishop's troops clattered over the cobblestones, nearing the square, Ansel broke off his ex-Michaelines and most of the Kheldour contingent to circle around the side while Ailin continued on to meet any official resistance in the square itself. Graham and Sighere remained with Queron and Father Derfel at the rear and kept their heads down, for Sighere's red hair was distinctive, even under a steel cap, though he had sacrificed his bushy red beard and moustache in the interests of passing unremarked.

The square before the cathedral was crowded, but mostly gathered along the side where the royal procession would leave. The great bell in the cathedral tower had begun tolling, signaling that the service inside was coming to a close, and Ailin had his men rein back to a walk as they entered the square.

The twenty *Custodes* knights who had escorted the royal party from the castle were formed up ready to return, their heads turning with interest at this unexpected arrival, several pointing at the banner Tieg bore. Men in the livery of Lord Ainslie were holding the horses of those inside. Ailin called his captain to his side and muttered something to him, keeping to a walk, then glanced obliquely at Tieg.

"Son, we're going to ride right up to that *Custodes* captain and brazen this out," he said. "Just stay by my side and don't look surprised at anything I say."

"Aye, sir," Tieg murmured, and silently sent the warning back to Queron as a *Custodes* officer broke off from his men and trotted out to meet them. He had already spotted Jesse among Ainslie's men.

"MacGregor of Valoret, Captain," Ailin said, before the man could speak. "We're here to relieve you. We met a galloper on the way in, and you're needed up the north road. You can pick up more men at *Arx Fidei*. Apparently the Kheldour lords are, indeed, headed toward Rhemuth."

"You've come from Valoret?" the man said. "But how—"

"We came by the east road, man," Ailin said. "I was summoned for the conclave to elect the new archbishop. We've been on forced march for nearly three days; you know the terrain on the central route. I can't ask these men to turn right around and ride north again. We'll take over your escort duties, and you can go ahead. I'll explain to the great lords."

The captain nodded, clearly reluctant, but not one to question the orders of his superiors.

"The command is yours, then, your Grace. You can move in right behind us. They should only be another quarter hour, at the most. I think they're just now taking the coffin down into the crypt."

Ailin saluted with his riding crop. "Thank you, Captain."

As the *Custodes* troop rode out, Ailin led the Valoret knights in right behind them, dispersing twenty of them along a long line facing the cathedral steps as soon as the *Custodes* men had disappeared. Lord Ainslie appeared in a wicket doorway as Ailin and his remaining ten knights dismounted and bade his men take the extra horses out of the way as he saw Sighere and Graham also dismounting, coming to meet them on the steps.

"Is it true?" he asked Sighere, also flicking a glance at Graham but ignoring the others.

For answer, Sighere pulled out his copy of the codicil and handed it to Ainslie, who made one quick scan and handed it back, grinning.

"Your other men are already in position, my lord. God, but it'll be good to have honest regents in this kingdom! Hubert and the royal party just went into the crypt. We've got maybe ten minutes to secure the area before they come out."

"Aye, guid, let's get started," Sighere murmured, already

moving them back inside. "Exactly who is in the royal party? By th' by, this is Bishop Ailin MacGregor. Wi'out his help, this wouldnae be possible. Obey his orders as ye would my own; he knows what he's doin'."

Nodding distracted acknowledgment, Ainslie continued on with Sighere and Graham, Queron and Father Derfel also falling in behind them as Ailin began dispersing his knights inside.

"In the royal party," Ainslie said, ticking them off on his fingers: "The queen and the young king, of course; Hubert, Rhun, Manfred, Tammaron, Abbot Secorim—who's been designated as the next Archbishop of Rhemuth, by the way. Cathan and the *Custodes* knight who guards him—they've done terrible things to him, Sighere. Oh, and four *Custodes* monks, who carried the coffin into the crypt. I don't think they'll give you much trouble."

"I dinnae think any o' them'll gie us *much* trouble," Sighere murmured, loosening his sword in its scabbard. "Let's clear th' cathedral an' get a welcoming committee ready, fer when they come oot."

In the cool and quiet of the crypt below, lit by torches and candles, the rite of interment moved toward its conclusion. As the *Custodes* monks lowered the king's coffin into the sarcophagus prepared for it, Hubert having blessed the place with holy water, Secorim began censing it, the sweet perfume of the incense smoke only slightly masking the charnel smell of the damp crypt, which eventually stretched nearly the length of the cathedral in a series of interlinked chambers.

"*Ego sum resurrectio et vita,*" Hubert intoned. I am the resurrection and the life; he who believes in me, even if he die, shall live; and whoever lives and believes in me, shall never die . . .

As Hubert continued with the Canticle of Zachariah, the monks answering him with the antiphon he had begun, Michaela let her thoughts wander—anything to keep from thinking about the slab of marble that Rhun and Manfred and Tammaron and the monks were slowly closing over the sarcophagus, sliding it into place; anything to keep from thinking about the man who lay in the coffin beneath it, whose lifeless body she had never even seen after it came home—

No. She did not want to remember him like that. Not bloodless and forever stilled, the grey eyes forever darkened, wrapped in his winding sheet and sealed in lead inside that coffin, for the long, hot journey back to Rhemuth from the place where he had died. Not with his hand cut from his body—the strong, graceful hand that should have been free to wield his kingship, the hand that often had pleasured—

She closed her eyes and made herself stop *that* line of remembering at once, briefly lifting one hand from Owain's shoulder to wipe at the tears from under her widow's veil. Owain stood directly before her, comforted within the circle of her arms, tears runneling down his face as he hugged the Papa knight to his breast. Cathan stood on her right, swaying slightly on his feet, the despicable Gallard de Breffni on his other side.

Beyond Rhysem's tomb were the tombs of three other recent Haldane kings: King Cinhil and now all three of his ill-fated sons. The carved effigies atop the tombs showed the occupants at their best, even the sickly Alroy depicted as a hale, handsome youth, cut off in the flower of his young manhood. She wondered how the artists would show Rhysem, who perhaps had been the bravest of them all . . .

"Dearest brothers and sisters," Hubert murmured, "let us faithfully and lovingly remember our brother Rhys Michael Alister, whom God has taken to Himself from the trials of this world . . ."

As all of them knelt for the final prayers, Cathan steadied his hand against the edge of Javan's sarcophagus, leaning his forehead against the cool stone.

That Rhysem, too, should have come to this, and so soon, still seemed so very unfair. Such courage should have enabled him to persevere. Would *nothing* ever break the stranglehold of the old regents? He blamed it partially on old King Cinhil, for having chosen so unwisely. After Cinhil's death, the fortunes of the Haldanes seemed to have sunk in ever-deepening spirals. He had hoped desperately that Rhysem might be the one to restore the Haldanes to their rightful prominence, after seeing Javan's fate; but even in the very best of circumstances, it would be many years before Rhysem's heir, the young Owain, would be ready to take up his father's dream.

"*Kyrie eleison . . . kyrie eleison . . . Christe eleison . . . Pater noster . . .*"

He could feel the leaden weight of his grief pressing on his chest, heightened by his physical weakness and the drugs they had given him, and a part of him tried to yield to blind, disconsolate weeping; but he used the words of the familiar prayers to force himself back to better balance.

Surely all was not yet lost. Friends were coming. Whether they would get here in time to make any difference remained to be seen; and whether Rhysem's last will could be enforced . . .

"A porti inferi."

"Erue, Domine, animam eius."

From the gate of hell—deliver his soul, O Lord. May he rest in peace . . . Amen.

"Domine, exaudi orationem meam . . ." Hubert prayed.

And Cathan echoed the prayer in his own intentions. *O Lord, hear my prayer, and let my cry come unto Thee. Avenge him, Lord. His enemies sacrificed him for their own ungodly ambitions, working their evil in Thy name. Strike them down, Lord. Give strength to those who would uphold his will and see his crown freed. Make me Thine instrument, Lord. Use my hands to right the wrongs done here. Please, Lord . . .*

"O Lord, we implore Thee to grant Thy mercy to this, Thy servant, Rhys Michael Alister, which Thou hast commanded to leave this world," Hubert prayed, in words that shortly made Cathan wonder whether the archbishop realized what he was asking for. "May he who held fast to Thy will by his intentions receive no punishment in return for his deeds, but a place in the land of light and peace, in union with the company of angels in Heaven. Through Christ our Lord. Amen."

"Amen," came the response.

"Thou great and omnipotent Judge of the living and the dead, before Whom we are all to appear after this short life, to render an account of our works. Let our hearts, we pray Thee, be deeply moved at this sight of death, and while we consign the body of Thy servant Rhys Michael Alister to the earth, let us be mindful of our own frailty and mortality, that walking always in Thy fear and in the ways of Thy Commandments, we may, after our departure from this world, experience a merciful judgment and rejoice in everlasting happiness. Amen."

"Eternal rest grant unto him, O Lord," Secorim said, taking over from Hubert.

"And let perpetual light shine upon him."

"May he rest in peace."

"Amen."

"May his soul and the souls of all the faithful departed, through the mercy of God, rest in peace."

"Amen."

The prayers completed, Hubert crossed himself and lumbered to his feet, pulling himself up against the king's tomb as the others rose. Great George continued tolling in the background. Secorim brought an unlit three-branched candelabrum from a side niche and set it on the tomb slab, and Hubert took up a taper and lit it from one of the torches, beckoning Michaela and Cathan to approach with little Owain.

"You may each light one of the candles, your Highness," he murmured, holding out the taper, "adding your prayers to ours."

Composing herself, Michaela folded her veil back over her crown, then bent to pick up Owain, settling him on her hip as she took the taper from Hubert and lit one of the end candles, then put the taper in his hand and guided him to light the center one.

"God bless Papa," she prompted softly. "Keep him safe with the angels. Amen."

"God bless Papa," Owain repeated dutifully, as she passed the taper to Cathan. "Mummy, angels all around here. They come to bring Papa back?"

The innocent words nearly made Cathan drop the taper, but Michaela only went a little paler and shook her head, not daring to acknowledge the flutter of unseen wings but silently thanking them for their presence—and praying that Hubert would not press the point of whether Owain could actually see angels.

"I don't think angels do that, darling," she whispered, under the murmur of Cathan hastily offering up a prayer of his own to cover for her, his hand shaking as he lit his candle. "Sometimes angels come to comfort us when we're very sad—and your guardian angel is always around when you need him. Maybe Papa's guardian angel came to say good-bye."

Owain frowned, but he had caught the mental warning from his mother not to pursue the subject and instead turned his eyes to the other sarcophagi in the tomb chamber as his mother started to set him down.

"We can go back upstairs now," Hubert said, gesturing toward the stair that led back up to the rear of the nave. "I don't know why the bell hasn't paused, so the years can be tolled."

"Mummy, wait," Owain said, holding back as his mother started to lead him toward the stairs. "Why Papa's place doesn't have a king on it?"

"What?"

He pointed at the other tombs. "Grandpapa Cinhil has a king on his place, an' Uncle Javan, an'—"

"I think he means an effigy," Hubert murmured indulgently, almost smiling as he glanced at the others. "Your Highness, the stonecutters must make one for your papa. They haven't had time yet."

Owain's rosy lips compressed in a pout. "My papa should have a king."

"He shall, I promise you—"

"Should have one *now*!"

"Your Highness, that isn't poss—"

"Mummy—"

"I may be able to solve this," Cathan murmured, coming over to scoop Owain into his arms. "Owain, Owain, listen to me, my brave little man. You mustn't cry. Listen to me."

He whispered in the boy's ear for several minutes, Owain's tears gradually subsiding as he listened, shortly beginning to nod his head.

"So, what do you think?" Cathan finally whispered, drawing back a little. "Would that be all right?"

Gravely Owain nodded. "Papa like that."

"All right. Shall I help you?"

At Owain's nod, Cathan carried him the few steps over to the empty tomb slab, where Owain gravely set his Papa knight in front of the candelabrum, facing the candles.

"My Papa knight is a king," he explained, as Hubert looked at him in question. "See his crown? He stay here until Papa gets a big king."

"But darling, won't you miss the Papa knight?" Michaela asked, taking one of his hands in hers and glancing at Cathan. "If you leave him here, he'll have to stay for quite a while— maybe months. If you miss him in the middle of the night, we can't just come down and get him."

"I still have the Uncle Cathan knight at home," Owain reminded her. "Uncle Cathan take care of me now."

" 'Uncle Cathan' may have other things to do," Manfred said under his breath, gesturing for Cathan to put the boy down. "Let's go, Drummond. We've been down here long enough. Gallard, take him upstairs."

Sick at heart, Cathan obeyed. He had eased his young nephew's immediate distress, but how long the regents would let him live to take further care of him remained to be seen. He gave his sister a forlorn glance as she took Owain's hand, but he turned dutifully to accompany Gallard up the stairs as the others fell in behind.

He could see the guard of honor drawn up to attention on either side of the stairwell as they ascended, though he did not remember that Hubert had assigned that many knights of his Valoret garrison. It was only as his shoulders came above the level of the top step and strong hands roughly jerked him and Gallard out of the stairwell, hands clapped over their mouths to stifle outcries, that he saw the longed-for faces among the Valoret men—and knew that the next hour would either see the House of Haldane dead or delivered.

CHAPTER THIRTY-FIVE

But if ye bite and devour one another, take heed that
ye be not consumed one of another.

—Galatians 5:15

Manfred drew back with a shout as Cathan and Gallard were snatched from right in front of him. Cursing, he shrank back from a sword thrust and started pushing back down the stairs as men in Valoret livery swarmed into the stairwell with drawn swords. Rhun had been following directly behind and spun to shoulder past Lior with a shove that nearly sent him tumbling backward, sweeping the queen and Owain back into the crypt and shouting for Tammaron.

Neither he nor Manfred could get their swords clear in the close confines of the stairwell, but the swords came out as soon as they had gained the open space of the crypt floor, whirling to confront the unexpected intruders. Tammaron was waiting to back them, sword also drawn, helping Lior hustle the queen and the young king into the hands of Hubert and Secorim, who drew them roughly behind the screen of the six unarmed *Custodes* monks.

There Hubert restrained the queen with a hand on her arm and Lior presumed to pick up and hold the frightened Owain. As knights in the surcoats of Valoret began pouring down into the crypt with drawn swords, the *Custodes* men and their hostages eased farther into the open arch of the next chamber, their three "protectors" on guard before them.

"Throw down your weapons!" shouted one of the Valoret knights, of which there were six. Emerging from the stair behind them came an armored, grey-haired man in a scarlet bishop's cope and purple cap, accompanied by Lord Ainslie and two knights in Ainslie's livery.

"MacGregor!" Hubert thundered, as he recognized his subordinate. "What the *devil* are you doing? Order those men to put away their swords immediately!"

"I can't do that, your Grace," Ailin said, as his knights fanned across the opening to the stair, interspersing themselves among the tombs. Sighere and Graham quietly joined Ainslie behind him, along with two men in priest's attire. "I am acting under the orders of lawful regents of Gwynedd."

"*I* am a lawful regent of Gwynedd," Hubert said haughtily. "Furthermore, I am your religious superior. You swore me a vow of obedience."

"I also swore to uphold the king and his laws—which includes lawfully executed decrees issued in his name." In his hand that wore the bishop's ring he held up an unfolded parchment document bearing a splotch of crimson sealing wax. "I believe that at least Lord Rhun has seen this in draft. This copy was duly signed and witnessed; I can produce the witness. Another like it has already been recorded in the cathedral archives at Valoret. It appoints Graham of Claibourne and Sighere of Marley as regents of Gwynedd. They have some questions to ask the *other* regents of Gwynedd, who were directly responsible for the death of the late king."

"That's a lie!" Manfred blustered, gesturing with his sword. "Who dares to say that?"

"I do, my lord." Queron stepped from behind Ailin, hands folded in the sleeves of his brown habit. "And the king himself said it, in his deathbed confession—after having been bled *four times* in less than a day. The operations were carried out by a *Custodes* monk called Brother Polidorus, but the king was quite clear that one Manfred MacInnis gave the order. And Rhun of Horthness acquiesced."

"I didn't!" Rhun blurted. "It was Polidorus who wanted it, and Lior—and they had me drugged when I tried to stop them. Ask anyone who was there. The king himself would tell you that, if he were here."

"It is precisely because he is *not* here that we are having this conversation, my lord!" Ailin said sharply. "These are extremely serious allegations—"

"Serious *lies!*" Lior said breathlessly, as Owain started to squirm in his arms. "Certainly, the king was bled—in accordance with accepted medical practice. His hand was festering;

he was racked with fever. When the bleeding did not relieve him, it became clear that the hand would have to come off. Unfortunately, he did not survive the shock of the surgery."

"The king had both his hands when he died," Queron said quietly. "Shall I lay *my* hand on his grave and swear it?"

"Who is that man?" Secorim demanded of Lior.

"Tell him, Father," Ailin said, before Lior could answer. "Tell him how you brought in Father Donatus to hear the king's last confession, because you and your clergy had placed yourselves in such ill repute that the king would rather risk his immortal soul by dying unshriven than receive the last sacraments from any *Custodes* priest."

"And is this priest any better?" Manfred said, pointing with his sword. "Can we trust any part of his testimony? What good is the word of a priest who breaks the seal of the confessional?"

"What good, indeed?" Ailin said softly. "Except that the king gave Father Donatus leave to reveal what he had been told, to bring his murderers to justice. Therefore, the seal has not been broken."

"That is not for you to decide!" Hubert said angrily, thrusting the queen into Secorim's grasp as he moved a few steps forward. "You have no authority here—or in any other place!" He stabbed a trembling forefinger at his subordinate.

"Ailin MacGregor, I hereby suspend you from your office and command you, on pain of excommunication, to withdraw these hostile forces from this place and submit yourself to canonical discipline. How *dare* you presume to judge these men?"

" 'Tis *I* who presume tae judge them, Archbishop," Duke Graham said mildly, setting his hands on his sword belt as he moved beside Ailin. Sighere also stepped forward on Ailin's other side, burly arms crossed on his chest. "As both regent an' duke in this kingdom, I hae the power o' high an' low justice, an' authority tae hear evidence an' render judgment. I charge you, Manfred MacInnis, Earl o' Culdi, an' you, Rhun o' Horthness, Earl o' Sheele, with high treason an' sacrilegious murder—"

"I don't recognize your authority to try me!" Manfred said contemptuously.

"I further find ye guilty o' these crimes an' declare yer lives forfeit," Graham continued. "Throw doon yer arms. Ye cannae escape. An' I wouldnae profane this holy place with yer blood—though 'twould be a fittin' end, here before the tomb o' the king whose sacred blood ye spilled."

"*Several* kings," Sighere added softly. "King Javan also died beneath the blades o' traitors."

Not a soul dared to move. Into the taut, expectant silence that settled after Sighere's words, not a sound intruded save the harsh breathing of the cornered men, Owain's muted protests as he struggled again in Lior's arms, and a single, stifled sob from Michaela. Then, to everyone's surprise, Rhun contemptuously tossed his sword to the floor, where its clangor reverberated through the stone chamber. He reached next to the dagger at his belt.

"Rhun, what are you doing?" Manfred demanded, gaping at him in astonishment, his sword slowly sinking at his side.

Even as he asked it, Rhun spun to plunge his dagger into Manfred's chest, ripping upward as he wrenched it out. Blood gushed from Manfred's mouth even as Michaela screamed and one of the Valoret knights started forward, but Rhun was already elbowing his way through the line of *Custodes* monks and grappling Owain from Lior's arms. He slashed the blade across the side of Lior's neck when the priest tried to stop him, bundling the struggling Owain under his arm and sprinting back along the vaulted chambers of the crypt. At the same time, a wild-eyed Tammaron roughly seized the queen by one arm and whirled her in front of him like a shield, laying his sword across her throat from behind.

When Cathan was snatched from the steps to the crypt, his immediate impulse to fight for his life died at once as he recognized Sir Robert Ainslie as his "captor," with other familiar faces of Lord Ainslie's levy pouring into the stairwell to back up those who had followed Bishop Ailin and his men into the crypt. And as Robert released him, though supporting him when his weakness would have made him collapse, he saw that no less a benefactor than his cousin Ansel had Gallard de Breffni in protesting custody, straddling his bent form and twisting one arm up behind him while his other hand clamped over his mouth to prevent him crying out.

"Kill him *now!*" Cathan gasped, eyes wide as he clung to Robert.

"You're sure?" Ansel said, very matter-of-factly.

"He helped hold Rhysem while they bled him," Cathan said, numbly shaking his head to force back the memory. "He's killed many others, over the years. And he would have killed me. Kill him."

Gallard had heard his death sentence and tried anew to struggle free, but the end was quick. Ansel's hands moved almost too quickly to see, twisting the man's head to one side and back with a sharp wrench and a soft, sickening crack. Then Ansel was letting the limp body sag to the floor, wiping his hands across his thighs, already turning to peer urgently down the stairwell. Cathan fought the gorge rising in his throat as another man calmly began dragging Gallard's body out of the way, and looked around gratefully as young Tieg was suddenly at his side, helping Robert ease him to a sitting position against the support of a thick stone pillar.

"I was warned you'd be in pretty bad shape," the young Healer murmured, slipping his hands to either side of Cathan's head. "Let me see you. I think I can help."

It was an order, not a request. A sudden sensation of vertigo made Cathan gasp and close his eyes, perception briefly blurred. Then someone was tipping his head back, pressing something against his lips.

"I want you to swallow this for me," Tieg's voice said softly, as a cool, minty liquid slid down his throat. "That's it. Again. I came prepared for several things they might have given you; this should clear your head and give you a jolt of energy in a minute or two. Your blood loss isn't serious, but the fatigue is. I can counter that temporarily. Just relax."

Cathan was somewhat aware of Tieg's mental touch this time, just before a wave of utter lethargy overcame him, but when he opened his eyes, he could almost imagine that the events of the past few days had never happened, at least so far as his body was concerned. He could feel his head clearing even as Robert helped him sit up, though Tieg was still monitoring with a hand clasped around one wrist.

"Cathan, come over here," Ansel called to him softly, from over nearer the stairwell. Around them and farther back in the cathedral, men in plain brigandines were helping Lord Ainslie's men clear the building. There were a few *Custodes* bodies here and there, but mostly people were more than willing to leave a place that suddenly had become an unknown battle zone. As Cathan scrambled over to join his half-brother, the great cathedral bell suddenly stopped ringing.

"Good," Ansel whispered. "Someone finally got to the bell

platform. Now, who, exactly, is down there besides Mika and the boy?"

Cathan peered down the stairwell. He could only see the backs of Graham and Sighere and Father Derfel, but he pictured the others in his mind's eye, as they had stood during the prayers beside Rhysem's grave.

"Manfred, Rhun, and Tammaron are armed," he replied. "There are six *Custodes* monks who might have weapons under their robes—knives, maybe. And Hubert and Secorim and Lior. What are they doing?"

"Talking. Arguing." Ansel motioned for one of Lord Ainslie's captains, who came to crouch beside him. "Is there another exit from the crypt?"

"Aye, m'lord. Up to the left of the high altar."

"Any other ways out of the cathedral, besides the main doors and the way I came in?"

"A side door in the south transept, leading into the cathedral close—to the Chapter House, and the archbishop's residence and such. Another door from the sacristy, that also goes—"

From the crypt below came a clang of steel against stone, then the sounds of scuffling and a chorus of exclamations and shouts.

"Rhun has the king!" an anguished shout came from the bowels of the crypt. "He's headed toward the other end! Don't let him get away!"

Cathan was already taking off down the nave, his useless sword banging against his legs until he steadied it with a hand, praying he would be in time—for Rhun, with his deeds now known and his life already forfeit, had no reason to spare any Haldane, even a four-year-old one.

In the crypt, Michaela trembled against her captor, trying only weakly to twist around to see where Rhun had taken her child, for Tammaron's fingers dug into her shoulder like iron, and the steel of his sword was pressed hard against her throat. Manfred was dead in a smear of his own blood on the floor before them, an expression of astonishment etched indelibly on his bloodless face, and two of the *Custodes* monks were trying in vain to stanch Lior's wound. The Valoret knights had started forward the instant Rhun stabbed Manfred, but Sighere had called them back sharply as soon as Tammaron seized the queen.

They stood well back now, swords lowered, glancing uneasily at Sighere for direction as he raised both hands toward Tammaron in a placating gesture. Graham had immediately yielded command to his more experienced uncle, shoving Father Derfel back up the stairs to safety, and Ailin was urgently waving back men who would have come down in Derfel's place, frantic not to do anything to trigger further violence on Tammaron's part. Queron had ducked down behind one of the tombs, now hidden from Tammaron's sight and hopefully forgotten in the confusion.

Tammaron looked around wildly at the force arrayed against him, slowly retreating with the queen toward the arch where Rhun had disappeared with the king.

"Just stay back! All of you, stay back!"

"Tammaron, are you mad?" Hubert gasped, backed up against one of the tombs, the china blue eyes wide and horrified. "She carries the next heir!"

"She carries the last Haldane king!" Tammaron replied, hysteria in his voice. "And I'll kill her and the child in her womb before I'll let myself be given over to a traitor's death."

"Tammaron, ye cannae mean tae do this," Sighere murmured, inching closer. "Killin' a pregnant woman is no in yer nature. An' what guid would it do ye, if ye did sich a deed? They'll tak the young king fra' Rhun. Ye cannae escape. It's o'er."

Nodding, wild-eyed, Tammaron inched that much closer to the arch. "Oh, it will be over, all right. I've finally figured it out. The lad is no true prince and therefore no true king—unless a MacInnis dynasty is to replace the Haldane one. Hubert, did your brother ever tell you about that?"

"Wha' d'ye mean?" Graham demanded, as Hubert's jaw gaped.

"Ask the queen," Tammaron said, leaning closer to her ear as the flat of his blade caressed her throat. "What was the threat we made to the king after his coronation, your Highness, to ensure that you and he started producing Haldane heirs?"

"Sweet *Jesu*, no," she whispered, for she knew full well to what he was referring and that it could not possibly be true.

"It was only known among the Five," Tammaron confided, "that if he did not do his duty, there were ample volunteers to deputize for him."

"No!" she sobbed.

"But the king was stubborn, and Manfred must have gotten

tired of waiting. He would have drugged the wine one night. I trust I can leave further details to your imagination?"

Deep in trance, behind the tomb where he hid, Queron Read Tammaron's truth and knew he lied.

"It isn't true!" Michaela sobbed.

"She isn't to blame," Tammaron went on. "She never knew. None of us knew until Manfred came back with the king's body. But why else do you think he let the king be killed, when he knew the codicil existed? Because he knew that the king's death, would put his own bastard on the throne! It's Owain MacInnis that Rhun's taken out of here."

It isn't, Mika, Queron's mind spoke in Michaela's. *It's Owain Haldane, and you know it. Could Manfred's bastard have assumed the Haldane potential? Tammaron's every word is a lie, the fabrication of a madman, and you're the only one who can stop him, and refute the lie.*

How?

Under cover of the mutterings and shiftings of feet that accompanied Tammaron's incredible revelation, Queron eased closer to the appalled Bishop Ailin, a part of his mind reaching out to controls he had set before, seeing through Ailin's eyes as his dialog continued with Michaela.

Kill him, Mika. You're the only one who can, before he kills you—and destroys your other son by killing his good name.

I don't know how, came her numb reply. *Queron, can't you—?*

I can't touch him, because I never have *touched him,* Queron sent back sharply. *But you're right there, with his arms around you and his sword at your throat, as close as a lover's kiss. You have the power. All you have to do is reach out with your mind . . .*

I can't—

I'm going to set a scenario through Bishop Ailin. No one will suspect there's been magic. Just follow his lead.

"Tammaron, you're a liar," Ailin said coldly. "That's the most ridiculous accusation I've ever heard. One only has to look at the boy to see that he's true Haldane."

"He's a bastard," Tammaron repeated. "He's Manfred's bastard, and he'll never sit on the throne. Rhun will see to that—and *I'll* kill the true heir before he can ever be born, if you don't give me safe conduct out of here with the queen."

"An' what then?" Sighere demanded. "D'ye think ye could

rule as regent, after this? Ye might have possession o' the bairn, but that's no all that makes a king."

"I'll be regent, or there'll be no one to be regent *for*," Tammaron muttered, shifting back another step with the queen, his blade still pressed hard against her throat. "I'll kill her—I swear I will."

"That you will not," Ailin said quietly. "God will not suffer this to happen."

"Will He not?"

"His wrath will fall upon you, Tammaron. The Haldanes are beloved of the Lord, divinely appointed."

"Pious propaganda, Bishop."

"If you harm one hair on the head of the queen, who carries one of His chosen kings, you will die."

"You can't know that!" Hysteria tinged the voice again, and the eyes had gone wide with fear.

"You will die!" Ailin repeated, stabbing an index finger at the quaking earl. "You commit sacrilege by even laying hand on the queen, especially in this place. God will strike you down, Tammaron! You will die!"

Now, Mika! Queron sent. *Reach your mind into his chest, and clasp his heart.*

Suddenly her focus came. She knew how to do it. But to take a life—

Do it, Mika—for Owain, for Rhysem, for Javan, for the child you carry. He deserves to die. It's an execution.

An execution . . .

Closing her eyes, as if she grew faint, she turned her mind to what must be done, reaching out, feeling the tendrils of thought curl around his heart.

"You will die, Tammaron!" she heard Ailin repeat.

And as she closed the fist of her thought, he did.

Cathan pounded down the nave, his sword banging against his legs, Ansel and half a dozen of his men right on his heels. Tieg's drug and his spell permitted the exertion, but Cathan knew he would pay, if he survived whatever he must do to stop Rhun. He and his pursuing band approached the transept crossing just in time to see Rhun burst from the other entrance to the crypt and dash toward the north transept, an indignantly struggling Owain under one arm and a bloody dagger in his free hand. Rhun cursed as he saw the would-be rescuers and disappeared into the transept, but when Cathan reached the spot, Rhun was nowhere to be seen.

"God damn, where did he go?" Ansel gasped, looking around wildly as his men fanned into the transept to begin searching in side chapels and behind pillars and piers, and Cathan stared mutely at the deserted transept.

From back up the nave, Robert came bounding breathlessly to a halt beside Cathan, also casting a glance around.

"He killed Manfred and wounded Lior, and Tammaron's got the queen."

"And Rhun's got the king," Cathan murmured. "But *where*?"

"Not here, m'lord," one of Ansel's men called, as Ansel himself poked under altar cloths with his sword, more and more frantic, and others also called out, "Nothing here."

But Cathan's attention had been suddenly diverted to a burly man investigating a little door standing ajar in the main support pier, at the northwest corner of the crossing. He was already trotting toward it with Robert, tugging at his sword belt, his eyes searching the arched colonnade of the triforium level high above, whose narrow access walk looked to run all around the transept and back along the length of the nave.

"Up there?" Robert asked, following his gaze, accepting the sheathed sword that Cathan thrust into his hands and surrendering his dagger—for Cathan had none of his own. The man investigating the doorway backed out at Cathan's approach, for his bulk had already prevented him from going any farther.

"He's mine," Cathan murmured, peering upward, hefting the dagger as he pressed past the fellow and set his foot on the first of the narrow treads.

The little spiral stair was very steep and very narrow, only dimly lit by occasional slits that looked down into the cathedral, invisible amid the carving that adorned the vast supporting pier. From somewhere above him, Cathan could hear the scrabble of booted feet and an occasional whimper, magnified by the sounding column of the tunnel of stone he climbed.

He was breathing hard by the time he reached the level of the triforium walk and cautiously poked his head out of the little stair to look left and right. There was no one in the long stretch of narrow colonnade that extended west along the nave, but just where the transept walk turned to cross the north transept end, he caught just a glimpse of moving black shadow. He launched himself in that direction, scrabbling half-sideways in the narrow passage, his dagger held along his thigh, straining for some further glimpse of Rhun and Owain.

He reached the northwest corner; they were waiting for him in the northeast corner, Owain sitting in one of the arched openings of the colonnade with his legs dangling over the edge, his back against Rhun's chest, Rhun's blade at his throat. He had lost his cap and coronet in the scuffle. He looked more affronted than afraid, but Cathan's heart sank at the thought of the forty- or fifty-foot drop below him, onto the unyielding marble mosaic of the floor below.

"You're very troublesome, Drummond," Rhun said, as Cathan began cautiously moving across the north end of the transept. "I should have killed you years ago, when I had the chance."

"Aye, you should've done," Cathan replied, trying to catch his breath, hoping he could keep Rhun talking while he figured out what he was going to do.

Something was not right about this scene, not right about how Rhun had acted down in the crypt. Manfred and Rhun had been close friends, despite their difference over whether to kill Rhysem. Part of that difference undoubtedly had been caused by Rhysem himself, as a result of the compulsions he finally had dared to set—subtle compulsions, that would not require Rhun to act too far out of character, lest someone suspect Deryni interference.

Until today. What happened in the crypt had been totally out of character. And it was not the first time, though it was the most blatant. The old Rhun would have had no qualms about having Rhysem bled to death, if it would further his power as a regent—but Rhun had tried to prevent it.

And then Cathan began to make the connection. It had to stem from that night when Rhysem had told Rhun of the codicil, to keep from being bled; and afterward, seizing the opportunity to take control of Rhun at last, he had spent quite a long time working deep in Rhun's mind. He had never revealed to Cathan precisely what he had done; but nothing he had ordered could possibly have permitted killing Owain.

"Rhun, you can't kill the boy," Cathan whispered, now certain he was on the right track. "You can't kill him. The king forbade you to let *him* come to harm, and you know he meant that for his son as well."

Rhun's eyes darted to the boy's black hair, just under his

chin, at the little legs dangling over the parapet, at the blade along the boy's throat.

"Pull him in and let him go, Rhun," Cathan whispered. "What was it the king ordered you to do? Did he tell you to kill the other regents when you got the chance?"

Rhun looked at him sharply, bewilderment suddenly in his eyes.

"I—killed Manfred. I didn't want to, but—I had to."

"But, didn't he deserve to die? He kept you from saving the king, when the *Custodes* decided to bleed him to death."

"I—I tried to stop them," Rhun whispered.

"I know. I was there. I couldn't stop them either."

Rhun swallowed, nervously turning the dagger against Owain's throat. Somehow the boy knew to keep very still and very quiet. Cathan wondered how much he understood of what he was hearing. Far below, a crowd was gathering, upturned faces white and anxious—Ansel, Robert, Lord Ainslie, Sighere, and Graham—all of them very quiet, bunching together beneath where Owain dangled, to try to break his fall if Rhun let go.

"You can stop *this*, Rhun, even though we couldn't stop the other," Cathan went on softly. "The boy doesn't have to die. If you let him live, God will not forget."

"I'll be already damned," Rhun whispered, turning his face away, knuckles whitening on the hilt of the dagger. And suddenly Cathan guessed what Rhysem's last instruction had been to Rhun.

"Rhun, did the king order you to kill yourself, after you'd killed as many of the other regents as you could?"

Rhun hugged the boy closer, burying his face in the black hair, the knife hand going farther around his neck, the blade no longer touching flesh.

"My own boy is ten," Rhun whispered. "I would have liked to see him grown up."

So would Rhysem, Cathan thought to himself, though he only said, "It's difficult for a boy without a father. I—hope to be a father to Owain. If you'll let me."

Slowly Rhun lifted his head to look at Cathan, a flash of the old cunning rekindling in his gaze.

"I might just give you that chance," he said softly. "There would be a price, of course."

"Name it."

Rhun compressed his lips, considering, then pulled the boy

back in from the parapet and set him on the floor in front of him, though the dagger remained near his throat, his other hand firmly on the boy's shoulder.

"You claim to serve the king's justice, do you not?"

Cathan nodded, wondering whether he dared try to grab Owain and yank him to safety before Rhun could cut his throat.

"And the king's justice demands my death, doesn't it, even though I've saved you having to execute Manfred and Lior?"

Again Cathan nodded.

"Well, I won't kneel down at the block or put my neck through a noose. I won't be taken, but I *will* try to take you with me. That's my price, if I let the boy go."

Cathan drew a deep breath, knowing he must accept but wondering whether he had any chance at all. Tieg's drug and spell were still working strongly in him, and he was half Rhun's age—which should make him quicker—but Rhun's extra years were years of experience, and Rhun outweighed him considerably, none of it flab.

"Let him go," he said evenly.

Smiling the old Rhun smile, the earl pulled Owain around behind him and gave him a shove.

"Get back out of the way, son," he said. "Uncle Cathan and Uncle Rhun are going to fight."

Cathan knew he was outclassed as soon as they closed. After Rhun blooded him the second time, he knew he was going to lose. He fought gamely on, though, because he had no choice; because there was always a chance that Rhun might make a mistake. But he never did.

Ducking to avoid a particularly vicious thrust, Cathan recoiled so hard that part of the stone colonnade gave way, opening a gap nearly as long as a man and sending debris raining over the edge to shatter on the marble below, scattering the onlookers. Cathan nearly followed it, but Rhun caught his sleeve and yanked him around to face another vicious upthrust, only just parried.

An immediate counterattack drew his blood again, more seriously than the previous two times. He tripped and went down, sprawled on his back and precariously near the edge—and Rhun was suddenly on top of him, driving his dagger toward Cathan's throat as Cathan tried desperately to block it, to slow it, his own knife hand pinned by Rhun's.

Except that suddenly Rhun's hand was releasing his knife

hand, shifting to grab a handful of his hair and jerk his head back to expose his throat. Most incredibly, it left Cathan's knife free to thrust upward unimpeded, directly under the arm, full to the hilt.

Somehow Rhun did not even seem surprised. He made no sound save a faint, bubbling gasp. His whole body tensed, as if trying to arch away from the blade, but a faint smile curved at his lips as the blade poised at Cathan's throat fell from nerveless fingers, and his other hand relaxed its grip on Cathan's hair, the light dying in his eyes as his full weight collapsed across Cathan's chest.

For a few heart-pounding seconds Cathan merely lay there, hardly daring to breathe, astonished both at what Rhun had done and that he himself was still alive. When, at length, he summoned the strength to try to shift free from under Rhun's weight, he had to push the body toward the edge, for the wall was close along his right side. The shift of weight pulled the body over—one leg was already over the edge—to fall like a sack of feed to the floor far below.

As Cathan rolled breathlessly onto his side to look down at the men crowding around the body, Owain came running to him with a squeal of relief, to fling his arms around his neck and bury his little face against Cathan's chest without regard to Rhun's blood.

CHAPTER THIRTY-SIX

And those which remain shall hear, and fear, and
shall henceforth commit no more any such evil
among you.

— Deuteronomy 19:20

With only Hubert left alive of the original regents who had set
out to make puppets of Gwynedd's kings more than a decade
before, the two regents appointed at such cost by the late king
immediately set about consolidating a new regency that would
provide responsible guidance for the king's young heir as he
grew into manhood. They chose to ignore any element of
magic that might have contributed to Tammaron's sudden
death—or if they did not precisely ignore it, they imputed such
intervention to the priest calling himself Donatus, who melted
away into the confusion even as Bishop Ailin exhorted thanksgiving for God's mercy—and simultaneously secured his own
place in Gwynedd's future. Obedient to the late king's instruction, Graham of Claibourne and Sighere of Marley summoned
Sir Cathan Drummond back to the crypt and took his oath as
regent on the very tomb of his late brother-in-law. His sister
looked on in joy and relief, and his young nephew held the
Papa knight in witness—though he left it on the tomb when
they headed back to the castle, for he still thought it proper
that his father should have a king on his tomb like his grandfather and his uncles.

Archbishop Hubert MacInnis was taken into custody and
eventually tried before the same council of bishops that soon
suspended him from office and eventually confirmed Ailin
MacGregor as his successor. As Archbishop and Primate, Ailin
gained an immediate seat on the new Regency Council, to the

413

great satisfaction of his fellow regents. One of his first acts as archbishop was to quietly bring back Bishop Dermot O'Beirne as his auxiliary in Valoret—for it was Dermot who had kept the lines of communication open during those years of planning for the crown's liberation from the great lords. Ailin dared not restore the Deryni Niallan, but those Deryni aware of Ailin's courage in even bringing back Dermot slept a little easier in their beds in the years that followed.

The outcome of Hubert's trial was rather less satisfying. Though most of his fellow bishops quickly became convinced of his treason, as the evidence mounted, they were loath to sully the titles and office he had borne by turning him over to secular authorities for certain execution—though several felt execution far too lenient. In the end, he was banished to close confinement in a distant religious house whose name and location were never made public, there to submit himself to a regimen of fasting and penance from which there was no earthly appeal, allowed no human contact save with a confessor and certain spiritual directors. He died in his bed within the year—peacefully, it was said, nearly half his former weight and bulk—never having repented any of his deeds.

Of the *Custodes Fidei* implicated by Cathan in the king's murder, only two came to trial. After a hearing before the bishops, Brother Polidorus and Father Magan were handed over to a secular court, tried, convicted, and eventually hanged; Lior had escaped trial by dying of the wound dealt him by Rhun.

Master Stevanus would have been pardoned, but was found to have died while in retreat at the Order's Mother House in Ramos, the result of overzealous indulgence in certain privations and disciplines customary within the Order—voluntary, of course, or so the abbot said. Four *Custodes* knights who had gone into retreat at about the same time also died under curious circumstances, but the abbot similarly declined to discuss the causes, invoking the confidentiality of the confessional to justify his silence. The abbey at Ramos was dissolved, its abbot given into the custody of the spiritually sound *Ordo Verbi Dei* for rehabilitation; the rest of the Ramos brethren were dispersed to the remaining houses of the Order.

The *Custodes* abbey at Rhemuth suffered a similar fate. Its former abbot, Father Secorim, expecting momentary confirmation as archbishop, was happy to settle for the auxiliary bishop's post under the circumstances, gladly giving his obedience to Alfred of Woodbourne, who had always been the previous archbishop's choice as successor. Cathan was dubious about letting Secorim remain at all, but nothing could be proven against him other than ill judgment in his choice of associates; and Secorim argued fairly eloquently that he could hardly be held responsible for being singled out by his previous superior for favor.

With the bishops' promotion of Secorim came their farthest-reaching decisions about the *Ordo Custodum Fidei*. Though they did not demand its total dissolution, the Order's ecclesiastical knights were disbanded and forbidden to re-form. To replace Paulin, the bishops designated the office of chancellor-general henceforth to hold the governing of the Order and confirmed Father Marcus Concannon in that office, charging him to refocus the Order to more accurately reflect their original purpose as guardians of the Faith.

To that end the Order would be permitted to retain its schools and other institutions of education. More particularly, *Arx Fidei* and the several other seminaries under its aegis were to continue; for on sober reflection, the current generation of the Church's hierarchy remained unconvinced that Deryni should be permitted priestly or episcopal authority, notwithstanding the more moderate opinions of Ailin and Dermot. Though many other of the Statutes of Ramos were rescinded in the months and years to follow, those laws forbidding the priesthood to Deryni were to remain in force for another two centuries, even when other excessively restrictive statutes against the Deryni eventually began to be ignored.

In the secular realm, the new Regency Council of Gwynedd likewise set about the necessary housecleaning. Lord Ainslie and his son Robert were appointed to the council by summer's end. Robert also married his "Liesel," thereby ensuring a quiet Deryni presence at Court for the foreseeable future. Sir Fulk Fitz-Arthur was recalled from his brother's court at Cassan, testified at the trials of the king's murderers, and was appointed a royal equerry in time to attend on the young king at his coronation in September. None of the other heirs of the former great lords were retained in royal service, but neither did they suffer the attainder and confiscation of their estates that might have followed on the crimes of their fathers. Harsher reprisals might have been more prudent.

Young Owain Haldane was crowned on Michaelmas, the sixth anniversary of his father's coronation and what would have been his father's twenty-second birthday, on the first day of a weeklong celebration the likes of which had not been seen since the coronation of his Uncle Alroy, more than a decade before. Neither Torenth nor Tolan sent an envoy, but the ten-year-old Duke of Cassan came with his parents to pledge his fealty to the new king, embarking upon a friendship with his new liege lord that would become both famous and tragic in years to come.

Richard Murdoch declined to attend, pleading indisposition, but most of the other heirs of the former great lords came and at least paid lip service to the new king and his regents. The coronation was also witnessed by many of the remaining heirs of Saint Camber, though none came openly, for the laws of Ramos were still in force. Not for nearly two centuries would so many Deryni again set foot in Rhemuth Cathedral.

Almost three months after Owain's coronation, on a snowy Saint Stephen's Day morn—seventh anniversary of the day a Haldane prince had led his new bride before the high altar to have their wedding vows made public—Gwynedd's widowed queen came privately to Rhemuth Cathedral, gowned and cloaked in black, heavily pregnant with the child her dead husband would never see. Atop her widow's veil she wore the silver coronet her husband had placed on her head on that long-ago day, and her hands bore a circlet of holly and ivy like her wedding wreath. Only her brother, her young son, and Archbishop Ailin accompanied her as she made her way into the crypt where half a year before they had laid her husband to rest in a featureless tomb.

"Mummy, look, there's a king in Papa's place!" Owain cried, as they reached the bottom of the steps.

She smiled as her son raced over to the tomb, which now bore a recumbent, life-sized figure carved out of warm alabaster, the raiment painted in bold heraldic colors—crimson and gold and sable. Owain had grown a hand-span in the last six months, but he still had to crane to see, stretching determinedly on tiptoes and trying to pull himself up until Cathan came to his rescue. He laughed with delight to see his Papa knight standing guard just at the figure's shoulder, and he retrieved it from its lonely vigil and clutched it to his breast as he gazed with satisfaction at the alabaster face, feasting his eyes on the crown, the sweep of crimson robe with the Haldane lion painted on the breast, and the carved sword lying quiet and potent under the folded hands.

"It looks like Papa," Owain whispered, his grey eyes shining. "Papa has a proper king now, just like Grandpapa Cinhil and Uncle Javan and Uncle Alroy. Take me to see them, too, Uncle Cathan. I want to see if they're as fine as my papa's."

Nodding his agreement, Cathan took him over to look at his grandfather's effigy, urging him to bow his head and say a prayer as his mother moved closer to her husband's tomb and Archbishop Ailin hung back to give her privacy. There was a *prie-dieu* on the other side, and she went to it and eased her ponderous body onto its cushioned kneeler, bowing her head over the bridal wreath for a moment before reaching out a hand to rest on his.

It was a good likeness. His face had never been so still or stern in life, but the black hair beneath the carved crown framed a visage undoubtedly Haldane. A glint of red and gold peeped from the hair at his right ear, and the sculptor had carved the Haldane brooch at his throat as well. She let her fingers feel the sleek coolness of it, shifting then to lightly brush an alabaster cheek.

My Rhysem, she spoke to him in her heart. *It's a fitting tribute. I wish they'd let you be the king you wanted to be. I wish—*

But it did no good to wish. All the wishing in the world could not bring him back. Rhys Michael Alister Haldane was dead, but his hopes and dreams must live on in the boy leaning down to pat the carved hand of another King of Gwynedd, the martyred Javan. Perhaps they would live as well in the other son she carried beneath her heart.

She smiled and laid a hand protectively on her abdomen, then set the wreath of holly and ivy on the folded hands of the effigy.

Sleep in peace, my darling, she whispered in her mind, as she touched her fingertips to her lips and then to his, in gentler farewell than circumstances had allowed the last time she left him here. *You gave me your love and your Haldane princes to mold into kings. With God's grace, the Haldane crown that you died to free will remain free upon Haldane brows for as long as there is a Gwynedd. God keep you, my love.*

She smiled as her son came running back to hug her, and had a smile, too, for Cathan and the archbishop as they gave ready hands to lead her out of that place of death and into a more hopeful future.

INDEX OF CHARACTERS*

---

*An asterisk indicates a character mentioned only in passing, possibly deceased.

ANSEL Irial MacRorie, Lord—grandson of Camber and a prime mover in the resistance against the former regents.

ARIELLA of Festil, Princess—slain (905) elder sister of the late King Imre and mother of his son, Mark or Marek.*

ARION of Torenth, King—Deryni King of Torenth and elder brother of Prince Miklos and Princess Charis.

ASCELIN, Father—a *Custodes* priest.

BONNER Sinclair, Lord—Earl of Tarleton; son of Lord Albertus and nephew of the Abbot-Bishop Paulin.

BORG—an archer in service of Manfred.

CAMBER Kyriell MacRorie, Saint—Deryni former Earl of Culdi; father of Joram and Evaine, grandfather of Rhysel and Tieg; canonized as Saint Camber in 906; sainthood rescinded by Council of Ramos in 917.

CAMLIN (Camber Allin) MacLean—young kinsman of Camber who survived crucifixion at Trurill, now part of Joram's underground.

CASHEL Murdoch, Sir—younger son of Murdoch of Carthane.

CATHAN Drummond, Sir—brother of Michaela and half-brother to Ansel; junior aide to Rhys Michael.

CHARIS, Princess—wife of Marek of Festil and mother of his son and heir.*

CHARLAN Kai Morgan, Sir—former squire and principal aide to King Javan, slain at his side in 922.*

CINHIL Donal Ifor Haldane, King—late King of Gwynedd (904–917); father of Alroy, Javan, and Rhys Michael.*

CLOYCE de Clarendon, Sir—a *Custodes* knight.

COLUMCILLE, Father—a priest at Lochalyn.*

CONCANNON, Father Marcus—*Custodes* chancellor-general in charge of seminary training for Gwynedd.*

CORBAN Howell, Lord—husband of Stacia of Eastmarch.

CORIS, Sir Sean—see *Sean Coris, Sir.*

COSIM—Miklos' personal physician/Healer.

CULLEN, Bishop Alister—see *Alister Cullen.*

CUSTODES FIDEI—*Ordo Custodum Fidei*, the Guardians of the Faith; religious Order founded by Paulin of Ramos to replace the Michaelines and reform ecclesiastical education in Gwynedd for the exclusion of Deryni. Mandate later extended to ferret out and eliminate Deryni by whatever means.

DAITHI, Father—a *Custodes* priest at Rhemuth; official King's Chaplain after Father Faelan.

DECLAN Carmody—a slain Deryni.*

DE COURCY—see *Etienne* and *Guiscard de Courcy.*

DEINIOL, Brother—assistant to Brother Polidorus.

DERFEL, Father—chaplain at Lochalyn Castle.

DERYNI (Der-ín-ee)—racial group gifted with paranormal/supernatural powers and abilities feared by many humans.

DIMITRI, Master—Deryni agent in Paulin's service.

DONAL, Master—a scribe at Rhemuth Castle.

DONATUS, Father—an alias of Dom Queron Kinevan.

DROGO de Palance, Sir—Rhun's castellan at Sheele.*

DRUMMOND—see *Cathan, Elinor, James,* and *Michaela Drummond.*

EDWARD MacInnis, Bishop—young Bishop of Grecotha; son of Earl Manfred and nephew to Archbishop Hubert.

EITHNE—a maid at Rhemuth Castle.

ELGIN—an Eastmarch captain.

ELINOR MacRorie Drummond—widow of Cathan MacRorie and mother of Ansel and Davin by him; mother of Michaela and Cathan by second marriage to James Drummond.*

ELSPETH—a maid at Rhemuth Castle.

EMBERT, Brother—a *Custodes* monk-physician.

EQUITES CUSTODUM FIDEI—Knights of the Guardians of the Faith; military arm of the *Custodes Fidei,* intended to replace the Michaelines.

ESTELLAN MacInnis, Lady—Manfred's wife and Countess of Culdi.

ETIENNE de Courcy, Baron—a southern lord, secretly Deryni, sent by Joram to infiltrate the Haldane Court in preparation for Javan's accession.*

EUGEN von Roslov—a herald in service of Prince Miklos of Torenth.

EVAINE MacRorie Thuryn, Lady—Deryni adept daughter of Camber, sister of Joram; widow of the Healer Rhys Thuryn; mother of Rhysel and Tieg.*

EWAN, Duke—Second Duke of Claibourne, treacherously deposed as one of original five regents of young King Alroy and slain; brother of Sighere and Hrorik, father of Graham.*

FABIUS, Brother—a *Custodes* monk at Saint Cassian's.

FAELAN, Father—murdered former confessor to King Javan.*

FANE Fitz-Arthur, Lord—eldest son of Earl Tammaron and husband of Richeldis, Heiress of Kierney.*

FITZ-ARTHUR—see *Fane, Fulk, Nieve, Quiric,* and *Tammaron Fitz-Arthur.*

FULK Fitz-Arthur, Sir—Rhys Michael's senior aide, son of Earl Tammaron.

FURSTAN—dynastic name of the ruling House of Torenth.

GABRILITES—priests and Healers of the Order of Saint Gabriel, an all-Deryni esoteric brotherhood founded in 745 and based at Saint Neot's Abbey until 917, when the Order was suppressed and many of its brethren slain; especially noted for the training of Healers.*

GALLARD de Breffni, Sir—a *Custodes* knight.

GIESELE MacLean, Lady—Co-Heiress of Kierney, sister of Richeldis; smothered to death at age 12.*

GRAHAM MacEwan, Duke—Third Duke of Claibourne; son of Ewan and nephew of Earls Hrorik and Sighere.

GUISCARD de Courcy, Sir—Deryni son of Baron Etienne, sent by Joram to infiltrate the Haldane Court in preparation for accession of Javan; aide to Javan and slain with him in 922.*

HALDANE—surname of the royal House of Gwynedd.

HALEX, Father—Abbot of *Arx Fidei* Abbey, a *Custodes* House.

HENRY of Rutherford, Sir—a knight in Rhun's service.

HOMBARD of Tarkent—Torenthi envoy in service of Prince Miklos.

HRORIK of Eastmarch, Lord—Earl of Eastmarch; middle son of Duke Sighere, uncle of Duke Graham, husband of Sudrey, father of Stacia.*

HUBERT MacInnis, Archbishop—Primate of Gwynedd and Archbishop of Valoret, one of Alroy's former regents; younger brother of Earl Manfred and uncle of Bishop Edward.

IMRE, King—fifth and last Festillic King of Gwynedd (900–904); father of Marek of Festil by his sister Ariella.*

IMRE of Festil, Prince—infant son of Marek and Princess Charis of Torenth.*

IOSIF—a guard at Rhemuth Castle.

IVER MacInnis—son of Manfred; Earl of Kierney by right of his wife, Lady Richeldis MacLean.

JAMES, Master—a Court physician.

JAMES Drummond, Lord—deceased father of Michaela and Cathan Drummond.*

JAVAN Jashan Urien Haldane, King—clubfooted younger twin of King Alroy, whom he succeeded; reigned 921–922. Treasonously slain in battle and succeeded by his younger brother, Prince Rhys Michael.*

JERVIS—household steward at Lochalyn Castle.

JESSE MacGregor, Sir—Deryni adept, eldest son and heir of Gregory of Ebor; part of Joram's underground.

JORAM MacRorie, Father—Deryni adept and youngest son of Camber; brother of Evaine; priest and Knight of the Order of Saint Michael; now coordinating resistance to the former regents and plotting to restore independence of the Haldane crown.

JOSHUA Delacroix, Lord—*Custodes* captain-general at Ramos.

KENNET of Rhorau, Sir—nephew of Termod of Rhorau and brother of Sudrey; killed with Duke Ewan's party in 918.*

KENNET Howell—infant son of Stacia of Eastmarch and Corban Howell.

KIMBALL, Father—*Custodes* Abbot of Saint Cassian's.

KINEVAN, Dom Queron—see *Queron Kinevan, Dom.*

KYLA, Lady—a poet.*

LIESEL—alias used by Rhysel Thuryn.

LIOR, Father—Inquisitor-General of the *Custodes Fidei.*

LIRIN Udaut, Lady—daughter of Constable Udaut; wife of Richard Murdoch, Earl of Carthane.

LORENZO, Brother—a bookbinder.*

MACGREGOR—surname adopted by Jesse, son of Gregory of Ebor.

MACGREGOR, Bishop Ailin—see *Ailin MacGregor.*

MACINNIS—see *Edward, Hubert, Iver,* and *Manfred MacInnis.*

MACLEAN—see *Camlin, Giesele,* and *Richeldis MacLean.*

MACRORIE—surname of Camber's family. See *Ansel, Camber, Evaine,* and *Joram.*

MAGAN, Father—a young *Custodes* priest, assistant to Lior.

MANFRED MacInnis, Lord—Earl of Culdi of second creation; a former regent; elder brother of Archbishop Hubert and father of Iver and Bishop Edward.

MARCUS Concannon, Father—Chancellor-General of the *Ordo Custodum Fidei*, in charge of all seminaries and other institutions of education in Gwynedd.

MAREK of Festil, Prince—Deryni posthumous son of Imre and his sister Ariella, and carrier of the Festillic line after his parents' deaths.

MICHAELA Drummond, Queen—daughter of Elinor and James, sister of Cathan; wife and queen of Rhys Michael Haldane; mother of Prince Owain Haldane.

MICHAELINES—priests, knights, and lay brothers of the Order of Saint Michael, a militant fighting and teaching Order, predominantly Deryni, formed during the reign of King Bearand Haldane to hold the Anvil of the Lord against Moorish incursions and defend the sea-lanes; suppressed under the Regency of King Alroy and outlawed thereafter.

MIKLOS von Furstan, Prince—Deryni younger brother of King Arion of Torenth, ally of Marek of Festil.

MURDOCH of Carthane, Lord—slain father of Richard Murdoch, Earl of Carthane; formerly a regent of King Alroy.*

MURRAY—an Eastmarch captain.

NIALLAN Trey, Bishop—outlawed Deryni Bishop of Dhassa; a confidant of Father Joram MacRorie.

NICHOLAS—a retainer at Lochalyn Castle.

NIEVE Fitz-Arthur, Lady—Tammaron's countess and mother of four sons by him; widow of the late Earl of Tarleton, by whom she bore Peter (later known as Lord Albertus) and Paulin (of Ramos).

O'NEILL, Lord Tavis—see *Tavis O'Neill, Lord.*

ORDO CUSTODUM FIDEI—see *Custodes Fidei.*

ORDO VERBI DEI—Order of the Word of God.

ORIEL, Master—a Healer in the forced service of the great lords, slain during palace coup of 922.*

ORISS, Archbishop Robert—Archbishop of Rhemuth and member of royal council.

OWAIN Javan Cinhil Haldane, Prince—four-year-old Crown Prince of Gwynedd, son of Rhys Michael and Michaela.

PAULIN (Sinclair) of Ramos—younger son of the Earl of Tarleton and stepson of Earl Tammaron; briefly Bishop of Stavenham before his resignation to head the *Ordo*

Custodum Fidei; brother of Albertus (Peter Sinclair), the Order's first Grand Master.

POLIDORUS, Brother—*Custodes* infirmarian at Saint Cassian's Abbey.

QUERON Kinevan, Dom—former Gabrilite Healer-priest and founder of the Servants of Saint Camber; confidant of Joram.

QUIRIC Fitz-Arthur—a squire at Court, son of Tammaron.

REGINA, Sister—a nun at Saint Ostrythe's.

REVAN, Master—human charismatic preacher working with a Deryni faction to save Deryni by blocking their powers via a kind of "baptism." Slain in 922 by his own former followers.*

RHUN of Horthness, Lord—called the Ruthless; Earl of Sheele of second creation and a former regent for King Alroy; husband of Agnes Murdoch; Vice-Marshal of Gwynedd.

RHYSEL Thuryn, Lady—daughter of Rhys Thuryn and Evaine MacRorie; as "Liesel," sent secretly to infiltrate Court as a maid to Queen Michaela.

RHYS MICHAEL Alister Haldane, King—youngest of King Cinhil's three sons; succeeded his brother Javan as King Rhys (reigned 922–928); husband of Michaela Drummond and father of Prince Owain.

RICHARD Murdoch, Lord—Earl of Carthane, eldest son of Murdoch.

RICHELDIS MacLean, Lady—Countess of Kierney in her own right, wife of Iver MacInnis.*

RICKART, Dom—Healer to Bishop Niallan and part of Joram's staff.

RONDEL, Sir—aide to Manfred.

SECORIM, Father—abbot of the *Custodes* chapter at Rhemuth.

SEAN Coris, Sir—son of Sighere, Earl of Marley.

SIGHERE, Lord—Earl of Marley; brother of Hrorik and uncle of Duke Graham; father of Sir Sean Coris.

SINCLAIR—surname of the Earls of Tarleton.

STACIA, Lady—daughter of Hrorik and Sudrey; Heiress of Eastmarch; wife of Corban and mother of Kennet.

STEVANUS, Master—a *Custodes* battle surgeon.

SUDREY of Rhorau, Lady—widow of Hrorik of Eastmarch;

niece of Termod of Rhorau and therefore a distant cousin of Marek of Festil; mother of Stacia.

TAMBERT Fitz-Arthur-Quinnell, Duke—First Duke of Cassan, now ten; son of Fane Fitz-Arthur and Princess Anne Quinnell.*

TAMMARON Fitz-Arthur, Earl—Chancellor of Gwynedd and a former regent for King Alroy; father of Fane, Fulk, and Quiric and grandfather of Duke Tambert.

TAVIS O'Neill—former Healer to Prince Javan and one of the few Healers able to block Deryni powers.*

TIEG Thuryn—Healer son of Rhys Thuryn and Evaine MacRorie.

TOMAIS d'Edergoll, Sir—former aide to Prince Rhys Michael, slain during coup of 922.

UDAUT, Lord—Constable of Gwynedd; father of Lirin.

VALENTIN—Marek's most senior captain.

WINIFRED, Sister—a nun at Saint Ostrythe's Convent.

INDEX OF PLACES

ALL SAINTS' CATHEDRAL—seat of the Archbishop of Valoret, Primate of All Gwynedd.

BELDOUR—capital of Torenth.

CAERRORIE—formerly Camber's principal residence as Earl of Culdi, a few hours' ride northeast of Valoret; now the seat of Manfred MacInnis, Earl of Culdi of the second creation.

CARTHANE—Richard Murdoch's earldom, south of Rhemuth, whose capital is Nyford.

CASHIEN—episcopal see to the west of Rhemuth.

CASSAN—former petty princedom ruled by Prince Ambert Quinnell; now a duchy of Gwynedd under its first duke, Tambert Fitz-Arthur-Quinnell.

CLAIBOURNE—principal city of Old Kheldour and first duchy of Gwynedd; seat of Graham, Third Duke of Claibourne.

CONNAIT, The—barbarian kingdom to the west, famous for its mercenaries.

COR CULDI—hereditary ancestral seat of the Earls of Culdi, near the city of Culdi, on the Gwynedd-Meara border.

CULLIECAIRN—Haldane stronghold—castle, town, and garrison—guarding the Coldoire Pass between Eastmarch and Tolan.

DESSE—port town south of Rhemuth.
DHASSA—traditionally neutral episcopal see east of Rhemuth, in the Lendour Mountains.

EASTMARCH—earldom held by Hrorik, middle son of Duke Sighere of Kheldour.
EBOR—earldom north of Valoret, now in abeyance, formerly held by Gregory, Jesse's father.

GRECOTHA—university city, former site of the Varnarite School; seat of the Bishop of Grecotha.
GWYNEDD—central of the Eleven Kingdoms and hub of Haldane power since 645, when the first Haldane High King began to unify the area; seat of the Festillic Dynasty, 822–904; restored to the Haldane line in 904 with the accession of Cinhil Haldane.

HORTHNESS—Barony of Rhun the Ruthless.
HOWICCE—kingdom to the southwest of Gwynedd; loosely allied with Llannedd.

KHELDISH RIDING—viceregality broken off Kheldour after its annexation by Duke Sighere and King Cinhil in 906.
KHELDOUR—small kingdom north of Gwynedd, now comprising the Duchy of Claibourne and the Earldoms of Marley and Eastmarch.
KIERNEY—earldom north of Culdi.

LLANNEDD—kingdom southwest of Gwynedd; loosely allied with Howicce.
LOCHALYN CASTLE—seat of Hrorik, Earl of Eastmarch.

MARBURY—episcopal see in the earldom of Marley.
MARLEY—small earldom carved out of Eastmarch for Sighere, youngest son of Duke Sighere.
MARLOR—barony of Manfred MacInnis.
MEARA—kingdom/princedom northwest of Gwynedd; nominally a vassal state of Gwynedd.
MOORYN—province at the far south of Gwynedd, including Carthmoor and Corwyn.

NYFORD—port city south of Rhemuth, seat of the Earls of Carthane; episcopal see for Carthane.

RAMOS—abbey town southwest of Valoret, where the Council of Ramos convened, winter of 917/918.

RHEMUTH—ancient capital of Gwynedd under the Haldanes; abandoned during Festillic Interregnum; restored under Cinhil and Alroy; secondary archbishopric for Gwynedd, junior to Valoret.

RHENDALL—lake region north of Gwynedd; territorial title given to the heir of the Duke of Claibourne.

SAINT CASSIAN'S ABBEY—a *Custodes* House on the Plain of Iomaire.

SAINT JARLATH'S ABBEY—Mother House of the Order of Saint Jarlath, on the southwestern edge of the Plain of Iomaire.

SAINT MARK'S ABBEY—monastery near Valoret.

SAINT NEOT'S ABBEY—stronghold of the Order of Saint Gabriel the Archangel, an all-Deryni esoteric Order specializing in the training of Healers; located in the Lendour highlands; destroyed by troops led by the Regent Rhun on Christmas Eve, 917.

SAINT OSTRYTHE'S CONVENT—small religious house lying between Ebor and Sheele.

SHEELE—seat of the Earldom of Sheele, north of Valoret.

STAVENHAM—episcopal see in the far north of Kheldour.

TOLAN—marriage portion of Princess Charis of Torenth, who married Marek of Festil; now a duchy.

TORENTH—powerful kingdom to the east of Gwynedd; origin of the Festillic line, who were rulers of Gwynedd 822–904; currently ruled by King Arion.

VALORET—Festillic capital of Gwynedd, 822–904, from which springs the primacy of its archbishop.

APPENDIX III

PARTIAL LINEAGE OF THE HALDANE KINGS

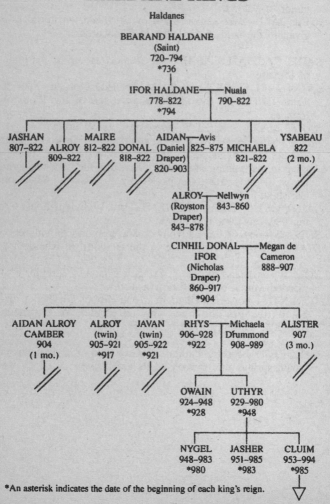

Haldanes

BEARAND HALDANE
(Saint)
720–794
*736

IFOR HALDANE —— Nuala
778–822   790–822
*794

JASHAN 807–822 · ALROY 809–822 · MAIRE 812–822 · DONAL 818–822 · AIDAN (Daniel Draper) 820–903 —— Avis · MICHAELA 821–822 · YSABEAU 822 (2 mo.)

ALROY (Royston Draper) 843–878 —— Nellwyn 843–860

CINHIL DONAL IFOR (Nicholas Draper) 860–917 *904 —— Megan de Cameron 888–907

AIDAN ALROY CAMBER 904 (1 mo.) · ALROY (twin) 905–921 *917 · JAVAN (twin) 905–922 *921 · RHYS 906–928 *922 —— Michaela Drummond 908–989 · ALISTER 907 (3 mo.)

OWAIN 924–948 *928 · UTHYR 929–980 *948

NYGEL 948–983 *980 · JASHER 951–985 *983 · CLUIM 953–994 *985

*An asterisk indicates the date of the beginning of each king's reign.

430

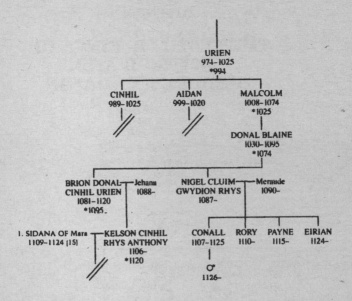

APPENDIX IV

THE FESTILLIC KINGS OF GWYNEDD AND THEIR DESCENDANTS

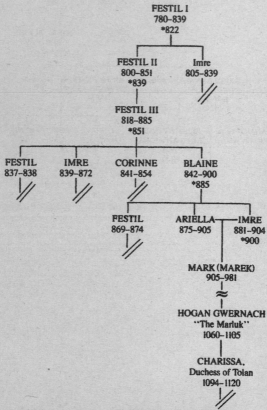

FESTIL I
780–839
*822

FESTIL II
800–851
*839

Imre
805–839

FESTIL III
818–885
*851

FESTIL
837–838

IMRE
839–872

CORINNE
841–854

BLAINE
842–900
*885

FESTIL
869–874

ARIELLA
875–905

IMRE
881–904
*900

MARK (MAREK)
905–981

HOGAN GWERNACH
"The Marluk"
1060–1105

CHARISSA,
Duchess of Tolan
1094–1120

*An asterisk indicates the date of the beginning of each king's reign.

PARTIAL LINEAGE OF THE MacRORIES

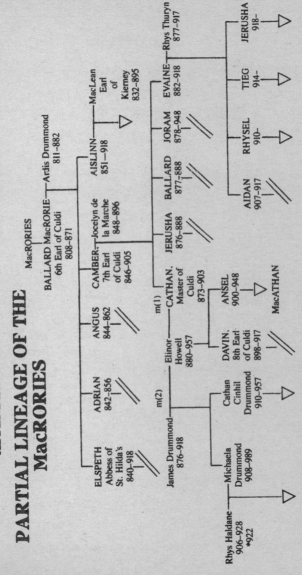

*An asterisk indicates the date of the beginning of each king's reign.

DEL REY ONLINE!

The Del Rey Internet Newsletter...

A monthly electronic publication, posted on the Internet, GEnie, CompuServe, BIX, various BBSs, and the Panix gopher (gopher.panix.com). It features hype-free descriptions of books that are new in the stores, a list of our upcoming books, special announcements, a signing/reading/convention-attendance schedule for Del Rey authors, "In Depth" essays in which professionals in the field (authors, artists, designers, sales people, etc.) talk about their jobs in science fiction, a question-and-answer section, behind-the-scenes looks at sf publishing, and more!

Online editorial presence:

Many of the Del Rey editors are online, on the Internet, GEnie, CompuServe, America Online, and Delphi. There is a Del Rey topic on GEnie and a Del Rey folder on America Online.

Our official e-mail address

for Del Rey Books is delrey@randomhouse.com

Internet information source!

A lot of Del Rey material is available to the Internet on a gopher server: all back issues and the current issue of the Del Rey Internet Newsletter, a description of the DRIN and summaries of all the issues' contents, sample chapters of upcoming or current books (readable or downloadable for free), submission requirements, mail-order information, and much more. We will be adding more items of all sorts (mostly new DRINs and sample chapters) regularly. The address of the gopher is gopher.panix.com

Why?

We at Del Rey realize that the networks are the medium of the future. That's where you'll find us promoting our books, socializing with others in the sf field, and—most importantly—making contact and sharing information with sf readers.

For more information, e-mail

delrey@randomhouse.com